THIRTY-SIX STEPS

Secrets & Searches

This is a work of fiction. All the characters and events portrayed in this book are either products of the author's imagination or are used fictitiously.

Thirty-Six Steps   *Secrets & Searches*

www.traciescheiding.com

ISBN: 978-0-6151-4234-0

First Edition: March 2007

Printed in the United States of America

To Bill. My best friend and husband.
Without you, I never would have found
the courage to chase my dreams.

Prologue
Birth

Cast out of the darkness of her mother's womb, she fell quickly into the light and flexed her fingers towards it. Her confused cries rang out from between her mother's thighs like high-pitched bells to signal her much anticipated arrival. However, on that day, there were no doctors to heed her call; no nurses or medications to dull the pain of the unusual birth.

The mother's only comfort came in the form of an old man's cigar smoke as it spiraled out from his darkened hiding place to tease her nostrils with its sweet, almost intoxicating, aroma. The man, her father, sat quietly in the corner and offered no assistance in the birth. He favored instead a sip of bourbon-soaked tea, a drink that was more bourbon than tea. As evidenced by the shotgun that laid across his lap, he was nervous; was worried about the tiny wiggling creature that had just made her debut.

To keep out the prying eyes of the townspeople, the windows had been boarded up two days prior; the nails had rusted in the walls without hesitation and waited for a reprieve that would be a long time coming. Already, sunlight was a strange memory to the cheeks of the woman; to the floors and to the walls of the aging farm house.

The young woman struggled to sit up and when she at last did so, she reached down to the child she had pushed into the world. In a state of fear and exhaustion, she knocked over the small table at her left and sent a tray of juniper beads to the ground where they scattered off in search of cracks in the wooden floor.

At the precise moment when the newborn's eyes fluttered open for the first time, a creeping scent of indescribable sweetness slowly began to fill the room. Finally, the house could no longer contain it. As it found the cracks and crevices amongst the shutters and doors, it seeped outwards in search of the light.

Above the woman's head, an anxious father paced. Beneath her feet, a tiny sprout broke free of the earth, a sprout that would forever seal the fate of the child and the father from which she had so effortlessly sprung.

Chapter One
Secrets & Searches

From a young age, Juniper Kelly was overwhelmed by an incredible thought. As she grew from a child into a teenager, the thought became her reality. She was, in fact, different than the other teens who lined the high school halls; was different than other *people* in general. It was nothing she could explain if asked about, and nothing she could prove with hard facts or tagged and bagged evidence, yet there it was. A lingering, almost nagging sensation that she was different, *special*, in some unexplained way.

To the naked human eye, Juniper appeared no different than other girls her age. She was tall and perfectly slender with hair that hung close to her cheeks in slight curls and wisps. By all accounts she was pretty, however Juniper herself felt plain and insignificant in appearance. Her black hair and brown eyes were nothing extraordinary upon first glance, but with closer inspection finer truths could be pinpointed.

It was the certain way her eyes reflected the light; it was an always-present glimmer that held steady even in the face of constant teasing and bad-natured ribbing from the kids at school, and when one looked further still into the depths of her, it became apparent to most that she was indeed different. For unspoken and sleeping at the very core of her, there was a light, firm and bright and waiting for the right moment to explode into greatness.

Juniper attributed her feelings of oddity to the stories that swirled about her head, stories that involved her birth and the father that had made it possible. Shrouded in mystery, the events surrounding the day of her grand appearance were a secret that Juniper's mother would shed no light upon. The curiosity followed Juniper through life, shadowed closely by questions about her father's identity.

Genealogy projects came and went, and took with them father/daughter dances and winter pageants that Juniper took no part in. Still, through it all, Penelope Kelly revealed nothing about her daughter's birth father.

Try as she might, and try she did, Juniper found it impossible to hate her mother for the secrets she kept. Instead she was only prompted to wonder why it was they were guarded so closely. Were they cloaked under years of pain? Were they hidden by a selfish desire on her mother's part to protect Juniper from some horrible truth?

The mysterious air that hung heavy over the entire story fueled the fires of Juniper's rampant imagination. When it was that she finally accepted the sad fact she might never know the truth, Juniper occupied her mind instead with fantastic, imaginative stories about her father and who he might be. She filled in the gaps of her life during afternoons spent in her room, until finally she had crafted an intricate web of mythology and memories that had never occurred. Still, she found that if she closed her eyes, she could almost see his face. Could almost see the two of them walking hand in hand along some distant river with the sun riding high upon their cheeks, rivaling only the laughter that lit their mouths and bared their teeth.

She dreamed of his face in detail, somnambulant reveries that came with a vivid intensity and left her soaked with sweat and curiosity. Juniper wondered what words her father might offer her as an apology for his absence if someday he *did* choose to return. And she longed for that; longed for a tearful reunion and a thorough explanation, but at that point in her life she would have settled for his name. A simple name to place with the mental image she had crafted so carefully over the years; a place to start searching for her own truths, unaided by her unwilling mother and a silent town.

She compared the likenesses and differences between herself and her mother and searched her eyes, her ears, her nose for clues to her own genetic makeup. If she didn't have her mother's nose, then it must be her fathers; her mother was a blonde, she herself had black wavy hair; over the years Juniper pieced together her father's image based upon her own facial characteristics.

She knew that he must be tall; Juniper herself was already 5'8" at just shy of sixteen. Her mother stood a slight 5'3" in bare feet; both of *her* parents had been roughly the same height. Other things she knew: his hair color was black, his eyes were probably brown, his mouth was wide and full; he had a sense of humor, and Juniper had inherited it. His cheekbones were most likely high, Juniper's matched; she wondered if he too was shy and introspective, a loner who preferred the comfort of a good book over the company of others.

Being a virtual outcast afforded Juniper too much time to think about his whereabouts and person. In a small southern town, hot under the penetrating sun of the remote forested area, Juniper grew to fill the shoes of the girl from the wrong side of the tracks; an outcast, tormented and made fun of by the other local kids.

When junior high finally ended and Juniper found herself with a chance at a fresh start, she moved on to the high school in the next county. The high school was closer to her house than the junior high had been, closer by several miles. In the weeks before the school year began, Juniper made the walk to the school several times to prepare her lazy legs for the soon-to-be daily trek through the town and over the bridge to the school. She walked the almost-mile distance in just under twenty minutes with a slow and even pace. Juniper found relief in silent walking, and found more relief still when she realized that her days of riding the bus were behind her. No more bubble gum on the bottom of her shoes, no more long and painful rides across gently rolling back roads, curled up and hidden in her seat to avoid the stares, whispers and insults of her classmates. She hoped that finally she'd be given the chance to improve her image, to start with a clean slate surrounded by fresh faces.

Unfortunately for Juniper, many of the elements that made junior high an exercise in torture would be following her to the new school, thanks to a last minute bid by the school board to re-align the area districts. In a rush decision, it was decided to combine Camden Falls High with East Lake High just two weeks before Juniper's sophomore year was to begin. When she heard the news, she cursed under her breath, a slip that narrowly avoided detection by her mother's finely tuned ears. She had quickly snapped her mouth shut and instead had kicked her brain into gear. With it up and running, she produced a series of frenzied thoughts and her anxiety over the new school year grew. She bit her nails short and walked a rut in the carpet of her room that led from the window to her bed. Juniper wasn't looking forward to facing the truth that things for her might not change at all.

For as much as trying to disappear had long since been a hobby of Juniper's, it was a hobby she'd been hoping to replace with something a tad bit more social.

On the first day of the new school year, Juniper woke early and dressed quickly in her thrift store duds. She checked out her appearance in the full-length bathroom mirror and smiled shakily at her reflection. Despite her best efforts to look like the other girls, she knew she'd still stick out like a sore thumb due to her odd sense of style and out-of-date wardrobe.

She gave herself a final once-over before she made her way downstairs to the kitchen where her mother had already started her own day. She remained quiet as she prepared her breakfast, then mulled over it with her head full of blazing thoughts about the day, about the *year*, to come. Her stomach was unsettled by the topic and she abandoned her oatmeal for a strong cup of black coffee. The caffeine did little to settle her and in the end, only upset her already-troubled stomach to a much greater degree.

Across from her at the table, her mother sat quietly, and sipped her own cup of coffee. Her lips were stained red with lipstick, the same red that graced the edge of her half-empty coffee mug. She was lost in her own world, in her own thoughts, and Juniper felt it unnecessary to trouble her further with her own doubts and concerns.

Juniper looked at the clock and tried without success to swallow away the knot that had developed in her throat. Finally, she resigned herself to the fact that it was time to leave the comforts of home if she hoped to make it to homeroom on time. Not wanting to start off the new year on the wrong foot by being late, she kissed her mother good-bye, gathered her bag of brand new binders and pens and left behind her two-story home at the edge of the great woods.

For the duration of the walk, Juniper hung her head low. She studied her class schedule several times and then stuffed it into her pocket only to retrieve it a moment later for another nervous glance. She had attended the orientation the week before, but Juniper still felt nervous about the idea of strange classrooms and new teachers. Unfamiliarity wasn't something she handled well, as she was most definitely a creature of comfort. Security in her surroundings was something Juniper sought after with much effort in the hopes of making her silent existence at least comfortable to live.

When Juniper first entered the front doors of the imposing three-story brick school that morning, she shifted nervously in her shoes and gulped past the still-present lump. The bell for homeroom was still some twenty minutes away from sounding and Juniper walked slowly to the locker bay in the east wing to try out her hand at both the lock and the combination.

She counted the numbers of the blue-faced lockers slowly as she passed them. Three-eleven, three-twelve, three-thirteen, and finally she found her own locker, three-fourteen. It was blue, metal, and waiting empty for her arrival. She smiled when the combination worked on the first try and the shaky, squeaky door shuddered open to reveal the beige emptiness inside. She let out a sigh of relief and in her throat, the lump lessened slightly in size.

One battle down, she thought. *Now if only the rest of the school year goes this well.*

She lowered her book bag to her side and unzipped the front pouch. Her mom had gone school supply crazy, and Juniper had found herself stocked up for years to come on ink pens of varying colors and pocketed folders. She unloaded a bulk of the supplies and filled the bottom cubby of the slender locker.

With her book bag significantly lighter, she made her way to her homeroom. She found it without difficulty and walked inside. The room was devoid of other students and Juniper was relieved that she was the first person to arrive.

She took a seat in the back of the room and noticed the teacher as she did so. He looked up, consulted the clock on the wall and smiled at Juniper warmly. She returned the gesture and then lowered her head to study her tightly clasped hands.

The bell rang before Juniper had realized that any time had passed at all, and the next time she looked up, she was surrounded by sleepy, grumpy faces. Some of them were familiar, others were not. She immediately noticed Erin Reid, and then found other faces she recognized. Wilson Pepperpot caught her eye and smiled, but Juniper looked away in embarrassment. She'd always had the feeling that the science-geek, redhead fancied her; boys were a topic Juniper knew nothing about, and she preferred it that way.

When roll call ended and the morning announcements had fizzled away, the bell rang and Juniper walked quickly to her first period Chemistry class. The rest of the day was a blur, and by the afternoon, smiles and laughter had returned to the hallways. The sullen mood of the student body lifted as it always did once everyone realized that there was no escape from the new school year, and acceptance was the best, and only, defense against the overwhelming influx of new information, faces and class schedules.

For the first few weeks of the new year, Juniper busied herself with adjusting to the new routine. By the end of the first month, she threw away her neatly printed class schedule, as she'd already memorized the quickest paths from point A to point B, and the order in which her classes came.

She was relieved that so far things seemed different. Not everyone leered at her, some people smiled, others asked to copy her perfectly penned notes and planned after school study groups. For a moment, Juniper was able to forget the secrets that surrounded her existence, and she felt almost normal. However, once the newness of the year wore off, a bit of the old crept quietly back in. At first it started simply. She would notice people whispering upon her approach, only to realize they silenced themselves when she came within earshot. She tried to convinced herself that she was being paranoid, but once the laughter rose up behind her back and feet were extended across aisles in an attempt to trip her up, she knew there was more to it than that.

The hallways were even more treacherous than the classrooms. Juniper kept her head down as she walked; the walls slipped by against a myriad of looks and rude comments, all of which she tried fruitlessly to ignore.

Juniper struggled through the first semester of the year, and by the time the spring weather rolled in, she felt almost comfortable in the high school environment. Comfortable aside from a few lingering factors that took the form of two boys, boys who still felt it their duty to make Juniper's life less livable. That day in particular, Juniper left her 4th period English class and walked slowly to her locker. She opened the tiny metal door with a flourish, and was grateful for the cover it provided her from the onslaught of students scurrying off to their next class.

Juniper slid her English book neatly into the nook it had abandoned earlier that morning and traded it for a World History book. She gave herself a glance in her small locker mirror, pulled her hair down further into her face to cloak her eyes and closed the door.

She turned on her heel without looking up, and instead she checked her watch. In doing so, she collided with a large and unmoving figure that stopped her fast in her tracks.

Juniper looked up, embarrassed by the collision. "Oh! I- I'm sorry, I didn't see anyone-" Her words fell away as soon as her eyes took focus on the stoic object and she found herself staring at a familiar antagonist.

"How can you see anything under all of that hair?" The boy took a strand of her black hair between his fingers and flipped it back over her shoulder with a quick flick of his wrist.

Juniper quickly shook the hair back into place with one subtle tilt of her head. The boy was no stranger; Juniper had grown up across the street from him for much of her life. That is until the previous summer when his family had moved across town to a larger home in a more affluent subdivision by the lake.

Since then, his behavior towards Juniper had become more aggressive and cold. She attributed that to the new crowd of people he'd found himself hanging out with since the move.

Juniper shuffled her books in her arms and moved her eyes to study the cracks between the grey and blue checkerboard tiles beneath her feet. "I'm sorry," she muttered again. "Look,

I've really gotta get to class now, so excuse me, please."

The boy, Jason Price, moved his arm out quickly and caught her at the wrist. "Just be more careful in the future, Junie. It helps to watch where you're going. You never know who you might run into." He threw her arm aside and snatched his hand quickly back to find the pocket of his jeans.

"Yeah, yeah, sorry."

Jason towered over her with his impressive height. He wore a cocky smile that he'd plastered across his narrow lips. His eyes were brown, thick and deep set, and, at the moment, they were narrowed in Juniper's direction. He reached up to push his shaggy brown locks back from his forehead, and then brushed the end of his sharp nose with his hand.

"Alright, apology accepted. Now go on, get outta here. I'm through with you." He paused to chuckle. "For now anyways."

Juniper nodded weakly, too tired of the familiar scene to argue or waste any of her breath in what she knew would be a vain attempt at ending his mission of making her life a wretched, miserable hell. Without another word she simply walked off and as she pulled away from the scene she pushed her shoulders high and put up her skin-thickening force field in preparation for the parting words she knew he'd volley.

"You know, you really are a weird girl, Junie. I'll be seein' you around. Oh, and uh, keep your chin up, would ya? You never know what kind of trouble you might run into." Jason was never one to disappoint.

Juniper cringed despite her thick protective shell, and clutched her books tighter to her chest as Jason's words hit her. She wondered if there was a cryptic meaning to his message, but pushed aside her thoughts as she wound her way through the halls to her next class in rapt silence. Around her hummed the constant whir of students as they passed her by without note, each on their own distinct path. They were all nothing more than a blur to her already pre-occupied mind.

Once inside the classroom, Juniper took her assigned seat in the back of the room, a seat in the row nearest the window. She sat slowly and brought her book bag down from her back and around to her feet. She unzipped it quickly and pulled out from the dark depths, her notebook and history text. She placed the book to the corner of her desk and lowered her head to further isolate herself from the rest of the students. She flipped the small, red notebook open casually and ignored the excited chatter around her as it swirled through the classroom. It was brought to her from the hallway as her fellow classmates escaped the corridor in pairs and trios, their arms heavy with books and papers. Her silent concentration, however, was short lived as a moment later Juniper's desk shook under the weight of a heavy text book that sent her own book sailing to the floor with a decisive thud.

Startled, Juniper looked up and her hand instinctively rushed to cover the page on which she'd been doodling.

Ben Maxwell settled into the seat next to her and retrieved her text book from the floor with a bow and a flourish. He held the book tightly between his thick fingers and grabbed his own from the corner of her desk with an insincere grimace.

He tossed his own hard-covered book to the surface of his desk and spoke slowly as the thump of the weight echoed away. "Well, look who we have here! If it isn't the one and only Juniper Kelly! Sorry 'bout that little *accident*, Junie. Would you believe that book just slipped *right* out of my hands?"

Juniper raised her eyes to meet his. "What are *you* doing here, Ben? As far as I know you aren't in this class."

He smiled, or more accurately, sneered. "This is my *new* history class, Junie. Got tossed right out of the other one." He lowered his voice and leaned towards her with a tight lipped message. "Word to the wise, Junie. Ms. Carol isn't fond of the insubordinate."

"Insubordinate? Get that one from your word of the day calendar, did you?" Juniper crossed her arms on the desk in front of her and indulged his sneer with a question. "So tell me, what did you do that got you kicked out of your other class?"

He laughed. "You mean you haven't heard? I thought the news would have been all over the school by now, but I guess maybe it's hard to see anything when you stare at your feet all the time. Anyway, long story short, I set my text book on fire. The sprinklers in the whole central building went off." With a slow steady motion he extended Juniper's book towards her. She moved to retrieve it and simultaneously Ben pulled his arm back. His smile widened and revealed his yellowed teeth. "I suppose it's a good thing that my dad is sheriff, eh?"

Juniper narrowed her eyes, her arm still extended towards him. Her palm was face up, open and waiting for the return of her text book. "Yeah, I guess you got lucky once again. I suppose congratulations are in order. Now can I *please* have my book?"

Ben looked at the book in his hands. "Oh, is this yours?" he asked innocently. He opened the cover and looked at the name stamped inside.

Juniper felt heat rise up to her neck. "You know it is so stop being a jerk."

Ben closed the book decisively and then tossed it onto her desk with an obvious attitude.

"Thanks." Juniper swallowed back the bile in her throat and returned her eyes to the college ruled page in front of her, hoping to avoid further conversation.

"Oh come on, what's a'matter, Junie?" Ben scooted his desk closer to hers. The metal legs screeched as they slid over the linoleum floor. "Don't you feel like talking today? I thought you'd be happy to see me! Lord knows you could use someone to talk to. Rumor has it you don't have any real friends, just that mother of yours. How is she by the way? Still as hot as ever, I assume."

Without looking up from her drawing Juniper issued a firm response to Ben's inquiry. "Don't talk about my mama and to answer your other question? No, as a matter of fact, I'm *not* happy to see you. And another thing? I really don't feel like talking. Not to you, anyway."

Ben scooted closer still and stopped only when Juniper felt his warm breath against her veil of hair. "What'cha drawing?" He craned his neck to look over the wall of Juniper's concealing arm. "What is that? A bird? I didn't know you fancied yourself to be an artist."

Juniper pulled the notebook further to the right side of her desk and closed it quickly. She looked at him, her eyes narrowed once again. "It's none of your business what I am or what I'm not," she snapped. "Just leave me alone, ok? I'm not going to ask you again."

Ben gasped in response to her comment. "Junie, I'm hurt!" He laughed a moment later and sat back in his chair where he pushed both of his oversized hands through his short, dirty-blonde hair. "I'll never understand why it is you don't like me. I've always tried my best to treat you the way you deserve to be treated."

"I deserve to be treated like shit?" Juniper made a disgusted noise. "Just do like I asked and leave me alone. You *and* Jason. Do you think you can do that for me?"

"But I thought we were old friends! Come on, we've known each other since 2nd grade, Mrs. Johnson's class... and now you don't even have time to chat with me?"

"The only reason you want to *chat* with me is to make me feel bad. And in case you've forgotten, you tormented me in 2nd grade, too. Not to mention in 3rd, 4th, 5th... Do I really have to continue here? Maybe all I have to say is *paste incident* to remind you of our less-than amicable history."

Ben thought over her words for a short moment before

he burst into laughter. "I'd completely forgotten about that."

"*I* certainly haven't forgotten it," Juniper said bitterly.

"Oh come on, even you have to admit that was funny! I mean, replacing your mayo with paste? It was *classic*! You have no idea how hard it was to pull that off with eagle eye Johnson watching my every move." He chuckled again and absently massaged his bare chin. "Say, can you even eat mayo yet?"

"I stay away from it as much as possible," she said dolefully.

"Ah, memories…" Ben put his arm around Juniper's shoulders and squeezed her closer to his person. "This is just the kind of relationship we have. I give, you take... It's symbiotic."

"Again with the big words. I didn't know you knew what a dictionary *was*, let alone opened one." Juniper shrugged his arm from her back. "As for our relationship, we *have* no relationship. *Period.* So please ,do me a favor and don't touch me again, got it?"

Ben placed his hand over his heart and tried his best to look hurt. "Is this how you talk to a friend?" he asked. "If so, it's no wonder you don't have any."

"You aren't my friend, Ben. We've already been through this numerous times."

Ben nodded and took a finger to tap his chin. "Oh, that's *right*. You don't *want* any friends do you, Junie? They might distract you from being a bitch."

"I don't need any friends," she spat through clenched teeth. Juniper scooted her desk closer to the window and further from Ben's with a screech.

"Oh, I see how it is. No, really." Ben shook his head and looked mildly insulted by Juniper's behavior. "Just ignore me then. I'm sure I'll be fine over here all alone in a new classroom with absolutely no one to talk to."

"I'm sure you'll find someone else to torment, your type

usually does," Juniper said as she prayed silently for the bell to ring, a bell that would bring a temporary end to Ben's attempts at pushing her buttons with his more than eager fingers.

Ben leaned over closer to Juniper with one last bomb to drop from his lips. "Say, I've been meaning to ask you about something... How is the search going?"

In spite of herself, Juniper indulged his cruelty one more time. "Search? What search? I don't know what you're talking about."

"Sure you do! The *search*. The search for your missing father, of course." His breath was hot and his lips were upturned at the corners to form a cruel smile. "Any luck yet? With tracking him down?"

Juniper's own lips snapped shut over her teeth and formed a taut line. She could feel the color as it rose quickly to her cheeks and she tried without success to will it back down to the soles of her shoes.

"Oh, what? Did I say something wrong? I didn't mean to upset you, I was just curious that's all. It's such a big mystery, and heck, there are a lot of people curious to find out who your daddy is. You know how gossip gets around a small town. People talk, people wonder." Ben pretended to mask his knowing cruelty under the guise of ignorance. A guise that Juniper knew wasn't a guise at all.

Juniper felt her lip begin to tremble, but she kept the reverberation from tainting her words. "I'm not going to ask you this again, ok? Leave me alone, please. *Please?* I've never done anything to you and I would appreciate it if you'd just leave me completely alone."

At the front of the room, the history teacher stood as the bell rang and he shifted his gaze down the aisle to Ben.

"Mr. Maxwell, I'll have to ask you to leave Miss Kelly alone and return your desk to its row for attendance, please."

Ben scooted back into his rightful location and Juniper

matched him by moving her own desk back into its proper place behind the thin blonde with the three heart-shaped moles on the back of her neck. When Mr. Halsey turned back to the board, Ben looked across the aisle at Juniper and lowered his voice from its earlier volume to a whisper. "I was just expressing concern, that's all.   After all, I know how much being abandoned by your old man bothers you. Jason's told me all about how you used to cry and moan about it. I get it, I mean how could it not bug you? You must think you were a pretty awful kid if your own *father* couldn't even stand to be around you."

Mr. Halsey cleared his throat. "Mr. Maxwell, if I have to warn you again about harassing Miss Kelly, you **will** be expelled from this classroom. Now I don't know if you're keeping count or not, but you're running out of history teachers at this school."

"Yes sir, sorry sir."

Mr. Halsey looked at Juniper; but she quickly looked away. "Are you alright, Miss Kelly?"

Juniper nodded, but soon felt her first tears creep to the ends of her lower eyelashes. They paused briefly before they took the plunge over her cheeks, and Juniper wiped at them furiously with her lip placed firmly between her teeth.

Beside her, Ben smiled and settled back in his seat. The look on his face gave up nothing if not his satisfaction over the sight of her tearful sadness and Juniper knew that silently he was breaking his own arm to pat himself on the back to commend a job well done.

"Juniper Kelly, may I see you for a moment, please." Mr. Halsey closed his lesson plan book as the bell rang and stepped around to the side of his desk. He sat lightly on the edge of the slab of thick oak and most of his weight sank quickly to his feet to hold him in place. He smiled and nodded at the crowd of students as they filed past him towards the door and reminded several of them about their oral presentations which were due the next day.

Juniper sat back down in her seat and held her hands in front of her on the surface of her desk. When the rest of the students had vacated the class, Mr. Halsey closed the door and took up his former position; perched at the corner of his desk.

"I've been meaning to have this conversation with you for awhile now, but you're always the first person out of here." Mr. Halsey motioned for Juniper to come closer and in response to his wave she picked up her book bag and did just that. She sat again, that time in the front row of desks.

"My next class is across campus, sir. I usually have to run to make it on time."

"I understand that, I do and I don't mean to keep you, I just feel as though there's something we should address, especially now, especially given our latest development." Mr. Halsey leaned forward. "First off, I have to say that you're one of my best students, Juniper. In fact, thanks to yesterday's quiz, you currently have the highest grade in the class."

"Is this why you're keeping me after? To tell me I'm too smart?"

Mr. Halsey laughed and his glasses bounced softly against the bridge of his nose. "No, no, nothing like that." He rubbed the beard on his chin absently with the fingers of his ring-less left hand. "It's just that.... well, pardon me if this sounds strange, but I've noticed that Mr. Maxwell and his friend Mr. Price give you trouble from time to time. Is that correct?"

Juniper shrugged and a well-trained strand of hair pushed forward to conceal her eyes from his view. "Sometimes, I guess, yeah. They're jerks, they do what jerks do. They pick on those less fortunate than they are."

"Look, Miss Kelly, I know all too well how hard it is to be a teenager. I was there myself once, and not so very long ago," he laughed. "As a matter of fact, I used to sit behind your mother in Chemistry class, you know, in this very high school."

"I didn't know you knew my mama."

He nodded and then jumped back to expressing his concern over the situation between herself and Ben. "I'm sure you want to know what my point is with this little speech and well... I just want to make sure that you know I'm here to help you, Juniper. In any way I can. And actually, I'm going to start helping by moving your seat away from Mr. Maxwell's."

"Thank you. I appreciate that, I do." Juniper studied the laces in her sneakers, uncertain of what else to say. She suddenly wished the floor tiles would crack and split and open up to suck her quickly down into the darkness of her own awkward embarrassment.

"I know it isn't much," he continued, "but it might help you get through *this* class at least, without being picked on I mean."

"T-Thanks and really, I appreciate this. But uh, may I go now, sir? I don't want to be late for my next class and like I said, it's all the way on the other side of campus." Juniper pulled her book bag up from the floor and held the straps in her palms so tightly that her knuckles bled white. The subject matter made her restless and she continued to avoid his gaze, favoring instead the speckles of color in the tiles beneath her feet.

"Yes, yes, of course. You may go now, I'm all finished here." He reached around on the desk behind him and pulled out a pad of bright yellow tardy slips. "I'll write you a note in case you're late to your next class." He scribbled something quickly across the thick pad of paper and tore off the sheet at the perforation with a flourish.

Juniper took it and managed to pull her lips into an

appreciative smile.   "Thanks, Mr. Halsey.   And again, I appreciate your concern and the seating change."

He nodded and his eyes sparkled with seriousness. "It's really not a problem, Miss Kelly. Just remember, you can come to me if you need to, alright? I also hope you know that anything we speak about in private will remain as such. *Private*."

"Alright."

"Ok, ok, get outta here. Oh, and if you remember, tell your mother Nick Halsey says hello."

Juniper nodded her response numbly and pulled herself to her feet. "Thanks again," she whispered. "I'll see you tomorrow."

He nodded and waved his hand dismissively in the face of her thank you. "When you come to class tomorrow, just go ahead and take the empty seat behind Karen Clary." Mr. Halsey paused. "Oh, and Miss Kelly...? If you're mother *does* happen to remember me-?" He shook his head and waved away his notion. "Never mind. Have a good afternoon and don't forget that your oral presentation is due Monday. I look forward to seeing what you've come up with."

"I won't forget." Juniper forced out yet another awkward smile and tossed her final parting words over her shoulder as she scurried towards the door and more importantly, to the hall beyond it. "See you tomorrow."

Once outside in the embarrassment-free arms of the hall, Juniper leaned against the cool white-painted brick wall and closed her eyes. She sighed and inhaled slowly before exhaling in much the same manner. She looked down at the tardy pass in her hand and then glanced down the hallway - three more periods to go and already she wanted nothing more than to run home and try to put the entire morning behind her.

Much to her dismay, Ben and Jason were standing several yards away. Jason was holding a pack of cigarettes in one hand and a text book in the other; Ben was pulling books from his locker with his own cigarette tucked behind his ear. Their conversation was muddied by the distance between them and Juniper turned quickly to face the other direction. She wanted nothing more than to avoid another confrontation. It wasn't something she was sure she could handle, as she was still reeling from Ben's hateful words at the beginning of Halsey's class. She could only guess that was what they were talking about, and was certain that her name had come up several times as Ben relayed his interaction with her to Jason's eager ears. Without another moment of hesitation, Juniper began walking towards the women's restroom at the end of the hall.

Please don't let them notice me, she thought. *Just let me get through the rest of this day without more of their crap. I don't know how much more I can take before I snap.*

To collect her thoughts and calm her nerves before she headed off to Biology, she ducked into the white-walled restroom. Relieved that her presence had gone unnoticed by the dastardly duo, Juniper sighed and made her way to the empty stall at the far side of the room. A gaggle of girls were hovering around the mirrors engaged in lively, inane chatter. One of them was smoking; another was re-applying lipstick. When she'd finished lining her lips with the bright red gloss, she smiled at her perfectly flawless reflection and rejoined the conversation. Juniper knew most of the girls only by name and nothing more. They were cheerleaders, the popular set that most girls wanted to be like and most guys wanted to be with.

They noticed her presence, but none of them said a thing in response to her disheveled appearance. Juniper wasn't surprised and she stepped into the tall-doored blue stall and latched the lock. She listened as the girls gathered their make-up and books and exited the bathroom in a cloud of laughter and innocuous babble about that weekend's upcoming football game with cross-town rivals, Whitewater High.

When they were gone, Juniper dropped her book bag to

the floor at her feet. She took a seat on the back of the toilet where she rested her head in her hands. She wanted to cry, but she held back, having already shed too many tears that day for her own taste. Instead she waited silently for the bell to ring and hoped against hope that Jason and Ben would have long-since scurried off to their next classes and left the hallways empty and emotional-landmine-free.

Fifteen minutes later, late and feeling only slightly better, she collected her demeanor and her thoughts and trudged off to her Biology lab. To her delight, the white-walled halls were empty of all life and the relief she felt was nearly tangible.

Thank God for small miracles, she thought, and with her book bag slung over her shoulder, she began the long walk across campus.

Chapter Two
Progress

When Juniper arrived home that afternoon, she was surprised to find her mother's car in the driveway. She skimmed her mental calendar and when she realized that it was Wednesday she quickly noted that her mother should have been at work. Her heart skipped a beat as it always did when faced with a deviation from the norm. She immediately assumed something was wrong and she quickened her pace to a jog. When she reached the patio she climbed the side steps to the kitchen door and pulled out her keys. The door was already unlocked and she quickly entered through the doorway where she dropped her book bag by the staircase and kicked off her shoes on the mat.

"Hey sweetheart, I'm in the kitchen," her mother called out. Her unexpected voice gave Juniper's heart a stir, and in the process, her heart increased its thump.

"What are you doing home? Is everything ok? You didn't go and get yourself fired did you?" Juniper crossed the hardwood entry way in her stocking feet and slid along the tile to the counter where she stopped abruptly next to her mother. "Well? Did you?"

Penelope Kelly was fixing up a cup of coffee, blonde and sweet, the only way she'd drink it. It was a habit that Juniper herself had inherited.

"Goodness no! Why would you think that? Everything's just fine, sweetheart. Karen- you remember her, right? She just needed an extra shift to make ends meet this month so I told her to finish out mine." Penelope leaned towards her daughter and placed a kiss on her forehead. "I was *more* than happy to make the sacrifice so that I might spend some quality time with my *favorite* person."

"You seem to be in a good mood," Juniper noted. "Did you have a good day?"

Penelope tilted her head from side to side. "Eh, I'm glad to be home, I'll say that much. What about you? How was school today?"

Juniper shrugged. "It was ok, nothing spectacular."

"Well, good." Penelope pushed a strand of fine blonde hair away from her forehead. "I suppose ok is better than horrible, isn't it?"

"Definitely better than horrible. Oh, and mama, while I'm thinking of it, do you remember Nick Halsey?" Juniper stuck her pinky in the sugar bowl and licked it clean.

Penelope smacked her hand lightly and placed the lid back onto the Tupperware bowl. "Nick Halsey...?" She repeated his name a second time under her breath and paused in thought. "The name sounds vaguely familiar. *Should* I remember him?"

Juniper nodded. "He's my history teacher. You know, Mr. Halsey. You met him at the PTA meeting last month. He happened to mention to me today that you two were in the same Chemistry class in high school.... He said he sat behind you or something."

Penelope shook her head. "I don't remember him, Junie, I'm sorry. Was I supposed to? Are you in trouble? I thought your history grades were top notch."

"Now look who's jumping to conclusions." Juniper shrugged. "But no, I'm not in trouble. He just wanted me to say hello to you, that's all. And between you and me? I get the distinct impression that he's got a crush on you and that he's *had* that crush since high school."

Penelope blushed. "Well that's nice, however I'm afraid I don't remember him. Is he cute? If so, feel free to get in trouble so that I might get called in for a conference."

Juniper groaned and scrunched up her face. "You're not seriously asking me to discuss the physical attributes of my *history teacher,* are you? Eww, mama. Just- *eww!*"

"What?" She laughed. "Does that mean he's dreadful? What are we talking about here? Buck teeth and an eye patch? Or perhaps he has some sort of ungodly horn growing from the side of his head?"

"Well no, but-" Juniper shook her head and laughed at the mental image her mother's playful joking had conjured. "He's decent, I guess, in comparison to horned pirates. But listen, can we not talk about this? It's *seriously* grossing me out."

"Fine, fine, we'll change the subject. I'll just dig out my yearbook later and look him up." Penelope smiled over the rim of her coffee mug, amused at Juniper's discomfort.

"So, anyway, moving on to slightly less disturbing subjects... we didn't get a chance to talk last night." Juniper smiled at her mother and quickly steered the conversation in a less unsettling direction. "I was in bed before you got home. That leaves me to assume that things must have gone pretty well. I mean, it's not like you to break curfew "

"You're right, it isn't. And I'm sorry about that, sweetheart. Dinner just ran a bit longer than I expected. The restaurant was packed."

"Oh, I don't *care* that you were late. In fact, I'm glad! After all, it's about time you went out on a date and had some fun. I just want all of the juicy details! So? Did you have a nice time? Did he kiss you good-night?" Juniper nudged her mother in the side with her elbow. "Come on, spill it! I want to know how it went."

"Well, dinner was excellent. He took me to this little Cantonese restaurant in Greenville. I have to say, the dim sum was out of this world. In fact, I was thinking that maybe soon you and I could drive out to the city for a meal. I really think you'd love it, it's much better than the China House in Tides

River." Penelope forced a tight-lipped smile in her daughter's direction, but dropped it when she noticed the disapproving look on Juniper's face. "What? What is it? Why are you looking at me like that? I had a nice time!"

Juniper relaxed her look of skepticism. "So do you think you'll ever see him again?"

"Ted?" Her mother shrugged. "He asked me out for dinner again next week, but I..." She shook her head. "To be honest with you, I just don't see the point in it."

"What do you mean? Why not?" Juniper asked. "He's a nice guy! Heck, even *I* liked him and you know how picky I am. Plus he's *really* cute and he has a great car. What was it? A Mercedes something or other? He's obviously got money *and* good taste. He picked you after all."

Penelope laughed. "Well, I'll tell you what... I'll keep his number and when you turn eighteen, then *you* can date him."

"He's not *my* type, mama. And I'm assuming by your attitude that he isn't yours either." Juniper sighed and clucked her tongue. "Well come on, out with it already, what's wrong with *this* one?"

When it came to dating, Juniper's mother had always been overly-picky, having in the past cited such reasons to dump men as poor table manners, bad fashion sense, and lousy taste in music. The one guy she *had* managed to see three times finally revealed to her his CD collection of nothing but adult contemporary only to be quickly shown the door.

"Dating is difficult, sweetheart. You can't just settle for any one person who happens to come along. The heart is a strange creature, girl. You can't tame her and you certainly can't predict her actions... but when it's right...?" Penelope smiled softly. "When it's *right*, you'll know it, and all of the pieces will fall neatly into place."

"Have you ever *known* it?" Juniper asked almost inaudibly. She shuffled her feet and crossed them over each other in an attempt at relaxing. "I mean, have you ever *really* been in love?"

Penelope cleared her throat and quickly drew closed the curtain on her memories, whatever they might have been. Still, no response came and after several drawn-out seconds, Juniper fished for an answer to her query.

"Mama?" Juniper questioned cautiously. "Are you ok? You look like you're a million miles away."

Penelope nodded and stirred herself from her thoughts. "Oh sorry, I- It's just that he's too old," she said finally.

"Too old?" Juniper furrowed her brow and cast her mother a quizzical glance. "What are you *talking* about?"

"Ted," Penelope said with a shake of her finger. "Ted's *way* too old for me."

"But he's hardly 40!" Juniper exclaimed. "Since when did 40 make a person over the hill?"

"I'm only 33, Junie," Penelope said firmly. "I'm not ready to start dating men in their 40s. Especially not *divorced* men with four children and enough emotional baggage to nicely fill up an RV! However, when you get to be a certain age I suppose that's all par for the course. And really, it's not like I'm in any position to judge. I have you and I certainly have my own baggage, it's just... It's *different* with Ted. His kids are young, infants practically, and the divorce was so recent that I could still make out the tan line on his ring finger!"

"Well what about Keith?" Juniper pressed. "Was that his name?"

"Keith?" Penelope repeated the name out loud and searched her mind. "Oh, you mean Kirk?"

"Kirk, that's it." Juniper snapped her fingers and shook them in her mother's direction. "What about him? You liked him, didn't you?"

"He lives too far away," she said simply.

Juniper shook her head and laughed. "It's like a 30

minute drive at worst!"

Penelope dried her long, thin fingers on the green and white checkered kitchen towel and placed it neatly back on the counter. Her hands found her hips when freed of the fabric and her eyes fell to rest upon Juniper's. "Thirty minutes *is* a long way for someone who works two jobs and has a teenage daughter to look after."

"You're just too picky, mama," Juniper said, "and don't try to deny it or I'll just remind you about Alex."

Penelope looked down and Juniper noticed the blush that rose to stain her pale, round cheeks. "Well really, could you blame me on that one, Junie? I mean seriously? There's just something *highly* unnatural about a 34 year old man who still lives with his perfectly able-bodied mother. Who lives in the *basement*, no less!"

"But other than that, he was perfect!"

"You just don't get it, do you?" Penelope sighed. "When I find the right person I won't have to settle or learn to accept anything. *Everything* will be perfect."

"You live in a fairy tale world," Juniper said softly. "There *are* no happy endings, mama. Not like the one you're waiting on."

"I hate to hear you say that, Junie." Penelope shook her head slowly from side to side. "I really hope I haven't given you that impression... that life *can't* be perfect." Penelope lightened the intense mood of the conversation with a soft laugh. "And, if I might ask, why does it matter to you all of a sudden whom I date or don't date?"

"It *doesn't* matter... I just-" Juniper collected her words carefully. "I just want you to be happy, mama. That's all."

"I *am* happy!" She faced her daughter and flashed her another wide, straight-toothed smile. "Really, I am! I have my health, I have two decent jobs and most importantly I have *you*. The best, albeit **nosiest**, daughter in all of South Carolina, and quite possibly the world. Now I ask, what more could I want?"

Juniper rolled her eyes. "I'm not nosy, I'm just concerned. I don't want you to not date because of me."

Penelope leaned against the counter and looked slightly defeated. "I'll admit that when you were younger, I didn't date because I didn't want to bring that stuff into the house. You were impressionable and I didn't want to give you the wrong idea about a lot of things, but now that you're older..." She sighed and shook her head softly, almost sadly. "I don't date because I don't *like* to date- and did it ever occur to you that maybe I genuinely *like* being single?"

"But don't you want to get married and have more children?" Juniper pried. "Don't you even want a chance at a perfect, normal life?"

"Is that what this is all about? You want a sister? Or maybe a brother?"

Juniper shrugged. "I don't know. I mean yeah, sometimes I do think it would be nice to have someone younger to play with, to teach things to and read to... And it would definitely be nice to have someone to think of as a father, even if that someone isn't my biological one."

Penelope reached out and smoothed her daughter's thick black hair. "I really should have gotten you that puppy when you were younger, shouldn't I?" Penelope, when she noticed the look of frustration on Juniper's face, dropped her joking. "Are you sure it's me that's lonely and not you?"

Juniper bit her lip. She didn't want to admit that there was some truth to her mother's accusation. "I'm not lonely," she said softly. "You know me, I like being a loner."

Penelope raised one eyebrow to scrutinize her daughter's words. "You're not lonely? Not in the least?" She smiled sympathetically. "Well, you could have fooled me, you know."

Juniper turned away from her mother and chose instead to face the cold comfort of the refrigerator. Her hands found the handle of the door and opened it. Bathed in the warm glow of the interior light, she popped her head inside and scanned the contents of the shelves. What she found amidst the soda and vegetables was an abrupt change in subject. "Say, did you happen to pick up more apples at the store like I asked? It's weird, but I've really been craving some sweet apples lately... and maybe if you're up to it we could put some of those apples in your famous apple pie-"

"I haven't been to the store yet and you know it. Now please, don't change the subject, we're talking here."

Juniper sighed and stood upright. With the turn of her wrist, she closed the fridge door and turned back to her mother's scrutinizing gaze. "I'm not changing the subject, I just thought we were done and I was moving on."

"Not done." Penelope shook her head. "Are the kids at school bothering you again? You always get testy with me like this when you've had a bad day and usually if you've had a bad day it's because of Jason or that other kid. So? Am I right?"

Juniper tossed her shoulders up and then allowed them to fall. "Sorta. Not really. It's nothing I feel like talking about."

"Well which is it? Sorta something or nothing really?" Penelope moved to the dining room table, her coffee in hand. She sat slowly and scooted the wooden legs of the chair across the tiles with a subtle screech. "Come, sit with me for a spell."

Juniper sighed and glanced wistfully towards the staircase. "I should really be getting started on my homework. I still have a lot of work left to do on my history project before Monday."

Penelope looked at the clock and clucked her tongue. "You have plenty of time for that. Now sit down here and talk to me for a few minutes. I promise I won't keep you long and if I do, you can ground me for the weekend."

Juniper followed her mother's pointing finger to the chair across from her and dolefully slid onto the cushion. "Ok,

I'll sit, but I don't know what it is exactly that you want me to tell you."

"The truth. Tell me the truth. That's all I've ever asked of you." Penelope held her hands over the coffee's rising steam and hardened her look of concern. "Are Jason and his buddies still picking on you?"

"Sometimes... but it's really not that bad, mama. You'd be amazed at how quickly a persons skin can toughen," she fibbed.

"Jason Price," she said with a sigh. "He used to be such a nice kid! Do you remember when you two were little? You'd play together all the time. Evelyn and I couldn't keep you two apart during the summer. We used to joke that someday you'd get married and have children of your own-"

"I remember." Juniper smiled and then shrugged it aside as the old memories were washed away by the current. "Things change, that's all. *People* change. It sucks, but it happens."

Somewhere, upstairs in her room, she still had a box full of childhood memorabilia. A walkie-talkie that she had used to communicate with Jason on late nights when children should have been sound asleep; photos; an old grass stained t-shirt, and the paper tiara she had worn at her 6th birthday party, the party where Jason had kissed her quickly and shyly at the corner of her mouth. It had been her first kiss, and Juniper was almost ready to declare that at the rate her social life had degraded, it might be her only one.

Yes, she did remember. She very clearly remembered every lazy, summer day of her youth. Days she'd spent running through water sprinklers with Jason behind her, days spent rolling on the soft wet grass and laughing as the blades stuck to their faces and tickled their noses. Sometimes she missed it, and always she wondered why it was Jason had taken such a strong stance against her.

They'd been best friends for much of their childhoods,

in fact. Then almost overnight it all changed and for a year they hardly spoke. When again they finally did, it was Jason who had done all of the talking as he'd flung insults and profanity, all at the behest of Ben Maxwell.

"I just wish I knew what happened to Jason to make him turn on you like he did! Maybe I should call Evelyn some time. Perhaps together the two of us could figure out-"

"Mama, please," Juniper groaned. "That's got to be one of the worst ideas I've *ever* heard."

Penelope didn't immediately respond to Juniper's protest as she was still mulling over the subject in her own mind. Her finger traced the rim of her mug absently. "I just hate to think he's fallen in with the wrong crowd," she said quietly. "But that's it, isn't it?"

"It's Ben. He does what he does because of Ben. He wants to impress him or something." Juniper had intentionally said his name quietly. The rest of her words dropped to the table where they slid fluid to the edge and fell directly into her mothers waiting lap.

"Ben? Ben...?" She considered his name thoughtfully. "Do I know him?"

"I don't think so."

Penelope took a sip of her coffee. Her eyes never left Juniper's face. "Oh, hey, what about that one girl? You used to hang out with her quite a bit. I liked her! Oh dear, what *was* her name?"

Juniper knew of whom it was her mother spoke. "Katie," she whispered softly. "Her name was Katie Greenup."

Katie had been one of the few people in Juniper's life that she'd considered to be a friend. Katie had also been an outcast, as her story was similar to Juniper's. An absent father, a lacking of self-esteem and a magnetism that drew cruelty from people like pliers extracting a splinter from a swollen, aching finger.

They had bonded quickly and had maintained a close friendship for several years until Katie's grandmother had fallen ill. It was then that she and her mother had been forced to move to Charlotte to help care for her. Juniper had cried for a week over the loss and at the time she'd thought for certain that she'd never recover.

"That's right! Katie!" her mother exclaimed. "Whatever happened to her? Did you guys have a falling out?"

"She moved to Charlotte, mama. Remember? It was almost two summers ago, now."

Penelope rubbed her forehead and looked all of a sudden weary. "Has it really been that long?"

"You work too much," Juniper said simply. She regretted uttering the words the moment that they slid past her lips and found life on the air between them.

Penelope's long hours had always been a sore spot with the both of them, and Juniper hadn't meant for her comment to sound like a bitter barb at that unchangeable fact.

Penelope nodded and sighed. "I know, I know... but what would you have me do? Move us back to that cramped apartment over the grocery and stock up on ramen noodles and chicken broth?"

"No, but-" Juniper cut herself off. She knew that anything she said would be overheard and ignored by her mother who had already begun to collect her defenses in preparation of firing her cannons.

"I don't know about you, but I certainly don't want to go back there," Penelope said firmly. "Things were rough and now our situation is good, well, it's *decent* at least. I can pay all of the bills and take care of us the way we need to be taken care of-"

"Mama, I'm not mad at you for working! I didn't mean to start this conversation again, I just miss you sometimes, and sometimes, you miss me and what's going on with me."

"I know I miss out on a lot, believe me I do." She rested

her mug of coffee on the table and checked the time. "Hey, I meant to ask you... do you want a ride to school tomorrow morning? I'm going in to work a bit later than usual and thought you might like a break from walking all that way."

Juniper shrugged. "Sure, if you've got time, I'd love that."

"For you, I always have time," Penelope said with a wink. "Now go on up and get started on your homework before supper. The food will be ready in 30 minutes or less."

Juniper groaned. "Pizza *again?*"

Penelope laughed and pushed herself back from the table in pursuit of the phone. "Hey, nothing but the best for my growing girl."

The next morning during the ride to school, Juniper slicked her lips with a thin layer of clear lip gloss and looked at her reflection in the passenger's side visor mirror. She crinkled her nose at the sight of her own plain-jane face, then looked at her mother's perfect profile.

Penelope Kelly had been blessed with all of the beauty Juniper herself could only hope for. Shiny, pin-straight blonde hair, wide blue eyes and as if that wasn't enough, her face was further accentuated with thick, perfectly-pink lips and naturally blush-stained cheeks that gave her a youthful, healthy glow. Even without any makeup, she was gorgeous. However, Juniper knew full well that behind the beautiful façade a troubled mind, and an even-more troubled past, brewed.

It was something she rarely ever brought up to her mother, and questions she'd never asked littered the ashtray like cigarette butts, unattended and forgotten. They smoldered and smoked in silence until finally they burned out from the absence of hope and eager lips to keep their cherries alive.

That morning, to her surprise, Juniper found that her lips

and mind had made an agreement to work in co-operation, and a subject she almost never broached grew heavy upon her tongue. "Hey mama? Can we talk?"

"Sure, sweetie. What's on your mind?" Penelope reached out to lower the volume of the radio and gave Juniper her full attention once the yammer of the morning DJs fell away. "I was wondering if you were ever going to say anything. You've hardly said two words since dinner last night."

"I've just been thinking a lot lately, that's all. And I know you probably won't answer this question, but I'm going to ask-"

"Is it about what I think it's about?" Penelope glanced over at her daughter briefly before she returned her slightly narrowed eyes to the road.

"Probably."

"Then you're right, I won't answer, so you should just save your breath until you think of something else to talk about."

Juniper pushed ahead with her question in spite of herself and her mother's obvious dissatisfaction. In a fevered rush, the words fell from her lips. "Do you still love my father? Is that why you can't commit to anyone else?"

Penelope's grip upon the steering wheel tightened instantly and visibly. "I don't know what to say to that, Junie. Or rather, I don't know what you *want* me to say."

"Look mama, I'm not asking for dad's name or his whereabouts or anything like that.... I just want to know if you still love him, that's all."

"Well I-" Penelope paused. "He gave me *you*... Because of that I suppose I'll always have a special place for him in my heart-"

"I know *that*, mama... but do you still *love* him after all of these years? Is that why you always find something wrong with every other guy you date? Because they aren't him? Because maybe you're waiting for him to come back someday?"

Penelope released a hollow laugh. "No, Junie, that's *not* why. There's no chance that I'll ever, that *we'll* ever, see your father again, so for me to still love him would not only be in vain, but it would also be *incredibly* foolish."

Juniper shifted in her seat and beneath the grip of the seatbelt her heart beat quickened. This was the most information about her father, and her mother's relationship with him, that she had ever been able to pry from her normally sealed-tight lips. "Why not?" she continued. "Tell me why not?"

"Why not *what?*" Penelope asked with a slight twinge of irritation to her voice.

Juniper licked her lips and forcibly held back the exasperation from her words. "Why won't we ever see him again, mama? What happened to him? Is he- is he *dead?*" Her heartbeat raced and it quickly filled her ears with its insistent ka-thunk beat.

"You know I don't like to talk about this." Penelope lowered the sun visor to deflect the early morning sun rays as they broke through the clouds and washed over the road and the pristine front windshield of the small, blue sedan.

"I know that, but mama, come *on*! I'm- I'm almost sixteen years old! I'm two years from being a legal adult!" She paused to gauge her mother's premature reaction to her words and continued when her expression remained unchanged. "I just want to know about my father. Like I said, you don't have to tell me his name or anything, I just want to know what he was like and I want to know why he left us. I think I deserve at least that much."

"He was a wonderful man, Juniper. Absolutely wonderful. He was tall, smart, raven-haired." She glanced at her daughter again and squinted through the sunlight. "Every time I look at you, I see pieces of him reflected in your eyes."

Juniper looked down at her lap having immediately sensed her mother's wistful sadness. "It must be hard for you to look at me," she whispered. "I'm like this giant, constant reminder of him."

"Sometimes it's hard, yes," she admitted before she added more to her statement in a lighter tone. "I do want you to know that if he could have stayed with us he would have, Junie."

"Really?" The hopelessness that had filled her drained slowly, but not completely, and around her ankles hung the cold, muddy waters of despair she'd known her entire life.

Penelope nodded. "Really truly."

"So was he in the military?" Juniper asked. "Is he a top secret spy or something?"

Penelope laughed. "No, he's not a spy."

"Then why couldn't he stay? There must have been some thing that took him away."

"Look, Junie, sweetheart, it's complicated, ok?" Penelope's frustration took hold of her and she forcefully pushed her hair back behind her ear and squinted at the road ahead. "Sometimes that's the way things are. Complicated and unchangeable and you have to learn to accept that. Some things are just out of your control no matter how much you wish they weren't."

Juniper knew better than to press the issue further and she slid instead into a new line of questioning. "So when was the last time you saw him? Dad, I mean."

"It was the day after you were born. That was the last time."

Juniper was stunned by her mother's casual admittance, and she continued her questioning with increasing speed and excitement. "So grandpa knew dad?"

Penelope nodded. "Grandpa was part of the reason your father and I couldn't be together, but only part. And, you know,

I hesitate at sharing that with you, I really do. The last thing I want to do is tarnish your memories of your grandfather. He loved you, Junie, very much. And you loved him, too."

Her grandfather had died of Alzheimer's when Juniper had been 3 years old. She hardly remembered him at all. In fact, the only strong memories she had of him were those of his final days. His ending had been torturous to watch and Juniper was glad that she'd been too young to recall it with any amount of real clarity. His mind had completely left him during the last few weeks and Juniper remembered how he had wandered through the house in a fever talking to people that didn't exist.

"Grandpa didn't like dad?" Juniper made a face. "But you said dad was a great guy. Why didn't grandpa like him if he was so great?"

"Junie." Her mother sighed, exasperated at her daughter's line of questioning. "I've have just about enough of the twenty questions already, so why don't you give it a rest before I get really angry with you, ok?"

"But mama," Juniper whined, "if I drop this now I'll never get you to talk about it again."

"No buts, young lady. Now we're changing the subject. No arguments." Penelope's eyes were narrowed beneath her wrinkled brow and a subject change followed swiftly behind the cold chill in the car as it swept over them both. "Just so you know, I'll be home later tonight than usual. It's inventory night at the store so go ahead and have dinner without me. I'll pick something up for myself on the way home."

"Oh, I see how it is! *You're* allowed to change the subject when the topic makes *you* uncomfortable, but you can't afford me the same luxury?"

Penelope groaned. "Junie, please! Must you ruin a perfectly good morning with an argument that we can easily avoid?"

Juniper crossed her arms angrily over her chest, but said

nothing further. Instead, she sat quietly and stared out of the window at the scenery that zipped by. It was all predictable, a landscape she'd watched race past her eyes a million times over. Tree, field, house, farm, tree... Juniper found herself wondering then what it would be like to live in a big city like Atlanta or Charleston, in a place that changed constantly and moved quickly, but she realized soon after that she couldn't even fathom a fast-paced life that took her away from Camden Falls. Deep inside, she knew that her heart would always be small town.

Again her thoughts drifted and they soon found themselves lingering over the issue her mother had ever-so-sternly put a lid on. She parted her lips to ask one last question, but try as she might to force the words out, they wouldn't come.

Instead, the question burned itself in to her forebrain with a red hot iron and a sizzle of smoke.

Where exactly did my father go? Juniper asked herself. *And why won't he come back for me? Isn't he the least bit curious about the person I've become?*

That night Juniper was awakened by the sound of her mother's car as it pulled into the driveway. Her eyes slowly peeled themselves open and crawled to consult with the clock on her dresser.

It was only then that Juniper realized she'd fallen asleep on the sofa with the TV on and the volume cranked. She yawned, found the time on the VCR and sat up slowly as she waited for her mother to enter the kitchen.

It had been shortly after ten when Juniper had heard her mother's engine shut off, and was shortly after 10:15 when Juniper finally stood and made her way to the kitchen to check on her mother's unusually delayed progress. She pushed apart two slats of the blinds on the kitchen door and peered out into the darkness; her eyes stumbled over her mother's silent, still form. She was leaning against the railing of the side patio with a distant look etched across her face.

Juniper unlocked the door and opened it slowly. Her mother turned and smiled at the steady creak and offered words as Juniper's bare feet stepped onto the hardwood deck.

"I'm sorry, sweetheart. Did I wake you?"

Juniper shrugged. "No, I uh, I fell asleep on the sofa after dinner. I needed to get up."

"Oh well... you should probably get to bed, then. I'll be in shortly." Penelope was lost to Juniper, wrapped up in her own thoughts and emotions to such a degree that Juniper wondered if she had even really heard her.

"Mama? Are you ok?"

Penelope sighed and pulled her eyes away from the forest trees. "Hmm? Oh, yeah... Yeah. I'm fine. I'm good."

"You sure? Work was ok? Because if you need to talk, I'm a good listener. You know that."

Her mother nodded and bypassed Juniper's concern. "Yeah, I know, but everything is ok," she whispered. "I just wanted to get a bit of fresh air. It's a nice night. A nice night."

Juniper stood her ground and her own eyes wandered over the field behind their house to the tree line just on the other side. "Hey mama? Have you ever been into the forest?"

Penelope inhaled slowly. "Yes. Once or twice."

"Well, I was thinking that I might explore it this weekend. You know, for lack of anything better to do. I've never really been in the woods and I figured a hike might do me some good considering that currently the only exercise I get is walking to school from time to time." Juniper watched her mother's features and prepared for a good talking to, however, Penelope remained silent. "I think the fresh air and change of scenery might be nice," she added. "And you *are* always telling me that I don't get enough time out of the house... Mama? Did you hear me, mama? I said-"

"I heard what you said," Penelope whispered. "And I've told you, haven't I? How dangerous the woods can be? That's especially true if you're alone out there. Don't be thinking that just because you're almost sixteen, the rules have changed. I still don't want you in those woods, you hear me?"

"I know that, mama, but come on! I can take care of myself! And sixteen... sixteen is practically grown up!"

"I was sixteen when I met your father. I was almost *seventeen* when I got pregnant with you." Penelope snapped her lips closed over her teeth as though unbelieving that her words had slipped out into the night.

"So uh... Where did you meet him? At school? Did he live around here?"

Penelope laughed. "He lived *around.*"

"Did you know the first time you saw him that you loved him?"

Penelope lowered her chin and shook it softly from side to side. "No, but soon thereafter the truth of my feelings became more than apparent."

"Did he love you, mama?"

Penelope's lower lip began to quiver. "He loved us *both* very much."

"Then *why* did he leave-"

"Because sometimes love isn't enough, Junie," Penelope snapped. She shook her head slowly and offered a sad sigh. "I'm sorry, I don't mean to be testy with you. It's just that I've had a really long day and I don't particularly want to end it the same way it began."

Juniper bit her lip and nodded. "It's ok, I understand." Juniper shoved her hands into the pockets of her jeans and changed the subject. "So are you coming in soon?"

Penelope nodded. "Soon, soon. Yes."

Juniper walked closer to her mother and leaned in to kiss her softly on the cheek. "Alright, but don't be long. It's chilly out here and you have to be up early tomorrow. Goodnight, mama."

"Night, Junie. Sleep well."

Juniper left her mother standing silent on the patio and made a quick retreat to her bedroom.

During her slow jog up the cool carpeted stairs, she made a decision. She *would* explore that forest and her mother would be none the wiser. After all, what she didn't know couldn't hurt her.

Juniper fell asleep with that very clichéd thought on the tip of her tongue and only moments before she drifted off into slumber did she realize that it was completely untrue.

What a person doesn't know *can* hurt them, and no one knew that better than Juniper herself.

The next day was Friday, one of Juniper's favorite days for obvious reasons, as it meant that the school week was nearly over. To her surprise, the duration of the morning passed quickly and without incident. Jason passed her in the hallway without even looking in her direction; Ben had done the same in the cafeteria at lunch, and he hadn't even bothered to show up for Mr. Halsey's class at all.

Juniper breathed a sigh of relief as she left her last class that afternoon and slipped away from the excited crowd of students. She fell in line with her familiar route; past the bleachers, through the hole in the fence and across the empty lot to the corner.

The walk home was shorter for Juniper than for most. Every day she made the mile walk in silence, and on that day in particular, she took special note of the forest as it loomed in the distance. Still, she passed it by.

She was too afraid to enter it alone, thanks in no small part to her mother's almost constant reminders that the forest was no place for a young lady to be. Being mindful of her mother's overprotective nature, Juniper had never penetrated its boundaries with anything more than her gaze.

A shiver ran down her spine that particular afternoon as she passed the path that led into the thickest part of the woods. It was a shiver unlike any she had ever felt before; different than other shivers, it was unique in a way that Juniper couldn't quite seem to place her finger on.

So powerful it was that it stopped Juniper's feet and forced her to give pause at the head of the dusty, dirt trail. For a long moment she stood there transfixed while her eyes wandered aimlessly down the path towards the trees.

She had heard the rumors, of course; the rumors of a hidden secret, of a strange creature, that the trees kept beneath their canopy. The stories had always intrigued Juniper, but until that moment, she herself had never seen or felt the need to search out the answers to the questions of a town.

With a gathered breath and a renewed sense of curiosity, she stepped gingerly onto the dirt path with one white sneaker; she did so softly as though testing the waters for their safety. However, before she could proceed further, she was forced to quickly recoil from her curiosity thanks to the sound of a car as it rapidly approached from her rear.

She turned to look back at the road to her right and noticed the familiar vehicle as it rounded the corner in a cloud of noise.

The stereo was booming on the old beat-up Cavalier and grew ever louder as it approached. The occupants of the car saw Juniper at the same moment that she identified them positively. They began to slow and Juniper began to walk in hopes of avoiding another uncalled for confrontation.

Juniper's hopes were soon dashed as the car pulled up next to her and shadowed her steps. Finally, the driver called out to her.

"Hey, stop would ya?" It was Ben, the only sophomore to have a car of his own, a beater his grandmother had left him in her will the fall before.

Juniper didn't stop or turn her head in his direction. "I can't be late getting home."

Jason leaned forward from the passenger's seat with a cigarette dangling from the fingers of his right hand. "Well, hop in, we'll give you a ride."

Juniper shook her head at the invitation. "No thanks, I like walking."

"Come on, it's hot out there," Jason insisted. "We promise we won't hurt ya."

Juniper again shook her head. "No... no really, I can't."

Two boys in the backseat chuckled; Juniper recognized neither of them. She quickened her pace and raised her chin in defiance of their inside jokes and hushed teasing; Ben gave the car a light increase in gas and continued his shadow of her steps.

"Fine, suit yourself, Junie." Ben reached for a cigarette of his own. Unlit, he let it hang between his lips. "But you can't say we didn't ask."

"Hey, one thing before we go. Do me a favor and throw this away for me, would ya?" Jason lobbed a can of soda across the front seat at Juniper and it flew past Ben and through the opened window of the vehicle.

Juniper jumped backwards on the sidewalk and yelped as the can hit her arm and the brown liquid spewed out across the sleeve and chest of her t-shirt.

The boys burst into uproarious laughter and Ben took off in a rush of squealing tires and booming bass.

Juniper sighed and dropped to her knees where she placed her books on the sidewalk in all of their dripping, liquid-stained glory.   With a sigh even heavier than her first, she brushed the liquid from the cover of her English book and rubbed her hands through the grass to alleviate the quickly-drying stickiness her flesh had found.

She looked down at her new blue shirt and grimaced; the brown pop had soaked her entire right sleeve and most of her chest and stomach.

Juniper wrung the liquid out of the cotton fabric with her hands, then rubbed her fingers on the dry, bottom, left corner of her shirt with a heavy sigh that carried all of the earmarks of defeat.

Finally, she stood with her sticky books held tight in her sticky arms. She looked back at the ominous dirt path one more time and held the gaze for but a fleeting moment before she quickly rushed towards the safety of home.

Chapter Three
Spring Cleaning

Much to Juniper's relief and unimaginable delight, the next day was Saturday.

However, to her chagrin, she woke earlier than she'd planned, and to an empty house. With sleepy, heavy legs and awkward feet she found her way downstairs from her bedroom in her post-sleep haze. Absently, she munched her way through half a box of Cheerios, forgoing both bowl and milk for bare hand. As she ate, she stared blankly at the cartoons on the living room TV and sat transfixed as the bright colors blended in front of her weary eyes and shifted in and out of focus. She yawned and changed the channel from the motley madness in favor of something less high-energy. She settled on a re-run of *I Love Lucy* and her eyes thanked her for the calm of the old black and white program.

When she'd finished her breakfast, she returned the box of cereal to the kitchen cupboard and hunched over in front of the open fridge in search of the milk. She found it behind a bottle of unopened wine and after she'd poured herself a tall glass she sat down at the counter to wash down the remnants of her dry breakfast.

Her mother had left a note for her there, a note that had been held in place by the edge of an empty coffee mug. The note, coffee ringed and wrinkled, reminded Juniper that it was the Saturday that her mother was picking up an extra shift at the optometrist's office at the mall in Greenville. Penelope had left the number of the store in case Juniper needed anything and had ended the note with an obligatory I love you. When she finished with it, Juniper crumpled the note and lobbed it towards the trash can. She missed, sighed and retrieved the stray piece of paper to place it into its proper and intended receptacle. As the paper wad fell amongst the rest of the refuse, she found herself wondering why it was that she seemed to be a miserable failure at everything she attempted.

That thought segued quickly to the events of the previous afternoon. Events that still clung to the front of Juniper's brain, try as she might to keep them pushed back to the periphery.

She just couldn't understand why they targeted her. Was it only because she didn't have a father or did other things factor into the equation? Was it her height? The house she lived in? The clothes she wore? Juniper looked down at her thin, long body in search of answers. She was lanky and tall, in fact, she was the tallest girl in her class and almost the entire school. She would be the first to admit that her clothes were out of style, and the first to confess that she did most of her shopping at the Good Will store in town. But how could she be found at fault for not having enough money to compete with the other girls in their overpriced mall-bought garb? For being tall? For not having a father?

Try as she might to make sense of it all, she couldn't wrap her mind around the cruelty her classmates, namely Jason and Ben, dished-out at her on an almost daily basis.

She sighed and reminded herself yet again that it was indeed the weekend. With that idea reaffirmed, Juniper made an active decision to push all of the unpleasantness from her mind so that she might focus solely upon the two days that were spread out before her ready to be claimed. Juniper, however, felt little like claiming anything as she stifled another exhausted yawn with her splayed fingers.

All night she'd tossed in her bed in a restless, dreamless sleep. Thoughts of the forest had plagued her throughout her rest, had haunted her with tight-lipped secrets that kept themselves heavily shrouded in darkness and mystery. Never before had she felt the need to explore the depths of the woods behind her house, but then, she felt almost as though something was calling her there. Something that she knew she couldn't ignore forever.

When she finished her milk and her stomach was undeniably full, she nodded to herself and confirmed the silent, determined decision she'd made the night prior as she had ascended the stairs to her room. The decision to penetrate the line of the forest and see once and for all exactly what was lurking beneath the lush canopy of the South Carolina trees behind her home. Of course she realized that her mission would be one she would carry out alone, but at that point in her life, she knew it was time to stop hiding and time to start searching for the answers that had always eluded her grasp. They were out there and for some reason she felt that they were closer than she could even imagine.

Determined like never before, Juniper pulled on her sneakers and quickly yanked her socks up to her knees beneath her jeans to shield her calves and shins from the tall, scratching weeds in the meadow that led to the forest entrance. She realized it was still early and that the sun remained hidden behind thick, dark clouds. In light of that, she grabbed a sweatshirt and set to work on gathering a small backpack. She packed it lightly with a sandwich, a book and a bottle of water. As an afterthought, she ran to her bedroom for one of the multi-colored scrunchies she kept on her dresser. She pulled her thick hair back from her face and secured it at the back of her head to keep the curled tendrils from assaulting her cheeks and vision.

She decided that instead of walking back to the path that jutted off from the main road, and thus drawing more attention to herself than was needed, she would cut through her own back yard and approach the woods from a different angle. For some reason, the leaves seemed to whisper less from that part of the forest, and Juniper felt it would be a safer place to start her exploring before she dared plunge into the deeper, darker, more boisterous parts of the trees.

On her steady approach to the woods, Juniper thought about many things. She wasn't a fearful person, but there was a rapidly multiplying part of her that was rethinking her decision to enter the woods without a friend. Of course, Juniper didn't really have any friends. Remembering that sad truth, she quickened her pace until finally she found herself only a few tiny steps away from the perimeter of the trees.

Juniper adjusted the book bag on her back and took a deep breath. Slowly she stepped onto the dirt and then placed the other foot in front of her first. Quickly her steps increased and soon she was speed walking across the fallen leaves and broken twigs.

Juniper broke into a run when she passed the next row of oak trees - past the juniper bushes whose name she bore, and past the subtle serpentine of the abandoned and forgotten creek. Her feet would find her answers, certain of that she was, and when finally she felt free amidst the cool embrace of the woods, the abandoned farm house stepped out from beneath the canopy of the trees in a bold maneuver and a display of trust. It presented itself without shame and heaved an almost visible sigh of relief when it saw her, as if to say *'you're home'*.

The farm house had been asleep in the thick of the forest brush for some time before finally Juniper discovered it that morning. Forgotten and hidden from the prying eyes of the world, it shone like a beacon through the treetops and finger-like branches of the giant old oak trees that surrounded it. With an almost siren-like call, it led her from the safety of her forest path to a road less traveled; to a road riddled with pock marks and overgrown brush.

As she approached, the three story farm house opened up in front of her and seemed almost to magically grow. She cut back the branches as she went with decisive snaps and pushed aside the thick shrubbery. She made her way towards the front porch of what was once a beautiful home with curiosity and a touch of anxiety.

She wondered who had lived there; wondered why they'd left and allowed the home to fall into such a sad state of forgotten splendor.

She glanced around quickly in search of the presence of other people, and when she found no one, she made the last dash through the muck of a make-shift rainstorm creek and hopped onto the first wooden step that led to the porch. Her footsteps made the old wood boards creak and moan beneath her weight, but she pressed onward until she reached the sunken porch.

The glass in the front door had been broken long ago, so long ago that most of the shards had crawled away and had fallen between the cracks of the porch leaving nary a trace of their existence behind.

She hesitated before she extended her fingers to the harsh surface of the rust-covered doorknob. When finally she did take it in her hand, her fingers were immediately stained orange, followed by her palm. She wrapped her hand tightly around the knob and let a short breath escape her lips before she twisted it.

The door caught on something, on time, on its own old age, *something*, and without stopping to question her actions, Juniper thrust her hip at the middle of the door while she simultaneously twisted the knob. A loud thump rose from the porch and lifted into the air; a gathering of nearby birds gave up the seclusion of the bushes and dissipated into the sky as their cries spread out amongst the trees, and then, beyond to the clouds.

She threw herself at the door several more times until finally it coughed and moved aside to allow her trespass.

Swiftly, she moved inside. Her curiosity held firm to her hand like an imaginary guide and pulled her along into what was once a living room.

As it was, stained with time and neglect, the room was nothing but a cobweb-covered dust bin with broken down furniture and broken glass jars littering its floors.

The scant amounts of light that managed to filter into the living room did so through a pair of yellowed lace curtains that hung over a series of nailed-in-place boards. The light streams were narrow, heavy with motes of dust that danced about in the glow of the spring morning. They swirled about Juniper quickly, as if to inspect her person and report back to a higher and unseen source.

Surprising to her later, was the fact that upon first glance of the living room, she didn't notice it. It. The oak. The giant tree that had grown up under the house, through the floor and had pushed everything aside in its favor.

Big as life and wider than it too, it grew from the center of the living room into the second story and disappeared beyond that into what Juniper assumed was the third floor attic.

She walked towards it slowly at first, in a state of disbelief. She'd never seen anything like it and ventured to guess that in all the years she would be afforded, she never would again.

Closer to it she found herself walking, each step filled with less trepidation than the one that had preceded it. When finally she was close enough to touch the tree, she did so. Sure enough, the feel of the bark beneath her fingers proved that it was real.

Her palm clung fast to the surface of the remarkable tree and she walked herself around its base, counting her steps heel-to-toe.

There were thirty-six steps in total.

Juniper stepped back when her circle had been

completed and looked up. With her mouth wide open she marveled at the sight. She was speechless and spellbound, and uncertain of exactly what it was she was witnessing.

Juniper ran into the house that evening, breathless and excited. She found her mother in the kitchen dishing dinner out onto two mismatched plates. Penelope looked up and smiled at the sound of her shoes, and a brief wave of relief crashed over her face.

"I was beginning to wonder if I'd been stood up," she said. "I'm glad you made it. And just in time, too!"

Saturday evening dinner had been a tradition for as long as Juniper could remember. Being a single mother, Penelope worked two jobs to make ends meet and that left the two of them with only Saturday evening and Sunday to reconnect.

Juniper always enjoyed the dinners, and that evening in particular she was famished and eager to fill her stomach, much as her head had been filled with questions and wonder over the appearance of the strange, tree-filled farm house.

"Sorry I'm running late," Juniper apologized. She rushed up to Penelope and placed a kiss on her cheek. "Is there anything I can do to help?"

Penelope's own smile widened from the sentiment. "I think I've got everything under control, but thank you for the offer, sweetie." She turned slightly and eyed Juniper suspiciously. "You seem to be in a good mood. Did you have a nice day?"

Juniper turned back towards the entryway and kicked her shoes off onto the rug. "Actually, I had a *great* day."

Her mother smiled; she was beautiful when she smiled. There was just something about the way her lips pulled themselves high at the corners that widened her face with life.

That night, she was wearing makeup. Her bright blue eyes were highlighted by eye shadow and mascara, and her blonde hair had been pulled back from her face with barrettes to even further accentuate her delicate features.

Juniper found herself smiling absently at her mother, and when she pulled herself from her thoughts, she spoke. "So how was your day?"

"Oh, you know... Same as usual." She waved her hand. "Just another day at the office. Long, but quiet for the most part. *However!* I don't care much to talk about it. Wouldn't want to bore you, but I *would* like to hear more about *your* day. Specifically I'd like to know where you've been hiding."

"Not hiding. I've just been out and about, enjoying the sunlight and the fresh air," Juniper said casually. She shrugged and realized quite suddenly that she wasn't yet prepared to confess her activities and discoveries. Mostly because she hadn't yet found the words or the courage to do so.

Juniper knew how her mother felt about the woods, and had proven that again just the previous night. She wouldn't be happy; in fact, Juniper was willing to bet that she would be quite the *opposite* of happy if she knew where Juniper had spent a large portion of the day. After she'd swallowed that truth to her stomach, Juniper let it dissolve and soak into her bloodstream. She wasn't going to worry her mother when there was no reason for it, and she had no plans to ruin their Saturday night dinner with a lecture and, ultimately, an argument.

"Well, good! I'm glad to hear you got out. Maybe now people will stop thinking I'm holding you hostage in here." Her mother placed the plates on the table and her hands found her hips. "Did I tell you? Just last week, Mrs. Murphy stopped me at the grocery to ask what had *happened* to you! As though you had vanished into thin air! Of course she's not the only one who's asked me about you. You remember Mr. Cooper, don't you? Nice fellow, grey hair, glasses... used to own the market?

Well, he asked me almost the exact same thing last month!"

"Oh mama," Juniper groaned. She rolled her eyes at her comments and assumed almost immediately that she was exaggerating her claims to back up her own point. "I get out! Maybe not as often as some kids do, but enough. Besides, I'm surprised anyone notices me at all. It's not like I'm one of the town's most beloved residents."

"It's a small town. Everyone is like a family here and you're part of that! As for you getting out... you go to school and that's about it as far as I tell," Penelope said softly. She placed the silverware on the table and grabbed her can of soda from the counter. "Get yourself something to drink, Junie. It's time to eat and thank goodness for that! I don't know about you, but I'm starving."

Juniper moved over to the fridge and pulled open the door. "You're never home to see what it is I do with my time," she grumbled under her breath.

Penelope sighed. With her keen sense of hearing, she'd easily picked up on Juniper's muttered response. "Do we *really* have to go through this again? You'll ruin the one nice dinner we get a week." Penelope took a sip of her soda and shook her head. "You know I have no choice about the hours I work. The bills don't pay themselves and with you college-bound in just a few short years we need all the money we can pick up."

"I told you I'd get a job," Juniper said softly. She walked slowly back to the table with her own can of soda and pulled out the chair across from her mother. "Mr. Wilkins is hiring at the bookstore in town, you know. It's only part-time for the summer. The pay wouldn't be great, but it would certainly help, and maybe then you could cut your hours at the mall."

"I don't want you working," Penelope said firmly. "I want you focusing on your future. On your *studies*."

"But it's for the *summer*, mama. No school, nothing to interfere with," Juniper protested. "Just promise me you'll think about it, ok?"

Penelope sighed and pushed a strand of escaped blonde hair behind her ear. "We'll talk about it more in depth at a later date. I'll speak with Mr. Wilkins some time this week and see exactly what kind of hours you'd be working, oh and another thing..." She tapped her forehead with the end of her fork. "How exactly would you get there? You can't walk two miles round trip every day for minimum wage."

"I'll get a ride," Juniper said.

"From whom?" Penelope tilted her head to the left and anticipated an answer.

"From someone... I don't know yet, but I'll figure something out." Juniper dug into the lasagna, smiled, and changed the subject. "This tastes great, mama."

"Yes, well, your grandma's recipe never fails," Penelope said in a sing-song voice. She took her own bite of the dish then sighed heavily. "I really wish you could have met her, Junie. You would have loved her. She was in a class all to herself."

Juniper had seen the pictures on her mother's dresser, pictures of the woman known only to her as Millicent Kelly. She had been a beautiful woman and Penelope bore a striking resemblance to her. From the few stories Juniper had heard about her grandmother, she had gleaned that she had been deeply religious.

Penelope winked at her daughter and plunged her fork into the lasagna. "Someday I'll teach you how to make this. It's not as hard as you might think. It just takes a little patience."

"I can't cook, mama," Juniper protested. "We know this. My D in Home Ec. *proved* it beyond all shadow of a doubt."

Penelope rolled her eyes at her daughter's stubborn resign. "You can always learn, Junie. And besides, I won't let this recipe die with me. It's tradition to pass it on to your children, and you know, another thing... Just because you aren't immediately good at something, it doesn't mean you give up."

"Well, for some people it does," Juniper muttered.

"But not you." Penelope leaned forward and looked her daughter straight in the eye. "And what does that mean anyway? For *some* people?" She let her voice trail off momentarily before it resumed. "I thought that I had raised you to be better than this. Never give up! That's the Kelly motto, after all."

Juniper rolled her eyes at her plate. "I'll remember that."

"I should hope that you do." Penelope chewed thoughtfully and then dabbed her napkin delicately at the corners of her mouth. "So where did you say you were all day?"

Juniper shrugged and swirled her fork through a thick deposit of tomato sauce. "Around."

"Secretive, are we?" Her lips twisted into a smile. "Are you meeting a boy? Is that what you're up to?"

Juniper shook her head. "What boy would meet with *me*, mama? I'm an outcast... a *freak*. People see me coming and they almost literally clear a path."

Juniper felt the uneasy silence creep in and join them at the table. The silence was perpetuated by her mother's contribution to its length. Penelope continued eating in silence as though she were collecting her words and forming her sentences with great, exacting care.

Juniper let the silence linger and nervously awaited her mother's reply to her assertion of her outcast status.

"I'm sure you're exaggerating," Penelope said finally. "You're a beautiful girl and I'm sure nobody thinks you're a *freak*."

"I'm not exaggerating, mama. I'm being serious here. I'm treated differently, as though I don't belong. You have to see it, you *have* to. You'd be blind not to notice."

Penelope took a sip of her drink before she countered. "The question is, do you *feel* different?" she asked.

Juniper looked up and met her mother's gaze.

"Sometimes... always."

"Oh, sweetheart. I'm sorry you feel that way." Her mother's eyes filled with sadness and a glimmer of understanding. "I wish there was something I could-"

"Why are *you* sorry, mama?" Juniper interrupted. "It's not your fault I'm a freak, is it?"

Penelope lowered her voice and leaned forward over the table. "You aren't a freak. Please stop using that word, because to me you're nothing but a blessing. Just as you've always been."

"I just wish I felt like a blessing. You know?"

Penelope nodded softly. "I know. I just think that if you made attempts at being a little more social you might not feel like such an outsider. There are plenty of school clubs and extracurricular activities you could get involved in. Surely you have an interest in something, right? Astronomy? The school paper? You're an excellent writer, I've always thought so." Penelope lowered her fork to her plate and put her bottom lip between her teeth as though contemplating something controversial. Finally, she spilled her thoughts. "You remember Diana Lovero, correct?"

"The woman you work with at the optometrist's office?" Juniper asked. She furrowed her brow and gave her mama a curious look. "Yeah. Why do you ask?"

"Well, her son is just slightly older than you are. He's a junior this year... maybe you know him. His name is Drew, Drew Lovero."

Juniper thought for a brief second before her mind conjured up the image of a tall, lanky boy with dark hair and sharp features. "He's on the basketball team, isn't he?"

"Yeah, and the Honor Roll, the track and field team, the French club... The only thing he's missing is a friend or two. You know, someone to talk with and hang out with on weekends. Anyway, I was telling Diana that you were much the same way, a loner-"

"Mama, no," Juniper groaned. "Are you setting me up?"

"No, no, it's not a date thing!" Penelope exclaimed. "It's a- a-" She searched carefully for the right words as evidenced by the hemming and hawing over Juniper's question.

"If you say play date I'm never speaking to you again."

Penelope laughed. "No, no, no... nothing like that. I just thought the both of you could use a friend. You have a lot more in common with this boy than you might think."

"Like what?" Juniper dared.

"Like a bunch of stuff, Junie, I don't know exactly *what!*" Penelope exclaimed.

"I bet we both have a pulse," Juniper said sarcastically. "Oh, and here's another amazing commonality! We go to the same school! Wow, mama, you're right, it's obviously fated, *written in the stars* that Drew and I become the best of friends. Maybe we'll even get married in a big lavish ceremony and have a dozen perfect babies that we'll raise in our multi-roomed mansion by the sea."

"Listen Miss Juniper, don't you get sassy with me!" Penelope warned in a sharp tone. "I'm just trying to help you out. I thought you might *like* having someone to hang out with besides yourself and your books."

"I appreciate your concern, mama, I really do. But you know me! I don't really mind being alone. Really, I promise."

Her mother sighed heavily and shook her head with a sense of defeat. "You know something, Junie? We both make *terrible* liars."

Juniper chose not to respond, and she and her mother continued their dinner in silence. The only sound in the room was that of the ticking clock on the kitchen wall that signaled each agonizing second with a painstaking click that said so much.

Over the course of the next several weeks, the excitement in the air grew to palpable levels in the hallways at school. Classes would be ending in a little more than a month and the weather was finally evening-out. The calm before the storm, everyone called it. That short period of time where the weather was steady before summer kicked in, the temperatures soared and the storms blew in with their intensity and humidity.

After two more afternoon encounters with Ben and Jason, Juniper took her new-found enjoyment of the woods and plotted a different route home. She followed an old dirt path from behind the school, around the creek and through the woods. It was quite a deal longer than her walk over the surface streets, but she found the air invigorating and the quiet wholly peaceful. The silence and serene setting of the forest gave her time to gather her thoughts and unwind from the day. It also allowed her the opportunity to stop in at the old farmhouse before she made the final walk across the sloping meadow to her back yard.

She stopped in at the abandoned house almost every day for the first several weeks after its discovery to clean up the glass and shake the dust from of the curtains. She even went so far as to squirrel away household cleaning supplies and to liberate her mother's broom from the pantry to aid her in her attempts to clean up the house. Juniper had every intention of making the silent farm house her secret getaway, a place where she could do as she wished without having to answer to anyone or make apologies for being who she was.

It was Saturday morning again, the third Saturday of April as a matter of fact, when Juniper waited anxiously for her mother to leave for work. As soon as her car left the driveway, Juniper left her room with an already-loaded back pack and bounded down the stairs to the kitchen. She had partially filled the bag with books and tapes, her current mission was to raid the kitchen for a hammer to remove the boards from the windows and for a strong-smelling cleanser that might help alleviate the heavy musty smell that still clung to the interior of the abandoned house. Over the years, the smell had soaked into the wood of the walls and floors so heavily that all other smells gave in to its aged intensity.

Juniper found a bottle of air freshener under the sink and shook it to check the level of the scented mist inside. She grimaced when she found that it was empty and she tossed the useless can aside in frustration. Thankful she had saved much of her lunch allowance for the week, she poured the contents of her pockets onto the countertop and counted the silver change. She cast the pennies aside and hoped the scant amount of money would be enough to afford her the air freshener the house so desperately needed. Quickly she gathered up the money and shoved it back into the pocket of her jeans.

She left her backpack at the side of the house and pulled her keys from her pocket to unlock the garage door. She heaved the heavy wood door up over her head with a *click-clack-click* and stepped into the garage. She spotted her mother's ten speed as it leaned against a tower of boxed toys and she grabbed it. She pushed up the kickstand with the side of her right foot and steered the bike out of the garage. She closed the door and jumped onto the banana seat, and after only a slight adjustment of the gears, she left the driveway and turned onto the sidewalk. She pedaled quickly to the next block and pulled up in front of the small general store at the corner of 4th and Adams. She had always looked upon the place fondly, as a sort of home away from home. She had few memories of her youth, but the ones that she had managed to retain were of the tiny apartment just above the small mom and pop market. Juniper and her mother had lived there briefly when she was a child until they'd finally moved into their current home.

She came to a stop near the front door of the market and looked up at the apartment window over the entrance. She smiled softly and wondered who, if anyone, lived there now. Her eyes finally left the frame of the tiny, green shuttered window and she locked the bike near the automatic door and ran inside. As she walked past the checkout counters, she pulled her change from her pocket to have it handy. She juggled it nervously in her palm, scanning the overhead signs for the cleaning supplies aisle.

She stopped briefly to look at the magazines, a picture of a cute boy catching her eye. She shook off the increase in her heartbeat and turned the corner to the next aisle. She found the air fresheners and scanned the different scents; finally she opted for an on-sale bottle of jasmine air freshener and hoped it would do the job. She shuffled up to the counter with her silver change splayed out over her palm, recently recounted for the umpteenth time.

Juniper stepped up to the checkout line behind Mr. Percival, the proprietor of the local real estate company, and he tipped his hat to her.

"Good morning, Miss Juniper," he said with his thick southern drawl. "Fancy seeing you here this fine morning."

Juniper flashed him a bright smile. "Morning, Mr. Percival. It's nice to see you."

The elderly man returned her gesture with a weak and shaky smile of his own. "It's mighty nice to see you, dear. You're growing into quite a beautiful young woman! Just like your mother! Speaking of, I ran into her last week... she said you're a bookworm. That you hardly get out of the house."

Juniper nodded and shifted her pose slightly and uncomfortably. "Yes, sir. That's right, sir."

He smiled again. "There's nothing wrong with reading. Just make sure you don't forget, Juniper, there *is* a world outside of your books that is plenty fit for exploring."

"I'm beginning to realize that, sir," Juniper said softly.

He pat her on the shoulder with one shaky hand and Juniper took note of the liver spots. She had a brief thought about the cruelty and curse of old age, but shook it quickly aside just as Mr. Percival turned his attention back to the checkout girl as she scanned his milk and read him his total. He paid quickly, waved to Juniper and exited the line with his gallon of paid-for milk. Juniper stepped up to the counter to take his place and pushed her air freshener towards the cashier.

"I'm sorry, sugar. I'm just closing out my drawer," the woman said, chewing her gum loudly and popping it between her teeth. "Step over to aisle 2. He'll take care of you there... I apologize about this, sweetheart, but the manager is a stickler about overtime."

"No problem." Juniper picked up the can of air freshener and retraced her steps back down the lane and then proceeded to the only other check out. She placed the can on the belt without looking up and she counted her change one last time to avoid any embarrassment due to lack of proper funds or an error in her own math.

"You're out and about awfully early for a Saturday," a familiar voice noted. "Big plans?" The scanner beeped as the air freshener's UPC code rolled past.

Juniper looked up slowly and Jason smiled back at her when their eyes met. "I didn't know you worked here," she said with mild disdain.

"I just started a few days ago," he said boastfully. "There's already talk about making me assistant manager when Darlene retires next month."

"Oh, well, how nice for you." Juniper handed him the correct amount of change and he placed the rung-up can of air freshener in a plastic bag. "Your parents must be *so* proud," she quipped. "It's not every day that someone finds their calling at seventeen."

"I'll pretend I didn't hear that," he said, and he changed the subject quickly. "Haven't seen much of you lately." He opened the register drawer and deposited the coins into their proper receptacles. "If I didn't know better, I'd say you've been avoiding us."

"Don't be silly." Juniper found that with age, it became easier to lie. "Why on *earth* would I be doing that?" she asked sweetly.

Jason handed her the bag containing the air freshener and let his hand linger in contact with hers. "You should pull your hair back more often. You ain't half-bad-lookin' when you're not hiding behind that mop."

Juniper took the plastic bag from his outstretched hand and shook her head. "Whatever, I- I gotta go," she muttered.

"I'll be seein' you, Junie." Jason folded his arms over his chest and flashed her a cocky half-grin. "Come back again real soon."

Without another word, Juniper rushed out of the store in such a hurry that one might have thought her feet were on fire. Once outside, she unlocked her bike with shaking hands and pedaled quickly away without looking back even once.

Chapter Four
Revelations

Juniper put her mother's bicycle safely back in the garage and pulled the door tight to the ground. She checked it twice to make sure everything was secure, and when she was satisfied that it was she rounded the side of the house to retrieve her book bag.

Without further hesitation she chucked the bag containing the air freshener into her backpack and began the gently sloping walk across the clearing to the woods. It only took five minutes if she hurried, ten if she took the time to stop and smell the wildflowers that grew in abundance behind her house.

That morning in particular, she was especially eager to explore the rest of the house and she kept her nose firmly in tact and on task. So far Juniper had only explored the first and second floors, never had she ventured into the attic. For a reason that escaped her, she knew that until that day she'd not been ready to climb that final staircase to the peak of the house. She assumed at first that the attic would be more of the same; the smell of decaying wood, spider webs spread out across everything like a finely woven blanket of filth, bugs scurrying from her footfalls to find safety in the darkness of the corners; but the more time she spent there, the more she wondered if her assumptions were false. The attic, she realized, just felt *different*. As odd as it sounded, it seemed almost *alive* and sometimes she almost felt as though it was watching her. Juniper knew that to calm her childish fears she would have to see the attic with her own eyes. Only then would she be able to put her anxiety to rest.

The book bag seemed to weigh her down that morning,

and rightly so. It was packed full of assorted items to both occupy and clean, when normally it only held a book and a few random college-ruled notebooks. Under its unusual weight and the heat of the morning sun, she'd already broken into a sweat by the time the house appeared in her line of sight. She huffed and puffed as she crossed the last few feet to the porch and wiped furiously at the rapidly accumulating beads of sweat at her brow line. She hoped the cool interior of the shadow-filled house might provide her some relief from the heat that was steadily creeping upwards as the day progressed; if it was already swelteringly hot before ten, Juniper could only wonder how unbearable the weather would be by noon.

She entered the house quietly and tossed her book bag to the floor. A dust cloud rose, expanded and fell exhausted back to the planks. Juniper pulled out the air freshener and began to spray the curtains liberally with a fine sweet scented mist. She bent at the waist to spray under the chairs and continued her search for the source of the offending odor that seemed almost to be part of the house itself. The broom she had stolen from her mother's pantry was resting against the wall undisturbed, and already it had been swathed with new spider webs spun by eager arachnids. Juniper grabbed it with her right hand and swept aside another pile of glass. The shards fell to the earth between the wood boards and disappeared from her sight. Satisfied for the time being with the slightly tidier appearance of the room, Juniper sat the broom back in its previous location and rounded the tree. She walked slowly around the right side of the massive oak and allowed her eyes to explore the early morning shadows that had curled up in the corners for a cat nap. Nothing seemed to be out of the ordinary; no lurking animals or creatures of any sort caught her attention and she relaxed slightly. With gathered breath, she glanced towards the staircase just to her left. It was tucked neatly away behind the tree and provided the only access to the second and third floors.

She paused at the base and her hand rested gently on the splintered wood banister as she contemplated her next move. She gulped at the shadows her eyes found at the top of the stairs and suddenly she remembered the flashlight she'd packed in her book bag for just such an occasion. Relieved to have recalled its presence, she ran to fetch it and retraced her steps back to the living room.

She flipped on the small battery-powered light and it jumped to life She moved back to the staircase and shined it up the side of the tree. The light disappeared into the leaves of the hungry canopy and Juniper retrieved it from the darkness with one movement of her wrist. She retrained the circle of light onto the steps just in front of her.

"Come on, Junie, you can do this. It's just an old abandoned house. There's nothing to be afraid of," she reassured herself out loud. With a renewed sense of purpose she nodded, bit her lip and climbed the first flight of stairs to the second floor. She held her breath until she reached the landing at the top. Once there she finally allowed herself the luxury of exhaling. She inhaled again a second later returned to holding her nervous air.

A strange thump rose from above her head and her footsteps quieted themselves at her ear's request.

Had there been a noise in the attic? Juniper's hand began to shake and the circular beam from the flashlight bounced uneasily over the floor. Nervous as she was, she mustered the strength to continue. She walked over the landing and turned to the staircase that led to the attic with a renewed reserve of courage.

The boards creaked under her feet and sounded much like the rest of the house, old and exhausted. So far, Juniper noted that her premature assumptions about the darker recesses of the house had proven correct. It was a lot more of the same. The same sounds, the same scent, and more of the same hastily crafted spider webs that jumped out at her hair and hands as she passed.

Juniper kept her flashlight focused on the top of the stairs as she steadily made her ascent to the third floor. The light cast shadows in odd places and caused her mind to play tricks on her. As she tried desperately to keep her head about her, her feet came to rest at the top of the stairs. Juniper assuaged her burgeoning concerns with silent admonishments and began to survey the attic surroundings.

The hallway was short and the ceiling was lower and more angular than those in the rest of the house. Two doors led off of the hallway; one went to the left, one went right. Both were closed off and silent. Juniper's heart thumped loudly in her ears and its beat prevented her from hearing anything else but it.

The first door Juniper tried, the one to her left, was locked tight. She pushed at it for several minutes while she grunted and puffed, but the door refused to budge.

She instead dropped to her knees and lowered her face to the ground. She shined the flashlight under the crack in the door and desperately tried to peer into the room that lay beyond.

Ornate legs of an old chair and a pile of dusty clothes were the only artifacts that Juniper could make out through the two inch crack between the floor and the bottom of the door. She sighed, pulled herself to a standing position and brushed the dust from the knees of her jeans. She turned around to face the other door and took a sharp breath into her lungs as her fingers reached out to the knob.

To her surprise, the door was unlocked and it opened easily into the room.

Juniper, the flashlight brought up to chest level and focused ahead of her, entered the room cautiously. She wielded the flashlight carefully and made sure to examine every shadow of the room that wasn't exposed by the soft light that filtered in through the uncharacteristically unobstructed window.

She realized immediately that the room was a bedroom. It contained a tiny bed, a nightstand and a three legged dresser that had once had four legs. The splintered wood furniture were the only items to be found inside the confines of the room. As her flashlight rolled past the bed, she noticed the fourth leg of the crippled dresser lying just beneath the headboard. It was splintered and broken.

That room was also the room that the tree had burst into as it fought to see the sky; from her new angle she was nearly at the top of it. The leaves jutted out into the room and scraped the ceiling; the highest branch, however, was bare and hung out over the room like an extended finger on an outstretched hand.

Juniper examined the branch with her flashlight. Upon her first scan of the tree, her eyes missed the shimmer of gold that the flashlight enhanced. On her second more careful pass, however, Juniper's eyes caught the sparkle and brought the light back to rest upon it. She tilted her head to the side and a curious look crept across her face as she inspected the tiny sparkle with narrowed eyes.

Without another thought, Juniper turned off the flashlight and shoved it into her pocket. She surveyed the branch and the contents of the room, and decided finally that the only way she could reach the shimmering object was to move the nightstand closer to the tree and, unavoidably, to the hole it appeared from.

She hesitated only briefly before she finally resigned and scooted the old wooden object as close to the gaping hole as she could without agitating the butterflies that lived in her stomach. She checked its integrity by shaking it and thumping its surface with her hands to make certain the surface was steady enough to support her weight. Satisfied, but still nervous, Juniper raised one sneaker to the surface of the small table and with a deep breath she pulled her other remaining foot up to meet the level of her first.

The night stand creaked, but held firm beneath her weight. Juniper's lips parted slightly and she breathed deeply the heavy air of the room; her heart was frantic in her chest.

On tip toes with extended fingers, Juniper reached out for the shiny, metallic object. She closed her eyes, sucked in her breath and stretched herself nearly flat to procure it. Finally, her fingers found victory as they closed around the item in question. She pulled it quickly to her chest and looked back up to the spot where it had been resting.

Something had been carved into the tree bark just behind where the item had been resting; it looked like initials and she could make out what appeared to be an A. Juniper squinted and leaned in for a better view, but when the nightstand shifted, her heart skipped a beat and she quickly recoiled in favor of firmer ground.

She stepped back off of the nightstand with her heart still pounding furiously in her chest and stumbled backwards towards the bed. She brushed off the edge of the worn mattress and sat down to collect her nerves. The metal coil springs squeaked loudly as they shifted to accommodate her, but held firm. When she'd calmed, her eyes shifted to her hand and she opened it slowly to reveal the trinket.

It was a silver, heart-shaped locket. It was tarnished and dusty from the cruel touch of time and she wondered who would have put such a thing in such a strange place.

Juniper found the hinge on the tiny object and then quickly found the latch. She opened the locket with little difficulty and revealed a dust-covered picture tucked away inside. Juniper drew her lips tight into a circle, closed her eyes and blew the dust aside.

When she re-opened her eyes and they found their focus, she had to rub them and look at the photo again before what she saw actually registered in her brain. She gasped at the realization of what she was seeing and her finger moved out to touch the photo to remove the last traces of the stubborn, lingering dust.

"Mama?" Juniper stared at the picture for several minutes in stunned silence, not sure of what to make of her discovery.

A noise behind her signaled her to turn. Her eyes darted nervously from wall, to floor, to corner and to door before she decided that her nerves and her mind had teamed up to play tricks on her.

A shiver ran down Juniper's spine a moment later, the sort of chill one gets when they are being watched, and for the first time since she'd found the house, she felt genuine fear creep into her veins and taint her blood with an icy chill. Quickly, she snapped the locket shut, shoved it into her front pocket and retreated to the first floor. She gathered the things she didn't want to leave behind and ran for home without hesitation.

She arrived on her own side porch in less than three minutes with her lungs and brain burning for two distinctly different reasons. It was a new record, she realized. A new record she hoped she'd never again have to match.

When Juniper finally managed to shake the uneasiness she had accumulated in the attic of the farm house, she went to her mother's bedroom and slipped inside. She rummaged through Penelope's jewelry box until she found an old and unused silver box chain. It was just what she'd hoped to find. Juniper pulled the locket from her jeans and opened it again to take another look at the photo inside.

The girl in the photo was definitely her mother. She was

young, probably not much older than Juniper was currently. Her hair was pulled back from her face and her eyes were looking off to the left at some unseen person or point. She looked wistful with her hands knotted at her stomach and her knees turned inwards beneath the hem of her dress. She took in all of the details of the black and white image one last time before she slid the locket onto the chain and fastened it around her neck.

She placed the charm under her shirt and the coolness of it hung like a stone at her chest. She decided not to mention her finding to her mother. Juniper knew her well, and knew that no matter what she was confronted with she would maintain her silence. However, Juniper's curiosity was biting at the back of her tongue. Questions came and went, bravery waned and waxed, but in the end she stuck firm to her initial decision to keep quiet about her discovery, pending further exploration.

For the rest of the afternoon, Juniper kept her thoughts and questions at bay by concentrating on her homework. She finished shortly after three, at which time she headed to the kitchen for a snack.

As soon as her hand touched the handle of the refrigerator door, the telephone rang shrilly from the counter. Juniper sighed and turned to answer it. She caught it on the second ring; her stomach growled.

"Hello?" Juniper did little to hide her irritation from the caller.

"Hey Junie. Thought I'd give you a call and see where you've been keeping yourself lately," the voice paused. "This is Ben, by the way. You know, in case you've forgotten me."

"How could I forget a louse like you?" Juniper asked sharply. "Just tell me what you want, would you? I don't want to waste my entire Saturday afternoon talking to *you* when all you're going to do is tease me mercilessly."

There was a silence; it sounded as though he was inhaling

and exhaling deeply. "Jason says he saw you this morning at the store," he said finally.

"Yeah? So? Is it a crime for me to shop?"

"Of course not. He was just sort of surprised to see you there, seeing as how you've kept yourself so scarce lately." Ben coughed and continued. "I just hadn't talked to you in awhile. Thought we might catch up. I could swing by for a bit if you're lonely. I've a car, but you already know that." He paused to cough once more. "Is your mother home?"

Juniper narrowed her eyes. "Yes, yes, she is and I'm not allowed company. I have chores," she fibbed.

"But if you *didn't* have chores...?" Juniper could almost hear him shrug. "Then maybe I could visit you? You see, I'm just curious about you, Junie, that's all. I want to know you better."

"Curious? About what?" Juniper asked sharply. "The only interest you've ever shown in me has been negative at best."

Ben sighed. "I just want to know about you. About your life, your family... I'm curious to know if all the stories are true."

Juniper felt a confused itch creep steadily across her face as simultaneously the feeling leaked from her face to her shoulders, "Wh-what stories?"

"Oh, you haven't heard?" Ben asked casually. "I thought for sure you'd have heard the buzz at school... It's followed you your entire life, ya know."

"I can't say I know what you're talking about." Juniper gulped and repeated her earlier question. She wondered if she was walking into a trap. "What stories? If you mean about the woods and the strange goings on, I'd hardly say that has anything to do with me."

"Well, maybe I shouldn't say. I mean, gee, Junie, I wouldn't want to upset your fragile mindset or anything like that."

Juniper felt a bite at her tongue. "Oh come on! That's exactly the reason you've called me. To upset me. So go on with it! Take your best shot and get it over with already. I'm getting bored."

Ben began slowly. "Well, if you really want to hear, I *suppose* I could tell you... but remember, you asked."

"Just get on with it." Juniper had long since grown irritated, and as much as she feared the truth, she feared even more being left to further linger in the darkness of ignorance.

"Come on, Junie. You know how this town is, how nothing is secret. This place has been buzzing for years about you and your mama. People have done the math! You weren't born in Table Rock, you were born right here in Camden Falls. There are people who remember when your mama got knocked up. They remember your grandparents, too. Especially that alcoholic grandpa of yours. After all, he used to own a fair portion of those woods behind your house before he just up and abandoned the whole lot one day. People around here remember it all and they talk, Junie. They talk and they know that something ain't right about the way things happened. They know that the strange goings-on in those woods are related to you somehow. We all know it, we can feel it."

Juniper didn't know how to respond.

"All of the strange noises in those woods, all of the rumors about an old homestead and a monster... It all relates to you and your mom and everybody is watching you two," Ben said softly. "We're all holding our breath and waiting for the other shoe to drop."

"I don't- I- I have to go," Juniper stuttered. She pulled the phone from her ear and placed the receiver back into the cradle with such force that the phone rang out shrilly in response. She stood there for a moment in a stunned silence staring at the phone as though it were a living, breathing beast.

Finally, she turned and fled the room and when she reached the security of her own bedroom, she threw herself onto the bed and cried into her pillow for she knew not what else to do.

Everything has been a lie, she thought sadly. *My entire life has been nothing but a series of lies, with each one bigger than the one that preceded it.*

The following Monday, Juniper arrived at school nearly a half hour earlier than normal. To pass the time she found an available bench in the quad and sat down with her book bag at her feet. She unzipped it slowly and rummaged through its contents. She pushed aside her unfinished homework in favor of *The Catcher in the Rye,* one of her favorite novels. She pulled out the small paperback book and smoothed the cover before she opened to her bookmark and plunged into the world of Holden Caulfield.

Time passed quickly while she read, and when she finally looked up from the pages of her book, the quad was filling with students. She surveyed the growing crowd, checked her watch for the time and returned to her book. A moment later she felt someone's eyes upon her and heard the footsteps of an approaching person. She didn't look up. Instead, she remained focused on the text in front of her. It was only a second later when a shadow fell across the page. Within moments, Ben and Jason came to rest on opposing sides of her with sneers and pointy elbows.

They sandwiched her in between them and afforded her little room. She pulled her arms in closer to her sides to avoid contact with them, but they only scooted closer. Around her, they proceeded to have a conversation as though she were as invisible as she'd always felt.

"So tell me... how was your weekend, Ben?" Jason lit a

cigarette without concern, inhaled deeply and exhaled the smoke directly in Juniper's face. "Didn't you have a baseball game Saturday afternoon?"

"Yeah, sure did. We beat the shit out of Table Rock, 8 to 3. It was practically a slaughter," Ben said. He nudged Juniper in the side with his sharp elbow, but didn't address her directly. "Too bad you couldn't make it, man. Kelly Willard was there looking hot as usual. She even asked me about you."

Jason chuckled. "She did, did she? Looks like I've gotten to her after all. I knew she'd succumb." He blew another spiral of smoke towards Juniper and leaned forward to get a better glimpse of Ben. "If you see her in study hall today, tell her to call me. I'm in the student directory."

Juniper coughed, snapped her book closed and stood, ready to make her escape. Before she could, Ben grabbed her by the wrist and twisted her arm to such an angle that she was instantly halted.

He pulled her unwillingly back into a seated position and finally addressed her directly. "We've missed you, Junie. Without you we don't know what to do with ourselves."

"I'm sure that between the two of you you've come up with *some* way to spend your time," Juniper said through grit teeth. "Surely there are other girls in this school you can torture with your presence."

Ben sneered, but otherwise ignored her comments. "So Junie, are you ever going to tell me why you had Mr. Halsey change your seating assignment in History class?"

"To get away from you," she admitted. "I know you two probably share a brain, but you couldn't figure that out for yourself?"

"You're such a bitch, Junie." Jason blew another cloud of smoke in her eyes. "Tell me, what have we ever done to deserve such treatment from our dear, sweet, friend, Juniper?"

"You really have to ask? All of that smoke must be

affecting your memory."

"Oh come on, let's all be friends," Jason said. "Life is too short for all of this unpleasantness."

"I'd rather not have friends if being friends with you is my only other alternative," Juniper spat.

"Ouch, burn," Ben laughed. "You're so cruel!" His fingers found her curls and laced themselves amongst them. "You know, you might have some people to hang out with if you'd lose the attitude."

Juniper sighed and struggled once again to stand, but Ben held tight to her forearm. "Let go of me," she said through grit teeth. "You're hurting me."

"Hurting you?" Ben tightened his grip instead of loosening it. "I didn't mean to hurt you. Just like I didn't *mean* to hurt you when I called you the other day. And while we're on that subject, have you been thinking about what I told you?"

"I haven't given it a second thought," she fibbed. "You're a liar and I don't believe a thing you say."

"Ask anyone, Junie. Everyone will tell you the same thing."

Jason chimed in. "I heard the stories from my parents."

Ben looked at Jason. "I got the heads up from my babysitter. You remember her, don't you, Jason? Alison Prescott?"

"Oh, now, *she* was hot," Jason said with a nod. "My first crush."

They high-fived over Juniper's head and she narrowed her eyes in obvious disgust.

"I've asked you to let go of me," Juniper said evenly. "If you don't, I'll file a sexual harassment complaint with Principal Baxter."

"Oooh, she's gonna tell on us, Ben. You'd better let her go. You don't wanna get in trouble," Jason said. He made an attempt to hold back his laughter over Juniper's idle threats, but his crooked, yellowing teeth released it a second later.

"Yeah, we don't want to get in *trouble*." Ben let go of Juniper's arm and leaned over until his breath was hot against her cheek. "We'll talk later," he sneered. "When we're away from all of these prying eyes. Because you and me? We've got some business to take care of."

Juniper shoved him away and grabbed her book bag. "Fuck you guys."

They laughed as she stalked off. Their profane comments followed her across the quad with their vulgarity; try as she might to ignore them, they made their way through her thickened skin.

Juniper noticed Mr. Halsey standing just outside the entrance to the West Wing, and he smiled upon her approach.

"Morning, Miss Kelly." He lowered his thick, black mug of coffee and glanced past her to the bench she'd abandoned. "How was your weekend?"

"Oh, hey, Mr. Halsey." Juniper stopped dead in her tracks and looked down at the grass briefly before she pulled her eyes back up to the history teacher's face. "My weekend was fine, thanks. Just fine. Yours?"

"Oh, fine, thanks for asking." He nodded towards Ben and Jason. They were still sitting on the wooden bench in the quad, both of them smoking. They were laughing at what Juniper could only assume was their treatment of her. "Are they bothering you again?" Mr. Halsey asked. "Mr. Maxwell and Mr. Price?"

Juniper allowed a short bitter laugh to escape her. "*Again?* I think you mean *still*."

He pushed his glasses up the bridge of his nose and lowered his voice to a whisper. "I know there isn't much I can do to stop them. Kids are cruel, especially at this age... but I'm sure I don't have to tell you that."

"No, you don't," Juniper said. She placed her hand over her mouth and cleared her throat, eager to change the subject.

"I told my mama you said hello, by the way."

A brief glimmer of hope arched its way across Mr. Halsey's forehead before he spoke. "Oh yeah?" He looked away from Jason and Ben and met Juniper's gaze. "What did she have to say?"

"Not much. She uh- she didn't remember you." Juniper watched Mr. Halsey's hope turn upside down and morph into a soft look of disappointment. Juniper quickly amended herself. "But she's been under a lot of stress lately... I'm sure she'd remember if she saw you."

"Sure, I'm sure she would." Mr. Halsey scratched his chin and looked once again to the bench. "Smoking on school grounds is punishable by detention," he said absently, then he shook his head softly and pat Juniper on the shoulder. "I'll see you in class this afternoon, Miss Kelly. Hang in there. These types of things usually blow over."

Juniper turned and watched Mr. Halsey as he walked over to Jason and extended his hand. Jason offered up his pack of cigarettes with a roll of his eyes and tossed his already lit cigarette into the grass carelessly. Mr. Halsey moved to stomp it out and Juniper turned her attention back towards the school building. She entered through the double-wide doorway slowly, certain that Ben and Jason were silently blaming her for ratting them out.

She looked down at her arm once she was inside under the invasive fluorescent lighting and found that the after-image of Ben's grip remained at her wrist. She grimaced at the sight and wondered what they would do next to make her life even more miserable than it already was.

Juniper ran through the moonlit clearing until finally her bare feet found the coolness of the earth. The trees shot up around her as they stretched from their daylight slumber into the ever expanding night. The path she had previously blazed to the abandoned farm house was wide and open, and it called her closer with whispers and words spoken in a tongue she had no knowledge of and couldn't understand.

The house was lit up like a proud Christmas tree upon her approach, and every window shone brightly with crisp, clean light. The smell of freshly baked vanilla cookies wafted from the kitchen, into the living room and escaped the house to the porch and beyond.

Juniper's nostrils flared as they took in the scent and she entered the house. Without pause, she went directly to the tree and dropped to her knees in front of it. She hesitated, prayed and finally her hands pulled back the planks at the base of the tree that hadn't already been broken and knocked out of place. They cracked in half and splintered easily, and Juniper tossed them aside. She stuck her hands into the earth below, the earth that was slightly hard and deathly cold.

She dug and clawed until her nails were broken and bleeding, until several inches of earth had been removed and shoved free. Her fingers finally found that which they were looking for when they hit cold metal. After several minutes more of fervent digging, Juniper had managed to free the small metal box from the firm grip of the seemingly unwilling to share ground.

She settled back on her haunches, set the box in the lap and fiddled with the lock. It finally gave way to her persistence and the lid popped open. It seemed almost relieved to be put to use after years of inactivity.

Inside was a Polaroid photo and a newspaper clipping; a small silver ball and a leather-bound book rounded out the motley collection of forgotten artifacts. Juniper examined the photo first and identified the woman as her mother. The man next to her, however, was someone Juniper had never before seen.   Nonetheless, she felt as though she knew him from somewhere. It was his eyes, she determined, and she stared into them as if waiting for something to happen, for some voice to call out to her from the shadows and whisper to her the truths she had always longed to hear.

However, no such voice came.

Juniper turned the picture over in her hands and on the back was written one word in a flowing, cursive script: Remember.

Juniper furrowed her brow, turned the picture back over then set it aside in favor of the mysterious book. She opened it slowly; pages were missing, the corners were tattered. Juniper squinted to make out the text, but soon realized it was hand-written in a language she couldn't identify. Before she had the chance to ponder it further, the room around her began its steady fade to black and into the middle of the abyss, she fell.

Juniper woke in a cold sweat with her hands and teeth trembling under the combined blow of the air conditioner and her vivid, heat-soaked dreams.

She flipped on the lamp next to her bed to shake the heavy blanket of night free of her bones. When she was fully awake, she reached for the glass of water at her bedside table and took several eager sips to wet her parched lips and throat. It was then that she noticed her hands. They were dirty; dirty and caked with dried blood and bits of brown earth; her nails were splintered and broken, and scratches had appeared on the palms and tops of her hands.

Juniper set the glass aside. Her hands shook from the realization the light had brought and she held them out in front of her. Her mouth fell open in disbelief as she inspected the tell-tale marks that covered her pale, thin fingers. Instantly, and as if on cue, her mind filled with a million burning questions.

It was only then that in the back of her mind her own tiny internal voice urged her to raise her head. She did so without knowing why.

It was then that she noticed it. Across her room on her dresser sat the dirty, beat-up metal box from her dream. At the sight of it, Juniper felt her heartbeat quicken as the truth began its casual settling over her bones.

It hadn't been a dream in totality; parts of it had very much been real.

She untangled herself from her bed sheets with a quickness; she was wide awake in view of her discovery. In the glow of the bedside lamp, Juniper noticed dirt ground into the carpet and a single green leaf fluttered down from her hair and passed her eyes to provide further proof of her somnambulant escapade.

Juniper threw her legs over the edge of the bed. She shivered from the shock of the cold air and from the sight of the rusty old box; a box that seemed to be looking at her, waiting patiently for her hands to inspect it.

Juniper crossed the room and noticed as she did so that her feet were nearly completely brown from her ankles to the tips of her toes. She curled her nails into the carpet and averted her eyes from the sight.

When she reached her desk, she took the cold metal box into her hands and held it carefully, firmly, with all ten fingers. Juniper carried it back to her bed and placed it carefully on her bed sheets. She drew in a breath and pulled her legs onto the bed and off of the floor.

Cross-legged and involved in a staring contest with the box, she sat silently for several minutes as she weighed her options. She could, as it were, either open the box, or, and the other was the option that currently carried the most weight, she could ignore its existence entirely. She could shove it under the bed or hide it behind her dresser, and she could chalk the entire thing up to a strange dream. However, as tempting as that was, she knew that she couldn't deny the truth of what had happened.

Sleepwalking, she said to herself silently. *I walked, in my sleep, all the way into the woods! Alone! At night! And now there's this box with a photo and a strange foreign book that I can't explain... This is all getting too weird. Maybe Ben is right. Maybe…*

Juniper drew in a deep breath, closed her eyes, and finally, she opened the box. She did so quickly with one swift and sweeping motion, but was afraid to re-open her eyes to take in the sights.

Come on, open your eyes! she screamed to herself. *The worst is over. The box is here now, in my room. I'm safe, it's safe. Just look! It could be empty or it could contain the answers I've always wanted.*

Juniper opened her right eye and peered down at the box. She caught a glimpse of the Polaroid photo as it rested atop the leather wrapped book. She knew instantly that her dream had been undeniably confirmed.

Everything in the box was at it had been in the dream. Upon realizing that through one squinted eye, Juniper opened the other and widened the pair to take in the sight her dream had already revealed to her.

With her hands shaking profusely, she examined the contents of the cold metal box more closely. The Polaroid was turned face down and Juniper pushed it closer to the glow of the 60 watt bulb on her bedside table. Once it was properly illuminated, she flipped it over.

The woman in the photo was definitely her mother, definitely the same woman in the locket. Juniper then noticed the pressure of the charm beneath her pajama top; it was almost as though the locket itself was alerting her to its presence, reminding her of the mystery she'd already found and strung onto a chain.

She leaned in closer to the photo. Her attention had been drawn to the man who stood just next to her mother. He was tall, over a foot taller than Penelope's bare feet height of 5'3". Juniper noticed immediately the size of the stranger's hands, hands which were knotted at his stomach. He appeared to be nervous for some unknown reason and Juniper squinted at him as if to ask him a million questions in the space of one look.

She sighed when no answers came and laid the picture aside. Her head had begun to ache at her temples and she knew it was only a matter of time before the pain spread out and down to encompass the whole of her head.

It was late, nearly 3am as told to her by the red, angry light of her bedside alarm. She suddenly realized that she was exhausted.

Juniper stifled a yawn, placed the photo back into the box and tucked the entire mystery neatly beneath her bed. She pulled the bed skirt back into place, flipped off the light and closed her eyes to sleep. It would all have to wait.

As an afterthought, she jumped up quickly, locked her bedroom door and placed a chair under the knob.

That's that, she said resolutely, and then slid back beneath the dirt-spotted sheets of her bed.

Juniper woke before her alarm the next morning and she showered quickly. She hoped to wash away the remnants of her early morning adventure before she encountered her mother.

Mud had collected between her toes and under her toenails and she scrubbed them clean as best she could. When she'd finished her thorough cleaning, she'd left nary a trace behind and she washed the last of the dirt down the drain in thick spirals. She was clean and devoid of reminders of the previous night.

When her shower was finished, Juniper was careful to clean the sides and bottom of the enclosed bathtub as an extra precaution, and she hoped her efforts would be enough to keep her mother from noticing anything out of the ordinary.

Juniper dressed almost as quickly as she'd showered and she left her hair to hang wet at her back as she ran to her bedroom to grab a pair of socks from her dresser. As confident as she was in her cleaning job, she still felt it best to cover her toes and keep them out of sight. Satisfied finally that her mess had been lidded, she jogged down the stairs to the kitchen. Halfway down the staircase, Juniper caught the glimmer of her locket. It was exposed and in plain sight at her chest. She gasped at her stupidity and quickly tucked the charm beneath her shirt.

In her back pocket she had placed the photo from the metal box. For what purpose, she wasn't certain. A confrontation wasn't something she actively considered, but the possibility of it dwelled at the back of her mind.

As Juniper approached, she found Penelope sipping coffee at the small, oval kitchen table. Juniper stepped into the kitchen quietly and reached towards the dish drainer for a clean coffee mug. She filled the cup quickly to the top, added a touch of sugar and then joined her mother at the table.

"Morning, mama." Juniper slid into her usual seat, forced a smile to her lips and glanced casually at the newspaper her mother had arranged and spread out across the table.

"Morning, sweetie." Penelope Kelly lowered the classified section from her line of sight and smiled at her daughter. "Sorry I didn't get home until after you were in bed last night."

Juniper shrugged. "S'ok."

"Well, maybe so, but I promise I'll be home on time tonight, you have my word." Penelope looked worried. Her brow was drawn down just slightly in a look of mild concern.

"You sure everything is ok? You look… *odd*."

"Oh, yeah, sure… everything's fine," Juniper replied, a reply that was a bit too enthusiastic for her mother, who increased the furrow of her brow tenfold.

"It's rare that you're in a good mood on a school day," Penelope surveyed. "Someone must be well rested."

Juniper sipped her coffee and winced as the hot liquid burnt her lower lip. She put the cup down quickly and choked out a response. "I'm just glad school is almost over for the year, that's all."

"Ah, I see." Penelope seemed satisfied with her daughter's response and returned her attention to her own cup of coffee.

"Do you think maybe I could get a ride to school this morning?" Juniper asked suddenly. She felt little like making the mile walk that morning, as she felt quite tired from her restless night.

"Sure thing," Penelope said with a nod. Her short blonde hair bounced over her shoulders in agreement with her mouth. "Hope you don't mind being a little early."

Juniper shrugged. "I don't mind. I have some things to finish up in the library anyway."

"Alright then. We'll leave when I finish my coffee." Penelope's eyes fell to rest upon Juniper's hands. "My goodness, what happened to your hands?"

Juniper suddenly felt embarrassed. She pulled her hands back from the table and hid them in her lap. "Oh, I was outside yesterday after school. Just messing around."

"Outside?" Penelope questioned. "*Where* outside?"

Juniper looked at her hands. To her surprise, the scratches were nearly gone. "Oh, just around."

"Juniper Marie Kelly."

"What?"

"Tell me where you were, young lady, and **don't** lie."

Juniper gulped.   "I took a walk around the neighborhood."

Penelope's eyes narrowed and her arms crossed at her chest. "I told you *not* to lie. You get **one** more chance to tell me the truth before I ground you for two weeks."

"Mama, come on, just drop it," Juniper sighed. "I'm fine, everything is fine... so why does it matter where I was?"

"It matters."

"Oh alright then! Geez! I was in the woods, ok? Is that what you wanted to hear?" Juniper wished immediately that she could pull back her angry words and swallow them down. Knowing that she couldn't, she cast her eyes to her mother and waited for the fallout.

A dark glimmer moved across Penelope's brow. "You've been in the woods? Alone?"

Juniper shook her head. "Don't worry, mama, really... there's no reason for you to be upset about this, I was just-"

"How can I not worry?" Penelope interrupted. Her voice had become excited with panic. "There are wild animals out there! Not to mention poison oak, poison ivy... the woods aren't a safe place to be alone!"

"I don't go alone, mama," Juniper fibbed. "I- I was with a friend of mine."

Penelope raised one perfectly plucked brow and thinly veiled her skepticism. "Oh yeah? Who? And you'd better not say it was a boy."

"Of course it's not a boy, mama." Juniper hated lying to her mother, but felt that this was her only recourse. Her eyes searched the kitchen and fell to rest on the catsup bottle she had left on the counter after her dinner the previous evening. "Cat," she blurted out. "Her name is Cat."

"Cat? Is she new in town, because I don't know any Cat's." Her mother's mind searched its database for previous mentions of this mysterious new friend; she came up empty and said as much. "This is the first time I've heard of this girl."

Juniper licked her lips. "She hasn't lived here long. Maybe a year, I don't remember-"

"Do I know her parents?"

Juniper shrugged. "I doubt it. She lives with her grandma."

Penelope nodded. "Oh, I see." She smiled softly, the smile she offered when she knew that Juniper was lying. Still, she said nothing more and held her accusations behind her lips.

Juniper forced out a small smile to match her mother's and she took another long sip of her finally cool-enough-to-drink coffee. "Don't worry, ok? Everything is fine. I'm making friends, I'm getting out of the house... this is exactly what you wanted, isn't it?"

Penelope still looked uncertain over the new development, but finally she nodded. "You're right. I *should* be happy that you've found someone to hang out with... and I *am* happy, it's just-" A familiar, wistful look took up residence behind her mother's eyes. "Just be careful, ok? Have fun, but please, *be careful.*"

"I promise I will be." Juniper reached across the table and gave her mother's hand a soft pat. "Try not to worry, ok? I'm a big girl."

"I'll try, but I *am* a mother, so no promises." Penelope winked, smiled softly and then returned to her previous look of concern. "You're sure everything is ok?"

"I'm sure, mama," Juniper soothed.

"Alright then, I'll not mention this again."

A moment later, Penelope finished her coffee and left the room to grab her purse and shoes. Juniper took the time to gather her books and she shoved them quickly into her book bag. She left the house without her mother and wandered onto the patio and down the stairs. In the driveway, she paused as inexplicably her attention was drawn to the woods.

She watched the trees for a moment. She was looking for something, *anything* out of the ordinary. She found nothing of the sort and dropped her shoulders in defeat. She completed her walk to the car where she waited in nervous silence for her mother.

Penelope came out of the house a moment later and paused to lock the door. She gave her hair a pat and adjusted a few stray strands she spied by observing her reflection in the glass. When she was satisfied with her appearance, she continued to the car. Juniper shifted uncomfortably as she approached and removed the photo from her back pocket. She glanced at it once, then turned it over in her lap. She folded her hands over it, just as her mother opened the door and slid into the driver's seat.

"You all set?" she asked.

Juniper nodded. "As ready as I'll ever be." She noticed her hands again at that point and cocked her head thoughtfully to the side as she inspected them. Already they looked better than they had just minutes prior at the dinner table.

Penelope started the car. "You know, your birthday is coming up soon." She adjusted the volume of the radio, checked her mirrors and put the car in reverse. "We haven't talked much about it."

Juniper nodded and glanced out her side mirror at the street behind them. "No, I guess we haven't," she murmured. Her eyes were fixed in a stare out of the passenger side window. From her sleep-walking escapades the night before, Juniper found herself to be almost too weary for conversation. Her sleepless night was most definitely catching up with her and suddenly she wished she'd finished that cup of coffee.

Her mother persisted. "You haven't told me what you want, ya know."

I want to know if the man in this photo is my father and where he is now, Juniper thought, but the words she finally offered up were much different from that. "There's nothing I really need, mama."

Penelope turned the volume of the radio down even further, until the chatter of the morning DJs was only slightly more than a hum. She sighed and clucked her tongue. "Honestly, isn't there a normal thing about you? Most kids have lists! Especially most kids who are turning 16! This is a special one, Junie."

Again, Juniper's response was a weak shrug.

"You only have a sweet sixteen once in your life and I think we should do something special." She paused to survey her daughter's mood and prodded her a moment later. "Are you even listening to me?"

"Hmm?" Juniper jerked her head around to face her mother, having been stirred from her own thoughts. "Oh, right, yeah... whatever you want is fine with me."

Again, Penelope sighed. "These days it seems like you're a million miles away."

"I'm right here, mama. I'm just-"

"What is it? I know something is bothering you. One minute you're pretending to be happy, the next you're sullen and silent, making no bones about your lousy mood."

Juniper loosened then re-gripped her hands. The picture was warm beneath her palms. It was as though it was aching to be addressed. Juniper finally mustered up her words. "I just have a lot going on right now, mama."

"Anything you care to clue me in on?"

Juniper shook her head.

"You can tell me anything, you know," Penelope said, still pushing the issue. "We're friends, Junie. I'm not just your mama. You know that, right?"

"Of course I do. You're my best friend, you always have been."

"Then why won't you talk to me?" Juniper could hear

the frustration as it seeped into her mother's words.

The photo pressed at her palms again and Juniper cleared her throat as if to dismiss its insistence.

"Are those boys still picking on you?" Penelope asked suddenly. "Jason and Ben?"

"Sometimes, yeah."

Penelope glanced over at her daughter with concern. "What are they doing exactly?"

"It's not important... I'm handling it." Juniper's eyes met with her mother's briefly and she pleaded silently for her to let the conversation drop. Penelope, however, did not.

"That Maxwell boy..." Penelope let out a slow whistle and shook her head. "He's a horrible rotten kid, *horrible*. He came into the office a few days ago for his yearly eye exam and he was nothing but a terror. He even had the nerve to ask me about you."

"What?" Juniper's one-word question was expelled in a high-pitched tone. "What did you tell him?"

"I told him you were fine, just fine... and then he proceeded to try on every pair of glasses in the shop, only to decide on contacts. He didn't even bother to put the glasses back on their displays! He just left them lying all about for *me* to put away. As if I have the time for that."

"He's a jerk," Juniper said softly. "A Grade A Certified asshole."

"Juniper," Penelope warned. "Watch your language, young lady."

Juniper shrugged weakly. "Sorry."

Penelope smiled in spite of her reprimand. "It's ok, *this time*... and for the record, I'd have to agree with you. He is an *asshole*." She paused momentarily before she launched into her next statement, and when she finally spoke, her voice was firm. "Ben will be coming in tomorrow to pick up his contacts. Do you want me to speak with him? I could tell him to leave you alon-"

"No!" Juniper exclaimed and then brought her demeanor back to calm. "No, no... don't make things worse, mama. If I have you fight my battles for me, then they'll pick on me for *that* too."

"I know... I know you're right," Penelope resigned, "but Junie, I just hate to see you upset."

"It's ok, really."

"It isn't ok. It's **not**." Penelope's voice softened. "What exactly is it that they do?"

Juniper shrugged yet again and decided that response to be her favorite of the day. "You don't really wanna know," she said quietly. She kept her eyes focused on the road ahead and hoped Penelope would sense her reticence and drop her interrogation.

"Of course I want to know," Penelope said with a firm nod. "Tell me. Maybe I can help! You know it wasn't that long ago that I was your age. Not as long ago as you like to think."

"They call me a freak, mama. They think I'm weird, they make fun of my height, they-" Juniper shook her head. "They make fun of me because I don't have a father. They call me, pardon my language, a *bastard*." Juniper's voice was barely audible by the time she uttered the last word.

Penelope gasped. "Are you kidding me?"

"No."

"Juniper! Why didn't you tell me? I could have-"

"Could have *what*, mama? What can you do to make them stop teasing me?" Juniper lowered her chin to her chest and spoke under her breath. "Besides telling me the truth about everything."

"How would that help?"

"I don't know!" Juniper exclaimed. She threw her arms up in exasperation, an action that caused the photo to flutter from her lap to the floorboard. She froze and then her arms fell limply back to her lap for lack of a better reaction.

"What was that?" Penelope glanced over and then looked back at the road.

"What was what?" Juniper asked innocently. She moved her right foot to cover the photo.

"You dropped something."

"No... No, I didn't."

"Why do you insist upon lying to me?"

Juniper grit her teeth and spoke through them. "Mama, I'm not lying. Just drop it, alright?"

Penelope drove the rest of the way to the high school in silence. She pulled into the student parking lot and coasted slowly to a stop at the curb. "We aren't finished here. We'll discuss this more when I get home tonight."

"What time?" Juniper pulled her book bag into her lap and with her right hand she casually scooped up the photo.

"About eight. If you get hungry before that, you can heat up the meatloaf in the fridge."

Juniper sucked in a deep breath and nodded as she did so. In her mind, a countdown began.

3...

"Have a good day, sweetheart." Penelope leaned over and placed a kiss on Juniper's forehead.

2...

"If you remember, invite Cat over for dinner. Some night this week would be great. I'd really like to meet her."

1...

Juniper nodded as she climbed out of the car and tossed her backpack over her shoulder. "Oh, one more thing..." Juniper produced the Polaroid picture from her sleeve and she tossed it onto the passenger's seat. "I think this belongs to you."

Chapter Five
Contact

On her way home that afternoon, Juniper took her, by that point, usual path through the forest. She found herself stopping from time to time to thrust her nose in the direction of a wildflower, as she paused to admire their beauty. Blue, pink, purple and white - the forest floor was a virtual canopy of color. Juniper found a pretty yellow bloom, plucked it and stuck it behind her ear. She felt prettier the instant she did so.

Juniper's upper arms and hands had slowly stiffened as the school day wore on and she currently found herself feeling tired and sleepy, thanks in no small part to her adventure the night before. She pulled her book bag along behind her in the dirt and thought only briefly about the disapproving look she would have surely gotten from her mother if she were there to witness it.

That book bag cost good money, young lady! she would have exclaimed. *You should learn to treat your things better than that!*

Juniper sighed at the appearance of her mother's reprimand and picked up her bag. She stretched and flexed her fingers as she tossed it over her shoulder and began to whistle to herself. Her unnamed whistle was soon met with response as a gathering of birds flew overhead and offered her a hello. They startled her with their cries at first and she laughed at her paranoia. She watched them for a moment, relaxed and then continued at her leisurely pace.

It was about that time when she heard it; the crack of branches at her back, branches that had most definitely been broken beneath the feet of an unknown follower. She turned quickly and her hair bounced frantically from shoulder to shoulder before it fell to rest at her back.

"Is someone there?" she called out. "Hello?"

Overhead, the wind whipped through the trees and woke them from their slumber. Juniper shivered and thought of monsters. Still, despite her fear, she called out again. "Look, I know someone is there... show yourself!"

Her plea was yet again met with silence.

Juniper, nervous and terrified by the thought of giant, unknown creatures, turned back to the path and continued her walk. Her leisurely pace, however had given way to a much quicker one.

When she finally reached the front porch of the farm house, she went in quickly and closed the door behind her. She peered out of the window, back down to the path, and waited for who or what had been following her to show themselves. Several minutes passed and the trees gave up no secrets; Juniper reluctantly turned away from the window and turned instead to the living room. She dropped her book bag near the tree and took her normal seat next to it. Still nervous, she kept her ears opened for unidentified sounds as she settled down amongst the planks.

She noticed then the broken floorboards and the collection of dirt at her feet; she wondered again how it was that she had managed to sleepwalk from her house to the tree in the middle of the night without waking even for a second. She supposed it would always be one of those things for which an answer was never provided. Juniper added it to her already large collection of other mysteries and sighed. It seemed some days as though answers would never come.

Juniper pulled out a book and opened to the page she'd earlier earmarked. She leaned her back against the tree and began to read. Several minutes passed before her uneasy feeling returned.

She was seated in the middle of a solitary shaft of sunlight, finally calming, when a darkness crept past the corner of her eye.

It was movement, and it came from the front porch in the form of scuttling shoes. That was followed by the sound of rocks as they slid over the rotting boards. A moment later her ears also heard the laugh of a distinctly male voice. Her blood began to chill.

Juniper's hands fell away from the book and slid quickly to rest on the cool surface of the floor. She braced herself, her heartbeat quickened and her ears perked up. The all-to-real sounds of voices, more than one, caught her ears again and held them tightly. At Juniper's best guess there were two, maybe three people outside, and they were circling the perimeter of the house.

Juniper dropped to her stomach and scooted back several feet into the darkness between the staircase and the tree trunk. From her position, she'd be able to clearly see the front door, but anyone who happened to enter the house wouldn't be able to see *her*, at least not until they were right on top of her. If the people, whomever they were, should happen to come inside, Juniper would wait until they passed her before she'd jump to find her legs and then the door. Still, despite the certainty of her own quickness, Juniper's heart increased its beat until she thought it was going to leap free of her ribs and arc across the floor before it came to a halt with a bloody, confused and decisive thump.

Two voices met up with a third as they completed their circle of the house and came to rest with their shoes on the front porch, just inches from the door. Juniper could see a shoed foot through the two inch opening she'd been afforded from her angle. A foot that moved, a second that followed and finally came the sound of a heavy creak as the door was heaved open and entry was made.

Juniper held back a gasp when she saw their faces, a gasp that came not out of surprise to their identities, but one that came from a growing sense of dread. She pulled her breath back into her lungs and studied the faces of the classmates she knew too well. She hoped to see within their eyes a glimpse of their intentions so that she might prepare herself for what lay ahead. However, to her dismay, she found nothing.

Ben and Jason had stopped just inside the doorway, and already their eyes were surveying the scene that had spread out before them.

"I can't believe we've never found this place before," Jason marveled as he pulled free of the older boy's shadow in favor of his own unobstructed glance around the living room.

"I told you this place existed! I knew it!" Ben turned his attention to the tree. "Look at this would ya. This old tree grew right up through the middle of the house!"

The third boy entered slowly behind Jason and Ben and peered between them. His brown eyes were wide in awe over the marvelous splendor of the giant oak tree. Juniper had to admit that it *was* a stunning sight, one that she too had been taken with the first time she'd seen it.

Juniper felt a sneeze tickle her nose before it passed as quickly as it had come. She was kneeling then, in the thick shadow of the tree only a few feet removed from the approaching boys.

"Hey Junie, you in here?" Ben called out. His voice whipped around the tree and found her well-hidden ears with its sharpness.

"Come out, come out wherever you are." Jason took another step closer to the tree. "We're not gonna hurt ya, Junie. We just wanna play house."

Ben snickered, but Jason shushed him and continued his calls. "*Juuuuunie*, wherever could you be hiding?"

Ben kicked at her book bag; Juniper heard her pencil case rattle. "We know you're here, so you might as well show yourself." More footsteps sounded and they grew ever closer to her crouched location.

Finally, feeling more than slightly defeated, she crawled out from her hiding spot and raised from her knees to her feet before either of the boys spotted her. Even though she was wary about her decision, she knew there was no use in hiding and felt it'd be best to get whatever teasing they were going to dish out, over and done with. Still, her voice caught and hesitated at the back of her throat before it finally spilled out into the semi-stagnant air. "W-Why are you following me?"

Ben found her first and his eyes came to rest upon her. "There you are! We were wondering where you'd gotten to."

Jason stepped in closer. His normally quasi-handsome face was twisted into a sneer. "Why were you hiding? You aren't scared of us are you?"

"I *wasn't* hiding," she fibbed. "I was reading and I didn't hear you guys come in."

"Sure, sure," Ben said. He sounded obviously unconvinced and he eyed her up, then down. "Quite a place you've got here. Quite a *strange* place." Ben's eyes left her and moved to the oak. He followed the line of it upwards and into the darkness. "I guess we know now where you've been keeping yourself lately."

Juniper shrugged. "I hang out here sometimes, yeah."

"What do you do up here all alone?" Jason asked. "Or maybe you *aren't* alone. Is this where you meet your *boy*friend?"

Ben chuckled. "Yeah, Junie, is this a little love nest for you and some unfortunate loser?"

Juniper felt her cheeks redden. "It's nothing like that," she said through grit teeth. "I read here. I listen to music, I do homework… It's my alone place. My *secret*."

"Well, not any more, it's not," Ben said. "You're being evicted. That is, unless of course you can play *nice*."

Jason chuckled; Ben did no such thing, instead he moved forward and advancing towards Juniper. She moved away from him instinctively, but stopped when her right side was pressed up against the cool and mighty trunk of the tree. The look on his face was one of strange frustration mixed with a dash of anger.

"What do you say, Junie? Can you be nice?"

"Yeah, but *you* can't," she whispered. She could feel his breath upon her cheek. It was warm and smelled of spearmint.

Ben clucked his tongue. "There's that attitude again! I swear, you really do need an adjustment."

The way his lips twisted around the final word of his sentence made her skin crawl. His eyes left hers then and moved down her face to her chest. He studied her in search of something. What that something was, Juniper had no idea and she felt herself stiffen under the scrutiny; *saw* him stiffen below the waist as the look of anger on his face morphed into a more dangerous emotion.   Juniper averted her eyes as a sickness quickly multiplied in her stomach. *Oh no. Oh, please, no. This isn't happening. Jason, no matter how much he doesn't like me… he won't let this happen. He'll say something.*

Ben pushed himself even closer. "Do you like to play house, Junie?" He was so close by that point that Juniper could feel his words hit her cheeks in tiny, warm puffs.

Juniper's eyes widened and met Ben's. He was smiling at her in an unfamiliar way; a shimmered of black flashed in him before it faded from his pupils entirely. The sight of it pushed her fear higher and she felt the acidity of the anxiety bite at the back of her throat.

"Hey, guys. Why don't you two step outside for a minute so's I can speak with Juniper here alone." Ben flung his words over his shoulder to the other boys without so much as even the slightest movement of his head. He kept his eyes trained on Juniper the entire time.

She felt her stomach turn and she lowered her hands to cover it. "Please, Ben… if there's something we need to discuss we can do it in front of them."

"No, Junie, I don't think we can. This is a... *private* matter."

"Oh come on, we don't-" Jason tried to protest, but was quickly shut down by the oldest boy's harsh words.

"Outside, **now**. Or I'll make sure you two regret not listening." Ben's tone had turned harsh under their opposition. "This'll only take a minute, alright? I just need to discuss something with our friend here."

Jason looked at the third boy and they shrugged at each other. He looked at Juniper, then found the back of Ben's head. "How long is this gonna take?"

"Don't know. A few minutes, I'd guess." Ben looked down at Juniper's chest. "I suppose that depends on how things go."

Juniper's heart raced into high gear. It clawed at her ribcage and prayed for an escape it knew it'd never find. "As much as I'd love to stay and chat, I *really* have to get going. Mama'll come looking for me if I'm not home soon." Juniper's feet found movement, only to be prematurely stopped as the oldest boy leveled his hand at chest height and blocked her path. His fingertips touched the base of the tree and acted as a gate that barred Juniper from moving any closer towards the exit.

Juniper looked past him and found Jason; he quickly looked away and without another word, he and the other boy turned for the door.

"Jason," Juniper whimpered. "Come on... *please*. Don't go."

The shaggy-haired boy hesitated, but didn't turn back. In a matter of seconds, they were through the doorway and on the porch. During the same seconds, Ben brought his arms down around Juniper and pulled her body to his.

"Did you really think Jason would listen to you over me?" he asked. "I can take him places. I can get him invited to all the cool parties, I can help him shake off his old nice-guy image. He *needs* me, Junie. He needs me to turn him into everything he could never be on his own."

"You're a sad, pathetic creep. You know that?"

"Is that what you really think?" He curled her hair around his thumb. "You're wrong, you know. I'm a decent guy once you get to know me. Maybe I'm a little misunderstood... and maybe, from time to time, I like to cause a little *trouble*... But I don't think that makes me bad."

"Maybe not," Juniper agreed. "But what you're about to do here? It makes you anything *but* decent."

Ben smiled wickedly. "Oh yeah? And just what is it that I'm about to do?"

"I d-don't know," she whispered. Her words were barely audible as they tripped over her stone-dry lips. "I don't want to think about it."

Ben moved his lips to her cheek where he allowed them to hover. "You're a cute girl. Do you know that? I mean, sure, you're a bit of a freak, but that doesn't mean you aren't pretty." He moved one hand from her back to her face and he cupped her cheek in his palm. "I know I've been pretty mean to you over the years, but I really do like you. I've wondered for awhile now what it would be like to..." Ben's words slipped away as he slid his lips to hers.

Juniper, not knowing what else to do, found his lower lip between her teeth and bit down.

"You bitch!" Ben pulled back in shock, but his arms didn't release her. Blood pushed to the surface of his lip where it beaded in a straight line before it plummeted down his chin. Ben's tongue found the wound and he sucked it clean. "I don't know why you have to fight this." His lips once again found the path to her cheek and he stained her flesh beneath him.

"Let me go!" Juniper shifted her shoulders from side to side in an attempt to break free, but Ben's grip was too strong.

"Just be still, Junie! This doesn't have to be difficult."

"Stop!" she screamed again. "Let go of me!"

Ben moved his hand from her cheek to her mouth. He covered it to suppress her screams. "Shhh, be quiet. This won't hurt. You might actually enjoy it."

Juniper widened her eyes in horror as Ben pressed her against the tree until her back was flat at the bark and her feet were fighting for level ground.

"You can't tell me you don't wonder what it's like to-" He said nothing more. It was as though the words had been drained from him and he'd been left empty of everything but the urge to touch and grab and paw at her flesh in his teenage, fevered passion.

Juniper closed her eyes as the zipper of her jeans was pulled down. Ben was eager to push her to the floor and when he'd succeeded in pulling her down, he climbed over her. Juniper felt her head smack hard against an exposed tree root, but she felt strangely disconnected from the pain. Juniper blinked once, twice and a third time before her sight re-aligned just in time to see the room go hazy.   Like a bad dream, she felt Ben moving over her. Her head began to ache and her legs were growing numb from their rigid, unyielding panic. The boy fought to free himself of his pants and with one hand he pushed Juniper's jeans down over her slender hips until they came to rest just below her knees.

"That's a good girl... don't fight it," he muttered. "It's alright."

Juniper was in shock. Her muscles had ceased their resistance of Ben's actions; her voice had dried up in her throat where it was eagerly swallowed by her panicked tongue. It burned as it slid down her throat and when it reached her stomach it dissolved into the acid and left her silent.

Her white panties were pushed aside to make room for his entry. His eyes, as he struggled to find her virginity, seemed hollow and weak. It was almost as though he himself were inside looking out, and had no real control over his own actions. Or maybe, just maybe, what she saw in his eyes was her own fear reflected back at her. Juniper couldn't decide what it was she saw and wasn't sure she wanted to know for certain.

Juniper's eyes fell shut as she waited for the penetration; the dizziness that had surrounded her seemed to morph into something quite different, something surreal all the same, but different none the less.

Then, as suddenly as the air had changed, Juniper felt something call to her and she re-opened her eyes in search of it. Her gaze moved past Ben and his silent concentration and raced up the long trunk of the tree. She moved past the second floor where the branches had grown through the hall and bedroom doorways; the third floor was the destination and her eyes rushed on quickly to attain the heights of it. And there, in the darkness, there was a second noise.

That time, Ben heard it too, and he stopped his futile attempts at his lascivious endeavor and looked upwards.

There was a stir in the rafters, a rattle that echoed down from the top of the house and shook the ground beneath them. Ben's fury shriveled quickly and he pulled himself free of his entanglement.

"What the fuck was that?" Ben zipped his pants quickly and shoved an out-turned pocket back into his jeans. "Is someone up there? I thought you were alone."

Juniper found herself engaged in prayer with eyes wide open and staring to the heavens. She prayed while Ben cursed and paced and debated about ascending the stairs to investigate the disturbance. She prayed as she slowly regained her senses and sat up in a shaky panic.

Ben found her again with his eyes, surveyed her partial nudity spilled out across the dirty wooden floor, and not knowing what else to do, he backed towards the door.

"I'm not sticking around to find out what the fuck that is... just know this isn't done!" He pointed a finger at her and his eyes moved again to the hole in the ceiling; to the tree that had carved it. "This isn't over, Junie... and so help me, if you tell anyone about what happened here-?" His threats fell to the wind as the noise from above sounded once again; that time it had moved closer to the first floor.

Without another word, Ben turned and ran; outside Juniper heard the voices of the other two boys pick up and assail him as he ran past them to find exit from the trees.

When the woods and the house fell back into silence, Juniper lifted herself up from the floor. Her hands were still shaking from the trauma of what had almost happened. They shook to such a degree that she found it hard to pull her jeans up; harder still to maneuver the zipper and press the button through the small, denim hole.

Then, in the turn of a screw, the atmosphere of the room changed yet again. From threatening to comforting, she felt the sensation wash over her like a warm curtain of water. Next, Juniper noticed the scent. The slightly musty, ever-present smell of the house had been almost instantly replaced by a warm and soothing note. It smelled vaguely of vanilla, vanilla that was so subtle she wasn't sure if it was real or if she was imagining it. It reminded her instantly of her dream the previous night, of the scent that had wafted from the house to meet her nose.

It was then that a tiny white *something* caught her eye. The something fluttered casually down from the ceiling and fell to rest at Juniper's feet with a flourish.

It was a single, white feather.

Juniper bent to pick it up and she examined it closely, curiously. It was too big to belong to any bird she'd ever seen, and she twirled it between the fingers of her left hand to inspect its size and shape further. Mid-twirl, she heard the noise above her again and she stepped slowly backwards from the tree with a creeping feeling of dread wriggling in her stomach like tightly wound worms in a rusty tin can.

That time, however, the noise was not unaccompanied. Instead, it brought with it a giant *something* that hardly made a noise as it sailed down the length of the tree. It landed on the wooden floor of the living room without so much as stirring the dust beneath its feet.

Juniper, uncertain of what to do or say, said nothing and jumped away from the creature. She stumbled in her fear and before she had time to correct her failing posture, she toppled straight to the ground. She cried out when she hit the splintering boards and the calm she'd so briefly reclaimed escaped her again. Her panic returned to its previous location in her forebrain and sought to quickly fill her lungs. She cried, softly at first, then more vigorously. Not like normal tears, they were hot and stinging and fell quickly from her eyes to her chin.

She was still sobbing when the unknown person stood slowly from its crouched position and turned to face her. Juniper wiped frantically at her tears, but despite her efforts she saw nothing of the person but a large black blob that was slowly moving closer.

"Don't cry, child. You're alright now. No one here is going to harm you, you've my word on that." The stranger's voice was deep and ever-so-slightly accented. He kneeled before her, just several feet removed from the spot where she was sitting in tears.

"W-Who are you?" she finally managed to croak out. "Please don't- don't hurt me."

"I promise, I won't hurt you." He extended his arm in her direction and she flinched before she recoiled completely. The stranger, unfazed by her reaction, made no retreat of his own. "Shh, it's fine. You're safe now, I swear to that."

The stranger used the long sleeve of his hooded cloak to dry the tears on Juniper's cheeks. He blotted at the corners of her eyes for several moments, before Juniper sucked in her breath and found the handle with which to turn off her salty faucet.

When her vision cleared and her chest stopped heaving, she was able to make out more details of the person in front of her. Even in his current crouching position he seemed like a giant, however Juniper couldn't be certain if his size was an illusion of her own creation or a fact of reality.

She noticed the scent then, the vanilla. She allowed herself a smile and then let her eyes roam the length of him. Upon closer inspection, Juniper noticed the tattered state of his cloak. There were holes near the floor-sweeping hem, frays and rubbed bare spots where the fabric had continually brushed against the harshness of the wood.

She could hear him breathing; could feel his eyes upon her even though she couldn't see them.

"I- I asked you a question," she said finally as her resolution returned. "Who are you? What are you doing here?"

When he responded, his words were slow. His hands, large and unencumbered by his cloak, were folded neatly over his bent right knee. "I'm simply someone who means you no harm. A friend, if you will."

"Does this *friend* have a name?" Juniper took the stranger's hand when he extended it towards her and she allowed herself to be pulled to her feet.

She brushed off her jeans and smiled up at him politely as if to silently thank him with her eyes.

"You may call me Azerial for now." He leaned forward into a strike of light which pulled his eyes from the darkness of his hood. "And you. You're Juniper."

Her eyes widened and her shock was apparent in her tone. "Yes! How did-?"

"Your name is on your book bag," he said gently. He held back a chuckle from tainting his words.

Juniper surrendered a nervous laugh. "That's my mama's thing. Like I'm ten or something. She even labels my shoes. I'm like, mama, how often do I take off my *shoes* in public? Even if I did, I'd surely not have them off long enough to get them confused with someone elses!"

The stranger didn't laugh, but Juniper sensed that he was smiling. She squinted at him and realized that her eyes were drawn to his, or more importantly, to the familiarity she found therein.

"What did you say your name was?" she asked him again, but then just as quickly she answered her own question. "Azerial was it?"

He nodded. "That's correct, yes."

Juniper mussed up her face. "What kind of a name is that?" she asked curiously. "Is it religious or something? It sounds religious."

Azerial finally offered a laugh. "I'll try not to be insulted, but I will ask *you* the same question. What kind of a name is Juniper?"

She felt a blush rise to her cheeks and she looked down at her feet to conceal it. "Point taken."

Azerial's voice regained its former firmness when next he spoke. "Are you sure you aren't injured?"

Juniper nodded. "I-I'm fine, thanks in no small part to you."

"Oh, well, I'm just glad you're alright." He took his eyes from hers briefly, only to promptly return them. "Do you mind if I ask *you* something, Juniper?"

Juniper shook her head and her curls bounced lazily over her shoulders. "No, I don't mind."

"Today isn't the first time you've been here, I know that much." He moved a hand into the darkness about his face, presumably to scratch his chin. "What I don't know, and would like to know, is *why* you're here."

"What do you mean? *Why?*" Juniper shrugged. "I don't have a reason to be here- I just..." She looked down at her feet then shuffled them nervously. The movement reminded her that she was still alive and in fact that her heart *was* still beating solidly within her chest. "I just stumbled upon this place and I come back because I like it here. That's all."

Azerial seemed satisfied with her answer and continued his interrogation from there. "So tell me, where are you from?"

Juniper pointed over her shoulder. "I just live about a half a mile from here, across the meadow."

"Is that right? Hmm... Interesting." Azerial seemed surprised by her response and it slowed his next question. "Have you lived there long?"

"Well yeah, but-" Juniper paused to clear her throat.. "Listen, I don't want to be rude, seeing as how you sorta saved me and all, but... who *are* you?"

"I already told you that. I'm a friend," he said quietly.

"Well... *friend*, if I may ask, what are *you* doing here? Certainly you don't live here." Juniper paused to view Azerial's demeanor. "Do you? Do you live here?"

"As a fact, I do," he admitted. "I've called this place home for many years now."

"Oh. I-I see." Juniper felt her cheeks flush, but despite her embarrassment, she was able to continue with her own line of questioning. "But- why? Why live *here* of all places? There can't be any electric or gas... don't you freeze in the winter? How do you eat? Do you shop?"

"You certainly ask a lot of questions," he said. He was chuckled just under his breath. "You remind me of someone I used to know." His voice turned heavy with sadness as he amended his statement. "But, I suppose you would."

"What?" A look of confusion hit her square in the forehead and bent her brow. "What does that mean?"

Azerial waved his hand. "You'll have to pardon me,

Juniper.   It's been quite some time since I've had visitors and my conversation skills are lacking." He extended one long cloth draped arm towards the kitchen. "I would offer you something to drink, but-"

Juniper held up her hand. "It's ok, really."

"Are you sure? There *is* a well out back." Azerial motioned towards the back of the farm house with one jerk of his neck. "I don't mind fetching you a glass-"

"No, really, I'm fine."

Azerial fell silent as if to prove his earlier comment about his degenerated social skills.

Juniper, her bravery having returned in the silence, took one step forward towards Azerial. As she did so, he took one step back. His eyes leapt back into the darkness, removed from the steady curtain-penetrating beam of filtered light.

"Are you human?" She immediately felt silly as soon as the words left her mouth.

Azerial laughed. "More or less."

That time, it was Juniper's turn to move away. Her surprise over his answer caught her at the breast bone like an insistent hand and moved her backwards towards the door.

"What are you then?" she finally asked, having given herself time to examine him again. She suddenly wished she hadn't turned down his offer of well water as her lips had gone dry, much as her palms had gone wet.

"I'm not certain you want me to answer that," Azerial said quietly. "The truth you seek isn't at all what you assume it to be."

"Let me see your face." Her words came out weak and less forceful than she'd hoped. On her second attempt she straightened her spine and injected her question with a quick-drying firmness. "You do *have* a face, right?"

"I do indeed." Again, Juniper sensed he was smiling.

She didn't relax; didn't relent. "Then take down your

hood and let me see what you look like."

"I don't think I should do that, Juniper. There are a lot of things that I'm not sure I should-" He stopped himself from speaking further and Juniper spoke up during the pause.

"Are you a criminal? Are you hiding from the law? Is that why you're out here all alone? Afraid you've been featured on *Cops* or something? I promise I won't turn you in, if you promise to not kill me," Juniper bargained. She had taken to twisting her hands nervously behind her back.

He laughed softly. "No, it's nothing like that I assure you."

"Then why are you hiding in this old house?" she asked suspiciously. "Normally, people don't hide away like this unless they're insane or dangerous-" She stepped backwards and her words began to shake. "Or b-both."

The sadness Juniper sensed he had been holding back finally freed itself from the knots at his tongue. "I stay here because I have not been afforded another option. Because for a person like me, there *is* no other place to go. I've a mission I must see to, a burden to bear in silent repentance."

Juniper was uncertain as to how to respond. She bit her lip and once again returned her eyes to her shoes. Once white, they were currently dusty and scuffed.

"I'm sorry if my words have caused you pause," he apologized softly.

"No, they haven't. I'm just thinking, is all."

"About what?" asked Azerial.

Juniper pulled at her fingers again. She stopped when she was satisfied that all of the pops in her knuckles had been freed. "Well, about you... about this house... About what happened here today. Or rather, almost happened."

"Ah," he said softly. "I would imagine it's a lot to take in, even without my adding to the mix."

She looked up at him suddenly. "You said that you *have*

to stay here. Why?"

"Because that's the way it works, Juniper." His words on the subject seemed almost final, but Juniper was unwilling to let him go at that.

She stepped closer to him and once again made an attempt to better assess what it was he was hiding beneath the cover of his hood. She stopped when the fingers of her right hand were within inches of touching the fabric of his sleeve.

Azerial recoiled and Juniper could sense his anxiety almost as strongly as if it were her own. "What more do you want from me?" he asked, and his voice suddenly turned defensive. "What more can I say?"

"I don't know," she admitted. "I just have this-this *feeling...*"

Again, Juniper could see his eyes and he spoke softly to her gaze. "There are some things you shouldn't know," he whispered. "It isn't the right time."

Juniper didn't give up and when the tips of her fingers met the scratchy fabric of his cloak, she felt a shock go through her. She released him and looked at the tips of her fingers. She searched them for any signs of fire or smoke, but she found none. Speechless, her eyes regained their former position.

"You should go, before it gets any later. Your mother will worry," said Azerial.

Juniper paused and her hand stopped and suspended in mid-air. "Mama will wait! But right now, I'm not leaving here until you show me what you're hiding."

"Juniper, please-"

She, ready to pull his hood back from his face, paused only when she saw another white feather. That one fell slowly from behind Azerial and it spiraled softly to a stop on the ground between his sandal-covered feet.

She pulled back her hand. "What are you?" she asked again. That time her voice broke over her tongue and caused her words to splinter outwards like ice spray from a freshly picked block.

"You already know the answer to that, don't you?" he asked her softly. "You're a smart girl. You almost have to be. That being said, I ask that you look to your heart, Juniper, and therein the truth shall be revealed."

He removed the cloak at long last and when it fell to the floor around him like an inky black puddle, he raised his eyes to meet Juniper's gaze. He seemed almost ashamed of the secrets he'd kept hidden just below the surface of his man-made facade, and after only a few brief moments of eye contact, he lowered his chin.

Juniper widened her eyes and felt her jaw go slack at the sight of him. At first glance she was almost able to overlook *them* and see only the man before her. She saw his slowly graying black hair, saw the deeply etched lines in his face that had been earned from years of reluctant worry. His mouth was wide like hers and his ears were flat and pinned close to his head. His cheekbones were high and pointed and further accentuated his pale, somewhat gaunt face. Beneath his thin swath of a shirt, his chest was bare and well-defined. His stomach heaved heavily in and out over the waist of his long black pants as he waited in uncomfortable silence for her inspection to cease.

He was the man in the photo, the one who had held himself so closely to her mother's side. Juniper gulped at the realization and brought herself to face the part of him she had been ignoring, the part that hadn't been revealed to her in the photo she had so carelessly left in her mother's care that very morning.

Spread out behind him were wings of white. The tops of

them stood just higher than his shoulders and the bottoms stopped just at his ankles.

Azerial, with much trepidation, took Juniper's hand in his and pressed it to the side of his face. "Look at me and you will see the answers just hidden from your view."

Juniper's hand was cold and clammy and stuck to the dryness of his cheek. Again, she felt a sharp jolt of electricity and she almost pulled her hand away, but Azerial's grip was firm and unrelenting.

The first vision came swiftly like darkness over a canyon bed. A room flashed before her mind's eye; a woman's cries followed by those of a newborn child followed. The almost wooden sound of something rolling out of earshot, like marbles set out across the surface of a concrete floor, came last.

Juniper's hand was then released from Azerial's fingers and it fell to her side where it rested quite restlessly.

"I held you for but a second on the day that you were born," he said softly. "You were beautiful. Perfect and oh so beautiful." For a moment, Juniper thought he might cry. However, he did not. Instead he quickly pulled his shaking lower lip back into alignment and straightened his posture.

"You were there? We were *here?*" Juniper's breath caught in her throat as Azerial's words sunk into her pores. She looked down at the ground to find stability, but the wooden floor was moving beneath her in waves. "You're an angel..." she said finally. The word escaped her in a bubble of disbelief and popped on the harsh air of reality that surrounded them. "An angel... An *angel?*"

With one long finger extended in the air, he corrected her. "I *was* an angel. Was," he said. "No longer is that the case."

"But the wings! You still have *them!*" Juniper exclaimed. She continued her struggle for air; for understanding. She felt as though she was losing the battle in both cases.

Azerial responded to her comment by bending and retrieving his cloak from the ground. He picked it up carefully, shook it out and then began to replace it. "The wings are one of the few reminders of the life I used to live."

Juniper found him again with her eyes; they traveled slowly to his face. "You were really there when I was born? Why? And why was I born here? Mama always told me that I was born at the hospital in Table Rock…"

Azerial looked away and lowered his head to his chest. "You were born on a Friday morning. For twenty five seconds, time stood still. The air refused to stir; the birds in the trees had tightly clamped their beaks… It was a strange day, a day I'll never forget."

"Born here." Juniper dropped both of her arms to her sides as though they were nothing more than cotton stuffed pillow cases. She looked around the living room again, her eyes now widened with curiosity about the other secrets the walls possessed.

"It didn't always look this way," Azerial was quick to say. "It used to be much nicer, but over the course of the past sixteen years I've been forced to burn most of the things left behind." He pointed to the other side of the living room. "I cannot tell you how many times I've stood on the spot where you were born and wondered where you were."

"Wait a second here… Let me get this straight…" Juniper's shaking left hand rose slowly to meet her temple. Once there she massaged the side of her head, as the pressure that had built steadily inside of her brain made it unbearable to think. "You're my mama's guardian angel or something?"

"Something, yes." Azerial cleared his throat and Juniper realized that her question had made him uncomfortable. The look on his face was not foreign to Juniper; she had seen much the same desperate look on her mother's face a million times.

"Ok, so if you're a guardian angel, then why are you

living here? Shouldn't you be in, you know…" Juniper rolled her eyes towards the ceiling. "*Heaven?*"

"I told you, I'm no longer an angel." Azerial had re-cocooned himself within the folds of his oversized cloak, but the hood he kept at his shoulders. "For hundreds of thousands of years I served God. I was a divine extension of a power so great no human could ever imagine it. When the heavens divided and the original angels fell, I remained true to the fight and took up flaming swords with the best of them. Flanked by Gabriel and Michael, I defended everything I loved with everything I had-" His shoulders slumped and his voice lessened. "It went on like that for longer than I can now imagine… and, in a moment of extreme weakness I made a decision. A decision to leave the kingdom, to strike out on my own."

"You fell?"

"I jumped," Azerial whispered. "I extended my arms at my sides and I dove into the darkness."

"When?"

"Seventeen years ago." He no longer appeared to be nervous. He had instead taken on the defeat of a person on a sinking boat who had accepted their lack of a life jacket.

"You fell here, then? And mama found you and-"

Azerial cleared his throat. "If you don't mind, I would prefer to continue this at another time, Juniper. It's only getting later and I-I should stop now before-"

Juniper interrupted him quickly and a touch of anger crept into her normally calm voice. "For my entire life I've been kept in the dark about the details of my own birth. Specifically about my father… and now I find you, someone who has the very information I've wanted, and you- you can't deny me! You just can't!" Juniper shook her head. "My own mother denies me! I understand her reasons, I do, but that doesn't stop the way I feel. *Strange.* As though my own life is being held hostage by things I can't change!"

Azerial stepped towards her. "I understand your pain, but I fear already that I've said too much. The pieces are there for you to place together, Juniper, if it is the truth you truly seek."

Juniper spoke slowly. "Tell me why you were there on the day I was born! Tell me why! Please..."

"It's a long story." His eyes were fixed on a location just above and to the right of where Juniper was standing with her hands on her hips and her eyes flaming.

Juniper spoke again, that time more firmly. "I've got nothing but time."

Azerial's shoulders rolled forward. He quickly retrieved them from their slump and pulled them upright once more. "You don't understand, Juniper. I don't keep this secret because I don't want to share, but rather because I- It's *complicated*, child. So very, *very*, complicated."

"Then explain it to me! *Make* me understand," Juniper pleaded. "Please, I beg you. Do me this one favor and I'll leave forever if that's what you want."

Chapter Six
Flash Light

"You *do* recognize me, don't you?" Azerial held the final piece of the puzzle over Juniper's head and dangled it close to her curiosity and growing understanding. "Somewhere in the back of your mind, your questions already have their answers. In my eyes, you see it, a spark of familiarity."

Juniper mouthed the words, and didn't realize at first that actual sound was coming from her lips. "Y-You're my... my *father?*"

Several moments of stunned and awkward silence filled the room. Outside, the crickets were serenading Juniper's revelations. They seemed oddly removed from the interior of the home, almost as though they wished to keep their distance from the blast zone.

"I know this must be a shock for you." Azerial lowered his voice. "I can only imagine how you must be feeling. All of the questions you have! Questions that I *will* answer, I promise you. But you must promise *me* that you'll be patient as I too am struggling."

She laughed at his words and the sound escaped her much like her earlier utterance; quickly and through no control of her own. "So it's true then? You're my father?"

He nodded. "Yes, it's true."

"My father is an angel." Juniper couldn't think of a more bizarre thing to say and then it came to her. "My father is a *fallen* angel."

"Like I said, I know it must be quite a shock, but-"

"A shock?" Juniper exclaimed, interrupting him again. She laughed and ran her nervous fingers through her hair. "Yeah, it's a shock... It's a hel- *heck* of a shock," she corrected herself. "It's funny, but I never thought finding the answers I wanted would create so many new questions."

"You will find that the truth is often like that, Juniper."

She shook her head softly from side to side, still trying desperately to process the information she'd been handed. "I-I always expected my father was someone, well... *different*, but this? This is just... *wow.*" Her voice had italicized the word before she forced it out. "Mama would never breathe a word about you... about any of the things I was too young to remember. Sh- She prefers it that way and now I think I get why that is."

"I'm afraid her unwillingness to share is at least partially my doing," Azerial said. He paused briefly to collect his thoughts before he continued his explanation. "I hope you don't find fault with her for her actions. She was protecting me, and I'm certain you can understand why."

"But protecting you from *me?* Your own child? Your flesh and blood? I don't understand why *I* was a threat to your safety. You're my father, no matter what you are. I'd never turn you over to anyone who might harm you!"

Azerial seemed to overlook her words and he continued instead down his own wooded path. "Your mother left me here with the idea that I was leaving earth and going back to Heaven. It was a lie I created to free her from her torment of-" He exhaled slowly, and as though walking through a darkened field of landmines, he was careful where he stepped. "She was forced to take you away, Juniper, and it was for the better. My presence in your life would have only made things more difficult... it wasn't right for me to rob a child of her innocence so that I might be a father- and what sort of a father would I have been? Trapped in this house with no hope of escape, trapped in this world-"

"You keep saying that! That you're *trapped* here, but- but what do you mean, *trapped here?*" Juniper chose that fragment to latch on to as his other words and thoughts still spun frenzied about her head, unable to be stopped and plucked down.

Azerial sighed and looked to the tree, a moment later his hand reached out to feel the bark. "For a fallen angel to be with a mortal woman...? It is considered a great sin. And for that union to bring about the birth of a child? There are certain things that happen in such a case... things that prevent me from leaving here, an obligation if you will."

"I don't understand."

Azerial sighed and quickly brought the side of his right hand to his brow; his left was still touching the bark of the tree trunk. "I apologize that I cannot explain this better. Please, bear with me."

"Was the house built around the tree?" she asked curiously. "I can't imagine why someone would do that, but at this point nothing would really surprise me." Her eyes roamed the trunk for several long seconds of contemplation, then went back to Azerial's down turned eyes. "I'm sorry, I don't mean to ask a million questions. You just have to understand my confusion."

He spoke beneath her gaze. "I understand it, believe me I do."

"Yeah, I guess you probably would understand." She shook her head to clear away her confusion. The act did little to help. "Anyway... this trapped talk... What do you mean?"

"Well, Juniper, you see... Two things happened the night that your mother and I-" He cut himself off to reconsider his phrasing. "Not only was a seed planted inside of her, but one also took root in the soil below where we stand. As you grew inside of your mother, the seed inside this very earth began to emulate you. On the day that you were born, the earth cracked and from beneath the dirt came a sprout."

Juniper looked at the giant oak; the amazement of her situation took her over again. "You mean to tell me that the tree has… that it's grown this tall in less than *sixteen years*?"

He made no movement and when he spoke his lips scarcely parted. "With God, all things are possible."

"But that doesn't explain why or how you're *trapped* here," Juniper continued. She rubbed her temples once more and realized that the soft circular motion did more good than she'd thought it might. "What does the tree *mean*?"

"The tree… the earth-" Azerial chuckled and Juniper wondered if that had been his intended reaction, because almost as quickly as the sound had erupted, he locked his jaw to prevent a follow up.

She realized suddenly that he was probably almost as nervous as she was, and instead of further prompting him to continue, she allowed him several anxiety-filled seconds to compose his thoughts. While she waited, she examined her fingernails; two were broken, another splintered. Tiny drops of blood had collected beneath the remaining nails and to conceal them she shoved both hands quickly into her pockets.

"The tree grows for a very specific purpose," he paused, nodded once at his own thoughts and forged onwards with a slightly heavier tone. "As I've stated, my act was a sin against God. An abomination that somewhat aligned me with the darker forces of this world. Pure I was, then tainted I became. As punishment, my life and that of the tree have been irrevocably bound to one another."

"What do you mean?" Juniper asked. "Bound how?"

He inhaled and then exhaled a shaky sigh. "I mean that I cannot stray very far from this spot without suffering great consequences."

Juniper furrowed her brow in confusion. "Then why don't you just chop down the tree? Wouldn't that free you from this bind?"

Azerial held up one hand to silence her. "As I said, my life and that of the tree are one. If the tree dies, I will also perish."

Juniper's eyes widened in alarm over Azerial's statement. "You'd die? Like... *die?*" She shook her head and gathered the breath that had quickly left her lungs. "There goes *my* idea, I guess. Wow... so then you really *are* trapped here."

Azerial nodded. "Indeed."

"So can you even leave the house?" Juniper asked.

Again, Azerial nodded. "I can, yes. Through trial and error I've established that a perimeter exists."

Juniper nodded. "I see... and this perimeter-"

Azerial quickly interrupted her. "Your mother... When I knew her, she was young, not much older than you are now," he paused. "She felt it her duty to show me as much of the world as she could, as a substitute for the real thing. I don't suppose she realized that I had seen much of it during my tenure in Heaven... Ah, but mostly she would read to me, and out of all the stories I heard, I was most fond of Superman. Are you familiar with Superman?" He continued after Juniper nodded. "Superman's weakness is, of course, kryptonite. When he comes in contact with it, his strength fails him, he falls to the ground and with prolonged exposure, he would die... it is much like this with the perimeter and I."

"So it's an invisible wall?"

Azerial contemplated her question carefully before he responded. "It is not so abrupt as to be considered a wall. It's much more akin to climbing a tall mountain. The higher one climbs, the thinner the air becomes, and the more difficult it is to continue the climb. Inevitably, a point is reached where any and all progress becomes physically impossible. So it is with the boundary. The further I get from the tree, the weaker I become, and the harder it is to proceed. If I stray too far..."

"Kryptonite, got it," Juniper interjected. "So uh, you said that you've sorta tested these boundaries. Well, tell me, exactly how far can you safely travel before you start feeling...

weakened?"

"Well, I know for certain that I can safely make it to the creek. I fish there often, usually by the moonlight. As I'm sure you can imagine, that's quite a challenge when the moon has tucked herself away," Azerial said with a chuckle.

"So the creek is within the perimeter," Juniper mused. She gave Azerial a hopeful look. "What about the road to the north? Have you ever-?"

"I can assume that I would be able to make it that far," Azerial said softly. "Although I'll admit that I've never strayed past the edge of the woods. As I'm sure you understand, the risk of being seen is too great for such-"

Juniper interrupted with a question. "But if you wanted to, you *could* visit my house, right?"

"Well, maybe, but-"

"Then you'll visit mama and you two can be re-united!" Juniper clapped her hands together at chest height and a smile leapt quickly to her lips. "She'd absolutely *love* to see you again, I know she would! Then you two could talk and you could explain-"

Azerial shook his head firmly, an action which caused his black hair to bounce at his shoulders. "Juniper, no. That will *never* happen."

Juniper's face fell instantly in accordance with her popped balloon of premature hope. "No? No? But why not? I don't understand-"

"No," Azerial said again, his voice steadier and more harsh than it had been the first time he'd denied her offer. "I promised myself that I wouldn't put Penny through it again."

Juniper let out a sound of mild disgust. "Put her through *what?* You two can be together now! Why couldn't you be? Everything is out in the open between *us*! There don't have to be any more secrets-"

"It's not that simple," said Azerial. "I don't stay away

only to shield *you* from the truth. I stay away so that your mother might be happy with someone else, with someone more her type. Someone who can care for her in the way she deserves to be cared for! I won't love her again only to break her heart, Juniper. I've done that once in this lifetime and once was more than enough."

Juniper pouted and continued her protest. "But it could be *different* this time!"

Azerial shook his head sadly. "It can't be different, it *won't* be different." He forced himself to recover from the sadness with a smile and his words came easily as though they were a speech he had been rehearsing for years. "I can hardly imagine it, the truth you're dealing with right now, all of these strange realizations about who I am, what you are... This weight I have placed upon your shoulders is nothing if not an unbearable reminder that life can be cruel in her surprises. I should have known that the truth would find us someday, and I was foolish to think I could deny you your heritage. Deny myself my own fate... That being said, it is understandable if you're angry, shocked, frightened... You should not be forced to just accept this quickly, without ample amounts of time to process the information."

Juniper bathed in his words until her skin could hold no more. His distraction had worked and Juniper changed the subject as a new question hit the front of her brain, freshly fallen from the circle of confusion about her. "So what am I?" she asked quietly. "I'm obviously not *normal*."

"You're my daughter," Azerial replied simply.

"Am *I* human?" Juniper asked, uncertain as to whether or not she wanted the answer.

"Of course you are," he said with a succinct nod.

Juniper, unsatisfied with his vague answer, crossed her arms over her chest and narrowed her eyes in his direction. "But?" she prompted.

Azerial sighed when he realized that Juniper was much like a dog with a bone, and that her grip upon the current subject would not be shaken until she was satisfied. "How much do you know about religion?" he asked.

"Little," Juniper admitted. "Mama took me to church when I was younger, but over the years, we just stopped going. I got the feeling it was hard for her. Being there, I mean. Now I guess I know why."

"First off, let me say that my appearance is deceiving if you wish to use it to judge my age," Azerial said. He cleared his throat and took a cautious step forward. "I'm older than all of mankind, if you must know the truth, but I digress, as there is a point in these words. During my tenure in heaven, I heard stories of other angels who had fallen and sinned with daughters of Eve, heard of the children born unto them. The children were legendary, giants amongst men and they were called the *Nephilim*."

"Is that what I am?" Juniper asked. She repeated the strange word slowly and it rolled awkwardly from the end of her tongue. *"Nephilim."*

"You are indeed a Nephilim," he said with a gentle, supportive smile. "You will, however, be relieved to know that you won't grow much taller than you currently are. The rumors of the Nephilim are highly exaggerated. I'm afraid that over the years they've been given a bad reputation. They've even been held responsible for famine, disease, destruction of all sorts. I've always felt that the Nephilim have their purpose as well as free will. Like any other creature, they have a choice as to their life path. Either they choose good, or they choose evil."

Juniper had looked up suddenly at the mention of her height. "How did you know I was self-conscious about my height?"

Azerial smiled softly. "Even though I'm no longer in the heavens, I maintain my halo and wings. With them I have certain *special* talents not afforded to most humans."

Juniper's thoughts froze, but not before a question formed. "You can read my mind, can't you?"

Azerial nodded and then chuckled at the look of shock on his daughter's face. "Your mother wasn't a huge fan of the ability."

"I can't say I'm fond of it either," Juniper muttered. She averted her eyes and tried to shake her thoughts loose in an attempt to clear her mind.

"I'm sorry if I've made you uncomfortable," Azerial said quietly. "If it makes you feel any better, I'll try my best to not read your thoughts any more."

Juniper looked at him curiously with her head tilted slightly to the left to survey the truth of his words. "You can do that? You can just turn the ability off like it has a switch of some sort?"

"Yes, of course. No divine ability is ever *continuously* active. In fact, prolonged use of any special gift will harm the user."

"Harm how?" Juniper asked.

"It varies, dependent upon the ability. But in this instance, if I were to read every thought you had, I would develop a headache. If I didn't stop at that point, the headache would worsen and eventually I would lose consciousness."

"I see," Juniper said softly. "So are there other powers? Does every angel have a different one?"

He moved his hand from side to side as though weighing her question, and his answer, on an imaginary scale. "There are many different abilities, but I'm not the only one who reads minds."

"Do *you* have any other abilities?" she asked. "Besides the mind reading thing, I mean."

He was slow to answer, but finally did. "All who wear the halo have the ability to self heal. The halo also acts as a sort of shield if I'm in danger, thus making it harder for me to be harmed. For instance, I can walk through a wall of fire and not be burned, just as long as my halo is *activated*, so to speak. Also, those who possess the wings are gifted with immortal life." He paused and took in a deep breath. "There is one *other* ability I possess. One that I believe you'll have a better understanding of."

"What's that?" Juniper asked.

"Well, in addition to being able to heal *myself*, I can heal others with my touch," he explained. "It's one of the more active powers that exist in divinity and the responsibility of it is not to be taken lightly."

Juniper wet her lips and nodded softly. "I-I think I understand." She looked at him once again with a quizzical tilt to her brow. A recently sprouted thought had reached out to tickle her tongue and despite her trepidation over hearing the answer, she allowed her mouth to form the words in spite of her fear. "So do *I* have special talents?" she asked. "Like you? I mean, I can't read minds, if I could I think I'd know it by now, but-"

Azerial's smile grew and he nodded towards her. "Look at your hands and you tell me."

Juniper did as she was instructed and pulled her broken-nailed fingers from their hiding. She gasped when she realized that already the cuts on her fingers had completely disappeared. She looked at her father, her mouth open wide.

"It's important for me to mention that any Nephilim will inherit some, or all, of their paternal parents' gifts. I've always wondered what it was you'd end up claiming for yourself."

"But I- *I* did that?" Her mouth was agape as her eyes continued their examination of her hands. "But I don't have a halo... How can I-?"

"The ability to heal oneself is not tied to possessing a halo in this instance," Azerial explained. "Of course, if you *did* have a halo, the ability would increase ten fold."

"I just can't believe this!" Juniper finally halted her self-exam and lowered her hands to her sides. "I can *heal* myself? This isn't a joke?"

"You've never noticed it before?" he asked. "I'm sure you're rarely sick."

Juniper thought for a moment and a slow realization began to form at the front of her mind. "I had the chicken pox for one day in 2nd grade," she said quietly. "*One* day."

"I'm surprised you had them that long!" Azerial said with a hearty laugh. "Your ability works on yourself, without your control or want, and on others when the situation warrants such an act by the laying on of hands."

"Did you ever tell my mama about this gift?" Juniper asked. "Did you ever heal *her*?"

"Only once," Azerial said quietly. He took a step closer to Juniper and left the tree at his back. "She twisted her ankle and I, not able to stand seeing her in pain, touched her and alleviated her suffering."

"Wow," Juniper whispered. "I c-can't believe this... This is like... I mean, I don't-" She bent at the waist; her head was spinning and she rested the palms of her sweating hands on her thighs to steady her failing posture. "I don't know what to say!"

"In time you'll come to terms with this, I promise." Azerial reached out and pushed a strand of Juniper's hair from her face. He secured it behind her ear and when next he spoke, his thick voice was softer. "You're handling this better than I ever could have hoped. Most people would have completely toppled under the weight of these things, but not you. Not you."

"It isn't easy," Juniper said, a tight laugh crawling up the length of her chest to her mouth. "I feel like I've been hit by a truck."

"Perhaps you should sit down," Azerial said. He stepped forward and put his arm around her shoulders. "Come, we can have a seat on the stair-"

"No, no, I'm fine," Juniper said. She forced her spine to straighten and when she stood tall, she smiled encouragingly at Azerial. "I just needed a second to collect my breath, that's all."

Azerial's smile was shaky. "Alright then, but it probably would be best if you returned to your home soon. I don't want you getting in trouble, and I'm afraid time has passed us by rather quickly."

"I know, and you're right. Mama *will* worry, but I- I don't want to leave! I have a million questions to ask you! I've been waiting my whole life for this and now here you are and here I am! I'm afraid if I leave here tonight, that I'll-" Juniper shook her head as her words caught in her throat.

"That you'll never see me again?" Azerial asked. He smoothed his palm across her upper back to calm her nerves. "Juniper, I've been here for seventeen years. I can promise you that I'll be here tomorrow and the day after that and yes, even the day after that." He glanced back at the tree and roamed it with his eyes. "She keeps me here, Juniper."

Juniper wasn't sure if Azerial was referring to the tree or to Penelope, but she chose not to question him on the meaning of his words. Instead, she looked up at him and studied the curve of his jaw with her eyes. "Can I ask just one more thing?"

"Anything," Azerial said softly. "I told you, I'll answer whatever questions I can."

Juniper nodded. "Are your abilities tied to the halo? I mean... if you somehow lost it or couldn't access it, would you still be able to read minds and heal? I assume so, because I certainly don't have a halo and apparently *I* can heal."

"Without my halo, I would lose everything. The mind reading, all aspects of the healing, *everything*." He dropped his hand from her back and turned to look at her head on. "For as much as we are alike, we're very different, Juniper. Unlike my power, yours isn't bound to the divine. It's only bound to *you*, to who and what you are. That means that no matter what happens, you'll never lose it."

"Weird," Juniper said.

Azerial chuckled and made a jerking motion towards the tree with his chin. "May I ask *you* something?"

"Of course," Juniper said. "Although I don't know what I could possibly tell you that you don't already know."

Azerial chuckled and pointed to the base of the tree. "I just want to ask that you make certain to keep my things safe."

Juniper blushed when she realized that he was referring to the rusty metal box she'd liberated the night before during her fevered mission. "Oh, I- I'm sorry about that. I'll bring it back tomorrow, I promise."

He held up his hand to quiet her apologies. "I understand, believe me. You were called to it, and don't worry about returning the things you've found. If you'd like to keep them, they're yours."

"Are you sure?" Juniper asked, her mouth still parted more than slightly.

"They have served their purpose," Azerial said, and he tossed her a wink. "You need them more than I."

Juniper finally fell silent, hushed by her own thoughts. Thoughts which were plentiful and exhausting to keep track of. She yawned.

"You should be getting home. I'm sure you have a lot to think about."

Juniper tried to protest, but Azerial shushed her and moved his oversized hands out in front of himself to further accentuate his point.

"We will see each other again," he said quietly. "I promise you, I'm going no where. Especially not now, not when we've finally been brought together."

Juniper smiled and inside of her chest she felt the unmistakable swell of happiness. "I'll see you again soon. I can't wait to get to know you better."

Azerial's own smile widened. "And I, Juniper, can't wait to know *you*. There's just one favor I have to ask of you before you go."

Juniper picked up her book bag from the base of the tree and hoisted it over her shoulder. "Sure! You need me to bring you something?"

"No, I uh- I need you to promise me that you won't tell your mother about me," Azerial said. His eyebrows lowered and his eyes widened with concern. "I don't want her to know that I'm here, that we've met... and I do hate having you lie to Penny, but I'm afraid there's no other way."

Juniper bit her lip and against her better judgment she nodded her agreement. "You have my word," she whispered. "I won't say a thing to mama about you. I promise."

Penelope was sitting at the kitchen table when Juniper arrived home that evening. She was staring at the photograph Juniper had left behind in the car that morning with a sullen, worried look etched firmly into her delicate features. Upon hearing Juniper's approach, Penelope dropped the photo to the table top where it fluttered to a casual rest.

"Junie, come here for a second," she said. Her voice was firm and Juniper braced herself for the impending argument. "Now," Penelope added, and Juniper slightly picked up her pace, more out of habit than out of want.

Juniper kicked off her shoes and expelled a sigh. "Can't this wait, mama? I'm tired and I haven't even started my homework yet."

"It won't take but a second," Penelope assured her. The

tone in her voice held a clear indication of what emotions were boiling just beneath her serene surface.   Fear, anger and annoyance to name but a few.

Juniper relented and entered the kitchen.   She realized that there was no way to avoid the conflict.   However, upon reaching the table, she didn't sit.   Instead she stood behind the dining room chair and placed her hands on the back to steady herself.   "What is it, mama?"

Penelope picked up the picture and held it up for Juniper to see.   "Where did you get this?" she asked.   "And I don't want to hear any lies.   I want the truth."

Juniper shrugged with one shoulder.   "I found it."

"Found it *where*?" Penelope asked sharply.   "In my room?   Have you been going through my things?"

Juniper narrowed her eyes.   "No, mama, I haven't.   I didn't find it in your room.   Just think about it for a second and I'm sure you'll figure it out."

Penelope nodded once and lowered her eyes to the surface of the table.   "I see," she whispered.   She sounded slightly defeated.   "Is that where you've been tonight?   In the woods?"

"Yes," Juniper whispered.   "I was reading there and I lost track of time."

Penelope didn't respond to Juniper's comment at first.   Instead she looked intently at the photo while her eyes seemingly drank in the details she'd forgotten so long ago.   "Is this all you've found or are there more surprises you're waiting to spring on me?"

"Why do you ask, mama?   What else are you hiding from me that you're so afraid I'll find?"   Juniper's words were thick with bitterness and she realized quite suddenly that she didn't care how she sounded.

"Juniper, don't talk to me with that tone!   I'm still your mother," warned Penelope.   Her eyes tightened their focus and nearly made Juniper shiver with their intensity. "Is there more?" she asked again.

Juniper apologized under her breath with words that were indiscernible and lacking in sincerity. "There's nothing else."

"You've been nosing around in places you shouldn't be nosing. Dangerous places," continued Penelope. "How many times have I told you that the woods aren't a safe place for a young girl to be? How many, Junie? Because quite frankly, I've lost count."

"Dangerous for whom, mama?" Juniper blurted out. "For me or you?"

Penelope had grown agitated. "I will not tell you again, Juniper. You will address me with the respect I am due as your mother."

"I'm sorry mama, but-" Juniper stopped herself and rolled her eyes. She'd suddenly lost the steam to fuel her argument. "Forget it, just forget it. I don't know why I'm wasting my breath because I know you'll never be straight with me about any of this."

Penelope sighed and within her sigh Juniper could clearly see that she had no intention of letting her daughter off the hook that easily. Her own boiling waters had produced more than enough steam to continue her lecture. "I know you're angry with me about a lot of things, but you have no right to snoop around behind my back like this. The things I keep from you I do for good reasons."

"You don't think I'm old enough to handle the truth, mama? Will I *ever* be old enough?" Juniper found her hands drawing themselves up tightly into fists at her sides as her temper flared. "Do you think I have no right to the truth? No *right* to know and meet my own father?" Juniper raised her voice louder still and surprised even herself with its volume. "It's my *life* we're talking about here. *My* father, *my* birth... it all leads back to that picture!"

Juniper's mother was silent for a moment and then finally she spoke. "So you assume that this man is your father?"

Juniper nodded.

"Jesus..." Penelope let her head rest temporarily in her hand before she raked her fingers through her hair. "I suppose since you already know the truth, there's no harm in admitting this much."

"What *harm* would it have done to tell me about him years ago? To at least show me his face?"

Penelope began to sob without warning as her anger turned quickly to fearful desperation. "I've done what I thought was best for you! For everyone concerned... you have to know that."

"I *thought* I knew that." Juniper's tone and volume had returned to its normal, unobtrusive level. "But everything is unraveling, mama. School, life, *us*... Every where I look to find answers I only find more questions and I've fought and wrestled with my own demons over these unanswered truths! And now, now that I'm onto something you're still putting up road blocks! I have a right to the truth, don't you think? After *all these years*, isn't it my right?"

"You're right, it is," her mother relented. "You do have a right to the truth, but in this situation, Junie, there are other factors to consider. Other *people* to consider."

"You mean dad?"

"I mean me! I mean everyone in this town!" Her mother had grown frustrated and she began to trip over her words in a frantic attempt to sooth her daughter's simmering anger. "If I tell you the truth... If it gets out-" She bit her lip and tossed over her words like a fish out of water. "Junie, I-"

"Forget it, mama. If you don't trust me, that's fine. I'll accept that." Juniper put up her hand then shrugged. "Besides, everything I've learned so far I've learned without your help. If this is the way you want it, then this is the way I'll continue to do things. Behind your back, without your assistance... and so help me, I **will** find out the truth you hide from me at every turn, I promise you that."

"Junie, I wish you'd give this up," Penelope pleaded. She was blotting at the corners of her eyes with a wrinkled, balled-up tissue she had pulled from the pocket of her jeans. She appeared smaller than Juniper had ever realized and she looked frail and slightly weak beneath the thin fabric of her cotton blouse.

"I can't give up, mama, I'm sorry." Juniper shook her head and when she continued, her tone had softened in consideration of her mother's apparent distress. "You don't understand, mama. You *know* who your parents were! *You* were never made fun of for being abandoned! You were never me and I'll **never** be you."

Juniper let her sharp words fall into her mother's lap where they waited for digestion. Juniper, however, did *not* wait, and instead she turned on her heel and stormed out of the kitchen. She hoped she might find solace in the comfort of her bedroom and knew that she needed some time alone to process all of the information that she had been given. Information that was more important than a photograph, more important even than the feelings of her own mother.

She locked the door at her back when she reached her room and then put a chair under the knob to further insure her seclusion. Satisfied that her barricade would be more than sufficient, she turned on the TV in hopes of blocking out any words her mother might force into the wood of her door.

To further insure herself against any attempts her mother might make to continue their unpleasant conversation, Juniper retrieved her Discman from the dresser and placed the headphones over her ears. She turned the volume up as loud as she could stand, and when she thought her eardrums might burst, she removed her finger from the volume wheel.

With her arms crossed over her chest and her back against the wall, she slowly slid to a sitting position to further consider the events that kept replaying themselves time and time again in her mind.

How could she possibly come to terms with the knowledge she had been handed? In all of her years, in all of the moments she'd considered the truth about her father, never once did she think that the reality would be almost more frightening than sitting in the darkness of ignorance. But it was; and not only was she frightened, Juniper found that she was also overwhelmed.

When nearly an hour had passed and her CD had expired, Juniper removed her headphones and slowly rose to her feet. She knew her mother would be asleep by that point, however restless that sleep might be. Her legs were weak when they carried her full weight and each step she took was more difficult than the one before it. She felt as though she were a hardened block of cement, awkward and uncertain in her footfalls. When finally she reached her desk, she turned on her computer and pulled out her chair without knowing exactly what it was she planned to do.

The operating system blinked on shortly after the monitor stirred and a moment later her desktop appeared. She double-clicked on the internet icon and a moment later the modem dialed out and a connection was made.

After several minutes and several searches, Juniper found what she was looking for and she clicked on the link. A black page loaded quickly, then white text appeared and slid gracefully to the bottom of the screen and out of sight.

Juniper leaned closer to the monitor and began to read. At first she read silently, but when the words became too large to contain, she found herself whispering them aloud.

"The origin of the Nephilim begins with the story of the

fallen angels. Originating in the Book of Enoch-" Juniper made a face and then scrolled further down the page until she saw a bold, red heading that stopped her. "The Book of Giants?" She read again out loud. "Another work concerned with the fallen Angels and Enoch... it was widely read in ancient Rome and Greece but only fragments of it, some still untranslated, exist today." Juniper sat back in her chair and allowed the information to soak in.

After several hours of exhausted and desperate reading, Juniper turned off the monitor when she realized that her confusion had crippled her. She didn't attempt to sleep that night, knowing that it wouldn't be possible to rest under the weight of the questions that filled her head. Still she found herself moving slowly towards her bed. Once there, she lowered herself to the soft and slightly creaking mattress. The ceiling above her spread out. The simplistic stucco swirl tapestry of beige soothed her enough to illicit a yawn, and before she even realized what was happening, she slipped into sleep.

When the sun came up the next morning, it fell across a quiet room. Juniper woke slowly and stretched into the new day. She didn't remember turning off the TV, but judging by its silent blackness she knew that at some point she must have. She was still fully dressed, right down to her socks, and when she threw back the blankets her eyes ran quickly to the alarm clock on her dresser.

The overly-bright red letters proclaimed it to be 9:43 a.m. Soon the realization that it was Wednesday rang heavily in Juniper's mind. She cursed under her breath and sat up slowly. It was nearly 3rd period already, and upon realizing that fact, Juniper relaxed slightly.

No point in rushing now, she thought, *I've already missed nearly half the day.*

She had a headache and she quickly relieved it. In all of

the years she'd rubbed her pain away, she'd never realized what it was she'd been doing. She dropped her hand to her side and sure enough, the dull ache at her temples had receded beneath her magical touch. Juniper licked her cracked lips and swallowed, and realized that her throat was raw from the yelling match with her mother the night before.

She rubbed her neck with one hand, and with the other she pushed her socks down over her heels until they dangled at the end of her toes. She stifled a yawn and looked absently around the room; in her inspection, she spotted a small, folded, yellow piece of paper beneath the chair she'd propped up beneath the door handle.

She already knew what it was, and generally what it said, but still Juniper crossed the room to retrieve the note. As she unfolded it, she blinked several times to encourage her eyes to prepare themselves for reading.

Junie,

I called you in sick to school this morning. Take today for yourself and relax. We'll discuss last night when I get home this evening. We have a lot to clear up. Anyway, it'll be another late night, so fix yourself something to eat for lunch and dinner. There's leftover meatloaf in the fridge.

Love, Mom

Juniper read the note again to fully process it and then she let the paper flutter from her fingertips to the floor. She moved the chair away from its post beneath the gold-plated knob, then cautiously unlocked the door of her bedroom and ventured into the hall. The house was quiet as she knew it would be and Juniper made her first act of the day a long, hot shower.

She lost herself in the rhythmic rain of the water from the shower head and found herself praying that it might absolve her. However, when the water ended she felt just as confused as ever, and she realized that she would have to settle for the fresh clean feeling the shower had left her. She stepped from the bath tub onto the soft green bath mat and grabbed a towel to quickly dry the water from her skin.

In the full-length mirror on the back of the bathroom door, Juniper caught a glimpse of herself. For a moment she was startled, due to the fact that her nerves were already on edge and frazzled from the unravel of her life. She laughed at herself when she realized that the intruder was merely her own reflection, however, upon viewing herself she almost wondered if the body she was looking at belonged to someone else.

She paused to examine her figure once her mind settled into the notion that the form moving before her was her own. Her 16th birthday was only days away and the graceful touch of womanhood had been busy to prepare her for the day. In ways she had missed, her body had curved and her breasts had grown; her hips had filled out and her stomach had expanded softly up from her waist to give way to a lean silhouette. Juniper looked away from her reflection with a growl in her stomach and heaved a t-shirt over her damp arms. She struggled to pull it into place and realized that in that struggle, there was a metaphor. Everything was changing, she realized, *everything* had become a struggle.

Her jeans slid easy up from the floor to find rest as her waist. She cinched them tight, zipped them into place, and shook out her legs until the cuffs fell at her ankles, unbundled.

With the entire day ahead of her, Juniper decided to relay the previous night's drama with her mother to Azerial. Before that, she grabbed a bagel from the fridge and toasted it. While she waited, she thumbed through the mail, threw the morning paper into the trash and tossed her weary feet into her newly-scuffed sneakers.

The bagel popped up from the toaster a short time later and Juniper scooped it up eagerly; she chewed on it slowly as she made the familiar walk across the meadow to the woods, and tried along the way to come up with a game plan for her second conversation with her father.

Over the years, she'd rehearsed what she'd say and do if ever given the chance at meeting him, but all of the questions she had prepared seemed trivial and silly in the harsh light of what was slowly becoming Juniper's long sought-after truth. Instead of normal average questions, strange and foreign ones had cropped up like weeds to choke her. To alleviate the heaviness of her thoughts, she stopped by the creek and admired the break of the bank as it careened through the thoughtless overgrowth of the wilderness. She found beauty in the idea that it found its way to the river blindly, and smiled at the comparison of herself to the creek.

Slowly she wandered on, and her eyes were constantly drawn to the surrounding trees of varying kind. She drank them into her - the sights and sounds of the natural din that she had never fully appreciated. She realized too, that she was connected to the forest much in the same way as Azerial, she'd just never known it until then. She'd perhaps felt it in some small way, yes, but *known* it? Not until that moment in her new state of awareness.

For once in her life, she felt as though she was on the right path and she intended fully to walk it lightly and with grace. The storm with her mother would pass, she finally knew her father and soon school would be over for the summer, an event that would provide her respite from the unrelenting and escalating torture of Ben and Jason.

As for what happened after that? Juniper realized that what life held for her behind the closed doors of the future, she didn't know, and couldn't know, but whatever it was, she would face it head on unburdened by the fear she'd so often felt the need to succumb to. After all, she felt it her duty. To make up for the Nephilim of the past who had gone bad, to prove that she could withstand the allure of darkness.

Her thoughts continued to carry her onward until the familiar part in the trees bowed a greeting upon her approach. That day, however, there was a difference in the house. A difference Juniper saw and heard clearly as her timid steps brought her nearer the porch and revealed a sight that instantly brought tears to her eyes.

It was a puppy, whimpering and writhing in pain, and as Juniper's feet hit the first step she saw why. He was injured to such a degree that Juniper had to look away or the bagel she'd just ingested would have surely returned to her mouth; already the flies had begun to buzz around the small animal; had paused to pick at the wound. A wound that was deep and wide and located on the right side of the animal. Muscle and guts were exposed, and the puppy's stomach shook as he suffered through the final agonizing moments before his death.

Juniper sobbed and moved closer to the dying animal. Something inside of her spurred her to do so, and she questioned it not. She realized that it would be her first chance at battling the fear she had vowed to conquer. As she kneeled on the splintering wood, the puppy looked at her with his sad brown eyes, whimpered once and even tried to muster a bark that came out sounding more like a helpless plea. Juniper shushed him as she moved closer, and with little trepidation, her hand found the top of his head. She smoothed his fur as she talked and she wondered if she was speaking to comfort herself or the puppy.

"It's going to be ok, little guy," Juniper said softly. Behind her eyes she felt tears began to struggle outwards. "Shh, it'll be over soon."

Her right hand found a spot above the dog's heart and

she pressed her fingertips into his blood soaked fur. Uncertain exactly of what it was she planned to do, she closed her eyes and found focus. She directed her energy and thoughts to the subject of the dying, wriggling dog and in a matter of moments, Juniper felt a tingle move slowly from her chest to her arms. From there, the energy shot quickly to her hands and a warm light began to radiate from her fingertips. Juniper opened her eyes to not only witness the sight, but to guide her fingers expertly over the length of the small animal's wounds.

Bright, white light encased her fingertips and slowly crept up to her knuckles and past them to her wrists. Juniper's hand moved down the length of the puppy's still body and covered every inch of him in warmth and light.

A moment later, the warming ended and the light faded until there was no proof it had ever existed. Juniper looked at her hands in amazement, then brought them to rest over her heart. The beating slowed to a normal rate and her breathing regulated. Her eyes were taken to the animal, most specifically to its horrible wound.

There was blood woven into the fur of the animal, but the wound itself was no more. To her shock, the gaping, bleeding gash was completely gone. Moreover, the dog was coherent. Judging by the look on its face, the shock of the injuries had faded only to be replaced by confusion. His head soon left the porch and was followed slowly by his body. He stood on all fours and then dropped to a sitting position. He looked at Juniper quizzically, and tilted his head to the left to survey her. A moment later he barked, wagged his tail and pushed his head into Juniper's knee as if he had come to terms with what had happened and was offering his thanks.

With a shaking hand and slight hesitation, Juniper stroked the dog. He sniffed her shoe and barked, and Juniper smiled, rubbing the dog behind his ears as she did so.

"It looks like I've made a new friend," she said, to which

the puppy seemed almost to nod before he barked again, that time in obvious agreement with Juniper's comment.

She suddenly realized where she was and her previous thoughts returned to her. She looked over her shoulder towards the front door of the farm house, and for a second she hesitated before she stood. Finally, she mustered up the courage to enter the house, and the puppy followed her closely.

"Azerial?" Juniper called out for her father at the base of the oak tree. Her voice echoed upwards and rattled the leaves on the branches as it went. "I need to speak with you."

The silent din of the overhead darkness broke like waves over the shore and a rush of activity replaced it. An opening door, a few heavy footsteps and then a moment later, Azerial appeared from the second floor. He took each of the remaining stairs of the rickety wooden staircase with great care until he was finally before her.

"What? No grand entrance?" she asked him. She found herself slightly disappointed that she hadn't been afforded the opportunity to witness his spectacular entrance again, that time with unfettered vision.

Azerial smiled when he saw her and shook his head. "It's really only impressive the first time, after that it's like I'm showing off." He winked at her to accentuate his joviality and his lips rose even more at the corners. "So what, pray tell, brings you here this beautiful morning?"

"More questions and more questions." Before Azerial had the chance to respond, Juniper continued and pointed at the puppy as she spoke. "Do you happen to know what *that* is?"

The dog had found his way to the base of the tree and was sniffing wildly at everything he could find to sniff.

"Well, let me see here," Azerial said as he scratched his chin thoughtfully. "Unless this is a trick question of some sort, I would say that's a dog. Or, a puppy, more specifically."

"It's no trick question, and you're right. He's a puppy,

but, he's not just your average, ordinary run of the mill puppy. Oh no! *This* puppy is a very, extraordinarily lucky pooch."

Azerial nodded and pulled her unspoken thoughts from her mind. "I have to assume that he's the first thing you've ever healed aside from yourself, yes?"

Juniper nodded and moved her attention from the exploring puppy to Azerial. "How did I know what to do? I just- I felt a heaviness in my chest and without considering what I was doing, I- There was this *light* and *warmth* and when it was over he was ok. Completely healed."

"I told you yesterday that you possessed this power," Azerial said flatly, not quite understanding her shock. "Why are you confused by what's happened?"

"I'm not confused, I'm just-" Juniper shook her head to clear the clutter of thoughts. "I guess I just wasn't expecting it to be like that, that's all."

"Like what?" Azerial asked.

"So..." She extended her hands in front of her and turned them over so that her palms were facing the ceiling. "*Powerful.*"

"Well, Juniper, your ability *is* a powerful one. Now that you've taken care of this little guy, you understand that. Of course it's hard to come to terms with. The realization that you can fix what goes wrong, that you can almost reverse time, revert life to a former state... Well, that's quite a thing to adjust oneself to."

"Why haven't I felt this before?" she asked softly, her words finding it difficult to impress themselves upon him with any real firmness.

"I assume that you have, at some point. But without the knowledge of *why* you were feeling it, you ignored it. You let your fear hold you back."

"Does mama know that I have-?"

"I cannot say for sure what it is your mother does or

doesn't know." Azerial brushed several specks of dust from the sleeve of his cloak and continued at a casual pace. "We had many conversations while she was pregnant with you. Conversations about who and what you would be, what your place was in the world. I told her many things, expressed to her many ideas and thoughts as to what you would become-"

"Do *you* know my fate?" Juniper asked quickly. "What am I supposed to do with this gift?"

Azerial kneeled next to the puppy and ran his fingers through the scruff on the back of his brown and white neck. "I'm afraid I don't know." Azerial looked up at Juniper, a subject change on his lips. "He needs a bath, and a name, you know. But other than that, he's a perfectly healthy little guy. Thanks to you, of course."

Juniper rolled her attention back to the puppy and allowed Azerial his distraction. "I really doubt mama will let me keep him. I've been asking for a pet for years."

"Well, if she doesn't, I'll keep him here with me. I could use a good companion."

Juniper cocked her head to the side and watched as her father played with the puppy; Azerial had even gone so far as to head butt the dog, and a second later he rolled him onto his back and vigorously rubbed his belly. Juniper opened her mouth to speak, but Azerial interjected his own thoughts in place of hers.

"Yes," he said softly. "This is the only special power you have."

"Are you *sure?* Because if there's even a *chance* that there's something else, I have to know."

He looked up at her, his eyes wide and truthful. "This is it. I'm sure." He gave the dog one last pat on the head before he pulled back his hands and rested them atop each other on his knee.

Juniper sighed. "I suppose this is enough."

"You will find, my girl, that it will be *more* than enough." Azerial stood and dusted the dirt from the hem of his tattered cloak. "Healers have a heavy burden to bear, Juniper. This is why most of them choose to keep their gift a secret. It's the same with mediums, seers... Those who are *truly* blessed choose not to exploit their talent, but instead they use it wisely, discreetly, and only in times of dire need."

"But some choose to share it, right?"

He nodded. "Yes. Some do."

Juniper could sense that there was more to the story, and she was quick to question him about it. "What happens to *them?*"

Azerial sighed and turned his face away from Juniper's. He chose instead to cast his eyes towards the tree where they proceeded to roam the bark for several moments before he spoke. "There are a lot of needy people in the world, Juniper. A lot of people who are terminally ill, a lot of people who can't walk, see, hear... People become desperate in the face of disease and they will go to nearly any lengths to achieve good health. If a healer is known, *proven*, he or she will find themselves being overwhelmed with requests. Heartbreaking pleas, letters... Most of the healers are kind folks. They give of themselves as much as they can, to make a difference in the world-"

"But?" she asked.

"But," he continued, "it all becomes too much. I've seen healers die in the middle of a healing, simply because they were too exhausted to continue. As I said yesterday, any overuse will be detrimental to the user. That applies to you as well." Azerial took a timely pause and pulled a finger across his brow to smooth it. "But still, there are others. I've seen people go insane from the pressure, self-imposed and otherwise, to cure all the afflicted people they can reach."

"Insane?" Juniper's heart skipped a beat at the mention of the word, and more so at the thought of the images it conjured.

He nodded.   "Normally, they end up committing suicide."

Juniper gulped, but found that the knot in her throat wouldn't dissipate. She coughed, hoping to dislodge it, but it remained, thick and hot and growing in size by the second. Her words came from around the knot, splintered and hoarse, and met back on the other side. "And those who keep their gift a secret?" she asked.

"Well... it isn't out of the ordinary for them to feel extreme guilt. Guilt over the fact that they've been given a gift they can't, or won't, share."

"What am I to do then?" Juniper asked softly. Her words were timid and wanted nothing more than to hide behind her jumble of impressive and overbearing thoughts. She felt a headache coming on and she pressed her fingers to her left temple. Immediately, the throbbing subsided.

Azerial finally looked at her again, and she was surprised to see that he was smiling. "Do you remember what I said last night? That everyone has a decision to make? Well, that applies here. To you."

"You can't tell me what you *think* I should do?" Her voice was tiny and weak.

"How would that be your decision?" he asked her. The puppy weaved himself around and through Azerial's legs and looked up at him with an obvious awe. He growled, however, as he sniffed at Azerial's wings, wings which were only slightly visible past the bottom hem of his thick, black cloak.

Juniper nodded and realized the truth in his question. Instead of pressing the issue, she chose instead to move on. "So anything living, I can heal?"

"Yes," he said simply. "People, animals, plants-"

"Plants?" Juniper asked in amazement. "You mean if I forget to water mama's plants I can just-"

"Zap," Azerial said. He extended one hand with fingers wide in illustration. "Although I don't suggest you go about using this power for trivial things. As I said, use it only when all other avenues have been exhausted. The power is too great to be used liberally and reserving your strength is always in your best interest."

"I'll remember that." Juniper looked down at the puppy again. He had taken a seated position between them and was still watching Azerial curiously. "Do I have to touch someone... to heal them, I mean?"

"It certainly helps, yes, but that wasn't your question was it?" Azerial rubbed his chin with his fingertips. "Well, the short answer is no."

"And the long answer?" Juniper asked.

He laughed and his chest shook from the intensity. "Is long. Long and confusing and probably best saved for another time-"

"No, *now*," Juniper insisted. "I want to know everything *now*."

"When you need to know, you'll know," said Azerial.

Juniper made a face at his cryptic response and placed her hands on her hips. "Do you remember what I said last night? You know, the bit about how I'm tired of people hiding things from me under the guise of protecting me?"

Azerial sighed and he nodded, as he realized that she'd found her loophole. "Fine, but sit down. You'll *want* to sit, trust me."

Juniper didn't know what to say, so she said nothing and dropped to a cross-legged, seated position on the floor. The puppy was still circling Azerial, obviously unhappy about something. She drummed her fingers on the wooden floor to coax the puppy's attention away from him and onto her. It worked, and the puppy looked over, distracted from his inspection of Azerial's wings. Finally, he left his side completely in favor of Juniper's outstretched hand and wiggling fingers.

Azerial thanked her with a nod and pulled his cloak tighter around him. He adjusted it slightly so that it fell closer to the ground and concealed his wings completely. He looked to the window and the light that came through the cracks in the nailed-up boards illuminated his face. Juniper smiled, and suddenly she was given a glimpse of what her mother must have seen all those years ago.

A strong chiseled face that gave an impressive profile; deep-set eyes that shimmered and burned like hot coals under the flashlight beam of the sun; cheekbones that were well-defined and high gave his face a regal look.

He sighed a moment later and then joined her on the floor. When he'd managed to pull his oversized legs into a comfortable position, he spoke. "The universe and all things in her are much bigger than you can ever imagine. Now, sometimes, I even find it hard to believe... Still, here I am, here *we* are, and your question should be answered, you're right about that much. You're certainly level-headed and intelligent enough to understand, so I will honor your request and comply with you completely."

"Thank you," Juniper said quickly. "I want you to know that I really appreciate this, and I do realize it's gotta be difficult for you too."

Azerial smiled softly. "See what I mean about that intelligence? That aside, I will gladly accept your thanks and offer you some of my own. Thank *you*, Juniper. For finding me here, for providing me with the opportunity to get to know someone I've so desperately wanted to know."

Juniper returned his smile with one of her own. She couldn't begin to express how wonderful it felt to finally have someone on her side, and she realized that with Azerial's mind-reading ability, the need to say such things out loud was almost definitely unnecessary.

"Anyway," Azerial said, breaking the heartfelt moment. "I've gotten off track, as I have a habit of doing." He cleared his throat and met her eyes with his own. "What you asked was if you could heal someone without touching them." He nodded. "Well, yes, you can, but not currently. You lack the proper... *tools* to do so, but when the time is right, you'll have what you need to do the job you're destined to do."

"Job? *Tools?*" Juniper asked. She skewed her face into a look of confusion. "What do you mean? You said you didn't know my destiny!"

Azerial leaned forward, holding her gaze. "I don't know your *ultimate* destiny, only a small fragment of the path you must follow to achieve it. I know that there will come a time when you put your gift to work. I don't know when, I just know that it *will* happen." He glanced at the tree over his right shoulder and sighed. "There are things you don't know about your birth, about what that birth brought about. The tree is only part of the story, the rest is... I hesitate at delving into the depths of this, as I don't think you're quite ready to accept or understand exactly how much of an impact your birth had upon this world."

"You said you'd be honest with me," Juniper said. "You told me that-"

"I know what I said, but you have to trust me when I say now that some things are bigger than you can imagine," Azerial explained. He reached out and placed his hand on her knee. "I cannot say anything, Juniper. Not a thing that might inhibit your free will. I don't want to take from you the choices that are yours to make."

"Then just tell me why I feel as though I was drawn here! Tell me why I left my bed in the middle of the night to dig beneath this tree for an old metal box! Tell me what it all means, what *I* mean."

Azerial sighed and pat her knee with his oversized hand. "You weren't brought to the tree to retrieve the box. The box is only the object that got in your way. What you were *really* drawn to is something *else* that lies beneath the tree, something far more important than an old photograph and a leather-wrapped book."

"What? What drew me here?" Juniper asked. "And what does it have to do with my destiny?"

Azerial closed his eyes and drew his hand back to meet the other in his lap. "I believe that I mentioned to you that what I allowed to happen was a sin. I passed along a divine trait to a human child, which caused an imbalance between the good and evil forces of the world. To compensate for that, evil was also allowed a birth."

"What?" Juniper asked. "I don't get what you're saying."

"As I stated, it's not something easily understood, or explained."

"Is the tree evil?" Juniper asked. She almost laughed at the notion, but judging by the look on Azerial's face she held back the sentiment.

"The tree keeps evil from sprouting," Azerial said simply. "It acts like a stopper, plugging the rift that developed at the time of your birth. A rift that is a direct portal to the shadow realm."

"S-Shadow realm?" Juniper furrowed her brow. "What's that?"

"It's the dimension from where the Shadows come," Azerial said softly. "It's separated from our own by a thin veil that sometimes sees tears, *rips*. These rips allow the Shadows to enter our world. Demons can also use them from time to time, to travel from one realm to the next."

"These Shadows... What do they do?"

"They have several jobs, but their main purpose is to take the souls of the damned to hell," Azerial explained. "In other instances, however, they seek to find a human host.

Someone they can latch onto that might give them a corporeal form."

"So they're demons?" Juniper asked.

"They're dark energy. Evil, yes... but demons? They aren't exactly that, no."

Juniper sighed. "I'm sorry, but I just don't understand what these Shadows have to do with *me*."

Azerial reached up to rub his left temple and Juniper wondered if he was alleviating the same headache that kept threatening her. "The reason you were drawn to the tree has to do with the fact that beneath is lies a Nexxus."

"A Nexxus? What on earth is *that?*" Juniper asked.

"That is what this doorway between worlds is called," Azerial said. "And beneath this tree, lies a conception Nexxus. A rift that was created to bring balance into the world."

"And that's why I was brought here?"

"That's what I suspect, yes."

"Can you tell me why that is?" Juniper scooted closer to Azerial and widened her eyes. "How does my destiny involve the Nexxus?"

Azerial wet his lips and leaned in. "You, my dear, are the only one who can close it," he said softly. "That's why you were brought here and that's why I'm telling you this now.... the fact that you were drawn to it so strongly must mean that the time is drawing near. The time when you'll be asked to fulfill part of your destiny. To set right what was put wrong."

"But I can't do it right now, can I?"

Azerial shook his head. "No."

"Because I don't have the right tools," Juniper said softly. She met Azerial's gaze. "What are the tools? I'm assuming the answer isn't hammer or screwdriver."

Azerial cleared his throat and pushed himself up from the floor to a standing position. "When the time comes, I will arm you with what you need." He rested his palm on the tree and glanced to the spot where the puppy had curled up for a nap in the shadows just off to their side.

Juniper studied him closely and in the silence she found her truth. "But I can close the Nexxus, can't I? That's what I have to do to fulfill part of my destiny?"

Azerial seemed impressed at her statement and displayed a smile. "You don't even need me here, do you?"

Juniper blushed. "You have *no* idea how much I've needed you, and for how long."

Azerial fell silent, and nodded with a slightly pleased look on his face. A look that seemed to express that he too was happy for the reunion and the time they were currently spending together.

"The time draws near, but is not upon us yet," Azerial said. Juniper wondered if he was addressing the tree or her.

The look on Azerial's face halted her from continuing with her questioning. He seemed to be deep in thought, as though contemplating something he could not express with words. When his look finally unfroze and began to twitch with activity, the subject changed and with it, the mood of the room also seemed to pick itself up and shake off the dust.

Birds could be heard outside again, as though they finally found it safe to continue their serenade.

Azerial turned to face the nearby kitchen window. "Shouldn't you be at school this morning?" he asked suddenly. He turned abruptly from the light and found her eyes once again.

Juniper stood and held fast to the spot where she had, until recently, been glued. She lowered her head and focused her eyes on her hands. She'd knotted them at her stomach in a display of nervousness. "Don't you already know the answer to that?"

Azerial nodded, almost sheepish in his admittance. "You had a fight with your mother last night."

Juniper shifted and shuffled her feet over the dusty floor. "It was a bad one... I don't think I've *ever* yelled at her like that before."

"But you kept me a secret." His voice was low. "I thank you for respecting my wishes."

"It wasn't easy, you know." Juniper bit her lip. "In fact, telling her about you was the *only* thing I wanted to do. But my mouth, it just couldn't form the words."

"I really do think this is for the best. At least for now. I just need time to think about everything." He nodded absently and Juniper wondered if he even realized he was doing it. A moment later he added to his nervous display when he began to pace the length of the living room in silence.

Juniper allowed him time and she stood silently by. She tried her hardest to keep her mind a blank slate.

He stopped finally, but didn't look at her as he spoke. "May I ask you something... about your mother?"

"Of course you can."

Azerial was slow to continue. "Well I- I find myself wondering if she's happy. Is she, Juniper? Is your mother happy?"

"I don't really know," she admitted. She shifted her weight uneasily from her left foot to her right. "I like to think so, but..." Juniper moved her head from side to side to display her ambivalence over the question. "She's lonely, I think, and she won't admit it, but- I think maybe part of it is because she misses *you*."

Azerial raised his head slowly, and only stopped when his eyes were focused firmly upon Juniper's. "I want to see her, Juniper. I want to see her face one more time. Will you take me to her?"

Chapter Seven
Second Chances

Azerial explained his request in more detail. While Juniper listened, her joy over an impending reunion faded with each word he spoke.

"I want to see her," he said quietly, as though the decision had been one he was slow and somewhat uncertain to come to. "But not in the way you're thinking," he added quickly.

"I don't understand," Juniper admitted. "What are you asking me to do?"

Azerial smiled softly. "I haven't seen her face in sixteen years, Juniper. If for one second I could see her, I think I might be able to live another sixteen years on her memory alone."

"So you want me to bring you a photo? What? Her driver's license? Something from a scrap book?"

He shook his head. "No, not exactly." He paused to clear his throat of the awkward nerves that had invaded him. "I want to see her, in person, but without her seeing *me*."

Juniper thought for a second and almost immediately her mind began working frantically to devise a plan that would make his request possible. Finally, it came to her.

"The kitchen window! Come to the kitchen window, you should be able to see in. You're *more* than tall enough." She surveyed his stature closely and then nodded at his height. "Tonight... she'll be home around 8. I'll keep her in the kitchen, away from the window, but you'll be able to see her."

Azerial nodded and pulled at his chin with his fingertips. "That might work," he said quietly. "It just might work."

Juniper bit her lip, hesitant to ask the question that was sitting squarely on the end of her tongue. "But why don't you just come in? Wouldn't you like to talk to her-?"

"Of course I would," he said quickly. "You shouldn't even have to ask me that."

"Then why *don't* you?" Juniper countered. "What would it hurt?"

Azerial sighed and his head lowered as if cued by an unseen force. "Because I *can't*. Because it isn't right to disrupt-"

"It isn't *right* for you to hide yourself from her!" Juniper was tired of arguing and as much as she wished to avoid upsetting yet another of her parents, she found that she just couldn't help herself. "You know something? I asked mama just the other day if she still loved you."

Azerial looked up suddenly, but remained silent in anticipation of her continuance.

"She wouldn't answer me. She told me that it would be foolish to still love you after all this time-"

"*See?*" Azerial erupted. "You would have me walk into a place where I'm not welcome?"

Juniper narrowed her eyes. "But don't you see? Her answer wasn't an answer at all! It was just something she said to get me to shut up! You don't know her like I do. I saw the look in her eyes, and I know she still loves you. She *has* to! And if you'd just spend five minutes with her, you'd see it."

Azerial shook his head firmly, as though he'd never been so opposed to any other idea in all of his existence. "It's too dangerous and already I'm risking a lot just by asking to see her."

"But if you're going to take a risk, shouldn't it be *really* worth it?"

He fell silent, as if he were pondering her words. He was torn, but in the end he stood firm. "You have to trust me, Juniper. It wouldn't be right."

Her shoulders slumped forward in an awkward defeat. "Fine... but if you change your mind-"

"I won't," he said softly. "I've given this much thought over the years. What I might do if the chance arose to speak with her again... I decided long ago that it be wrong of me to bring all of this back to her."

Juniper continued as though she hadn't heard him at all. "If you change your mind, she'll be there."

"Thank you," he said. "For everything you've done and are trying to do. I don't want you to think I don't appreciate it, because I do."

She shrugged. "I'm not just doing it for you, you know."

"I know," he said softly, and a brief smile rose to his lips. "There's nothing wrong with being selfish about this. After all, it's something you've wanted for a very long time."

Juniper felt tears well in her eyes, and she nodded. "Yeah. It is."

"I'm sorry I can't give it to you. But," Azerial said, walking towards her, "all is not lost. We have each other, and you have answers to your questions. Progress has been made, yes?"

Again, she nodded.

"Hey, kiddo..." Azerial reached out and took her chin in his hand. He forced her eyes to meet his and when he held her gaze, he smiled almost sympathetically. "Promise me you won't be sad, ok?"

Juniper wanted to hug him, wanted to feel his arms around her, but she resisted.

Azerial sensed her hesitation and smiled, taking it upon himself to extend his arms in her direction. Juniper smelled it again, the subtle vanilla that seemed to radiate from Azerial's very skin. She was calmed by it, and fell without pause into her father's waiting arms.

"I've waited a long time for this," Azerial said, his words parting Juniper's hair and washing over her. She relaxed, pulled back and with a smile at her lips she addressed him finally.

"You aren't the only one... *dad*." Juniper froze at the sound of the word that was nothing but foreign to her tongue. "I'm s-sorry. I didn't mean to- I mean, I know that we hardly know each other, but is it ok if I call you that? If it isn't, I-"

Azerial held her tighter and choked off her words. He pulled her so close that Juniper thought for a second that she might shatter into a thousand pieces.

"It's more than ok..." he whispered into her hair. "More than ok."

When Juniper finally made her way home that afternoon, she left Azerial deep in his thoughts. The as-of-yet nameless puppy fell into step beside her during the walk, his tongue and tail both wagging happily.

Upon arrival at her house, Juniper unlocked the door and carefully opened it. She pushed open the storm door and without a word or a spark of an invitation, the puppy scampered into the kitchen.

His nails clicked against the linoleum floor as he walked the perimeter of the room, sniffing under chairs and in corners as he went.

"What am I going to do with you?" she asked the puppy. He turned and looked at her with wide sad eyes and gave her a muffled bark.

She smiled. "Well, thanks for your help... and believe me, you've been a huge one." She sighed and her hands placed themselves on her hips in a pose she attributed mostly with her mother. "Are you hungry? I imagine a near-death experience takes a lot out of you."

The puppy continued to ignore her, favoring instead the idea of crawling under the table in pursuit of a wisp of dust.

Juniper turned to the fridge and rummaged through the contents, she looked down a moment later to find the puppy sitting between her feet gazing up at her. "See anything good?" she asked him.

"Bark!"

"Yeah, my thoughts exactly." Juniper closed the refrigerator door. "I'll tell ya what, I'll get you some water, give you a bath and when mama gets home we'll decide what to do with you."

"Bark!"

"Good." Juniper rubbed the top of the dog's head, "I'm glad you're ok with this."

She pulled a bowl down from the cabinet and held it under the faucet until it was filled to the brim with cool water. She sat it carefully on the floor next to the stove and kneeled down next to it. "Come on, it's just water, boy."

The dog approached cautiously. At first he sniffed, then he snarled at the bowl.

"I didn't like the pattern either, don't look at me."

Finally, the dog relaxed and began to lap up the water. Juniper sat back and watched, cross-legged on the kitchen floor.

"Do you understand what happened to you, puppy?" asked Juniper.

The dog continued drinking and paid her no attention.

She sighed and rested her chin in her hand. "I'm not sure exactly how I did it, little guy, but I saved your life today." She laughed at the sound of the words as they passed her lips and became real. "The kids at school thought I was a freak *before*! Imagine what they would say about me if they knew I could heal the sick and injured." She shook her head and freed herself of her faint smile. "They'd probably burn me at the stake as a witch."

The dog looked up at her quizzically and then turned his attention back to the water.

"You sure are thirsty! Again, I apologize for the lack of food... I really wasn't expecting company, you know. At least not four-legged company... or well, *any* company, really." She chewed a piece of dead skin free from her lip. "Come on, guy, let's get you cleaned up. There's no *way* mama will let me keep you if you're covered in dried blood."

By the time her mother arrived home that night, Juniper had managed to bathe the still-nameless puppy and she'd fashioned him a makeshift bed out of old bed linens and a cardboard box she'd dug out of the garage. Currently, the dog was asleep in the living room, curled up on a blue cotton blanket Juniper used to carry with her as a child. Her mother had called it her security blanket, however Juniper preferred to think of it as her cape, as it was that blanket she'd been wearing around her neck when she'd decided to jump over the railing of the stairs in a failed attempt at flight. Lucky for Juniper, an end table broke her fall and not her bones. She had been six at the time, a difficult year for Juniper *and* her mother, as she remembered. Her mother had lost her job in the spring and money had been tight for many of the following months. Juniper remembered that on several different occasions that year, she'd walked in on her mother only to find her in tears. It had upset her then, and still, seeing her mother cry evoked much the same emotion.

It was partially because of that, that Juniper felt so horrible about the fight with her mother. She missed the days when she'd told her everything, when she'd shared every detail of her life with her. Juniper knew that it hadn't been so long ago that they'd been each other's sole confidants, but to her it felt like years.

Juniper's thoughts were suddenly fractured by the sound of her mother's keys as they jingled just outside the kitchen door. When Juniper heard the key in the lock a moment later, she jumped to her feet, ready to head her off at the pass in an attempt to soften the blow about their unexpected house guest.

Juniper reached the kitchen just as Penelope closed the door at her back and tossed her keys on the counter.

"Hey... mama. Hi."

Penelope jumped. "Goodness, you scared me!" She sat her purse on the counter with her left hand, her right still clutched her chest.

"Sorry," Juniper apologized. "I'm just happy to see you."

Penelope kicked off her heels and reached down to straighten the seam at the toe of her pantyhose. "You're feeling better then?"

"I don't know if better is the word for it," she said. "I'd say *different* fits the bill more accurately."

"Well, so long as you've managed to calm down a bit after last night I don't see why we can't talk about this now, in a civilized manner." Penelope ran her hands through her hair and her thoughts drifted as she did so. "You wouldn't believe the day I've had, Junie. Just when I thought things were slowing down, we'd get hit with another rush of calls or drop-ins... people just expect to get in to see the doctor without an appointment and are pissed when I tell them it isn't possible." She stopped talking, and her finger extended to point at the bowl on the floor. "Why is that there?"

"That's actually what I was going to talk to you about, mama."

"Junie..." Her mother put one hand on her hip and tilted her head to the side. "What have you done?"

"He followed me home, mama, I swear. He's a charming little guy and I just *know* that if you give him half a chance you'll grow to love him!"

"Right, right, and in time, I'll wonder what we ever did without him." Penelope rolled her eyes and unbuttoned her blazer. "We are talking about a dog, right? I'm not going to walk into the living room to find a horse or a pig or anything am

I?"

"He's a dog. A *small* dog," Juniper added.

"You know, I must have asked papa for a pet a million times, but every animal I brought through the door left through the door. The only dogs we ever had were his coon-huntin' hounds. Dreadful things, no fun at all to play with."

Juniper saw her approach and took it. "So then how can you deny me the very same thing that you were denied?"

Penelope bit her lip. "Where did you say you found him?"

"That's not important, mama, I'm just asking you to let me keep him. Please? As a favor to me, to *him*." Juniper shook her head and sighed. "I just don't know where else he'll go if he can't stay here."

"How about you take him back to the place where you found him? How do you know he doesn't already have a family?" Penelope scratched her chin absently. "If he has a family, we should take him to the pound. People always check the pounds when a pet goes missing."

"Mama! They'll gas him there and you know it!" Juniper tugged at her mother's sleeve, a pout rising to her lips. "Just come see him, won't you? Humor me, alright?"

She sighed, pulled off her jacket, and tossed it over the back of the chair. "Fine, I'll look, but I'm promising nothing."

Juniper spun on her heel and headed towards the living room. Her excited chatter sailed back over her shoulder as she walked. "You're just going to love him, I know it. He's smart and clean- I already bathed him and checked him for fleas and ticks. He's in great health. I'd even venture to say he's in *perfect* health."

"What about food?" Penelope asked. "Has he eaten?"

"I gave him water and a piece of lunch meat. I was hoping maybe you'd take me to the store. You know, for food, maybe a toy or a bone or something-"

"Oh Junie! I don't know about this!" Penelope shook her head. "Is this your way of softening me about last night? I wasn't mad at you then and I'm not mad at you now."

"This isn't about last night," Juniper protested.

"Then why the sudden need for a pet?" asked Penelope curiously.

Juniper shrugged. "It's not like I went looking for him. It just *happened*. It's almost like he found *me*, mama. There's a reason he's here, I know it."

Penelope nodded as she carefully considered Juniper's words. "I see... and this *reason*,... It's nothing you could tell me about, is it?"

Juniper bit her lip. "It's not that I don't *want* to tell you. I just have to come up with a way to say everything."

"If you need help, though, you'll ask me?" Her statement was hopeful.

Juniper nodded vigorously. "Of course I will, mama. You should know that! I love you, I trust you, and I'll always turn to you if I'm in trouble. But for right now, I'm ok. I have everything under control. There's just some stuff that I have to do on my own, discover on my own. In a way I'm glad you've kept me in the dark about so many things... had I been told the truth earlier, it would have been hard to handle. But now that I'm living it? Things are coming to me more naturally. It feels *right*." Juniper bent to pick up the puppy and she held him to her chest. "Look at him, would you! Just look at his cute little puppy face! How can you resist him?"

"Junie, I don't know." Penelope leaned towards the puppy and extended her hand. "A dog is a lot of work, Junie."

"I know, but I'll take good care of him. I promise."

Penelope sighed when she realized that she was helpless to resist the pleas of both Juniper and the whimpering puppy. "Oh, alright. Fine, fine... you can keep him, but if you can't handle the responsibility you'll have to find him a new home.

And I still think it would be wise to put an ad in the paper, just to make absolute certain he doesn't already have a family who misses him."

"And if no one responds?"

Penelope sighed again; her voice was filled with the sound of defeat. "If no one responds then you can keep him."

Juniper placed the puppy back into the blanket where he curled up and drifted back to sleep as if he had never been disturbed. "Oh! Thank you, mama, really! You don't know how much this means to me."

"This is on a trial basis, Junie," her mother warned. "If I think you can't handle it, or if I end up taking all the responsibility-"

Juniper threw her arms around her mother's neck to prematurely end her lecture. "I love you, mama. I promise I won't let you down!"

"Oh, Junie." Penelope stroked her daughter's hair and then buried her face within the curls. "You know I love you too. No matter what."

Juniper pulled away as her thoughts of the puppy situation broke through the rotted wood ceiling of her mind. "Hey mama? I've always been a healthy person, haven't I?"

Penelope skewed her face into a tight look of confusion. "What an *odd* question!" She paused to ponder her answer, before finally coughing it up. "Yeah, I suppose you *have* always been extraordinarily healthy. Any reason why you're asking?"

"Remember when I had the chicken pox?" Juniper continued.

"You had chicken pox?" Penelope searched her thoughts, then snapped her fingers. "Why, that's right, you *did*! For less than 24 hours, if I remember correctly."

Juniper reached for her mother's hand. "There's something I have to tell you and I think you should sit down to hear it. It's uh- it's heavy."

The look of confusion on Penelope's face was etched deeply into her features. *"Ooob-kay.* You're not pregnant, are you? Please tell me that's not it. I don't think I could take it."

"No! *God* no! I've never even really kissed a boy!"

Penelope's free hand fluttered up and covered her heart. "Oh, thank goodness for- wait, what do you mean? Never even really-?"

"Mama! Focus! This has nothing to do with boys or sex." Juniper squeezed her mother's fingers between her own and held her gaze. "It's nothing bad, I promise. Well, not *really*. Just let me get this out now before I lose my nerve, ok? This isn't easy for me to say."

"Ok, you're *really* frightening me here," Penelope said, still she allowed Juniper to lead her to the kitchen table.

Juniper released her mother's hand and pulled out a chair. She sat slowly, cleared her throat and tried desperately to gather her words before she continued. She cast a sideways glance at the clock and noted the time.

It was fifteen minutes until eight; fifteen minutes until Azerial arrived as planned to get a glimpse of Penelope. A look that was both well-earned and long overdue. Juniper realized that in that moment she was more nervous for him than for herself.

Penelope had seated herself across from Juniper and she held her hands on top of each other, clasped and white-knuckled. She was obviously anxious and Juniper knew she couldn't keep her waiting much longer, *or* back out of the corner she had painted herself into with her dramatics.

She licked her lips and prepared to launch her words. "Have you ever wondered *why* I'm so healthy?" she asked. "Have you ever given it much thought?"

"More of this?" Penelope sighed, yet appeared relieved. "You had me worried!"

"Mama, please, let me talk." Juniper pleaded with her

mother using first words, then her eyes. In light of her daughter's seriousness, Penelope quickly snapped her lips shut over her teeth.   She nodded and motioned for Juniper to continue. "I've never been sick for more than a few hours at a time, mama. I've never needed medication for anything, not even a headache... and you know, like you, I never really thought much about why that was. I guess I just assumed that I was lucky, you know? That I'd been blessed with a good immune system."

"But there's more to it than that," Juniper continued. "And until recently, I had no idea what that was or *why* I was so healthy." She used a pause to examine her mother's face; Penelope was stone silent.

"And now?" Penelope finally asked. "Now you think you know why that is?"

"Yeah, I do.   And I know this is going to sound weird..." Juniper took in a deep breath. "But is there anything *wrong* with you right now?"

"What? Wrong with *me*?" Penelope shook her head; her confusion was nearly tangible. "Well... no. I'm fine. I feel *fine*. And what do you mean exactly, wrong with me?"

Juniper made a dissatisfied face. "No headache?   Or maybe a toothache? An ingrown hair? *Anything* at all?"

Penelope shook her head slowly, then stopped suddenly and in mid-shake. "Well, I do have this." Penelope moved her left hand across the table and exposed it to Juniper's sight.

A thick blotch of a purple bruise sat presumptuously on the side of her mother's hand.

"It happened at work yesterday," she explained. "I was in a rush, I misjudged the distance between the door frame and my hand-" She reddened slightly. "What is this about?"

Juniper took her mother's hand in both of hers and pressed them together around it.   "I don't know how to say what it is that I have to say and that's why I'm just going to *show* you."

"Juniper? What's going on?" Penelope's eyes had widened and she tried to jerk her hand away from Juniper's grasp.

Juniper didn't release her and instead tightened her grip. "Trust me, mama. It's ok."

Penelope stopped her fingers from wiggling; her jaw went slack a moment later when the brief glimmer of healing light passed from Juniper's hands to her own.

"W-what just happened?" Penelope tried again to pull her hand away. That time Juniper obliged her and she unlocked her fingers to allow her mother's to wriggle away.

"Look at your hand." Juniper said quietly, so quietly that she felt it necessary to repeat herself. "Go on... Look at it."

Penelope moved her eyes slowly from Juniper's face, slower still from Juniper's chin to her own hand. She gasped at what she saw, or rather, at what she *didn't*. Shocked, her right hand jumped out to inspect the left. "What in the world-? How did you-?"

Their eyes met again. Juniper smiled; Penelope, however, was too speechless to respond in kind. Her shock was apparent and her face was long and blank like a wiped-clean slate.

"I can heal people, mama," Juniper whispered. "I can heal myself, I healed the puppy... and now I've healed you."

Penelope sat back in her chair. Her hands massaged each other absently for several drawn-out seconds before she finally realized her nervous action and allowed her arms to drop to her lap like two limp, rag dolls. "Juniper, I- I don't know what to say! I wasn't expecting this! This is- it's amazing."

"Just say that you don't think I'm a freak. Say that you love me no matter what I am." Juniper felt her lower lip begin to tremble. Her sudden onset of tears surprised her, but she didn't attempt to hold them back.

"Oh, baby!" Penelope's own lip began to tremble and she jumped quickly to her feet. She rounded the small dinner table and fell to her knees at Juniper's side.

Juniper turned and threw her arms around Penelope's neck. "I was so afraid to talk to you about this. I was afraid you wouldn't love me any more if you knew."

"Shhh, sweetheart! That's just silly! When have I ever given you the impression that I'd stop loving you for *any* reason?" Penelope held her tight and spoke into her hair. "I will *always* love you, Juniper. No matter what. You're my daughter, for goodness sake! This doesn't change anything." She pulled back and placed her hands on Juniper's shoulders. "You, young lady, are the best thing that ever happened to me. You've never been, nor will you *ever be* a freak. Not in my book."

Juniper pulled her hands across her eyes and then wiped her tears on her jeans. "This is why the puppy is so important. He was nearly dead when I found him and I healed him. I *healed* him, mama. That's why you just *have* to let me keep him. He's already part of the family as I see it."

Penelope stood, and kissed her daughter on the forehead as she did so. "I'm glad you've shared this with me. For so long I've feared that you'd eventually grow up and stop telling me things... for so long I've waited for the day. And I'll tell you, Junie, for the past few months, I've thought it was upon me. I thought I'd lost you or at least that I was going to."

"I'm sorry I've been distant, mama."

"Don't apologize. I understand, I do." She paused to wipe away a few of her own tears that had steadily accumulated at the corners of her eyes. "So tell me one thing... How did you figure out that you could do this? That you could heal?"

Juniper gulped. She wasn't sure how to explain it without mentioning her father's name. "I just... *put it together*," she whispered. "I just figured it out one day."

"Well I- I can see how you might figure out how to heal yourself, I mean- I don't know why *I* didn't see it... Maybe I didn't want to, or maybe I *do* work too much. So much that you've grown up right under my nose and I've had my eyes shut the whole damn time." Penelope rubbed her eyes with her fingers as she tried to come to terms with the truth Juniper had placed before her. "But what I don't understand is how you knew that you could heal others. How...? How does one come to that realization? Was the puppy the first thing you used this gift on, other than yourself of course? I hate to ask all of these questions, but you've given me quite a lot to swallow here... Although..." Penelope's voice dropped sharply into shadow and she shook her head to free the unspoken words from the tangle of her lips and tongue.

Juniper was about to speak, but much to her relief, she was cut off by a knock at the kitchen door. Juniper looked at the clock with a wrinkle at her brow. It was 7:50 and her heart was running laps around her lungs.

"Someone has lousy timing! Any idea who on earth it could be?" Penelope asked. She stood and cast her own glance at the clock. She wiped at her eyes again in preparation for company, then blotted at the corners with her fingertips. "Were *you* expecting someone?"

Juniper bit her lip and shook her head. She hated to taint their truthful exchange with a lie, but knew no other way. "N-No, not expecting anyone, but I'll, uh... I'll answer it. You sit down, relax for a minute. You've had a rough day." She shot past her mother, smiling falsely as she did so. She only hoped her smile didn't look as forced and frightened as it felt.

Dad? she asked herself as she crossed the tile floor in three steps to find the door knob at her palm. *Have you changed your mind about seeing mama in person?*

Her heart skipped a beat as her fingers parted the slats in the blinds to reveal the mystery guest. Her wonder subsided when she saw that it was only Mr. Halsey. His attention was directed away from the door and down the driveway to the street beyond and his lips were drawn together into what appeared to be a nervous whistle.

"Who is it?" Penelope asked. She came up behind Juniper with her hands once again clasped tightly in front of her.

"It's my history teacher, Mr. Halsey..." Juniper let her voice trail off as she twisted the doorknob. She pulled the door inward carefully and peered around the edge. "Mr. Halsey? Can I help you?"

Stirred from his patient wait, Mr. Halsey pulled open the screen door and smiled cheerfully at Juniper. "Miss Kelly," he said. "I hope I'm not disturbing you or your mother this evening."

"Oh, well, actually, we *are* in the middle of something," Juniper said. She stepped onto the doorstep and glanced towards the driveway; towards Mr. Halsey's beat-up red pickup that she recognized from the teacher's parking lot at school. "What can I do for you?"

Mr. Halsey straightened his blue and green striped tie and glanced past Juniper into the well-lit kitchen beyond. "Well, I was hoping I might have a word with you about today's assignment, but if you're busy-"

"Junie? Who is it?" Penelope asked. She put a hand on Juniper's shoulder and squinted into the darkness of the side porch. "Can I help you, sir?"

Mr. Halsey's expression changed quickly from one of seriousness to one of shy embarrassment. "Ms. Kelly, yes? I'm Juniper's history teacher, Mr. Halsey. I was just in the area and thought I'd stop by and make sure Juniper was going to be in class tomorrow."

"Oh, well how thoughtful of you!" Penelope exclaimed. She brushed Juniper's hair from her face and put an arm around her shoulders. "I think she'll be in there tomorrow. It was just a 24 hour bug and it seems to have passed."

"Good, good," Mr. Halsey said softly. "I'm glad to hear it."

"Was that it?" Juniper asked abruptly. "If so, thanks for stopping by. I appreciate your concern and I'll see you tomorrow in class-"

"Juniper Kelly!" Penelope exclaimed. "Don't you think you're being awfully rude? Mr. Halsey has gone out of his way to check in on you and here you are rushing him off."

Juniper felt her cheeks flare with color. "Sorry, mama... Mr. Halsey. I don't know *where* my manners have gotten to."

"Why don't you come in for a minute, Mr. Halsey," Penelope said. "You'll have to excuse Junie. Sometimes she forgets her manners."

Juniper pushed open the screen door further and motioned him inside. "I'm sorry, Mr. Halsey. Please, come in."

Mr. Halsey smiled at her warmly and lowered his head as he entered. Juniper noticed immediately the scent of his cologne; she also noticed the spit-shined shoes, dress slacks and button down shirt he wore somewhat awkwardly. Ordinarily, Juniper would consider Mr. Halsey dressed up if he bothered to comb his hair. His current appearance was most certainly a departure from the norm for him, and not only did he appear to be uncomfortable, but he also appeared to be out of place. It was almost as though in the middle of some random night, a pack of elves had invaded his closet and replaced everything he owned with the wardrobe of another man. A financier, a CPA; and now it was a cruel reality that Mr. Halsey was forced to live with.

He smiled at her again when he raised his head and a moment later he pulled out a tri-folded piece of paper from the breast pocket of his shirt and offered it to Juniper. "Here's today's homework assignment."

Penelope had stepped into place behind her daughter and had put one hand upon her shoulder. "Aren't you going to properly introduce me, Junie?"

"Oh, you two already know each other," Juniper said dismissively. She shoved the paper into the front pocket of her jeans and glanced once more to the clock. "Don't you remember, mama? You two went to high school together... I even mentioned him to you not long ago."

Mr. Halsey nodded towards Penelope. "I'm not surprised you don't remember me. I've never made much of a lasting impression, I'm afraid."

"Oh, I'm sure that isn't true!" Penelope said. She smiled warmly and studied Mr. Halsey's face for signs of recognition. "Halsey, right? You're Nick?"

He relaxed and an easy smile slid over his lips. "Yeah, that's right. We had Chemistry class together sophomore year and English our junior year, well uh, that is to say until you *left*."

Penelope nodded once, then, as if hit by a ton of bricks that stirred her memories, she clapped her hands together. "You saved me from blowing up the lab, didn't you?"

He smiled and blushed slightly as he did so. "Yes, ma'am, that was me."

Penelope waved her hand. "Ma'am? Oh please! For an old friend it's Penelope! And you'll be glad to know, I've never touched another Bunsen burner."

"The town thanks you," Mr. Halsey chuckled. "And since we're on a first name basis, I'll have to ask that you call me Nick. Mr. Halsey is my father."

Juniper interrupted, her eyes having once against noticed the time as it grew dangerously closer to eight. "So, uh, thank you for coming all the way over here to bring me this assignment. You really didn't have to."

Mr. Halsey begrudgingly tore his eyes from Penelope. "Oh, it was really no problem. I also wanted to let you know that we're having a quiz tomorrow on chapters seven and eight. With finals right around the corner, I didn't want my best student to fall behind."

"That was awfully kind of you, Nick." Penelope looked over her shoulder to the coffee maker. "Listen, I don't have any coffee brewed, but I can make a quick pot if you'd like to join me for a cup. Maybe we can catch up on these past sixteen years."

Juniper turned to face her mama. She was standing effectively in between her and Mr. Halsey. "Oh, mama, I'm sure he can't stay. He's a busy man and we're busy women. Remember, we still have to go to the store in a bit, and we haven't even had dinner."

"Juniper!" Penelope's voice was filled with a shocked surprise over her daughter's short behavior. "You're being rude again. I thought I told you about that."

"Am I really being rude?" She turned back to Mr. Halsey and offered a sheepish grin. "I'm sorry, I'm not trying to be."

"Oh, I understand, Juniper. You have things to do, and I certainly don't want to keep you from them."

Juniper sighed internally; externally she flashed a nervous smile. "Well, I guess I'll see you tomorrow then. *In class.*" Juniper took him carefully at the elbow as she tried unsuccessfully to steer him towards the door. She was, however, stopped cold in her tracks by her mother's firm voice.

"Juniper Marie Kelly! I want you to leave the poor guy alone! I offered him coffee and he accepted coffee."

Juniper sighed and released Mr. Halsey's arm. "Yes, ma'am," she grumbled.

"Why don't you order a pizza for dinner, sweetheart?" Penelope asked. She pointed towards the fridge with her thumb; her eyes were otherwise occupied with Mr. Halsey. "I think there's a $3.00 off coupon on the fridge for a large pizza from Tony's. If you call now we might actually get it tonight. Go ahead and order whatever you like... just make sure you hold the onions."

Juniper pouted and wanted to protest, but the look in her mother's eyes quickly changed her plans. "Yes, ma'am," she muttered.

Juniper drug her feet across the tile, and picked up the phone. She dialed the number of the town's only pizza joint by memory and while the phone rang she turned back to face the table. A look of disgust spread thinly across her lips at the sight she saw. Her mother and Mr. Halsey were settling down at the kitchen table across from each other, laughing like old friends over a joke Juniper had missed in her sullen mood.

"Tony's Pizza. How can I help you?"

Juniper frowned heavily into the mouthpiece of the phone. "I'll have one large supreme pizza, please. And can you make sure that has *extra* onions?"

When Juniper hung up the phone she slipped out the kitchen door completely unnoticed by her mama, and hopefully by Mr. Halsey. The screen door latched softly behind her and she winced slightly from the sound of the wooden shudder as the frame fell back into its rightful place. She crossed her fingers at her side and hoped she hadn't drawn any unwanted attention from the attentive adults hunched over the kitchen table; she made a face at the good times she'd left behind and made her way to the edge of the porch.

Her eyes adjusted slowly to the dark night around her and to balance herself against the darkness she reached out her hand and grabbed the railing of the porch. She squinted down at the yard in search of Azerial and suddenly wished she could call out to him. She knew, however, that it wouldn't be safe to do so as long as the bumbling history teacher was on the premises.

When finally her eyes made their peace with the inky black night, she was able to focus on the kitchen window, or more specifically, on the area just beneath it.

"Is that you?" she hissed. She crept slowly down the steps to the grass and paused at the base. "Dad? You there?"

The dark figure moved and pulled itself only slightly upright. "I'm here."

Juniper relaxed and walked over to her father's semi-crouched position. She smiled nervously when her eyes found his beneath the cover of his hood. "I didn't think you'd actually come, but I'm glad you did."

"Yes, well, I'm beginning to wish that I hadn't come," he admitted. There was a sadness in his voice that carried with it a trace of jealousy. "Who is that? With your mother?" He jerked his head towards the window.

Juniper rolled her eyes. "That's my history teacher. Mr. Halsey."

"Are they-?" Azerial sighed. "Are they dating? I know I've no right to be jealous or questioning of this, but I-"

"Oh *goodness*, no!" Juniper laughed softly. "They went to high school together, that's all."

"I see. So they're friends, then? *Just* friends?" Azerial turned his head from her and his features were lost beneath the cover of the cloak.. Even without seeing his face, Juniper knew that he was unconvinced by her words.

"I wouldn't even call them that, really. I mean, he has a bit of a crush on her, has since high school, but mama is so picky. This is actually the first time they've spoken in practically forever! Talk about lousy timing though, right? I mean tonight of all nights he had to stop by." Juniper tried to gauge her father's reaction to her rambling monologue, but couldn't get a fix on his emotions. "Really, dad. There's *nothing* romantic going on there. I promise."

Azerial nodded, but he remained silent for a long moment. He finally broke the awkwardness with a woeful resignation. "Well... I've seen what it was I came to see. I should be going now, before someone sees something they shouldn't."

"Wait!" Juniper exclaimed. "You can't go yet! You have to tell me how it feels to see her again."

"How do you *think* it feels?" he asked. He glanced back at the kitchen window; his eyes fixed upon her mother's face. "It's the most exquisite pain I've experienced, if we're being honest. To be so close to her, yet unable to reach out. Unable to hold her, to touch her, to talk to her for even a *second*... Oh, that face, that *smile*! I've dreamed of her so many times since the morning she left that I could fill a dozen lifetimes." He shook his head and broke free of the melancholic ties that held him. He laughed softly as he turned from the light and faced Juniper again. "I wouldn't have thought it possible, but she's even more beautiful than I remembered."

"I'm sorry that-" Juniper started, but she was quickly cut off.

"No reason to be." Azerial's voice was firm and sounded slightly worn. "Well... off I go. I hope that I see you soon, Juniper. As I said, I have to get back now. It isn't safe for me *out here*."

Juniper nodded, albeit reluctantly. "Yeah, sure... I understand and I'll come see you as soon as I can. Finals are next week, so I have a lot of studying to do, but I'll visit as often as I can."

"Good. I look forward to every minute I get to spend with you."

An awkward silence snaked between them before Azerial swept in and placed a kiss on Juniper's forehead. He hit nearly exactly the same spot Juniper's mother had kissed just earlier that evening. She thought it to be an odd coincidence, but she said nothing about it. She assumed that she didn't have to, as her thought had probably already invaded Azerial's mind.

"Sleep well, Juniper. Have a good day tomorrow at school."

"I will," she said with a frown. She reached out suddenly and grabbed her father's sleeve as he began to pass her by. "Are you *sure* you're ok?"

"Of course I am," he said gently, trying to convince the both of him with his answer. "I saw what I wanted to see. What I *needed* to see. Worry yourself no further with thoughts of this as at least now I've a recent memory to warm this tired heart."

And then, with his sentiment complete, he left her. In his wake, his words lingered. They remained alive on the air like fireflies of nostalgia long after he himself had blended into the shadows of the distant meadow as he made his quick retreat back to the aged farm house.

Deciding then not to interrupt her mother and Mr. Halsey's conversation, Juniper took a seat on the bottom stair of the porch and placed her chin into her hands. She sighed heavily and her chest rose and fell violently once, then again when she realized that one sigh hadn't nearly been enough to express her frustration.

She just couldn't believe her rotten luck.

One minute everything had been on track and the very next the train was bent like a slinky at the side of the tracks, smoking and broken.

She looked up at the sky and her thoughts leapt from her mind to the cosmos beyond. She hoped they found their way home, to a friendly ethereal ear that might be able to alleviate the extreme exhaustion and confusion she was feeling over the unfolding situation.

But, she said to herself quietly, *at least I told mama about the healing. At least she knows about that. This will buy me some time. Mama'll chalk every occurrence of strange behavior over the past few months up to the healing and the keeping of that secret... maybe she'll be satisfied with that and...*

And what? she asked herself. *And I'll never have to tell her about dad still being earth-bound?*

Juniper sighed when she realized she had no answers; and instead of her mind jumping in with the right plan, her stomach rumbled a hungry reply.

Behind her, the kitchen door pulled open and the screen came outwards with an even creak.

"She's out here," Mr. Halsey said, obviously alerting Juniper's mother to her whereabouts. He stepped cautiously onto the porch a second later and addressed her directly. "Your mother was wondering where you got to. I told her you probably stepped out for a bit of fresh air, seeing as you spent all day sick and cooped up indoors." He waited for a response and when Juniper gave him nothing, he continued cautiously with a question. "Do you mind if I join you for a second? I think we should discuss a few things."

"You can sit if you'd like, I don't mind. I just thought I'd get wait out here for the pizza." She paused and looked up at the twinkling sky. "Besides that, it's a nice night."

Mr. Halsey inhaled deeply. "It is, isn't it? I've always loved this time of year in the south."

Juniper nodded. "Yeah, me too. Everything seems so alive."

Mr. Halsey stepped onto the top stair. He finally sat when he reached the step just above the one where Juniper was perched. "So uh... This is weird, isn't it?"

Juniper glanced up at him and shrugged. "A little, maybe."

"I know you're upset with me," he said quietly. "I do want to apologize to you."

"It's ok. No reason to apologize. You knew her before I did," said Juniper.

Mr. Halsey shifted on the step and pulled his pant legs up to accommodate his bent knees. "I won't be your teacher for much longer, you know."

"Does this mean I'm passing your class?"

He laughed nervously. "I told you, Juniper, you're my top student. Unless you bomb the final you've got your A."

Juniper didn't respond right away, instead she allowed her thoughts time to fully marinate in their own venomous juices. "Why don't we just cut to the chase here. I know you like my mama, Mr. Halsey. And I also know you're interested in dating her. But I have to tell you, it's not a wise idea."

Mr. Halsey coughed. "Why not?"

"Well..." Juniper licked her lips to unstuck her forthcoming fib. "I wasn't going to say anything... ya know, because I didn't want to jinx it... *but* there's a pretty good chance my dad might be coming back into the picture."

"Oh," Mr. Halsey muttered. He nodded a moment later. "I see. I uh... I didn't know that."

"Yeah, well, it's a fairly new development so uh, it might be best if you held off with the advances. You know, just to see if this pans out." Juniper paused for dramatic effect. "I just want her to be happy and I'm sure you want that for her too, don't you Mr. Halsey?"

"Yes, of course I do... of course." He lowered his head and chuckled to himself. "I feel silly. And your mother didn't mention a thing about this which makes me feel even *more* foolish. What she must think of me!"

Juniper was hit with a sudden pang of guilt, but she swallowed it away. "I'm sorry, Mr. Halsey. I thought mama would have said something."

"Well... She didn't. Not a word." Mr. Halsey sighed and looked straight ahead at the driveway. "I guess I should probably be going then."

"You aren't staying for pizza?" Juniper asked innocently. "There'll be plenty."

"No, no, it's getting late and I've already taken up enough of your time." He stood and dusted off his pants. "Besides, you have some studying to do. Remember, quiz tomorrow."

Juniper followed his lead and pushed herself to her feet. She nodded and made a cross over her heart. "I promise I'll be ready. You can count on me."

"I know that I can. Please do tell your mother that I said good-bye, Miss Kelly." He looked back at the house wistfully one last time before he bid his final farewell and walked to his truck. He fumbled with the keys for a second before he found the right one and slipped into the cab. The engine turned over slowly and noisily a moment later and the sound drew Penelope from the kitchen.

Juniper had barely the time to sit back down, before she heard the storm door open. A second later the screen door popped outward and Penelope emerged onto the patio.

"Where is he going?" she asked. "I thought he was staying for pizza."

Juniper shrugged and feigned stupidity. "He said something about having tests to grade. Guess he forgot about them."

"Oh, I see." Penelope sounded slightly disappointed, but she recovered quickly. "How much longer until dinner arrives?"

"Not long, I guess."

Penelope stepped onto the porch and the screen door snapped shut behind her with a metallic click. "So tell me, what do you think of him?"

"Who?" Juniper asked, slow at first to realize about whom her mother was speaking. "Mr. Halsey?"

"Yes, Mr. Halsey," she said. "Is he a good teacher?"

Juniper nodded.   "Well yeah, but, I don't think you should marry him or anything."

"Well, goodness no!" Penelope said with a laugh. "But what would be wrong with me having dinner with him some time? When school ends next Thursday, you'll no longer be in his class."

"I don't know, mama. You know how you are when it comes to men. You always find some reason to dump 'em." Juniper shook her head and leveled her charges. "What if you guys break up and he gets his revenge on you by withholding a glowing recommendation for me for my college applications? He could, quite possibly, keep me out of the schools I *really* want to go to. I mean, you *could* date him and *I* could end up at Greenville Community instead of Harvard or Oxford. With my bargain basement education I'll be lucky to find work as a fry chef at some crappy fast food restaurant. But hey, maybe if I work hard enough I might make employee of the month. I figure *that* career will last until the tragic yet unavoidable grease fire burns nearly 80% of my body."

Penelope laughed and took a seat next to Juniper on the steps. "Oh stop it, would you?   Where do you get these stories?"

Juniper fell silent and shrugged. "I'm just saying that I don't think it's a good idea to date him, that's all."

"He doesn't seem to be a vengeful sort of a guy. I really don't think he'd punish you if things between him and I went south," Penelope said softly,. She laughed a moment later almost as quietly. "If anything were to ever happen, that is."

Juniper saw the familiar round headlights of the pizza delivery vehicle and she sighed, eager for a subject change. She needed time to consider her options.

Penelope rushed inside to grab the coupon and the money from her purse. Juniper stood slowly and leaned against the hand rail, one hand over her eyes to shield them from the glare of Tony's delivery car.

She knew she would find a certain amount of joy that night in seeing her mother's face twitch at the sight of the extra onions. She, for now, would take her victories where she could get them.

The next morning when Juniper arrived at school she felt a knot form in her stomach at the sight of Mr. Halsey's pickup in the teacher's parking lot.

She sighed heavily and adjusted the weight of her backpack on her shoulders before she entered the west wing of the nearly desolate school.

She enjoyed the silence to be found in the hallways at the early hour, especially that morning when her mind was cluttered with a million tattered thoughts. After the pizza had been paid for and eaten the previous night, the hour had been too late to continue the conversation Mr. Halsey had interrupted with his impromptu visit. Penelope hadn't brought the revelation back up and Juniper had let it go in favor of brushing up for the history quiz Mr. Halsey had clued her in on.

She hadn't slept well; between the tossing and the turning she felt as though she'd only tucked a few minutes of actual shut-eye beneath her proverbial belt. Tired and groggy, Juniper shuffled down the hallway towards the central common area of the west wing. Homeroom wouldn't begin for another hour and Juniper planned to use the time to read and finish up the last of her homework without the usual distractions she found at home. Between the TV, radio and her internet-connected computer, Juniper wondered how she ever got anything done at all. Without her morning block of free time to organize her school work, she knew she'd never maintain her straight A average.

That morning she found a seat in the middle of the west wing lobby, a seat conveniently placed just across the way from her homeroom and first period class. She settled into her seat with little difficulty and pulled her legs up beneath her to begin her silent study.

She opened her book bag and slowly pulled out her history book. She almost couldn't bear the sight of it, as even the cover of the simple hardback book reminded her of her conversation with Mr. Halsey the night before. She felt bad for having lied to him, but had managed to justify her actions several times over on the almost-mile walk that morning. Still, she felt guilty and uneasy and already wasn't looking forward to seeing him in class that morning.

No sooner than she'd cracked the cover, did she hear someone clear their throat just behind her.

Instinct forced her to look up and much to her dismay she found herself staring straight at Mr. Halsey.

Immediately, every muscle in Juniper's body tensed up. She re-closed the history book with a soft thud and sighed as she did so. "Good Morning, Mr. Halsey," she said as cheerfully as possible. "I thought I was the only person crazy enough to get here this early."

"I enjoy the quiet," he replied simply. He moved around from behind the bench and sat down next to Juniper. He looked around nervously as if he were checking the lobby for signs of life. When he was satisfied that they were alone, he spoke.

"I just wanted to apologize again for last night." He looked down at his lap and his nervous hands gripped the bottom of his dark blue tie. "It was extremely unprofessional of me to do what I did and I hope that we can put it behind us."

"It's ok, really. And for what it's worth, I really did appreciate you bringing me the study sheet. I can't afford to fall behind at this point in the school year, not when I've worked so hard to get to where I am."

"Right, of course and you're welcome, but I have to confess, Juniper..." He looked at his hands and smoothed them over his knees. "I only used that study sheet as an excuse to see your mother."

"Oh, I know that," Juniper said softly. "I've known you were interested in my mama since the day you asked me to tell her hello."

Mr. Halsey's cheeks turned a brilliant shade of red. "I'm that obvious, am I?"

"Well..." Juniper bobbed her head slightly from side to side. "Yeah. You are. But it's ok. Mama's beautiful. A lot of guys take an interest in her. It's something I've gotten used to."

Mr. Halsey chuckled and awkwardly patted her knee. "I'm sure that's true. And for what it's worth, I appreciate your honesty."

"Any time," Juniper said. She opened the text book again and nodded towards the page. "I hate to cut this short but I really should get back to studying. You don't want me fail the last quiz of the year, do you?"

Mr. Halsey stood and straightened his tie, a nervous habit Juniper hadn't noticed until then. "Of course I don't. And so you know, there's not a finer subject you could be studying." He turned on his heel and began to walk off, but he turned back a second later with a slight air of hesitation about him. "I hope you get what it is you want, Miss Kelly. You'll be happy to know that I won't stand in the way of it. If your father *is* coming back, then I wish him and your mother the best of luck."

"Thanks," Juniper said weakly. She shifted on the bench, uncomfortable with the subject matter. An uncomfortable air that must have come across on her face loud and clear.

Mr. Halsey cleared his throat and forced himself to smile.

"Have a good morning, Miss Kelly. I'll see you in class later this morning."

Juniper only nodded and she watched him leave with a heavy guilt gripping her throat. She sighed heavily and looked back at the text book spread across her lap. The words were blurred on the page and the subject matter was all but lost to her tired mind and eyes.

In that moment, Juniper couldn't think of anything less fascinating than the War of 1812.

Chapter Eight
Paths and Choices

When Juniper arrived at the farm house that afternoon she found Azerial in his tiny attic room. He was sitting cross legged beneath the outstretched branch of the giant oak tree where he appeared to be deep in meditation. His cloak was drawn tight around him and his hood was pulled up and over his head to all but completely conceal his face. Juniper couldn't tell if his eyes were open or closed and she hesitated, not wanting to break his concentration. Azerial, however, spoke as soon as Juniper stepped through the doorway and into the room.

"I wasn't sure you'd make it today." He pushed his hood back from his head and his long, black hair spilled out over his broad shoulders. With a slight turn of his chin he shook the black waves back from his face and produced a warm smile.

"I can't stay long," Juniper replied. "I just wanted to pop in and make sure that you're really ok. You know after last night. I know things were a little awkward and I've been thinking about it all day."

Azerial smiled softly, but Juniper could sense that the action was merely a front to mask his true emotions. With the wave of his hand he motioned her closer. "Please, come in and have a seat."

Juniper crossed the creaking floorboards to the bed and perched on the edge of it. She clasped her hands in front of her and stared at them until she almost felt she was staring straight *through* them.

"I believe that I already told you how it is, Junie. I'm *fine* with last night." He smiled again and that time his emotion appeared almost genuine. "I saw her, I saw my Penny, and that was all I needed. Just to see her face again. Just one last time."

"Yeah, I know," Juniper said. "I mean, that *is* what you keep saying, after all. But you know you can't lie to me, right? I might not be able to read minds like you can and we might not know each other *that* well just yet, but I know what I heard. And do you know what that was? Hurt. I heard *hurt* in your voice last night. And just now? I *saw* it in your eyes."

Azerial sighed and dropped his chin lower to his chest. "I will admit something here, Juniper. Something that I probably shouldn't as it's dangerous to entertain such thoughts."

"There are no dangerous thoughts, only dangerous actions," Juniper said matter-of-factly.

His shoulders rolled backwards and pulled his spine straight. "Seeing your mother last night- seeing her made me want more. Of her, of what we once had... And believe me, I've considered *many* dangerous things since last night."

"Like talking to her face to face?"

Azerial nodded and met her eyes somewhat reluctantly. "Yes. Like talking to her face to face."

Juniper held his gaze and volleyed a question onto his side of the court. "Then why don't you? Why don't you come home with me right now? We can wait for mama to get in from work and then you two can talk and straighten everything out."

He shook his head, and a moment later his defiance became obvious in the tilt of his words. "I'm afraid I can't do that. Your mother... She wouldn't understand this, Juniper. There's no way that she could forgive me for lying to her all of those years ago."

I think," Juniper started slowly, "that maybe *you* need to forgive *yourself.*"

Azerial looked up suddenly, as though her words had hit him square in the chest. When he changed the subject a second later with addressing it further, Juniper knew that her arrow had hit its target.

"I wanted to ask you this yesterday, but I wasn't afforded the opportunity," Azerial cleared his throat. "When you healed the puppy... could you control the power?"

Juniper wrinkled her brow as she considered his query. "I think so, yeah." She turned her hands palm up with her fingers still laced together. "I didn't know exactly what I was doing, though. Everything sort of moved in slow-motion."

"But you did it?" he asked. "You moved your hands and were able to feel where the source of the injury was?"

She swallowed thickly and nodded her head. Her hair fell into her eyes and she quickly pushed it back. "Yeah, yeah I could. I did. And when I knew he was alright, that he was *fixed*, it just- stopped. You know, it was weird. It sorta felt like I'd always been doing it, *healing*, I mean. It was like it was a completely natural thing for me to do."

It was Azerial's turn to nod. "That's good. That means that you're ready for this power you have. You've matured into it as you were meant to. However, I feel as though I must caution you once again not to waste this gift. By that I mean, don't use it unless the situation absolutely warrants it."

Juniper gulped and looked down at the toes of her shoes. "That's actually another reason I stopped by today... To uh... to tell you that I used it again last night," she whispered. "I sort of told mama. About my *gift*. I was afraid that if I didn't *show* her, she wouldn't believe me."

Azerial smiled softly, an action that surprised her. "Your logic was sound and there's no fault to be found with your actions." He paused as another of her thoughts entered his mind. "She handled it better than you expected," he guessed correctly.

"Yeah. She really did! I mean, I don't know exactly how I *thought* she'd react, but I think it went well. All things considered." Juniper shrugged. "She really seemed ok with it. Almost like she'd been expecting it."

"Well..." Azerial placed his hands out at his sides and rested his palms on the wooden floor. "You mustn't forget, your mother has a bit of experience with this sort of stuff."

"I know. I think I just assumed that it would scare her."

"If I remember correctly, your mother's not a woman who is easily scared," Azerial said, and he added a laugh to the end of his statement before he continued. "Your mother marched right out into the woods, at night no less, armed with nothing but a lantern to call me out of my hiding. For all she knew, I was a psychopath, or worse yet, a demon... But that didn't faze her a bit. Of course she *was* shocked by me, at first anyway. She came around to the idea of what I was fairly quickly, though."

Juniper smiled at the thought of her mother flushing an angel out of his hidden enclave. "What was she like? When she was my age?" she asked.

A smile crept across his lips. "She was the most beautiful creature I'd ever seen. Smart, strong, full of life... You remind me of her quite a bit."

Juniper felt her cheeks redden beneath the compliment. "Mama says I look a lot like you."

He tilted his head to the side to better study her features. "I suppose it all depends on what side of the fence you're on, doesn't it?"

"Maybe." Juniper lowered her voice. "You just said that I shouldn't use my gift unless the situation warrants it. I'm pretty sure I understand what you mean, but should I not heal myself? Do I have a choice in that? Will something bad happen to me if I abuse the gift?"

"Your body will heal its own self naturally, without prompting by you." Azerial shifted from side to side and tugged his cloak out from beneath him to further free his movements. "As for healing your mother... Well, as I said, I understand why you did it. Nothing *bad* is going to happen to you because of it.

I just mean to caution you against healing every little thing you see. This gift is powerful and should be used only when all other methods fail."

Juniper nodded. "I understand. And I promise you, right here, right now, that I'll stick to that." She made a cross over her heart, which prompted Azerial to smile.

"Good. I trust that you will. After all, you've proven to me that you're a good kid. Penelope raised you right as I knew she would." Azerial paused, and when he spoke again his voice had taken on a new element of darkness. "Just remember not to push your limits. Your body can heal itself, yes, but there is a ceiling on the power. I don't want you thinking that you can jump from a 20 story building head first and survive the impact. After all, you are still human. The healing power you possess can easily be outweighed by heavy trauma."

Juniper looked at her hands and nodded slowly. "I *was* wondering something, though. C-Can I bring people back from the dead?"

"I'm glad you asked," he said, and he shook his head as a follow up. "The answer is no. Once the heart has fallen silent, there is nothing you can do to return its beat."

"But right up until the heart stops... I *can* save someone's life?"

"Yes," admitted Azerial. "Until the last beat, there's hope."

"Wow..." Juniper flexed her fingers then folded them to her palms. "I always wanted super powers, you know, as a kid. But now that I have them?"

"It's a big responsibility, isn't it?" He leaned closer and lowered his own voice. "Now you understand why the lure to do evil with the power is so great."

"So what... I can't give life, but I can take it?"

Azerial swallowed and shifted uncomfortably. "Yes."

"But, how? Why?"

"How? Well certainly you can figure that out! Knowing what you now know about how your ability works I'm sure you can answer your own question if you give it some thought."

Juniper squinted one eye as she considered the possibilities. "Well... when I'm healing someone I take their sickness, their *energy*, into myself and purify it before flushing it back into them. I *guess* to do harm to a person I could steal their energy and not give it back?"

"Very good," Azerial said. He nodded softly and his hair fell towards his chest. "I knew you could figure it out. And now that you know how, I have to make you promise that you never will."

Juniper's eyes widened in view of her father's request. "I can't imagine killing someone, not even for a second! How could you think that I could? That I *would?*"

"I don't think that you would, but still, you have to be cautioned. You *have* to be careful, Juniper. If your emotions get the better of you, *dark emotions*... anger, fear, greed... you might find yourself tempted to do that which you now say you never would. Believe me when I say that it only takes one second to change teams. I have seen it happen many, *many* times."

Juniper shook her head defiantly. "Oh no! I would never... *never!* Maybe other people succumb to evil, but not me!" She was slightly upset that Azerial would even consider such a thing about her and she felt like something had hit her square in the gut. "You don't seriously think that I would do that, right?" She shook her head. "Because I wouldn't. I swear it."

Azerial's forehead creased with a worried wrinkle and the hard look in his eyes melted quickly under the summer-hot heat of Juniper's defensive response. "I never meant to imply that I thought you would be lured towards evil, not for a **second**. Please, don't be upset. I merely felt it my duty to warn you, to squelch any feelings of hatred you might have towards a fellow human. Namely Ben Maxwell."

"You think I'd kill Ben?" she asked incredulously. "I know we both know what he was planning to do to me, but I wouldn't kill him to get revenge! That would be taking things a little too far... Now don't get me wrong, I've thought about getting back at him, but I've never considered *murder*! Just what sort of person do you think I am?"

"I think you're a wonderful person–"

"But you still think I'm a loose cannon! Even though you said that it was *my* choice as to whether or not I chose good or evil! Do you suddenly think I'm predisposed to following in the footsteps of every Nephilim who's taken the wrong path?"

"Juniper, no, I never–"

"Yeah, well, that's what it sounds like to me and if you'll excuse me, I've gotta go now."

"Juniper, wait, please. You're taking this all in the wrong way. I didn't intend for you to get upset."

But it was too late for words of explanation. Already Juniper's hands were knotted into fists at her sides and her form was rigid and unyielding. She had looked away from him and her eyes were crawling up the bark of the tree. She was counting, slowly and under her breath, trying desperately to regain herself. She knew that Azerial didn't doubt her, but there was still that insecure part of herself that lived on and lingered in the pit of her stomach. The part that would forever seek to make her mother, and now Azerial, proud.

When Juniper looked back in his direction, Azerial had stood. She, in her pseudo-meditative state, hadn't realized that he had moved at all. When she finally unclenched her jaw and fists, he spoke. Juniper jumped, startled at how quietly and quickly he had come to be by her side.

He placed his hand on her shoulders and he lowered his head until their foreheads were almost touching. His voice was low and had lost all the joviality she'd come to love. "Juniper, you're my daughter. You're *Penelope's* daughter. Knowing this, I know in my heart of hearts that you're one of the good guys. I just have to stress to you how important it is that you realize the magnitude of the gift you possess. I have to make absolute *certain* that I teach you, *educate* you, and instill in you the ability to do good and *only* good. As I said, it takes only a second to cross that line, and once it has been crossed, it cannot be undone. This is the way things are."

Juniper knew that he was speaking from experience, and the last bit of her anger dissipated. A tiny thought in the back of her head had grown quickly and bloomed, and left no room for resentment. Juniper plucked the question quickly, wanting to get the chance to actually ask it before Azerial read her mind and answered.

"Couldn't I, instead of hurting someone trying to harm me, couldn't I heal them instead? Exorcise them, so to speak?"

"Of course you could!" Azerial nodded several times in rapid succession and seemed proud of her conclusion. "Extracting evil and battling it are two *very* different things."

Hesitantly, Juniper continued. "May I ask you something else?"

"You want to know why I left Heaven." Azerial's look was one of calm serenity. He closed his eyes and appeared to be caught up in a particularly vivid memory.

"Do you regret leaving?" Juniper asked cautiously. She had been hesitant to disrupt his silence, but the words had prompted her to do so.

"I have had moments, yes, where I regretted my actions. But over the years, my faith has repaired herself. I understand that the events that transpired must have done so for a reason."

"What do you mean?"

"I mean to say that I think *you* happened for a reason. God has a plan, after all." Azerial glanced up and then shook his head. "You've heard the saying about how He works in "mysterious ways", yes?" He nodded, but said nothing more on the topic.

Juniper took the silence to consider his words and found that she was less confident in the idea of fate than Azerial seemed to be. In fact the whole of it made her feel rather uncomfortable. There was something about the idea of destiny that left Juniper unsettled; something just didn't seem right about feeling as though no matter what you decide, you've still made the choice intended. Free will was the idea that Juniper subscribed to and nothing could shake her faith in it.

Azerial tapped into her thoughts and shattered his own silence. "I believe the two can work together in harmony," he said. "Fate and free will, I mean."

Juniper smiled, and she took her father's hand in hers. She liked the way it felt to be near him; enjoyed feeling like a small child when his large paw encircled her delicate hand and nearly concealed it entirely within his palm.

"Does God still talk to you?" she asked. Her question was almost a whisper.

"God..." He looked up with a faint smile resting atop his lips. "These days God and I have a *strange* relationship, my dear. I am faithful to Him as ever, yet we are estranged by my personal decisions."

"How do you survive here? All alone with no one to talk to? With no food?"

"You'd be surprised how good I am at catching fish in the creek."

Juniper laughed. "With a spear?"

He shook the long sleeves of the cloak free of his hands and held them up for her to witness. "I have an even *better* tool right here."

"Impressive," she said with a smile. "Father-daughter fishing trips will be much more interesting this way."

Azerial chuckled and looked over at her with an

adoration Juniper had never witnessed. "I must say, I'm pleased that you're adjusting to this all so well."

Juniper shrugged in response. "What choice do I have?"

"There are always choices, Juniper, even when it seems that there are none." His lips twisted into a calm smile. "God always provides more than one path."

"But is there a plan? For me?"

He weighed his words carefully before he unleashed them. "As I said, I believe that fate and free will are sisters. There is a *desired* path for every creature. Whether or not that destiny is fulfilled is up to the individual."

"And you're *sure* that you don't know what my desired path is? Absolutely sure?"

"Absolutely sure, yes."

"Am *I* supposed to know what it is?" Juniper asked quietly.

Azerial shook his head. "No, I'm afraid not. The journey is the important part, as well as the lessons learned along the way. If you knew now your ultimate path, knew the steps it would take to achieve it, you would choose to avoid all of the pitfalls and mistakes that make you inherently human, and wiser."

"Free will," Juniper whispered.

Azerial nodded. "Free will." He glanced upward towards the ceiling and smiled. "He's real big on that, you see"

"So God *is* a he?"

"Well, no. I didn't say that, not really." Azerial tilted his head from side to side. "God isn't really male *or* female. God is both, God is neither."

"Does He visit us? Down here?" asked Juniper.

Azerial shook his head. "There is no need for such a journey on his part for He is *everything*, Juniper. He is you, me, the flowers, the trees… the very *air* we breath. God is *everything*, thus the need to visit earth is unnecessary as he is always *here.*"

"Busy guy," Juniper commented softly.

Azerial chuckled in response to her uttered comment. "Yes, yes he is. It's extremely hard to get an appointment with Him, that's for certain."

Juniper smiled, a subject change at her lips. "Mama is letting me keep the dog and I think I've decided on a name."

"Spot? Or maybe Champ?" Azerial smiled and let out a slight chuckle. "I've always been partial to Fido, personally."

Juniper rolled her eyes at Azerial's joking suggestions. "I was thinking of calling him Sam."

"Sam?" Azerial paused briefly, then questioned her choice. "Why Sam?"

Juniper blushed and lowered her chin. "When I was little I always wanted a pet. A kitten, a puppy... I didn't care. But mama said that we didn't have enough time to take care of a pet, that it was a big responsibility. So instead of a pet she gave me a large stuffed teddy bear, hoping that would fill the void. I named him Sam, and Sam and I went everywhere together. I fed him part of my dinner, I tucked him in at night and I always told myself that if I ever had a *real* pet someday, I'd name *him* Sam in honor of that teddy bear."

"Sam sounds like a fine name," Azerial said. "If I might ask, what happened to the teddy bear?"

Juniper's smile turned wistful. "Oh, he went on to a better place a few years ago. He'd been re-stuffed and patched so many times, that finally, there was nothing we could do for him. I still have what's left of him, but I don't play with him any more."

Azerial put his arm around her shoulders. "I understand how hard it can be to let go of things that once meant so much."

Juniper smiled faintly and knew that he spoke the truth. "I bet you do." She brought her wrist watch up and checked the time. As much as she hated to face the fact that the real world spun on around them, she knew she had to attend to it. "I really hate to run off, but if I don't get Sam fed and walked before mama gets home, she'll reconsider her decision to let me keep him."

Azerial laughed and squeezed her lightly. "Then by all means, go on then. I certainly don't want to keep you."

Juniper kissed him impulsively on the cheek. His stubble was scratchy against her lips and chin and elicited a slight tickle. "I'll try to stop by tomorrow if I can."

"Good," Azerial said through his wide-mouthed grin. "Because I have something I'd like to give you."

The next afternoon was Friday, the last Friday of the school year. Monday would begin the final week of classes, four half-days that would be comprised of final exams and year-end goodbyes; goodbyes that would carry the students from the classroom to summer vacations and part-time jobs.

As relieved as Juniper was to find herself at the end of another school year, she had to admit that she was slightly disappointed to see it end as the approaching season of summer was her least favorite. The weather played a major role in that, but mostly Juniper found that she grew bored of her self-imposed isolation by the end of June.

She still hoped to take the job at the bookstore, but her mother had never again broached the subject. Juniper had taken that as her answer, and as upset as she was about it, she understood that taking the position was impractical. After all, her mother had been right. It was a long walk to the bookstore, a walk that would take Juniper several hours, even if she walked as fast as she could.

All she could do was hope that something opened up at the grocery store, but even that wasn't an ideal solution. There, she knew, she'd have to deal with Jason and his near constant personal attacks and snide remarks.

As she walked through the woods that afternoon on her way to the farm house, Juniper realized that it had been several days since she had seen either Ben or Jason. At first she assumed that they were also studying for finals, but then she realized how silly that line of thinking was. She doubted very much that either of them knew what a text book was, let alone what to do with one.

When Juniper finally arrived at the farm house she went immediately upstairs to the small, third floor bedroom that Azerial called his own.

The door was closed when she got there and she knocked firmly to announce her arrival. She was always careful to respect his privacy, as she realized that it was something he'd grown quite accustomed to in his years of solitude.

It was only a moment later before Juniper heard the familiar swish of Azerial's cloak as he approached the door.

"It's me, Junie," she said. "Are you busy? If you are I can come back later... I just thought I'd pop in on my way home and say hey."

The door opened slowly, then fully, and Azerial stepped aside to welcome her into the room. His face was wearing a smile. "I was wondering if I'd see you today! Come in, come in! I'm glad you're here."

The temperature outside the house was made stunningly obvious by the heavy, choking air inside the room. Juniper found herself gasping for breath and a few beads of sweat automatically appeared at her brow.

She wiped them away with the back of her hand. "Whew, it's warm in here!" she breathed. "You can definitely tell summer is fast on the way."

"Is it really that warm?" Azerial asked. He was dressed in his normal attire; long black pants and his long black cloak.

He didn't seem to notice the heat and was sweat-free and calm looking.

Juniper nodded as vigorously as the heat would allow. "It's sweltering in here! I don't know how you can stand it."

He shrugged one heavy shoulder. "I suppose I've gotten used to it. Would you be more comfortable downstairs?"

"Yeah, I would. Is that ok with you?"

"Sure, sure! It's not a problem at all." He nodded once, and motioned for Juniper to exit the room. He followed closely at her heels and closed the door behind him with a click. "I seem to have lost track of time today. You surprised me. I wasn't expecting you for another hour or two."

"Well, I *am* a little earlier than normal." Juniper hit the second floor landing and rounded the corner to the final set of twelve stairs. "My last period was just a review, for the final on Tuesday. The teacher let us leave when we finished."

"Speaking of teachers... What was your mother's friend's name? Have he and your mother seen each other lately?"

Juniper bit her lip to keep from letting loose a smile over her father's not-so-subtle display of jealousy. Even though Azerial was behind her and unable to see her face, she knew very well that his keen senses would quickly find the smile in her words.

She pushed her happiness over Azerial's jealousy aside and answered his question as vaguely as possible. "His name is Mr. Halsey. *Nick* Halsey. I don't think they've seen each other since he stopped by the house, but I know he'd certainly *like* to see her again. As for mama... well, she expressed a passing interest in him, but I don't think it'll go any further than that."

Juniper took the last step of the staircase with a small jump. When her feet were firm at the floor she moved closer to the tree to allow Azerial the room to pass her by.

He went quickly to the front of the house where he

latched the door. From there he surveyed the rest of the windows in the dimly-lit living room to make certain he was keenly concealed from the outside world.

When he was satisfied that the secret of his presence was well-kept he turned to face her. His face was slanted with a look of curiosity. "That isn't your doing is it?" he asked. "Their inability to get things together for a real date?"

Juniper blushed, and try as she might to suppress her thoughts, they tumbled to her forebrain and neatly exposed her interference in the would-be pairing. Knowing that her guilty secret was no longer tightly contained, she spoke and owned up to the dirty deed. "I might have said *something* that led Mr. Halsey to believe that mama was about to be otherwise engaged."

Azerial didn't chuckle as Juniper had expected he would. Instead, his face grew stern and stormy. "Why would you prevent your mother from being happy? It was a very selfish thing to do."

Juniper looked down at her feet. "I know it was and I feel guilty about it, I do. I just thought that if I pushed him out of the picture for a bit it might give you and mama time to talk, because I really do believe that you two could-"

"Could what?" Azerial asked. His voice was sharp and angry; it was an odd combination that Juniper hadn't previously been privy to. "You think your mother and I are going to live happily ever after? Is that what you think?"

Juniper didn't look up; didn't respond.

In the silence of her embarrassment, Azerial continued in the same thick and angry voice. "I know that most children have dreams of seeing their separated parents get back together, and in some cases, that outcome is possible... even likely. But this time? The *game* is different, the *rules* are different. It's silly for you to hold out hope for us. Absolutely silly."

When her shell-shocked shame dissipated, Juniper finally

addressed him. "Yesterday, when I asked you to tell me about mama when she was my age... We got sidetracked, but from what you *did* say, I could tell how much you still care for her. And just from the few things I've gotten her to say about you, I know that she still-"

"I will **not** discuss this with you again, do you understand me? Instead I will say that sometimes love is not enough. It wasn't enough to keep me from falling, it wasn't enough to keep your mother and I together and it isn't enough to reunite us now."

"I don't understand why you're so against this!" Juniper exclaimed, her voice climbing quickly to the status of yelling. "There's a *real* chance that you could have what you want! That we could all have what we want! But you're being stubborn and foolish and-"

"Juniper, sweetheart... I realize that we haven't known each other for very long, but I absolutely *cannot* let you speak to me this way! I'm the adult, which means that I'm the one who decides what's right and what's wrong and that's what I'm doing here."

"But that's not fair! I should get some say in this! And what about mama? She's an adult! Where's her say? Doesn't her opinion matter?"

"A lot of things about life aren't fair," he retorted. "Do you think I like that it has to be this way?"

"If you don't like it then change it!" she screamed. Her frustration manifested in the form of bright red pools that quickly stained her cheeks and dripped down to her neck and upper chest. "Please, dad! Do something to change this! It doesn't have to be-"

"I can't change this!" Azerial bellowed. So gruff was his tone that Juniper found herself stumbling backwards with a gasp lodged firmly in her chest.

Azerial spoke again. His voice was still tense, but

seemed to be softening in light of her shock. "Do not push this subject with me again, Juniper. I will not tolerate it."

"Fine!" Juniper spat. "I won't ever again mention how *stupid* you're being, not **ever** again!" With her anger having gotten the better of her, Juniper turned for the door. She didn't know what else to do or say and in the absence of such things she ran for the door.

Azerial called out to her. "Juniper! Where are you going?"

"I'm g-going home," she said shakily. Her trembling fingers fumbled with the latch on the front door as she tried desperately to hold back the sobs that were multiplying within her chest.

"Juniper, please don't go," Azerial said softly. "We've both let our tempers get the better of us... we should talk this through." In spite of his plea, he remained motionless. It was obvious to Juniper that he had chosen to allow her to leave if leaving was the decision she made.

Juniper finally heard the click of the lock over the echo of her frantic heartbeat and she pulled the door open so quickly in her agitated state that she nearly hit herself in the face. Just outside the doorway with her hand on the knob, she paused long enough to offer up her parting words.

"Without love, what is there?" she asked. "When you figure out the answer to that, let me know."

Azerial, having no idea what to say, said nothing, and Juniper closed the door behind her with almost as much force as she had used to open it. When she stepped onto the burnt-brown grass she broke into a run, and kept up the pace all the way home. She stopped only when she'd reached the privacy of her pink-painted bedroom.

Once securely tucked away inside, she crumbled to the floor and dissolved quickly into tears.

Juniper spent her Saturday studying for her fast-approaching finals. She looked at the clock on her nightstand a dozen times before noon and debated as to whether or not she would visit Azerial or keep her distance.

She was still upset about their conversation the previous day and Juniper realized that the main reason she was so upset by his words, was because she knew they were true.

Sometimes, just maybe love *wasn't* enough. Maybe, out of all of the great things love could do, it couldn't reunite her parents and it couldn't bridge the gap between heaven and earth.

Juniper, however, still held out hope and supposed that she always would.

By two that afternoon she had studied to the point of being cross-eyed. She pushed aside her books in favor of the TV, but when she realized there was nothing on of any interest, she quickly clicked the set off.

She rolled onto her back and the mattress squeaked softly as she did so. Her eyes found the swirl plaster ceiling and she traced the ridges and lines for several moments in silence. It was something she had done since the first night in her new bedroom.

Had it really been 12 years? Juniper felt younger than 16, but much older at the very same time.

Again, she found that her thoughts drifted back to Azerial. Her mind still buzzed with a million questions; things she had meant to ask him and things she'd wanted to explore in more depth. Mostly, she wanted to know more about her mother and the grandfather she barely remembered at all.

The whole idea of her mother having had a secret life excited Juniper and almost made her envious. There was also a part of her that felt angry as it was almost as though she didn't know her mother at all. For how could you know someone when they hid such a huge part of themselves from you?

Juniper found herself once again toying with the idea of telling her mother about Azerial. No matter how much she thought about it and rehearsed the scene in her head, she couldn't quite imagine what her mother's reaction would be. But, Juniper knew that she couldn't betray her father's trust no matter how much she might want to. She just had to trust that someday he would change his mind about staying away and confess to Penelope the truth of what he had done.

She also had to trust that her mother would be able to forgive him for what he had done, all for the sake of love and sacrifice.

Too tired to think and too exhausted to study, Juniper found herself wandering from her room to the kitchen. She took the stairs by two and was surprised when she found that the house was empty.

Outside the windows and doors of the small two-story house, the skies had opened up and a deluge of rain had escaped the clouds. Juniper sighed when she heard the thunder and cast a short-lived glance at her rain boots by the kitchen door.

No, she told herself. *I'll just stay here and study; relax. There'll be plenty of time to clear things up with dad and plenty of time to ask him all of the questions I want to ask him! It's not as though he's going anywhere.*

Juniper sighed at the conclusion of her internal debate. She knew that the nagging voice inside of her head was right, that it *would* be best if she kept her distance, at least for a little while. She knew most likely that he wasn't upset with her for running off like she had, but she also knew that there was nothing wrong with a little time for reflection. Maybe in his isolation he'd see that she was right; or maybe *she* would finally resign herself to the fact that *he* was.

Juniper had barely sat down at the kitchen table when she heard Penelope's car pull into the driveway. The kitchen window was partially open and a few minutes later Juniper heard her mother humming as she slammed the car door and headed towards the deck.

When the door opened, Penelope's exhausted voice entered first. "Juniper, a little help here, please. Help!" she squealed. Sam barked at the sound of the squeak and Juniper scrambled quickly to her feet.

Penelope's arms were loaded with groceries. She carried two plastic bags around each wrist and two paper bags in her arms. Over her head she'd thrown her purse strap and the bag dangled down the middle of her back. With her left foot she held Sam back from escaping through the opened door as he'd lately been so eager to do.

Witnessing her mother's precarious balancing act, Juniper swept in quickly and grabbed the two rain-spotted brown paper bags while she simultaneously shooed Sam from the kitchen with a stern admonishment. The puppy ran off reluctantly, reached the carpet in the living room and turned to watch the unfolding scene with a slightly amused, slightly questioning look on his face.

"Sorry to yell at you, Junie," Penelope apologized. She lifted her arms to the counter and pulled her wrists out of the plastic straps that had already begun to cut off her circulation. "I didn't think I had this much stuff until I tried to open the door! And of course, it didn't decide to start raining until I turned onto our street."

"It's ok. No reason to apologize." Juniper began to unpack the bags and sorted the food into four separate piles. Freezer, fridge, non-perishable and miscellaneous. "I've been studying all day," she said. "I'm currently taking a much deserved break."

"Oh, wonderful, then my timing is actually good for once!" Penelope opened the refrigerator door and pulled out a half-empty carton of milk. She removed the lid and sniffed it carefully. A moment later her face wrinkled and she shoved the carton in Juniper's direction. "Do me a favor and smell this for me."

"God, mama. Why do you do this to me?" Juniper put her hand out to reject the carton and turned her head. "I can smell it from here! Throw it out!"

Penelope set the carton on the counter disdainfully and shoved aside a few more things in the fridge to make room for the groceries that Juniper had nearly finished sorting.

"So, do you wanna hear who I ran into at the grocery today?" Penelope asked. She turned and one hand went to her hip.

Juniper gulped and already knew by the post her mother had struck that she was in trouble for *something*. "Uh, sure, yeah. Who'd you run into?"

"Nick Halsey," she said breezily. "And you know, he did the oddest thing!"

Juniper gulped. "Oh yeah? W-What?"

"He wished me good luck," Penelope said casually. She turned her attention back to the fridge and bent at the waist to pull out a carton of Chinese that had been living on the bottom shelf for weeks. "You know, I couldn't figure out why he'd do such a thing! Do *you* have any idea why he'd do that, Junie? Any idea at all?"

Juniper froze and tightened her grip on the bottle of ketchup in her hands. "I don't know, mama," she said quietly. "Maybe he was confused about something."

"It wouldn't have anything to do with me and your father, would it?" Penelope closed the refrigerator door and turned to face Juniper. She crossed her arms over her chest and narrowed one eye. "Well, young lady? Is there anything you'd like to say in your defense?"

Juniper nervously cleared her throat to buy herself time. When the clock ran out on her hesitation, she said the first thing that came to mind. "Well, it's- I just-"

Brilliant, she chastised herself. *So much for talking yourself out of this one.*

Juniper shook her head as she realized that there was no way out of the web she'd woven and she headed towards her only recourse. "I'm sorry, mama. I know it was an awful thing to do."

"I just don't understand why on *earth* you'd do something like this! It's not like you to lie!"

"I'm sorry," Juniper repeated. She had finally set the bottle of ketchup on the counter to let her hands hang free at her sides.

"You should be sorry! Honestly, why would you spread stories like that?"

"I didn't *spread* anything. I just lied to *one* person," Juniper protested. "It's not like I took out a full page ad in the Gazette!"

"Juniper, you know as well as I do that when you say something to one person in this town, you might as *well* take out an advertisement." Penelope shook her head and clucked her tongue. "So come on, out with it! Why did you do it? Can you just tell me that much?"

"I don't know why I did it!" Juniper exclaimed in frustration. "I guess it just made me uncomfortable. You know, you and my *teacher.* My teacher, mama! It's just *weird.*"

Penelope drew her lips into a pout. "He'll only be your teacher for a few more days. And since when is it your business who I date? As long as I'm respectful of your boundaries and tasteful in my actions, how is it your concern?"

"Well, it's not, but-" Juniper stopped talking and released a weighty sigh. She was too tired to argue any more, and on top of that she was tired of lying and was *tired* of being *tired.*

"Listen, Junie, I appreciate that you care about me. But

bringing your father into this...?" She shook her head and suddenly appeared more melancholic that Juniper could remember having seen her in recent history. "You know... I've been giving your father a lot of thought lately, sweetheart. Do you wanna know what I've been thinking?"

Juniper looked up with curiosity and met her mother's eyes. She didn't say anything. She didn't have to.

Penelope reached out and smoothed Juniper's hair with her hand. "Junie, what your father and I had was *very* special. Being with him? It was probably one of the happiest times I've seen, or *will* see, but I'm afraid that it's all in the past. And you were right, you know. When you said that I was lonely *and* when you said that I was avoiding becoming serious with anyone because I still loved your father."

Juniper's heart skipped a beat.

"I do still love him, and I venture to guess that I always will. But he's *gone*, sweetheart. He left a long time ago and he isn't coming back." She sucked in her breath and appeared to dig within herself to gather the remains of her courage. "I've also been thinking that it's time to tell you... to tell you *everything*. I'm working my way up to it, I am. It's just very difficult for me to-" Her gaze wandered and for a moment Juniper thought her mother was going to dissolve into tears. However, a moment later, the glaze in her eyes passed and she blinked away any would-be salty emotion. "It's hard for me to talk about it, that's all."

"I don't know what to say," Juniper whispered. A more accurate statement she'd never made, as at that moment a million different thoughts were racing through her mind.

Penelope dropped her hand to Juniper's shoulder. "Just be patient with me, would you? Understand how difficult this is, how *hard* it is for me to put into words the way I felt about your father. But I promise you, Junie, I'll tell you everything soon enough and I think it'll make a lot of sense... Well, as much sense as it possibly can." She paused to read her daughter's face. "Are you ok?"

Juniper nodded, but quickly recanted with a shake of her head. "No. No, I'm not ok. There's something I have to tell you, mama. Something important." She couldn't hold back the truth about Azerial any longer as the words were threatening to break her jaw with their weight.

"And I, dear, have to tell *you* something," Penelope said with a smile. "*I* have a date tonight. With Nick."

Juniper felt the color drain from her face. "What did you say?"

"I know it's short notice and I know you aren't crazy about this, but I'm excited." Penelope plastered a hopeful smile across her face. "Be excited for me, please?"

Juniper turned away from her mother's smile and busied herself with the collection of the canned goods on the counter. She nodded as she stacked the cans neatly, and when she was certain that her voice wouldn't crack, she whispered her response. "That's great, mama. That's just great."

Penelope sighed, obviously relieved that Juniper hadn't unleashed upon her a tirade about her choice in companion. A second later she interrupted Juniper's thoughts. "*Now*, what was it that you wanted to tell me, sweetheart?"

"Oh... it's nothing, mama," Juniper lied. "It's not important."

Juniper avoided her mother as much as possible for the rest of the weekend. She just couldn't stand to see her smiling and didn't want to hear any of the details about her date with Mr. Halsey. She simply couldn't stomach the idea of the two of them together and she most certainly couldn't think about the possibility of her history teacher becoming a permanent fixture around the house.

As it was, in just two days, Juniper had already seen him twice. Both times she had ignored him and had offered him only a nod before she rushed off under the guise of studying.

She just didn't like having him around. He didn't *fit* into the life that she and her mother had worked so hard to make; he was an outsider and Juniper took personal offense to his presence.

She knew that she was being too harsh on him, but she just didn't care to correct her childish attitude. As she saw it, everything was falling apart thanks to him and she was helpless to stop it.

In addition to the general uncomfortable nature of her home life, she was also worried about final exams. Luckily though, her first day of testing on Monday passed quickly and she felt confident that she'd more than passed her English exam and had done reasonably well with Chemistry. Juniper only had two classes that day and was lucky enough to have had both exams in the morning. That meant that she was out of school by 11:30, and without realizing where it was she was going when she left the solitary brick schoolhouse on the hill, her feet took her directly to the farm house for an overdue apology.

She hesitated about one hundred feet away from the farm house and stopped to admire the impressive structure. In the daylight it looked almost normal. It was, without question, most definitely abandoned, but for all the house had been through in the past 16 years it looked almost livable. Anyone who might happen upon the house would never suspect that just inside of the third floor window lived an angel named Azerial.

Juniper finally traversed the remaining distance to the house and she entered quickly through the front door when she reached it. As was customary, she gave a quick, sweeping glance over her shoulder as an extra security measure to make certain she hadn't been followed.

She wasn't sure what Jason and Ben might do if they found out about Azerial, and she certainly wasn't eager to find out.

Hurriedly she slipped inside and hardly made a sound as she did so. Once in the living room, she was surprised to find Azerial descending the stairs.

He smiled when he saw her and didn't seem all that shocked to find her there. "I was wondering how long you'd stay mad," he said lightly. "I'm glad it wasn't all that long."

Juniper flushed. "Just so you know, I wasn't *mad*. I was just upset, and I want to apologize for rushing off like I did. It was childish of me and I'm sorry."

Azerial shook his head slowly. "Expressing your emotions isn't childish. However, I do wish you wouldn't have stayed away so long. I was worried, and on top of that, I missed you a great deal. I've become quite accustomed to having you around, you know."

"I didn't mean to worry you. I've just been studying a lot, and staying in my room to avoid the rain."

"Ah, yes, the weather has been nasty." He shrugged with one shoulder and adjusted the fall of his cloak. "Although, I must say, I've always enjoyed the rain. Everything old is new again, washed cleaned."

Juniper felt her lips slide into a smile. "I think I did well on my exams today."

"Ah, well! Of course you did!" Azerial tapped his temple with his thumb and chuckled. "After all, dear, you have good genes."

Juniper winked. "Yeah, that must be it."

"Oh! I have something for you. That's actually why I was on my way down here. To retrieve it. I think I mentioned it to you the other day, but then, well-" He shrugged and extended his hand towards Juniper. When she took it, he pulled her into a one armed hug. "Now don't get your hopes up. It's not much, but I think you'll like it nonetheless." He steered her around to the other side of the living room and stopped just in front of a large, dust-covered curio cabinet.

"I'm not sure I deserve a present after how I acted the other day."

"That's all in the past now," Azerial said cheerfully. "Let us never speak of it again! Now, where was I? Oh yes! You stay right here and keep your eyes closed until I say you can open them. Got it?"

Juniper did as Azerial requested, but couldn't hide her curious smile. "Just what are you up to?"

He chuckled airily. "Just keep those eyes closed, young lady. You'll see soon enough what I'm up to."

Juniper squeezed her eyes shut tightly, all the while listening anxiously to the sounds of Azerial's labored breathing; sounds which were accompanied by the sounds of a heavy *something* scooting slowly across the wood-plank floor.

A moment later when the noises ceased, Azerial's voice materialized in front of her. "Alright, Miss Juniper, you may open your eyes now."

Juniper peeled back her eyelids and brought her eyes in to focus on a framed photo that Azerial held proudly in front of him.

"Tada!" he exclaimed cheerfully. "This photo has been a great comfort to me, Juniper. However, in honor of your fast approaching sixteenth birthday, I thought you might like to have this for yourself."

Juniper's fingers reached out for the frame and Azerial relinquished it from his grip. "Is that us?" she asked incredulously. "I can't believe it! It *is* us!"

The color photo was worn by the touch of time and one of the corners was missing. Several thick scratches had come to rest over the bottom half of the image, but in spite of them, the subjects of the photo were in tact.

Azerial was pictured wearing his typical attire of black, concealing clothing. Next to him stood a young, fresh faced Penelope who cradled in her arms a small bundle that Juniper could only assume was herself.

"It's the only picture I ever had of you... but now that I have the real thing?" He shrugged and smiled softly. "Well, I no longer need this and thought you might enjoy having it."

Juniper looked at him, smiled and returned her gaze to the picture. "Do you know how many times I *prayed* to find something like this? I don't know what to say, I-" She broke off and shook her head in disbelief over the gift she'd been handed. "Thank you! Thank you for this! You've no idea what it means to me."

Azerial beamed at her favorable reaction. "I'd hoped you'd like it. And I hope that you'll accept it as an early birthday present. I'm afraid that I have nothing more to offer you."

"Oh, dad... I... do I like it? How can you even ask me that? I **love** it!" Juniper held the picture in her right hand and threw her left arm around her father's neck. "I hope you'll believe me when I say that this is the best birthday present I've ever been given."

"I just wish that I could do more." His words were wistful and filled with longing. Longing and a need to make up for his absence from her life in every possible way.

Juniper dismissed his self-doubt. "Finally getting the chance to know you is more than enough of a present. Really." She paused and chewed at her lip thoughtfully. "Well, I suppose that isn't *entirely* true. There is one other tiny, *little*, thing that I'd like to have."

"Dare I ask?" Azerial laughed. His laughter ceased when he saw his daughter's serious expression. "Well, come on with it. What do you want?"

Juniper swallowed, looked at the picture again and spoke

softly. "Well, this Saturday, as I'm sure you know, is my *actual* birthday. Mama and I are fixing a big dinner and she's buying a cake... It'll be just the two of us, as usual, but this year I was hoping that maybe I could have *both* my parents there."

Azerial stepped back and put both hands up as if to shield himself from her outrageous request. "No, I'm afraid I can't. I wish that I could, but I just... *can't*. We've already been through this, the reasons why I cannot honor your request. And after our argument the other day you'd still ask me this?! No. No, and you knew that would be my answer."

"Do you say no only because you lied to mama about going back to heaven?"

"I say no because she would never understand why I did what I did. *I* don't understand sometimes... so how on earth can I expect *her* to?" His eyes pled with hers for understanding. "Don't you see how hard it would be for us both? But especially for her... to know that all of these years I was right here? No more than a stone's throw from her own back door?"

"I'm not saying that what you did was right, but I understand *why* you did it!" She sighed as her frustration grew within her. "Believe me, dad, I know it was hard for you both, it had to have been! But I don't blame you for lying to her, and I don't believe she will either."

Sadly, slowly, he shook his head. "I wish I had as much faith in your mother's forgiveness as you seem to have."

"I *have* known her longer. And well, actually-" Juniper shook her head and discontinued her recant of her mother's oh-so-recent confessions. "Forget it," she said. "It's not important."

"No. Tell me. What were you going to say?" He touched her forearm to spur her onwards when her hesitation lingered on. "What is it, Juniper? Talk to me."

"Well, I'm sure you remember Mr. Halsey, right? And you remember how I tried to scare him away from mama?" She gulped and at her waist her hands knotted "It seems my little plan backfired. Mama found out what I did and now she's-she's sorta dating him."

Azerial's face fell. "What?"

"She's dating him. My *history* teacher! And after what she said..." Juniper looked away, but peeked at Azerial to make sure he had taken her well-placed bait.

"What did she say?" he asked. Concern crept steadily into his throat and took up residence there. "Juniper? Talk to me! What did your mother say?"

"She said that I was right," Juniper said quietly. "She said that I was right when I accused her of still loving you."

Azerial took careful note of her words. He seemed to be more taken aback by them than Juniper had assumed her would be. "She said that?" he asked finally. "She really said that she still loves me?"

Juniper nodded.

Azerial said nothing. He turned away from Juniper's eyes and words and faced the window instead. Several drawn out moments passed before Azerial dared to speak. "You *really* think she would understand?" he asked. There was hope in his voice, a hope that had previously been buried beneath a mound of unfortunately placed dirt.

Juniper nodded again. "As I see it, it's now or never. If you wait any longer it could be too late."

Azerial sighed and his chin lowered to his chest. "I don't know how I would even begin to explain myself..."

"The most difficult of speeches begins with one word," Juniper interrupted. She approached Azerial slowly and when she reached him she placed her palm flat against his back. "But wouldn't you rather know? One way or the other?"

He said nothing.

After a too-long pause, Juniper broached the subject again and threw her earlier question back into the ring. "So will you come to my birthday dinner? On Saturday night?"

Azerial hesitated in his answer. "I don't know, Juniper. I fear being seen by people other than you and your mother. There's danger out there, danger too great to comprehend. I'm afraid of what might happen if I'm spotted."

"That isn't all you fear," Juniper said softly. "Look, dad... I may not be able to read thoughts like you can, but anyone could hear it, that sound in your voice. It's unmistakable."

He turned back to her briefly. "I can't believe that I'm considering this for even a second."

"And *I* can't believe you're being so stubborn," she countered.

"Now you know where you get it," he retorted. He turned away once again as if he was attempting to conceal his soul from her prying eyes. "I do still love your mother, Juniper. As much as I would love to see her again, it's safer to wonder what might have been rather than face what is."

"So that's it, then?" Juniper asked. "You're just going to be a coward?"

"I know that you don't really think of me as a coward," Azerial said. "Your harsh words are meant to goad me. I assure you they won't."

Juniper sighed. "Then if words won't work, tell me what will?"

"Nothing."

"Nothing?" Juniper shook her head, unable to accept his answer. "You told me, **you** *told me*, that we all have choices, that we all have a desired path. How is it that you're so certain that setting things right with mama is outside of your path?"

Azerial said nothing and Juniper took that as her chance to continue weakening his defenses.

"Are you really willing to let this chance pass you by? Because if you are, if you're ok with living here in this house cut off from everyone, then I won't press you about this again. But if you aren't happy, if you aren't willing to ignore this opportunity to make things right, then do this. Because there's always a choice, *dad*."

Azerial drew his gaze from the shadows and met Juniper's eyes. "What time should I be ready?" he asked.

"Eight o'clock." Her heartbeat doubled and she found it increasingly difficult to keep a lid on her surprise and excitement.

"You'll help me clean up? Get me some new clothes and trim my hair?" He looked down at his tattered cloak and appeared for the first time to be self-conscious about his attire. "I can't very well see her again looking like this, now can I?"

Juniper nodded vigorously with wide, tear-brimmed eyes. "Whatever you need, I'll get it."

"Alright, I'll do it. I'll be there." He sighed and ran a hand through his hair. "I can't believe I'm agreeing to this. I must be out of my mind."

"It's going to be ok, you'll see! She's going to be absolutely thrilled to see you again."

Azerial drew in a deep breath. "There's just one condition. You'll have to tell her that I'm coming. Have you thought about that?"

"I have," said Juniper.

"And?"

She shrugged. "I haven't decided exactly what to say just yet, but I will, and soon. As I see it, that's the easy part, that's the part *you* don't have to worry about. So don't give it another thought, ok? Just focus on what *you're* going to say."

"I've been practicing that speech for years," he said quietly. "I believe that I have it memorized by now, Juniper."

Chapter Nine
Rope Burn

That Wednesday afternoon, with just 3 days before her birthday and the much-anticipated reunion dinner, Juniper went to the farm house carrying with her an oversized bag of toiletries and clothes. The clothes she had bought the previous day at the Good Will store in town. She had spent nearly all of the birthday money she had received from her Great Aunt Trudy in Grand Rapids on the items, but felt it was definitely worth it. After all, Azerial had to make a good impression. A lot was riding on the impending dinner, and even though her mother didn't know it yet, life as they knew it was about to completely and irrevocably change.

Juniper had guessed at the proper sizes of the clothing and had finally decided upon a simple pair of brown slacks, a beige button-down shirt and a dark blue, lightly pinstriped tie. Also in her possession she carried shaving cream, a razor and a pair of scissors. All of the things Azerial had requested to ready himself for the big night.

Juniper thought about the modifications she would have to make to the shirt to accommodate Azerial's wings as she made the familiar trek to the farm house and decided that the best method would likely be to cut two slits up the back of the shirt. So wrapped up in her thoughts she was, that she didn't notice the screen door of the farm house and the fact that it was hanging wide open until she was standing on the rickety front porch.

The sight was most definitely uncommon and it caused Juniper's heart to skip in her chest and jump to her throat. Still, she entered the house and clutched the bag closer to her chest in hopes of calming her excited heart under the pressure of its weight.

"Azerial? I've brought some of the things you asked for... clean clothes, a shaving razor..." Her words echoed through the empty house and traveled up the length of the tree trunk to the attic. "Hello? Are you here?"

Juniper set the grocery bag of belongings on the wooden side table and climbed the stairs slowly to the attic. Along the way she listened for any unusual sounds, but heard nothing that further raised her awareness. When Azerial's third floor bedroom door finally came into sight, it was closed tightly per usual. Juniper raised her fist to knock when her feet finally found pause before it.

"Are you in there? It's me..." She knocked softly the first time, paused, then rapped again with more force. "Hello? I brought you the things you asked for. I thought we might see about getting you cleaned up a bit."

Juniper heard a muffled voice inside the room, then saw the shadow of feet move past the door. She stepped back, and a frown sprouted to her lips. "Is everything ok? If this is a bad time, I could come back after dinner."

A moment later, the door swung inwards as a response to her words. Juniper, taken aback by the abruptness of the movement, stumbled backwards over the uneven, wooden floor.

"We were beginning to worry about you, Junie." Ben stepped forward from the shadows of the room and grabbed her by the arm. Juniper let out a surprised yelp as he jerked her into Azerial's bedroom. The force of his action nearly pulled her off of her feet entirely.

"What's going on?" Juniper asked. She tried to hold back the panic that was threatening to pour into her voice; she felt unsuccessful, and when Jason appeared at Ben's side, she knew she was destined to fail at its containment. "What's are you *doing* here?"

"The question is, Junie, what are *you* doing here? If you'll remember, I think we evicted you." Jason elbowed a third, younger boy in the ribs and laughed as if he'd suddenly remembered some crucial fact. "Oh, *that's* right! You're here to see your imaginary friend."

"He's not imaginary!" Juniper exclaimed as her emotions got the better of her. "He's very much real and you'll find that out when he gets here."

"Even better!" Ben said with a hearty laugh. "I personally can't *wait* to meet this mystery person! I'm curious to know more about this homeless bum you've grown so attached to."

Jason rubbed his hands together and sneered at Juniper's defiance. "We've been here for hours and we haven't seen anyone."

Juniper jerked her arm to free herself from Ben's grasp, but he didn't relent. Juniper stomped her feet in frustration. "Damnit, Ben! *Let me **go**!*"

"Not a chance of that happening, I'm afraid. Not until we get some answers." Ben looked at the other boys and nodded in their direction. "Come on, would ya? Give me a hand here. She's stronger than she looks." Ben pulled Juniper closer to his body and held both of her arms at the wrists. "We're going to have a little fun today, Junie. Hope you don't have any pressing plans."

Jason came around behind her and grabbed her at the waist. "Just hold still, Junie. This'll hurt a lot less if you don't struggle."

Juniper felt her feet lose touch with the ground as the boys picked her up; her feet kicked out and downwards as they searched desperately for the familiarity of the sturdy, wood planks. "What are you *doing*? Let go of me!"

"Get the rope!" Ben yelled to the youngest boy, the one that Juniper didn't recognize and couldn't name. She did know, however, that he was the same boy that had accompanied Ben and Jason in their last assault, and he appeared to be at least a year younger than they were, than she was.

Ben tossed Juniper onto the bed face down and the rusty box spring spoke out in protest. "This doesn't have to hurt, Junie. Just co-operate with us and everything, *everyone*, will be just fine."

She felt her arms being twisted behind her back and a moment later she felt the itch of the rope as they secured her wrists. When they were satisfied with the knots at her arms, they moved on to bind her ankles.

"Get her up," Ben commanded. He grabbed her by the shoulders while Jason moved to catch her at the knees.

"Are you guys completely *crazy*? Why are you doing this? You've lost your minds!" Juniper wiggled her fingers and feet wildly as she desperately tried to squirm her way out of the ropes. She realized soon enough that her actions were fruitless and stopped her struggle in hopes of preserving her strength. They would, she knew, make a mistake in judgment, and she'd have to be ready to capitalize upon it.

"Stop *fucking* moving!" Ben bellowed. He grabbed her head and placed one palm on her forehead and the other on the back of her neck. "I'm not going to tell you this again, Junie. Just play along and you'll get out of this alive."

Jason moved quickly and jumped onto the nightstand. He pulled a third piece of rope down from the thick tree branch that hung out over the room some nine feet above their heads. He made certain Juniper saw it before he released it and let it swing gently over the floor. The rope had been fashioned into a noose.

"Fucking come on with it," Ben barked. "She's a fighter, this one!" He and the nameless third boy lifted Juniper onto the nightstand next to Jason and held her firmly at the waist and knees.

Jason, with his hands shaking like mad, lowered the

noose to Juniper's forehead. Their eyes met briefly and within his pupils Juniper caught a glimpse of her own frightened reflection. Jason looked away from her as quickly as he could manage and Juniper could sense in him a tiny kernel of regret and fear. Ben, on the other hand, seemed to lack even the smallest shred of decency and in illustration of that he tightened his grip on her mid-section. Jason continued his forward movement and in the flip of his wrist he released his grip on the rope. It fell to rest at Juniper's shoulders and the weight of it seemed heavier than anything she could remember having felt.

Juniper felt the tightening of the noose around her throat as Jason pulled the coiled knot to the base of her skull. Juniper felt her airway begin to constrict with trapped words and breath as the boy struggled to pull the rope even tighter to the back of her neck.

Jason abandoned Azerial's night stand in favor of the floor when he was satisfied with his work. Juniper stood tall and firm in her shoes against the slight slack in the rope that brushed her shoulder. Standing there, free of their hands, she worked quickly to get a grip on the situation at hand.

"You might as well get comfortable, Junie." Ben moved around in front of the night stand and sneered up at her with a look of twisted satisfaction. "You're going to be up there until you tell us what we want to know. If you talk, then we'll let you down. However, if you *don't*, we'll kick this night stand right out from under your feet," he threatened. A sneer spread across his wide, slightly dirty face. "You know what'll happen after that, right?" He put his hands around his throat and stuck out his tongue to illustrate.

Juniper closed her eyes at the sight of him. *This can't be happening. This has to be a nightmare! It's just a sick, twisted, nightmare and any second I'm going to wake up safe in my own bed.*

"The choice is yours, Junie," Ben said. His voice pulled Juniper away from her delusion of safety and placed her feet back into the proverbial fire of reality. "You can either tell us what we want to know, or you can have your neck snapped," Ben continued.

She opened her eyes. "What exactly do you want to know?" Her words were slow and cautious as they passed through her narrowed throat. "I don't know what you could possibly want from me."

"We want to know what you are." Ben stood directly in front of her with his eyes directed up at her face.

"Are you a witch?" Jason asked accusingly. "Is that why you spend all of your time out here alone? Are you casting spells and riding brooms or something?"

Ben chimed in where Jason left off. "You know what happens to witches, don't you?"

"Yeah, do *you?*" Juniper sneered. She hoped that they'd soon tire of their game and remove the noose from her neck. Still, Juniper's heart was thumping wildly inside of her chest. She knew the longer she kept them talking, the longer they'd keep their feet from the legs of the night stand.

At that moment, when the silence in the room was at its heaviest, a cold strike of wind sailed up through the hole in the floor and caught Juniper hard on the back. She shivered and shook and the night stand beneath her feet creaked under her shifting weight.

On the air, a thought possessed her and Azerial's words came back to whisper in her ear.

"....you have to be careful, Juniper. If your emotions get the better of you, dark emotions... anger, fear, greed... you might find yourself tempted..."

Ben spoke again. His words were quick to pierce the water of her thoughts like a steadily skipping stone. "So how *did* you do it? Was it some sort of magic? If it wasn't witchcraft, it was something like it."

"How did I do *what?*" The bitterness in Juniper's voice

had given way to concern over her precarious situation. "I don't know what you're talking about!"

"We saw you! We fucking *saw* you!" Jason extended one long and slightly crooked finger in her direction, then wagged it to and fro to emphasize his point. "With our own eyes!"

"We saw that mean old dog attack the puppy," the third boy said softly. He stepped forward and stopped when he was next to Jason's slightly shaking shoulders. "We watched from behind the trees and we all knew it. We *knew* that puppy was going to die. We saw it collapse on the front porch of this house."

"Then *you* showed up." Jason still held his finger in a point at Juniper. "Suddenly that mutt was running around like nothing ever happened."

The overall tone of the room darkened. The humid, heavy air became choking in its intensity.

Ben moved closer and stopped only when he was inches from the night stand. He brought his left foot out in front of him and rested it on the front, right leg. "I'll ask you again, Juniper. What are you? And how did you save that dog?"

Juniper felt the stand shift slightly from the pressure of Ben's foot and her panic became apparent. "Jesu- Just let me **down**! Let me down and I'll tell you everything, I promise."

"And if we *don't* let you down?" Jason asked, his arms crossed over his chest.

Juniper swallowed thickly and her thoughts returned again to her conversation with Azerial. Thoughts that Juniper knew were dangerous even to entertain.

But really… what could it hurt? she asked herself silently. *I mean, so what if I was to weaken them a bit? I don't want to kill them, I just want to give myself a bit of an advantage seeing as I'm currently at quite a great one. Now if only I can turn just a little so that my hands-*

Juniper closed her eyes and prayed to silence her own

thoughts. "Please! *Please*, let me down."

"We can't trust you," Jason said firmly. "How can we trust you when we don't know what you *are?*"

Juniper tried to swallow again, but her fear had grown like cotton to cover her gums and teeth. It was quickly coating her tongue, but still she managed to choke out a cry. "I- I'm just a girl!"

Ben and Jason exchanged glances, as if for the first time realizing that she might be just that. The third boy interjected himself into their thoughts and then disrupted them with his tiny, fragile voice.

"I don't want to do this any more," he whined. "I think you'd better let her down. I don't wanna get in trouble!"

"We're not letting her go until she tells us the **truth**," Ben snapped. He didn't even afford the boy a sideways glance; his eyes were locked with Juniper's.

"I told you the truth, I did!" Juniper sobbed. The noise caught in her throat and spilled back down into her stomach where it rumbled uneasily. "I'm just a girl! An average, *ordinary* girl."

"Average girls can't heal dying dogs," Jason said.

"Average girls don't spend all of their time in a run-down old house in the woods all alone. Not unless they're up to something," Ben added.

The third boy cast his eyes downward and repeated his earlier opposition. "I want to go *home.*"

"We'll all go home," Jason began, his words frustrated, "safe and sound as soon as *Juniper* tells us how she did what she did."

Ben turned his attention back to the frightened girl. "So come on, quit fucking around and tell us."

Juniper's eyelids closed to shield herself from his cold stare. She remained silent.

"Are we to take this silence as your decision?" Ben asked.

"I've decided nothing.   There's just nothing to tell," Juniper said softly.

"You're a liar," Jason sneered. He moved forward and shoved Ben aside in his anger. His eyes were wide, engraved with a panicked frenzy. "You're not human... you're not *normal*. All of the rumors are true about you. You're not like us."

"If you aren't a witch, then you're something else... Are you an alien?" Ben asked. "Or maybe a demon?"

Jason continued where Ben's accusations left off. "You can't be a ghost." He poked her hard on the right thigh with his bony finger. "You seem real enough to me."

Juniper whimpered as the night stand creaked. "Please... *let me down...*" The ropes at her wrists had begun to dig into her flesh with their itchy hotness; it felt like she'd been left out in the sun to bake. "If all you wanted to do was scare me, then you've succeeded, ok? Good job."

"You should be scared!" Jason said loudly. "I'm *glad* you're scared! Because now that we know about you, we'll be watching you. Waiting for you to work your voodoo again... And when we have proof of what you are, and we *will* get proof, we'll out you to the entire town."

"And what then?" Juniper asked.   "I'm run out of here? I'm killed by an angry mob of townspeople with pitchforks and flaming torches like I'm some sort of medieval monster?"

Again, wind rushed up the base of the tree and temporarily relieved the heavy heat of the attic room. With it, the air and its coolness ushered in a dark *something* that Juniper watched as it arced away from the oak and over the room. It, whatever it was, hung over their bodies unnoticed by all eyes but hers. It carried with it a sense of foreboding; a creeping, sentient, sensation that fell to materialize in the words of the nameless, younger boy.

As the shadow hit his flesh it seemed almost to be absorbed by his pores. His eyes temporarily lost their blue.

They flashed black and then white before they returned to their normal hue. "You won't leave this town," he said softly. By the look in his once-again blue eyes, Juniper could tell that the words he'd spoken had frightened him. His mouth extended, his eyes widened and his hands reached up to find the sides of his face. It was almost as if he was trying to prove to himself that the movement of his lips had been real and not imagined.

Ben and Jason's eyes joined Juniper's as they fell to rest upon him. They said nothing and Juniper knew it was because they knew not what to do.

The younger boy spoke again, his voice quieter still. "None of us will make it out alive if we don't stop this."

"What are you *talking* about?" Ben's voice took on a subtle shake beneath its base as it finally reappeared from the troubled void of his silent throat.

The boy looked up suddenly. A shadow moved across his face and then disappeared. Juniper watched it dissolve into the wall. "I want to go home," the boy whined. "*Now.*"

"Shut up, wait... what did you just say?" Jason asked.

"I *said,* I want to go-"

"*Before* that," Ben said, obviously agitated. "What did you say *before* that?"

The boy's cheeks puffed out and his lower lip began to tremble. "You guys, I'm not having fun any more."

"Shut up! And don't cry!" Ben warned.

The boy burst into tears on the spot and ran from the room. Ben moved to chase him, but Jason grabbed his arm.

"Let him go," Jason instructed.

"What if he tells-"

"He won't," Jason said firmly. "He won't. He's just a kid, he knows if he mentions this to anyone you'll beat the shit out of him."

Ben nodded, then turned his full attention back to Juniper, not missing a beat. He kicked the leg of the nightstand, whether by accident or on purpose, from her vantage point, Juniper couldn't tell.

The stand shook under her feet and she cried out. "For the love of God, please let me down!"

"Tell us what you did!" Ben screamed back at her; he kicked the leg of the night stand again and sent it another inch closer to the edge of the gaping hole.

"I just put my hand on his chest!" she screamed. "I was comforting him... checking his wounds!" She licked at her lips furiously, but no dampness was provided them. "The next thing I knew he jumped up! I don't know what-" She hiccupped. "-happened."

Jason put his hand on Ben's shoulder. "Hey, whoa! Chill out, man. Ok? We agreed we were just going to scare her a bit."

Ben shook his head; his dirty blonde locks bounced over his forehead. "I don't care about that! I know she's not telling us the truth! I refuse to let her lie any more."

Juniper wiggled the tips of her fingers; they were numb and throbbing from the tightness of the ropes. She kept her lips shut as behind her eyes her mind whirred with a million fragmented thoughts.

"Well then, what are we going to do? Wait here all night until she cracks?" Jason asked. "Because let's face it, man. That might never happen. I mean, I know you don't want to consider it, but maybe she's telling us the truth."

Ben shook his head and wrinkled his slightly crooked, slightly pointed noise. "No, no... she isn't. And if we have to stay here all night? Then so be it. If that's what it takes, I'm more than willing to wait it out." He paused and smiled up at Juniper's docile form. It was a wicked, twisted grin that he produced; a grin that made Juniper's blood run cold. "I suppose we *could* just leave her here alone to think about what she's done."

"What?" Jason asked. His eyes widened with what Juniper perceived to be alarm.

"You heard me." Ben's smile brightened. "We'll leave her here for a few hours, by herself. We'll come back after supper and see if she's more willing to talk to us then, you know, after she's weighed her options."

"No, please... You can't do that..." Juniper's voice was all but lost and the temptation to harm them had once again risen up inside of her like an angry, feral, beast. She quickly forced it away and drowned it at the bottom of her anxious, fluttering stomach. She knew without a doubt that it would resurface; realized that each time it did so, it was harder to resist.

Ben, with one swift and surprising movement, jumped onto the surface of the night stand and pushed his face to within inches of Juniper's. The night stand creaked from their combined weight, but to Juniper's relief, it didn't move closer to the hole.

Ben said nothing for a moment and chose only to observe her face with his deep, green eyes. It was almost as though he was memorizing every line, every pore on her face in an attempt to crawl within her skin. When finally he spoke, his words were filled with a cold discomfort that chilled Juniper to the bone.

"Let's see if your *magic* can get you out of this, what do you think of that? Or maybe, just maybe this mysterious friend of yours will sweep in and save the day." Ben chuckled. "That is of course if he even *exists*. Maybe you're just crazy. Maybe you spend all of your time out here talking to yourself."

Juniper's blood froze in her veins; her heart nearly stopped soon after. "You can't do this to me. I've never done anything to you to deserve this."

Ben sneered at her remark with obvious disdain. "I'm afraid I don't have a choice, Junie. You've not left me with one." He pulled back, but his eyes remained locked with hers.

"Come on Jason, let's get out of here."

Jason moved slowly towards the door without so much as a word escaping his lips.

"Hang tight, Junie. We'll be back." Ben hopped down off of the night stand and shoved Jason towards the door. Over his shoulder, he called back at her. "Do be careful, Junie. Your life is in *your* hands now."

"You can't do this!" Juniper cried. "Jason! Jason, you know me! You can't let him do this! I know you don't want to be part of this! There's some decency left in you, I know it!"

Jason looked back, and for a second, Juniper found a brief glimmer of regret in his eyes. He didn't speak and Ben's anxious arms allowed him no choice of his own. Their noisy, paired footsteps left the room and then the hallway and Juniper listened with growing dread as their steps echoed loudly on the staircase as they descended to the first floor.

"Please! You guys!" Juniper's voice cracked and then under her breath, new words formed. "Where are you, dad? Where *are* you?"

Time passed in spurts, both quick and slow. Juniper's knees had grown weak from standing; both her neck and her wrists were raw from the constant nag of the ropes, as her wounds were given no reprieve from the pressure to heal.

Outside the window, Juniper watched as the sky faded from light into dark; the animals were on the prowl throughout the forest and in the distance a coyote cried out to the stoic moon.

Inside the lonely darkness of the house, all was still. Juniper's words and cries had dried out upon her tongue, and with no one and nothing to cry out to, they found no reason to make the journey from her throat to her cracked lips.

Finally, some hours later, a voice in the distance raised her head. She drifted in and out of consciousness and for a moment in the persistence of silence, Juniper imagined that she had mistakenly heard the voice below. But again the noise came, and was followed soon by the approaching echo of footsteps. Juniper pulled her chin up from her chest and turned it towards the open doorway, to the hallway just beyond.

Juniper almost cried out for help, but her fear got the better of her. What if it was Jason and Ben? What if it was a transient or a psychopath; someone who still would bring harm to her bones?

She bit her lip without realizing it and within seconds she tasted blood, metallic and warm. She wiggled her toes inside of her shoes and wished the ropes around her ankles would disappear and take with them the others that bound her tight to her current position. She wasn't sure how much longer she could stand up against her full body exhaustion.

A short time later, a figure moved into the doorway. Juniper's eyes fought to focus, but the darkness of the room, coupled with her exhaustion, made it nearly impossible to make out the shadowy features of the approaching figure. The impressive stranger stepped forward and finally her lips released a sob. "Who's there?"

"Juniper?" It was Azerial. He moved quickly into the room and over to the table that preserved her life. "Junie! Oh my- What's going on? Who's done this to you?"

Too weak and parched to speak, Juniper said nothing. When Azerial spotted the noose around her neck he worked quickly to loosen the knot. A moment later he raised the rope from around her head and let it swing freely into the dark air around them.

When she was completely freed of her tether, Juniper collapsed into Azerial's waiting arms. Instantly, the pressure of the tightly coiled rope abandoned the tenderness of her throat and allowed her the deep breath she had longed to inhale. Her legs banged against the surface of the night stand as Azerial pulled her down. Shortly thereafter they hit the floor beneath her.

"Dad," Juniper gasped. "It-"

"Shh," Azerial said softly. "It's alright now. Don't talk just yet." He unknotted the ropes at her wrists and ankles and tossed them aside. His hands were warm and gentle and within his grasp Juniper felt safe.

Suddenly, the emotion overwhelmed her and the tears came without pause.

Azerial held her tightly in his arms and released her shaking shoulders long enough to push the hood back from his face. "Junie... Junie, look at me! What's happened? What's going on here?"

"Where-" Her words fragmented in the back of her mouth and she tried a second time to piece them together. "Where were you?" she croaked. "I've been here all day... evening... I was worried. Scared."

"Oh, sweetheart. I'm so sorry, so sorry. I was- I was at the creek. I was fishing, cleaning myself up a bit..." He held her shoulders in his hands and forced her to look up. "Tell me what happened here today."

"It was Ben... Ben and Jason. They saw me-" she whispered. "They saw me heal Sam and when I got here today they were already here waiting for me. They accused me of being a witch."

"They hung you up there like that and left you?" Azerial asked incredulously.

Juniper nodded weakly. Her head was nearly too heavy for her severely weakened neck to support its weight. "They said they'd come back, but that was hours ago."

Azerial said nothing, but Juniper could sense his boiling anger. He let go of Juniper's shoulders and she wilted into the ground like a flower deprived of water.

"Where might I find these boys?" Azerial asked.

Juniper raised her hands to investigate her neck. "Why? What are you going to do?"

Azerial paced the length of the room in silence. His lips moved, yet provided no sound. Finally, he stopped in mid stride and turned back to address her directly. "I don't know yet, but I do know that I have to do *something*."

"What can you do? You can't out yourself to take care of a couple of high school punks!"

"And I can't continue to let them torture you like this!" His eyes were filled with concern, with rage and confusion. "I can't do nothing and let them kill you! You're too important! Not just to me and your mother, but to the world."

Juniper pulled herself from the ground into a sitting position. Her head was still spinning as her mind fought to return to its senses. "But you can't harm them. It's not who you are."

"Then what am I supposed to do?" His voice was full of desperation, a feeling Juniper assumed he was no stranger to.

"You do nothing," Juniper whispered. "You do nothing and you let me handle this in my own way, in my own time."

"Junie, I- I don't know that I can do that." Azerial's eyes were damp, his voice labored. "They mean you such harm, and now that they know... or *think* they know...? They're dangerous to us both."

Juniper nodded her agreement. "I know that, dad, believe me I do... but you can't drag them from their houses and beat them senseless! You have to know what would happen to you! And I promise you, it would be a million times worse than anything that could possibly happen to me."

He sighed and in doing so he admitted without words that he knew she was right and that he was, in fact, helpless.

"Have a little faith, dad," Juniper said. "I know you have

plenty tucked away beneath those wings somewhere. Just have some in me." Juniper again touched the skin around her neck; she winced, and her fingers recoiled quickly at the feel of the sting. Azerial watched her from the opposing side of the room.

"I do have faith in you, but in those boys? I must admit that I've nothing in my heart for them but revulsion." He stopped pacing and focused on her with narrowed, serious eyes. "And the next time they pull a stunt like this? I promise nothing."

"They won't try anything like this again," Juniper said softly. "When they see me at school tomorrow walking around like nothing happened-"

Azerial raised an eyebrow and quickly interrupted. "You think they'll find you less fascinating when they find that you're unwounded?"

Juniper shrugged and realized that her comment had been at least partially silly. "I guess not, but-" She pushed one frustrated hand to her forehead and held it there as though its support were needed to keep her brain from falling out of the top of her head. "I can't exactly tell myself that behind every closed door, around every corner, they're going to be waiting for me. Can I?"

"Of course not," Azerial said firmly. "That would be no way to live."

"Then I just have to tell myself that everything is going to be ok. That they'll be frightened of me - that maybe they'll cross to the other side of the hall when they see me coming." Juniper smiled to prove her strength of character to Azerial. "I'm not afraid of them, not any more. That means *you* shouldn't be either."

"I'm more afraid *for* them," he said sharply. He turned away and nodded as he did so. He pushed up the sleeves of his cloak from his forearms to just past his elbows. "If they come back here tonight, or *ever* again, I'll make absolute certain that they regret that decision."

Juniper's eyed widened involuntarily. "You won't kill-"

He waved his hand quickly and dismissively to halt her. "No, no, of course not, never! However, there are a lot of things one can do just short of murder to convince someone that their presence isn't wanted."

Juniper relaxed and looked down at her lap. The shadows had collected in the corners of the room and she sought to avoid them; they almost seemed alive and their presence reminded Juniper of an earlier scene. She suddenly recalled the comments of the third boy and her head was pulled sharply up. "Dad?"

"Yeah, Junie."

"The Nexxus is blocked, isn't it?" she asked softly. "I mean, the tree keeps it *completely* blocked, right?"

He nodded. "Yes. Why do you ask?" He turned back to face her, a strange and almost curious look on his face.

"Well, I- *earlier,* when Ben and Jason were here, they had a third boy with them. The same one who came when Ben almost-" Juniper drew in a sharp breath and hoped that it spoke the words she could not. "At one point, the boy got a strange look on his face. It sort of seemed like he was being controlled by someone, some*thing* else. He said that none of us would make it out alive. That we would- that we'd all *die* here."

Azerial seemed to ponder her words with much thought, and when Juniper thought he was going to speak he only moved his hand up to tap nervously at the side of his mouth. "The other night, when you dug up the box-"

"You don't think I opened a hole to the Nexxus, do you?" Juniper's hand flew up to cover her mouth. "Is that what happened? Did the shadows possess him?"

"Well, I can't say for certain, but-" Azerial looked up suddenly. "Did the boy look as though he knew what it was he was saying?"

"No, that's just the thing!" Juniper exclaimed. "When he was saying it, his eyes were wide. Like he was shocked that his lips were moving..."

"And when he returned to normal?" Azerial asked.

"Ben and Jason questioned him about what he said, but he didn't remember, or at least he claimed not to."

"I see." Azerial drummed his fingertips against his chin. "In the morning I'll check the perimeter of the tree, see if I can find anything that might lead me to believe that this is what happened." He paused and re-aligned his thoughts. "But for tonight, it can wait. If they did possess the boy-"

"Do you think that's what happened to Ben too? I mean... when he was- when he was *over* me, I saw a look in his eyes. It was almost as though he was inside himself, unable to stop what he was doing."

"It's possible, however I don't want to jump to conclusions, especially not at this hour when we're both weary. But rest assured that I will address these concerns, as they're troubling not only for you, but me as well."

Juniper nodded and said nothing further on the subject. She sensed that Azerial was somewhat eager to change the subject, and a moment later her assumption proved to be correct.

Azerial spoke suddenly and seemingly realized something important that he'd managed to overlook in the tense moments immediately following her rescue. "You didn't use your powers tonight." It wasn't a question, but a statement.

She shook her head. "No. But don't think the temptation wasn't there. It was. Just as you said it would be."

"I'm proud of you," he said quickly. "Not that I thought for a second that you would give in."

"I told you I was one of the good guys, I meant that."

He smiled wide and broke the tense mood of the room. "And you wonder how it is that you remind me so much of your mother."

Juniper blushed. "How do you mean?"

He chuckled and Juniper wondered what conjured memory had elicited such a sweet and lilting sound. "She was always very strong, very willful. I see a lot of her in you."

"Speaking of mama..." Juniper's throat was aching as her words scratched past it. "She's bound to be worried about me."

"I'll escort you home in a moment, but before I do that you need to rest for a bit longer." Azerial went to her and knelt on the floor at her side. "Are you feeling any better yet?"

She nodded past the dizziness. "A bit."

"You're lying," he said with a knowing smile. "You can't hide from me."

Juniper twisted her mouth into a teasing, dissatisfied mess. "I really hate when you read my mind."

He lips twitched into a wider smile. "I'm sorry. I try not to, but it's almost impossible to stop myself. Your thoughts are strong. Our *bond* is strong."

Juniper held her hands out to examine her wrists. "So when exactly will this healing start happening? I can't let mama see this."

"You've been through a lot." He reached for her hand and massaged her palm with his thick, coarse fingers. "Give your body and mind time to find each other again. They will pull themselves in line and you'll be fine by morning."

"But I have to see mama tonight!" Juniper whined. "She'll want to talk... She'll ask me where I've been! Not to mention the fact that she'll *definitely* scold me for not letting Sam out after school."

"Shh..." Azerial pushed a finger to her lips. "This isn't how one recovers from trauma."

"I know, but I can only imagine what mama would do if she found out what happened here tonight."

"Ben and Jason would be on their way to jail, as they

should be," said Azerial.

"Or mama would be," Juniper said quietly, her eyes again focused upon her wrists.

Azerial chuckled softly. "That's also a likely outcome." He leaned in and kissed her forehead. "Do you want me to heal you? I will, you know. All you have to do is ask."

Juniper reached out for him and squeezed his hand when she found it with her fingers. "I don't want you to use your gift. I'm not going to die."

"That isn't the point," Azerial whispered. He gently wrapped his fingers around her wrists and closed his eyes. "You don't want your mother to see your pain, and that I understand."

A slow warming sensation crept from his fingertips to her skin and coated her wrists in a radiant white light. When he released her, her flesh had been re-stitched into a perfect tapestry of pores and unbroken veins.

"So that's what it feels like?" she asked. A smile touched her lips as her fingers explored Azerial's handy work. "You did a good job. I'm impressed!"

"I have had many years of practice," Azerial murmured. His left hand moved to her neck and his fingertips found the worst of her wound. "In time, you will be able to heal others as quickly as I've healed you." He moved his hand to the side of her face when the light dissipated. "The old adage proves true, Juniper. Practice does indeed make perfect."

Juniper shook her head gently from side to side in amazement of Azerial's healing touch. Only then did the true gravity of her gift assail her.

"Thank you," she whispered. "You didn't have to do that."

"I *wanted* to do that," Azerial said. "I've been absent from your life for nearly sixteen years. There isn't much I can do to make up for that, but what I *can* do is be here for you now when you need me. Tonight, you needed me."

Juniper smiled and looked up to meet his eyes. "Ya know, I suddenly don't care about aliens."

"What?" Azerial was puzzled by her abrupt subject change and expressed as much through the knitting of his thick, black brows.

Juniper noticed his confusion and launched quickly into her explanation. "When I was younger, about ten or so, I saw something hovering over the tree line one night. It was a strange object… silver and smooth and perfectly elliptical as far as I could tell. You know, a *typical* UFO. I must have watched it for about five minutes before it finally zoomed off into the distance. From that point on, I wondered about it. What it was, where it was from, if we were alone in the universe… Now, suddenly, it's no longer important. Now that I'm possibly the only one of *my kind*, I feel a greater need to seek out others like me… to find a purpose? To find *some*thing, I'm not sure *what* just yet, but *something.*"

Azerial nodded his understanding. "I'll let you in on a secret." He lowered his voice to a whisper and leaned in closer to find her ear. "There *is* life in other places. Fantastic creatures, big *and* small. After all, God is a wonderfully creative artist with boundless imagination and power! It has always puzzled me that humans were so arrogant as to think they were unique."

"Will we ever know this? As a planet?"

Azerial shrugged. "Maybe. But only if a certain level of enlightenment is reached by the general populace."

Juniper let his words sink in and they muddied her mind with their presence. She pushed them aside until her slate was clean and then returned to a previous page. "So do you think there are other Nephilim out there somewhere?"

Azerial shook his head. "I'm sure I don't know the answer to that." He fiddled with the sleeve of his cloak until he had straightened it flat against his arm; he seemed ever-so-slightly uncomfortable. "I no longer have certain security clearances, you see, but fallen angels aren't as rare as one might think. It happens from time to time, not often, mind you, but the chance that there are others like you on this planet? Well, I'd say it's a good one. In fact, I know of an angel who left the Heavens only a few years before I did. Of course what he's done with himself since then I can only guess."

"How can I find him? *Them?*" asked Juniper. "Is there some sort of a bat signal or something that I can send up? Some sort of a divine flare?"

His chuckle came effortlessly to his lips. "I'm afraid not."

"Would I know one if I met one?" she asked. "Would I sense what they were? Or feel a connection like the one I felt with you?"

"I think your senses would definitely pick up on it, yes, but I can't say for certain. There are quite a few powerful gifts out there, you know. Some of which allow the user to essentially cloak themselves. Not only from sight, but from perception entirely."

"Are there a *lot* of different powers?"

"Too many to name," he said softly. "None more *or* less important than the others." Azerial surprised her as he pulled her into a hug. "I'm exhausting you with all of this talk! We'll continue this another time, for now you should get your rest."

But Juniper found that she couldn't rest. Questions persisted behind the unopened doors in her mind, doors that hid from her in darkness of her current exhaustion.

"Just one more question?"

"Just *one* more."

"Can people tell that I'm not..." She lowered her voice to shield her words from whom, she didn't know. "Is it obvious that I'm not completely human?"

"No." He pulled back from her and brushed the side of his hand over her cheek. "Your genetic difference is nothing that can be observed. The appearance of the Nephilim is something that has long since been exaggerated. Your height is a clue, but a lot of people are tall."

An earlier topic came back to her mind. "What will Jason and Ben do next?"

"I thought we agreed to just one more question?"

Juniper blushed. "Sorry."

"It's alright. I didn't expect that would be the end of it." He winked and pushed her hair behind her ear. "As for Ben and Jason... Well, I don't know what they'll do next. I wish I *did* know, but I'm afraid I don't."

"I just wish I knew what to expect, that's all. I just don't like this feeling. It's like helplessness... or frustration. I don't even really know how to describe it." Juniper's head suddenly began to throb. "Anyway... I should be getting home. I can't think about this any more tonight, it's too much."

Azerial nodded and pulled himself to his feet. He helped Juniper to hers and supported her weight with his strong arms and back. "I'll walk you home," he announced. "This is no time for you to make the journey alone."

"Are you sure it's safe?"

"I'm sure of nothing, but this is a risk I'm willing to take."

Juniper's smile was weary when it appeared. "Thank you. For everything."

Azerial bowed and placed a kiss on her cheek. "You owe me nothing more than that which you've already given so freely."

Chapter Ten
The Telling of Truths

Juniper hugged Azerial good-bye in the privacy between the sleeping houses and thanked him for the escort with a kiss placed directly at the middle of his forehead. He smiled, squeezed her hand, and disappeared into the shadows of the early-summer night without even the sound of one footfall to mark his retreat.

As Juniper slowly climbed the stairs of the side porch, she noticed the lights were still on in the living room and kitchen; she cringed at the prospect of an interrogation from her mother, but knew that it was almost inevitable. Sucking up her breath and nerve, she twisted the door knob and entered the house cautiously. She looked left down the hall to the kitchen, then right to the living room. Her mother was sitting on the sofa with a bowl of ice cream in her lap and her feet propped up on the coffee table. The TV was on, but the volume was low. Sam was asleep on the cushion next to her, curled up tight inside of his dreams.

Juniper's mother looked over when she heard the door. Her attention was pulled back to the TV only briefly before she caught Juniper's gaze once again. "It's about time you decided to come home! Do you mind telling me where on earth you've *been*?" she asked. "I've been worried sick about you! Do you even know what time it is?"

Juniper's head began to spin from Penelope's rapid-fire questioning. "I'm sorry I'm so late, mama, and I know you're probably eighty-four kinds of pissed off, but I'm *really* tired. I promise, in the morning, you can yell at me for as long as you'd like, but right now I'd like to just go to my room and **sleep**." Juniper knew her request would go unheeded, but felt she at least had to try to avoid the interrogation. She stayed hidden in the darkness of the unlit hallway as she waited for her mother's response; she found that she was afraid her eyes would reveal the things she herself was not yet ready to.

"It's after midnight, young lady, and on a school night no less!" The spoon clinked against the side of the small, porcelain, bowl as her mother set it down on the coffee table and stood. Her hands went immediately to her hips and Juniper had to wonder if a woman's DNA changed to include that imposing pose the moment one gave birth. "I thought you knew the rules!" Penelope continued. "Curfew is ten thirty and if you're going to be later than that you *call*!"

"I said I was sorry. I'm *sorry*." Juniper bowed her head and tucked her hands behind her back. "How many times can I apologize before you believe that I'm being genuine?"

Her mother sighed and pushed one hand up to massage her right temple. Her voice had all but completely drained of its anger and had instead filled with concern by the time it found Juniper's ears again. "Well, are you alright? Look at me! Let me see you."

"I'm fine," Juniper fibbed. "I'm just tired."

"Where have you been?" Penelope asked. She left the living room in favor of the kitchen and narrowed her eyes to survey Juniper closely. "Have you been out by yourself?"

Juniper shook her head and met her mother's gaze with reluctant eyes. "No. I've not been alone."

"Then *where* have you been?" she asked again. "And are you *sure* you're alright? You look funny. You *sound* funny."

"I'm sure that I'm fine. I was just studying for finals and I lost track of-"

"Are you on drugs, Junie?" Penelope asked with a concerned tongue. "If you are, it's ok... Well, it's not *ok*, but you can tell me and we'll work through-"

"Mama, stop," Juniper said flatly. "I'm not on drugs. I

told you, I just lost track of the time."

Her mother opened her mouth to speak again, but Juniper jumped in to stop her. "And to answer your *next* question... No, I haven't been drinking, either."

Penelope's lips sealed over her teeth; she raised a hand in the air and shook her head. Juniper could tell that she was too exhausted to fight. "Fine, fine. Just get some rest and don't let this happen again. Do you hear me, young lady?"

Juniper nodded, but said nothing more. She headed somberly for the staircase and when she reached it her hand found the banister and took pause. She turned back to face her mother.

"What's wrong, sweetheart?"

Juniper licked her lips and used the awkward silence to muster all of her reserved courage. "I'm just wondering... Why didn't you tell me?"

Her mother's pretty face became etched with a look of confusion. "Tell you what?"

"Why didn't you tell me about my father?"

Penelope sighed and rolled her eyes. "Oh Junie, not this again. Not *now!*"

"No, mama, **now**. Because this time it's different," she whispered. "It's different because I know who he is. I know *what* he is."

Penelope's mouth dropped open; even in the darkness of the kitchen, Juniper could see the color slowly drain from her mother's cheeks. When Penelope finally spoke her words trickled out slowly as a hoarse and disbelieving whisper. "What did you just say?"

"I *said* that I know what dad is. What *I* am."

"But- how did you-?"

"-find out the secret you've been keeping from me for almost sixteen years?"

Penelope nodded and ventured closer to the stairs.

"Junie, I- I don't know what to say!"

"How about you apologize for keeping this from me?"

"I did what I thought was best-" Penelope extended a hand. "Please, you have to understand."

"Understand, mama?" Juniper scoffed. "Oh, I understand, believe me. I understand that you didn't think I was strong enough or mature enough to be trusted with the truth about my own parentage."

"That isn't it," Penelope whispered. Her lower lip trembled under the weight of her words. "Who told you about this? Who have you been talking to? Because no one knows about this except for-"

"Dad told me," she whispered. "I made him tell me everything."

Penelope's eyes went wide as the fullest of moons. "Azy? But how did you-?"

"I've been spending time with him." Juniper's voice lost its sharp edge as her confession tumbled forth. "You could have told me what he was. I would have understood, mama."

"How could- But-" Penelope tried again to find the proper words to convey her shock, but instead she only managed a question. "Would you have believed me?" Her voice was small and thin, a prisoner to the thoughts and questions that were slowly piling up on top of each other like an out-of-control highway collision.

Juniper turned away from her mother's query. "I just wanted you to know that I was with dad tonight and that I'm ok. I know we're both pretty tired, so we'll talk more about this in the morning… when we can both think a bit clearly."

"But Junie, wait, I-"

She didn't stop, but her mother's words did. Juniper continued her climb up the carpet covered stairs and she counted each one silently in her head until she reached the landing at the top. For a moment, she almost turned back, but she thought better of that and quickly reconsidered.   Instead, Juniper merely shook her head and made her way in silence to her room.   Once inside, she threw herself onto her bed and fell easily into a dark and dreamless sleep

The next morning when Juniper woke she wasn't surprised to find that her head was pounding and her muscles were aching.   As she tossed back the blankets and sat up to stretch, she noticed that outside of her window the skies were overcast.   Accentuating the grey morning were fat drops of angry rain that were furiously assailing the glass panes.   To her dismay, the bad weather had become a common sight, one that seemed to almost mimic her general mood as of late.

If it hadn't been the last day of the school year, and if she hadn't one last final to take, Juniper would have ignored the alarm and rolled back over, favoring instead the warmth and comfort of her blankets.   That morning, however, laziness was not a luxury she could afford.

She dressed quickly, but didn't bother with a shower. She figured she'd be out of her exam by nine, and with no reason to hang around the school after that, she'd be home by 9:30 to start another summer vacation of isolation.

After she was completely dressed, she poked her head into the hallway.   She looked left, then right, and when she was certain the coast was clear she dashed to the bathroom and closed the door behind her, going so far as to lock it.

Alone in the white cleanliness of the tiny room, Juniper turned on the harsh, fluorescent light and leaned towards the full length mirror on the back of the door.   Her fingers found her neck first and pulled down the collar of her t-shirt to inspect the area where the damage had been.   She wasn't surprised to see that the rubbed-raw rope wound was completely gone, thanks in totality to Azerial's healing the night prior. Upon further inspection, she found that her wrists too were pale and unblemished. In fact, all signs of the near-hanging were gone and remained only as memories in Juniper's slightly shell-shocked mind. Still, despite the smoothness of her flesh, she decided that the long-sleeve shirt she had chosen was still in order. After all, she realized that it was just as dangerous to be seen *without* the wounds as it was *with* them. It all depended on the company she found herself in.

Satisfied that she could easily pass her mother's daylight inspection, Juniper left the bathroom and made the familiar walk to the kitchen. She could hear that her mother was on the phone as she descended the stairs and Juniper's stomach turned. She could tell by Penelope's sweetened tone that she was talking to Mr. Halsey.

As much as Juniper didn't want to face him, it was the day of her history exam. All week she'd been dreading it, and in that precise moment she found that she was more apprehensive about it than she'd ever thought possible. Not only would Mr. Halsey be there to set her nerves on edge, but Ben Maxwell would be in attendance as well. At that point, Juniper could only hope that Ben would skip the exam and lessen her emotional pain tenfold. She suspected, however, that if Ben made it to only one exam that week, it would be *that* one, if only to torture her.

Juniper wondered if Ben had ever returned to the farm house; wondered if he would be shocked to see her in class per usual looking none the worse for wear.

Engrossed in her thoughts, Juniper breezed past her mother without even the slightest acknowledgment. She made a beeline to the coffee pot and reached for a mug from the cabinet. She fumbled through the motley collection of cups before she located her favorite oversized, blue ceramic mug tucked neatly in the back of the cupboard.

As Juniper prepared her extra-sweet beverage, she thought back to the events of the previous night. As much as Ben and Jason's actions had frightened her, she found that she was less upset about the whole ordeal than she'd assumed she would be. Instead, the thought that spread pervasively throughout her mind was that of the angry confession she'd handed to her mother the night before. She found that she felt little relief over the fact that she'd finally said what she'd wanted to say for so long. It was something she found to be quite odd until she realized that the truth was sometimes even more frightening than lies. But there it was, the truth, out in the open and waiting between herself and her mother impatiently. It was hard for Juniper to wrap her head around the reality that Penelope finally knew that Azerial was on Earth. Perhaps more importantly, Juniper became aware of the fact that her mother had most likely realized that she'd been spending time with *him* and not some imaginary friend like Juniper had led her to believe.

Juniper gulped in light of her realizations. She absent-mindedly took a sip of her steaming coffee and winced as the hot liquid met, then burnt, her lips. She frowned heavily and lowered the mug to the counter to cool.

It was only a short moment later that Penelope came up behind her and gently cleared her throat to gain her attention. She had ended her phone conversation abruptly a few seconds earlier, and since that point, she had carried a nervous look about her.

"Good morning," Penelope said tersely. She retrieved her own coffee mug from the counter and pulled it close to her chest. The mug had already, at some earlier point, been filled to the brim with piping hot liquid.

"Morning," Juniper muttered. She didn't meet her mother's eye and instead kept her focus on the steam as it poured from the surface of her coffee.

"Did you sleep well?"

Juniper shrugged. "So-so, I guess."

"Are you excited? It being the last day of school and all?"

"Yeah, sure. I'm *real* excited, can't you tell?" Juniper forced herself to smile a wholly unconvincing smile.

Penelope sighed at the sight of it. Juniper knew that her mother was trying to tip-toe around the only matter she wanted to address; could tell that she was uneasy in almost every way imaginable. Finally, Penelope got around to broaching the subject Juniper knew she'd been mulling all night. "Listen, Junie... I'm just going to cut to the chase and jump right in. Now I'll admit, I was hoping that we could save this conversation for tonight, but-"

"Mama, *please*... I can't talk about this right now." Juniper finally faced her mother, but the moment she did, she realized that she had not been prepared to see her.

Penelope's normally gorgeous face appeared hollow, and the circles she carried under her eyes were deep and heavy with color. She looked exhausted, and it seemed as though she had been recently crying, that is if Juniper were only to judge her by the red-rimmed look she wore. Faced with the reality of her mother's torment, she suddenly regretted the way she'd behaved the night before, and realized that the way she'd chosen to break the news about Azerial had been wrong and done in a moment of anger and frustration.

Perhaps I am weak, Juniper thought sadly. *Maybe Azerial has reason for his concerns about me and my strength... or lack thereof.*

Penelope started to speak again once her words were collected neatly beneath her tongue, spring-loaded and waiting for the perfect launch window. "I can't *not* talk about this, Junie." Penelope brought the coffee cup to her lips, but decided against actually drinking any of the liquid. Instead, she merely held it close to her chin and basked in the rising steam. "I didn't sleep all night, you know. I don't know how I could have, I mean... if what you said is true, I-"

"Mama... *please*," Juniper repeated. "We'll talk about this later, because right now I have to get to school. My history exam is this morning and I didn't sleep well last night either... So please, *please*, don't make me do this right now because I can't. I just *can't*."

Penelope nodded weakly. Her head bobbed easily as though emptied of its thoughts. She finally took a slow sip of her coffee and then changed the subject against her own wishes and better judgment. "Well, do you want a ride to school this morning? It's still raining out there... has been all night."

Juniper shook her head. Her hair tumbled over her left shoulder and fell neatly across the side of her face that had been exposed to her mother. "No, that's ok. The walk will do me good."

"Are you sure? It's really no problem."

Juniper nodded and took such a large drink of her coffee that she almost choked. She coughed when her throat was clear and nodded again. "I'm positive. I need the fresh air this morning... I need to think."

"Yeah, right, *think*." Penelope's sigh was elongated and wispy. "I think I could use a little time to do that myself. Or maybe I just need a drink. Is it too early to drink?" She laughed nervously, much like Juniper imagined she might on a first date.

"You don't drink, mama."

"It seems like a fine time to start." Her smile was weak and nervous, as was the chuckle that followed. She dropped her gaze to examine the liquid in her cup and submitted for its approval her dissipating and awkward laughter. She stirred the coffee to dissolve it completely and glanced up just as Juniper turned and crossed the kitchen to the door.

Juniper shoved her feet into a pair of black sandals. "I suppose it's happy hour *somewhere*," she muttered.

"Juniper, I-" Penelope set her coffee cup on the counter, and one nervous hand found her hip. She tilted her head until her chin rested at her chest. "No, nothing. Just... Just have a good morning and good luck with your final."

"Thanks." Juniper shoved one hand into the pocket of her jeans; the other lifted her book bag from the floor and tossed it over her shoulder. "Any love notes for teacher you want me to pass on?"

Penelope raised her head and exposed her tear streaked cheeks. "We'll talk later, ok? About *every*thing."

Juniper squinted in examination of her mother. "*Everything?*"

Penelope nodded and raised one weak hand to wipe at her eyes. "I've decided that I'm not going to work today. I've already called in sick, because frankly that's exactly what I am. So after school... *please* come straight home. I think I've found my words, Junie, and I'm ready to tell you everything."

"But?" Juniper asked.

"But-" Penelope drew in a long, shaky breath and found her daughter's wide and disbelieving eyes. "In exchange, you have to tell *me* everything. Everything you've been keeping from me for the past few weeks."

Juniper said nothing as she pulled her hair out from beneath her book bag. She distributed her raven curls evenly over her shoulders and used the time it bought her to consider her mother's request. When she finished, she gave up her words. "Ok. You've got a deal. We exchange the truth for the truth." Her fingers felt strangely disconnected from her hand as they found the doorknob and twisted it slowly. Before she stepped onto the side porch, she paused. "I'll be home in a few hours. Make sure you have a full pot of coffee brewed. I've a feeling we'll both need it."

Once outside, Juniper shivered and she suddenly wished that she'd grabbed a light jacket on her way out the door. The morning was uncharacteristically cool and Juniper felt strangely out of place in between the rain drops and the quiet discontent of the sleepy town. As she walked, the rain lightened to a mere drizzle and she slowed her steps to a more normal, mostly casual pace.

She had no idea how she'd ever be able to keep her thoughts on the Civil War when the only war on her mind was the one that was waiting for her at the kitchen table in her own home.

Before she even realized it, her sleepy thoughts had carried her to the entrance of the High School. She yawned and looked around at the empty, sleepy campus in search of signs of life. She immediately felt better in the isolation she found and decided to sit outside of Mr. Halsey's classroom with her back against the wall to help keep herself upright. The allure to sleep on the long beckoning benches in the lobby had been so great that Juniper had for a moment paused next to them to weigh her options. Finally, she'd realized that staying awake was in her best interest.

Outside of the dark, closed-door classroom, she opened her text book. Historical dates and names swam through the thick, soupy, warmth of her brain not wanting to be plucked free of the mire. She was fuzzy about the overwhelming list of Civil War battles and their significance, but try as she might to study, the words refused to stand still upon the page and preferred instead to dance about hypnotically.

After her fourth consecutive yawn, Juniper closed her book and rested her head upon it. The position was uncomfortable at best, but she didn't pull herself upright; couldn't pull herself upright. She felt as though her spine had been suddenly and surgically removed from her body, a procedure that left her as nothing more than a helpless, straw-filled, rag doll.

It wasn't long before footsteps approached from her left.

At the sound of the dusty, shuffling, feet Juniper found that her bones had been promptly returned.

She sat up and hoped to see some innocuous, unimportant person, but instead her eyes found the familiar form of Mr. Halsey.

He pulled his keys from his pocket and when he noticed her, he nodded and flashed her a tight, brief smile. He seemed surprised to see her; surprised and ever so slightly uncomfortable.

Juniper shoved her text book back into her bag and stood up. She looked down at the floor and counted the speckles in the tile just beneath her feet until she heard the pop of the lock.

"Good morning, Miss Kelly." Mr. Halsey pushed open the classroom door and reached inside to flip on the light. He himself remained in the hallway.

Juniper coaxed a smile to her lips and responded to his greeting with as much enthusiasm as she could muster. "Morning."

"Ready for the exam?" he asked. He motioned with his briefcase for Juniper to enter the classroom before him.

She did so slowly. Her feet, she discovered, were almost unwilling to move. "I'm as ready as I'll ever be."

He followed her into the room and their paths diverged quickly. Juniper took her seat in the second row by the wall and Mr. Halsey went for his desk. He set his briefcase on the solid wooden surface and then leaned against it. "So... This is a bit awkward, isn't it?"

"Oh, not at all. My mama dates my teachers *all* the time. Why, just last year it was Mr. Griffin and the year before that-"

Mr. Halsey was quick to interrupt. "Juniper, please. I like your mother and I'm sorry if that makes you uneasy."

"Can we not talk about this?" Her eyes were already blazing with anger and she knew that if she didn't change the subject soon she'd say something that she might come to regret.

"Of course, of course. I know this isn't the time *or* the place to discuss, it's unprofessional of me." He cleared his throat and straightened his tie. With an almost tangible awkwardness he turned from her and pulled out his chair. It screeched as the legs were pulled across the over-waxed floor before it fell silent. He sat and pulled his briefcase towards him. "If you need any help reviewing, just ask. I'll be more than happy to answer any last minute questions you might have."

Juniper bit her lip. She wanted to take him up on the offer, but found she was unable to ask him to make good on it. Whether her hesitation found root in fear or anger, she couldn't decide. Finally though, she cleared her throat and roused his attention from an impressive stack of papers.

He looked up a moment later, first drawn to the window, then to Juniper. "Did you need something?"

"Well uh, yeah. I'm having some trouble keeping all of the significant battles in the Civil War straight..." She rubbed her forehead and then motioned to the text book in front of her with a frustrated sigh. "It's all a jumble and I don't know where my notes on this chapter disappeared to, or I'd use those."

Mr. Halsey smiled warmly. "Well, as you remember, we only studied the ten largest battles of the Civil War. That cuts out a lot of the lesser battles, so you don't have to concern yourself with those. Just remember the order in which the battles happened *and* which was the largest. If you can do that you'll be just fine."

"But that's just it! I can't remember them all!"

"Well, ok, just stay calm and we'll walk through them. Now remember if you will, the first battle we studied was one of the more obscure of the ten. On top of that it had the smallest number of casualties."

"Alright. Uh... it has to be Fort Donelson. Right?"

He smiled and snapped his fingers. "There you have it!

That's absolutely right!" He stood and walked towards her. He stopped when he reached the seat across the aisle from her. He took a seat in the tiny, cramped desk and leaned towards her. "Now we're on a roll! After Donelson you have Shiloh, then Manassas-"

"Followed   by   Antietam,   Stones   River, Chancellorsville..." She nodded and let loose her first genuine smile of the day. The information was beginning to come back to her as her brain decided to finally wake up. She silently and sarcastically thanked the coffee she'd had that morning for having taken its sweet time before it had decided to kick in. "I think I've got it now."

"Let's make sure of that! Now tell me, what was the largest battle we addressed?"

"Gettysburg, with over 50,000 casualties."

Mr. Halsey's smile widened and he reached across the aisle to pat her hand. "You're going to do just fine, Miss Kelly. Just fine."

Juniper looked up from her intense study of her hands and met his eyes. "Listen, Mr. H. I'm sorry I've been a real pain in the butt to you lately. I'm also sorry that I lied to you. You know, about mama and my father getting back together."

"Hey, it's all forgiven. Water under the bridge, as they say."

Juniper cleared her throat and nodded. "Yeah, right, but still, I wanted you to know that I feel bad about it."

"I know you do. You're a good kid and I think I understand why you did it. You just wanted to protect your mama."

Juniper chuckled. "Actually, sir, I just wanted to protect *you*. My mama can be quite a bit to handle sometimes."

Mr. Halsey laughed heartily. "I certainly appreciate that."

"Hey, no problem." Juniper looked away from him and found the bold-black words of her text book. "Anyway, I think

I'm going to go over this stuff a little more before the bell."

"It certainly couldn't hurt." He stood and looked relieved to be free of the confining student desk. "If you need anything else, just ask."

"Thanks. I appreciate it." Juniper smiled weakly and then looked back at her book. The words had finally stopped moving in front of her, but the urge to immerse herself in history was no where to be found.

She found herself thinking about her mother, about Azerial, and she wondered exactly where all of the chips would land when they finally stopped spinning in mid-air. She glanced up at Mr. Halsey once more and shook her head at the hunched over, slightly-geeky history teacher.

Poor guy, she thought, *he really is a nice man.*

As much as she wanted her parents to reunite, she didn't look forward to Mr. Halsey's feelings being hurt, if that were to be the case. He had been a great source of support to her at the beginning of the school year, and he'd done nothing but try to help her escape the evil clutches of Ben and Jason as much as he could. She had appreciated it then, and she definitely appreciated it now.

At that point, other students began wandering into the classroom. Most of them looked as sleepy as Juniper did, and most looked even more anxious than she felt. She considered that to be quite a feat, as she was certain she must look dreadful, all things taken into consideration.

She glanced down at her hands and pulled her sleeves down to her knuckles. She suddenly felt self-conscious, even though she knew that the wounds that had marked her skin were long gone. At five minutes before the bell, most of her fellow classmates were seated and chatting nervously as they quickly reviewed the last four chapters of the text book. As Juniper scanned the box-like classroom, she noticed that only one face was missing from the crowd.

Juniper stared at Ben's empty seat and felt a bit of relief wriggle through her. The bell was slated to ring in less than two minutes, and as per the rule of the school, the classroom door would be locked and no students would be admitted to the exam after that point.

Please, please, she begged with her eyes cast upwards. *Let Ben not show up today!*

At the front of the classroom, Mr. Halsey stood. His arm was full of thick-looking exams, all neatly stapled together and sorted. He looked at the clock, smiled at a few of the weary students encouragingly and instructed them all to take out their pencils and put away their books.

A few students groaned and the room filled with the sound of shuffling papers and last minute questions. Juniper had already put her things away and she sat quietly, anxiously, with her hands folded over each other. Her pencil tray was full of pencils, all sharpened and at the ready.

The clock ticked over to 7:14am and the noise drew her eyes to the minute hand. The classroom was nearly silent and Juniper dropped her eyes from the clock on the wall to the doorway just below it.

A moment later, as if on cue, Ben rushed into the room. He hurried to his seat and seemingly didn't even notice Juniper until he was already seated. As soon as his butt hit the blue, plastic seat, he casually glanced over at her desk. When he found her sitting there calmly, hands clasped in front of her, his look of surprise was obvious and eclipsed the smug look he'd previously been wearing.

Their eyes met, and his widened. Juniper found herself smiling softly at him as if to revel in her triumph over his cruelty.

The bell rang out above their heads and in doing so, it broke their gaze. Mr. Halsey cleared his throat and turned to close the door. The lock clicked shut and he turned back to address the class.

"Good morning, everyone! I'm glad that you all made it on time today." He surveyed the rows of students and scanned them for empty seats. "Since it looks like everyone is here, I won't bother taking attendance. I'm just going to go ahead and let you guys get started on this. I do, however, want to go over a few things first. Just some standard rules and regulations, nothing I'm sure you haven't already heard half a dozen times this week. First, this is a closed book test, so make sure you've put everything away. Cheaters will fail automatically and be ejected from the room immediately. There is to be no talking and *absolutely* no going through your book bags, so please make sure that you have your pencils and erasers out now before we begin." He paused and allowed a few students the time to do a last minute check of their supplies before he continued. "Now, I'm sure you've all heard the horror stories about my final, but I assure you, it's **much** *worse* than anything you could have imagined. There are three different copies of the test, just to further dissuade you from copying off of your neighbor. Use only #2 pencils and when you finish you may hand in your papers and text books and leave. Oh, and enjoy your summer, everyone. I hope to see *some* of you in the fall in American History."

A cheer went up from the students and Mr. Halsey smiled at them. "I'll assume the ruckus is for summer vacation and *not* for American History."

A few nervous giggles erupted from the other side of the room before everyone fell silent.

"Alright, if everyone is ready, we'll get started so we can get finished. Good luck to everyone, not that any of you will need it." He winked at Juniper and then handed out the exams by row. They were passed back slowly and when Juniper got hers she turned it over right away and wrote her name in the spot provided for it on the upper right hand side of the page.

She felt a chill slice through her as she read the first question and she looked up and over towards the window. Her eyes were captured by the firm and almost disbelieving stare of Ben Maxwell before they ever reached the glass barrier on the far side of the room.

She looked away quickly, but felt that his eyes were still trained directly upon her. A moment later, the feeling passed, and Juniper relaxed slightly. She read the first question three more times before it made sense, then she made an uneasy guess.

The rest of the exam, however, went better than the first question. Juniper felt confident in her answers and filled in the bubbles on the scan sheet with heavy, circular marks. When she finished with the seventy-five question nightmare, she looked up to check the progress of her classmates.

Everyone else was still buried in the test, their heads drawn close to their desktops in determination.

Juniper checked her answers quickly and retraced a few of the bubbles as she went to make certain that they were all obvious and legible. When she was sure she'd done all she could do, she rose to her feet and picked up her test. Mr. Halsey looked up from his book and then consulted with the clock.

Juniper placed her exam face down on his desk and leaned towards him. "It was easier than I expected," she whispered. "You must be losing your touch."

He picked up her test with a smile on his lips. "Then I'm looking at an A+ paper, I take it?"

She nodded, winked, and returned to her desk where she quickly collected her things. Across the room, Ben shifted uncomfortably in his seat.

On her way to the door, Juniper placed her text book on the edge of Mr. Halsey's desk. "Enjoy your summer," she said quietly, to which Mr. Halsey responded with a smile.

"I'm sure I'll be seeing you sooner rather than later," he said. "Have a good summer, Miss Kelly."

Juniper nodded weakly. "Thanks. I'll certainly try." She glanced back over her shoulder and Ben quickly removed his eyes from her and placed them back on his paper.

Juniper smiled at her history teacher again, then quickly escaped the classroom. Outside in the quiet hallway, she stopped to catch her breath. As much as she wanted to leave school behind for the year, she dreaded what awaited her at home.

The truth.

Penelope and Sam were in the kitchen when Juniper arrived home in record time.

She was out of breath and exhausted, due to the fact that for most of the journey home, she'd decided to run. She'd also decided to take the more direct path through town, which meant overlooking the woods and her routine visits with her father. Juniper had been afraid that Ben would follow her and she wasn't certain that she could stop herself from lashing out at him if he confronted her about the night before.

When she slammed the kitchen door behind her, Penelope's head whipped around to face her.

"You're home earlier than I expected." Penelope had taken the time to apply some make-up in an attempt to lessen the exaggerated appearance of the dark circles under her eyes. She'd also changed out of her pajamas and into a pair of jeans and a t-shirt. She seemed almost relaxed, but Juniper knew that wasn't the case.

Sam barked his greeting to Juniper and she went to him. She dropped to her knees next to the dog and brought him into her arms and up to her face. She rubbed her nose against his ears and kissed him on top of the head before she put him back on the floor where he quickly scampered away.

Juniper stood slowly and her mother's face appeared over the surface of the table as she did so. She looked almost peaceful, surprising when one considered the story she was keeping just behind her lips.

"I think it went well," Juniper said quietly. She avoided the subject at hand for another minute while she settled into a chair and steadied her nerves.

"That's great. I'm sure you did... *great*." Penelope nodded towards the table. "I made coffee, as requested."

Until then, Juniper hadn't noticed the two steaming cups of coffee on the table. Penelope pushed one towards her daughter and she took it, thanked her and met her gaze.

"So... where to begin," Penelope said. Juniper wasn't sure if her words were a blanket statement or a question.

Juniper ran a finger along the rim of her cup. "Mama, I just want to say, before you say *any*thing else, that I appreciate how hard this is for you."

Penelope nodded and forced a tight smile. "Thank you."

"Whenever you'd like to begin, feel free."

"Right." Penelope looked at the clock and then looked down at Sam. He had returned and was sitting next to her chair. He gazed up at her anxiously which spurred her to drop a hand to her side. She rubbed him behind his ears and in a matter of seconds he fell over onto his side in a happy, furry puddle of low barks and pants.

"If I might," she began slowly. "I'd like to ask *you* a few things first."

Juniper had expected as much. "Sure, anything. I'm done with keeping secrets."

The air between them was electric and Penelope held her words back until they were finely tuned to her standards. "Last night, you said-" She broke off and tried again a moment later to finish her sentence. "You said that you were with your father."

"Yeah, I did." Juniper searched her mother's eyes for a pre-mature response, but came up empty. Penelope was blank with the settling of the unsettling news.

"I see. And how long have you been spending time with him?" she asked.

"A while..." Juniper shrugged. "I don't know exactly. A few weeks, I guess."

"I should have *known*. I should have sensed that he was back..." Her head rolled forward and Juniper thought for a second that she was going to cry. She didn't and a second later she continued. "Juniper, sweetheart, why didn't you tell me this sooner?"

"Because he asked me not to," she whispered. "He didn't want to upset you."

"I see." She nodded and looked away as she did so. Her eyes seemed to focus on the window that overlooked the driveway. "May I ask where you met him?"

"In the woods."

"At the farm house, then?"

"Yes."

"Uh huh." Penelope paused. "Just how much has your father told you? About *us*?"

"Bits and pieces." Juniper wanted to reach out for her mother's hand, but her fingers were glued to the table top by the idea that they might be rejected.

"You know, it's suddenly all starting to make sense now. You finding out about your gift, the picture, the questions, the late nights and secrets." Penelope surprised Juniper by laughing. "You don't have a friend named Cat, do you?"

Juniper shook her head. "No, mama."

"I knew it, you know." She shook one long slender finger in Juniper's direction, however, she held onto her smile.

"I just never imagined where you *really* were all those times... *all those times?* God, I've been in the dark for *ages*, haven't I?"

"I'm sorry, mama. Really. I *wanted* to tell you the truth, so many times, but I could never find the right words."

"Why are you telling me now? Why last night? Why?"

The question Juniper had been dreading finally appeared and she squinted from the harsh light of it. Her answer was well-rehearsed, as it had been floating through her mind for much of the morning.

"Well I uh- I sort of asked dad if he would join us for my birthday dinner this weekend. He wasn't too keen on the idea at first, but after a little bit of begging and coaxing, he agreed. But there was a condition."

"A condition?"

"Yeah. He wanted me to tell you everything. About him, about us... he didn't want his appearance at dinner to be a surprise. He wanted you to have time to prepare."

"I see."

"Now before you say anything, I want you to know how much it means to me for him to do this. This is what I want for my birthday, nothing more, nothing less. Just one dinner with *both* of my parents in attendance... And I know you might be angry with him for various reasons, but I hope that maybe you can-"

"Can what?" Penelope raised one eyebrow, and her voice turned sharp. "Can *what*, Junie? What do you want to happen here?"

"I just want a normal birthday dinner!" Juniper exclaimed. "One night with both of my parents. One night where I can pretend to be an average, run of the mill, *normal* person."

Penelope shook her head. "There is *no* normal to be had where your father is concerned."

Juniper gulped and began work on digesting her mother's

final-sounding words. When she had swallowed them to the pit of her upset stomach, she raised one shaking hand to her neck. She found the silver chain with her fingers and pulled the locket from beneath her shirt. Penelope was still looking at the table top; one finger on her left had absently traced the grain of the wood. She appeared to be deep in thought; Juniper could only guess what a tumultuous place her mother's brain was at that moment.

Juniper removed the necklace from her neck. Her fingers fumbled with the tiny clasp for only a second. When finally it fell free, she clasped the whole of the object at her palm and moved her hand towards her mother. Juniper pushed open her fingers and displayed the locket on her palm for her mother to inspect.

Penelope's eyes found it slowly and when they drank in the realization of what it was they were seeing, she looked up. "Where did you get that?" she whispered. Her mouth fell open and her fingers moved towards the small silver trinket.

"I found it in the attic of the farm house. Azerial kept it all these years... to remind him of you. Of *us*."

Penelope picked up the locket. The shake of her hands was outweighed only by the shake in her voice. "I never thought I'd see this again! I thought I'd lost it forever." She opened the clasp of the locket and smiled at the photo inside. "My goodness, would you look at me. So young, so... *scared*." She tapped the photo with her fingernail. "I'd just found out I was pregnant a few days before this was taken. I still hadn't told your grandpa yet. Only Azerial and I knew the truth... I was so afraid... I actually wanted us to run away together, you know. I wanted the two of us to leave this place and raise you together. Somewhere, *anywhere*, but here."

"Do you ever wonder what life would have been like? If we *could* have been together?"

A wisp of a smile graced Penelope's lips before it

retreated. "Every day," she whispered. "Only every *single* day do I wonder."

"I have to ask you this, mama… Do you want to see him again?"

Penelope was slow to answer. "I don't know," she finally admitted. "For sixteen years now, I've resigned myself to the fact that I would never see him again, *never.* And now, he's here and-" She looked over suddenly as an irresistible question found her mind. "How long has he been back? Why did he *come* back?"

Juniper looked down at her coffee. "I think those questions are better asked of him."

Penelope narrowed her eyes. "But you know the answers, don't you?"

Juniper swallowed thickly. Her throat felt almost as tight as it had the night before when the noose had been holding her upright in the darkness of the attic. "I know that he misses you and I know that he's looking forward to Saturday night almost as much as I am."

Penelope sighed and reached up to massage her temples. "After you left this morning, I showered and changed and then I sat back down here, *right here.* I haven't moved since. I can't seem to do *anything* but sit here and wonder and think and try to make sense of all this. And I spent time rehearsing what I would say to you. How I'd tell you my side of the story, the whole damn, sordid story... And you know what? I'm still no closer to having the perfect words now than I was 16 years ago. I thought for sure I'd figure it out. I thought I'd one day just *know* what to say, but I... *This,* Junie, is the day I've dreaded since the moment I first held you in my arms."

"Just say what's in your heart, mama."

Penelope folded her hands together and gave her daughter a serious look. "First of all, you should know that Azerial and I made the decision mutually to keep the truth from you. You mustn't blame him for not being there for you just like you can't blame *me* for keeping him away. Our situation was an odd one and we did what we thought was best at the time. We may have been wrong, but we can't change that now." She re-wet her lips before she continued. "I'm not sure where I should even begin when it comes to explaining this."

"How about you start at the beginning, mama?" suggested Juniper. "It seems to me it would be the best place."

"Well, I-" Penelope cleared her throat. "It's hard to say where the beginning *is*. It's either the day I met your father, or the day before."

"Start with the day you met dad," Juniper said quietly. "It seems like the most logical place. If you ask me, that is... but it's your story, mama. Start where you feel comfortable."

Penelope nodded absently. Already her lip had begun to tremble. "You have to be patient with me, Junie. As I've already said, even though I always knew this day would come, I find that I'm ill prepared."

"At least you *had* a chance to prepare. I just wandered into an old farm house and the next thing I knew, boom! Wings and feathers and mythology and I find out that I'm..." Juniper shook her head, uncertain of where to go from there. "I find out that I've got this great power and a destiny... and... and a father. A *father!*"

"I know it must have been a shock for you. I can't even imagine how much of one." Penelope's eyes were eclipsed with a growing sadness. "I've wanted nothing more than to protect you from all of this, but I see now that I was foolish to have tried. If I would have just been straight with you from the beginning... Would that have made things any better? I don't know... any more I don't know *any*thing."

"I can't say what the right choices were, or what the *wrong* ones were. And I'm not judging you for the decisions you and dad made. Who's to say that you weren't right with the way you handled it? There's no way we'll ever know."

Penelope looked at her folded hands which rested uneasily at the surface of the table. "I really have raised you well. You've grown into a wonderful young woman. I'm very proud of you, Juniper. Very proud."

Juniper's eyes grew heavy with emotion over her mother's compliment. "You've been a wonderful mother and I love you. I wouldn't be who I am today without your strength."

Penelope reached out for her hand. "You're a beautiful person, Junie, and I thank God for you every day."

Juniper squeezed her mother's hand and smiled. "So uh… are you ready to tell me your side of the story now?"

Penelope pushed herself back from the table and clapped her hands once in front of her. "I'll tell you everything, but listen closely, because I'm not sure than I can say this more than once. The words are heavy and my lips are weak… to repeat myself might require a strength I'm not certain I possess."

Chapter Eleven
Penelope's Story

Your father fell to earth nearly 17 years ago. There was no net to catch him, and no tether to pull him back into the heavens from which he came. He confessed that in the early moments of his new-found confusion, he cried out for God's assistance only to be met with silence. That was the first time he felt genuine fear, he told me later.

When I asked him why he had chosen to leave Heaven, he never gave me a straight answer. Sometimes he claimed it had been an accident, a grievous mistake; other times he admitted that the decision had been his to make, and made it he had.

Immediately following his decent, he found himself lost in the woods. He slept in trees, caught fish from the creek, and prayed for hours on end, asking to be forgiven. Again, silence. Naked and exhausted, flooded with emotions he'd never felt before, he wandered in circles for days before he found our house. It was still another few days after that before I found him out there.

The odd noises were loudest at night. Long after papa had passed out from the whiskey, I would hear the rustling of the leaves and the howling of papa's dogs. It made me uneasy, but more than that, it made me curious.

It was his cries that I finally responded to. One night I'd finally had enough of the noise and the wondering, and I threw my books aside in frustration. I dressed quickly and left the house, all the while still having no idea what it was I intended to do.

But I knew that something was out there. Something that had *been* out there for several days; something that I just *knew* I had to see for myself.

So I mustered all of the courage I had within me and I took papa's lantern from the hook on the front porch. With my coat pulled tight around me, feet shoved quickly into house shoes, I headed out into the night in search of the cause of the mysterious noises

For nearly an hour I searched. I went so far as to turn over rocks in my pursuit of the truth! It seemed, though, that every time I was close to discovering something, that *some*thing would move around to be behind me. I would spin on my heels with an ah-ha at my lips, but my eyes never saw a thing. It wasn't until I was nearly ready to give up that I saw something move out of the corner of my right eye.

I turned quickly to my right and brought the lantern around in front of me. I directed it towards the source of the movement I'd seen. My voice shook as I spoke, and now I can scarcely remember how it was I found words at all.

I was terrified, you see. I'd always been terrified of the forest, ever since that day I got lost. Gosh, I couldn't have been any older than 5 when I wandered away that afternoon. I had been chasing butterflies, you see, and before I'd realized it, I'd followed one particularly large butterfly into a remote and unfamiliar part of the forest. Even after mama found me I cried for two days.

But there I was! Terrified and shaking, outside in the forest in the middle of the night, unarmed and facing the very real prospect of an unidentified creature watching my every move.

Still, I called out to it. "Who's there?" I took a cautious step forward in my moment of bravery and I spoke again, "I know someone is there. Show yourself! I've a gun here," I lied, "and I'm not afraid to use it."

Slowly something began to materialize out of the darkness, a light that, to this very day, I cannot accurately describe.   The richness of it was unearthly; it seemed to convey emotion to me and I was immediately put at ease in the presence of it.

He approached slowly, naked and unashamed.   I turned my head in embarrassment, not for him, but for myself.   I was just 16 and never had I seen a man naked!   But there he was... and at first my mind didn't put the pieces of the puzzle together; I didn't see the wings or understand what they were until he was only a dozen or so feet away.

His eyes could read me, could see to the depths of me that I only wished I could explore!   I nearly buckled under the weight of his presence, but by the grace of God I managed to stay standing.

"Who are you?"   I asked him, expecting a logical answer to my completely silly question.   It was more than obvious what he was, and what I should have asked instead was "Where have you been?"   I'd prayed for something to happen to me, Junie. Something big and wonderful, something to save me from the routine of caring for papa and going to school.   Something to save me from my small-town future and my loneliness.   And boom, he was there.

He was slow to respond to me at first, saving his words until he was close enough to see my face in the glow of the lantern light.   He smiled before he said a thing, and then he extended his hand towards me.

In spite of my trepidation, I took it and asked my silly question again, "Who are you?" This time he seemed to understand what I was really asking.

He lowered his head and he closed his eyes.   A moment later he released my hand, "My name is Azerial."   I remember wondering why he had let go of me, and I wished that he hadn't.

"What kind of name is that?"   There I was in the presence of an angel and all I could think to do was question him about the origins of his name.

I remember my relief when I saw his lips twitch upwards into a smile, as though he got that question a lot and wasn't offended that I'd asked.   However, he didn't answer my question, asking one of his own instead.   I said my first name quietly, "Penelope," I said it again, the next time adding my last name, "Penelope Kelly."

"Well, Penelope Kelly, it's a pleasure to meet you."

I felt color rise into my cheeks as he watched me.   I felt as though I were a book and he was reading my every word with the skill and adeptness of a literary scholar.

"Could you tell me where I am?" He asked me quietly, so quietly in fact that I had to ask him to repeat himself twice before I finally heard the question.

"Just outside of Camden Falls, South Carolina," I told him.   "The United States," I added.   I had no idea what angels did or didn't know about geography and figured that I would make it as easy to understand as possible.

He took in the information as if he were having difficulties processing the news of his whereabouts.   Finally he offered conversation, for which I was thankful.   He asked me if I knew what he was.

I nodded and answered him quickly, not wanting him to think that I was a moron.   "An angel."   My words were soft-spoken; I actually feared being wrong, I feared for a second that I was crazy!   Or worse yet, that he was a demon and not really an angel at all.

I noticed then that he was shivering and I touched his arm to ascertain the truth of his condition.   As I'd suspected, he was ice cold to the touch.   I couldn't figure out how I hadn't noticed it when I had held his hand earlier in the meeting, as he was practically frozen to death.   I took off my coat then and offered it to him, but soon I realized that my noble effort was a feeble attempt at warming him.   My coat was too small to cover him, his wings were huge, *he* was huge, and I was a sixteen year old girl who could knock herself over with her own coughs. Still he took the jacket from me and wrapped his hands inside of it.   He thanked me for the kind gesture and I told him to think nothing of it.

"Being cold is a new sensation," he confessed.   Our eyes met again and he smiled at me.   I looked away from him though, unable to maintain the gaze without turning an even deeper shade of red.   I was still embarrassed for myself at the sight of his nudity, but not only that- his eyes saw right through me, made me feel as though I didn't exist, yet at the very same time, made me feel as though I were *all* that existed.

I don't know if this makes sense to you, Juniper, but I hope that you can at least gather a bit of a feel for the magnitude of his presence in my life.   He was something else, and I was lucky to have him.

But I'm getting off track and I've finally hit my groove. Where was I? Oh, yes, well everything happened quickly from there.   Initially, it began with my father's old cloak.   I gave it to him, happily surprised to find that it fit him nearly perfectly and concealed his wings almost fully.   He was grateful for the treatment and I was grateful to have a special new friend.

I felt as though maybe my life *did* have purpose, and that I was standing on the precipice of discovering what that was. In many ways I was correct.   What began that night ultimately culminated in your birth.   Being your mother is what my purpose was.   My burden has always been great.   Raising you right, doing the best that I could to instill in you faith and a sense of right and wrong, not ever knowing why it was I felt as though I were grooming you for greatness..   But I have always done it blindly, without knowing why, because I have faith. Faith that your father gave me with one blink of his eyes.

I was saved by him, quite honestly.   Or maybe we saved each other, in a way.

After he was finally warmed by the fire, there was the

matter of protecting him from discovery and harm until he could figure out exactly what it was he was going to do.   I wasn't about to leave him shivering on the doorstep to sort it all out, but I couldn't very well trust that my father wouldn't give him up to the law.

You have to understand that after mother died, father lost his faith in God and religion. He turned instead to the bottle. Whiskey mostly, and to this very day it's the only scent that reminds me of him.   I had no idea what papa would say about having an angel as a house guest, and with the dire straits we were in financially, I couldn't trust that papa wouldn't turn Azerial over to the government for a nice chunk of change.

But lucky for me, it so happened that father, by that hour of night, was already passed out in his bed fully clothed. It was my nightly ritual to remove his shoes and pull a blanket over him.   Every night, Juniper.   Every single one.   It was exhausting to deal with, but more exhausting still to hide his obvious problem from the prying eyes of the town.

To be on the safe side, I went in the house alone at first. I checked on papa again, tucked him in with a kiss on his forehead and I closed his bedroom door.   As an extra precaution, I placed a chair from the hallway in front of his door so that I would hear if he was coming out of his room.

Azerial warmed by the fire while I brewed coffee. He'd never had any before, he said, but he loved the smell. In fact, I don't believe I ever saw him take a sip of the coffee that night. He would simply hold the cup to his face, inhale deeply and smile. I liked his smile. Even that first night I wanted to kiss him. It was as though nothing else mattered in the whole of the world, nothing but him and me.   I can't really explain it accurately to this day, but even in the early days of our relationship I sort of knew where things would ultimately lead.

Later I would find out that he could read my thoughts. I was embarrassed in hindsight. It's funny, but it's true. I was embarrassed for all of the impure thoughts I'd had, and many there had been.   All of those nights that I spent avoiding sleep in favor of his company.   Reading to him, mostly.   Poems, novels... I must have read him *Wuthering Heights* half a dozen times.   And when he fell asleep, I'd watch him.   I studied his face, every pore I memorized, every line I traced with my mind a million times.   He looked so young.   I found it hard to fathom how old he really was.

For nearly a year it was like that.   He hid, I taught him about literature and history; we were nearly caught by papa so many times that I eventually lost count.   Still, somehow we managed to conceal the secret from everyone.

As the months passed, our relationship changed from one of friendship to awkward lust.   We kissed a few times before we fell asleep.   I would wake up in the mornings to find his arms around me.   I would lie in his embrace unmoving, not wanting to stir him.   The longer he slept, the longer I felt safe, but as soon as his eyes opened he would recoil from me with his eyes downcast and closed.

It was September when before I knew it, school started. It was my junior year, and as much as I was looking forward to it, I had no idea what I'd do when high school eventually ended. Going away to college was out of the question.   We couldn't afford it and I couldn't fathom the idea of leaving Azerial behind, or worse yet, losing him entirely.

Aside from school, September also brought harvest time. Because of this, papa was rarely home until the late hours of the night.   He would stumble in from the fields already drunk and slurring his speech.   I would sit with him until he passed out and then rush upstairs to lock myself away with Azerial.

The night it happened, I had taken special measures to make sure I looked nice.   I fixed my hair, I wore makeup, and I found an old dress of mama's in the closet that brought out the color of my eyes.   When he saw me, his eyes widened and his jaw fell slack.   He recovered from his surprise quickly and shoved it down inside of him.   As usual, I picked up a book and began reading to him.   He was sitting cross-legged on my bed with his eyes closed, listening closely to the words I was spilling. I can't remember what book it was for the life of me.   Many times I've pondered it, but nothing comes to mind.   What I do remember is pausing to look at him, to examine his serenity with a subtle appreciative smile.

When my words stopped, his eyes opened.   Without giving my actions any more thought, I placed the book on the floor next to me and stood slowly.   Just as carefully, I made my way to where he was sitting on the bed.   I took a seat next to him and reached out to take his hand in mine.

It was Azerial who spoke first.   "We mustn't."   He'd already read my mind, and if that hadn't been enough to confirm his suspicions about my intentions, the look on my face certainly must have been.

I put my finger to his lips to silence his words and soon replaced it with my lips.   At first he resisted the pressure I placed on him, but the second kiss he gave to me willingly.

The moments turned into long and breathless minutes. The innocent fluttering kisses turned into long embraces.   I buried my face in his feathers, marveling at the feel of them upon my cheeks, praying silently that I would never again experience life without him in it.

"You smell like vanilla," I told him; my breath was warm against his skin and my confessions came easily, "I love the way you smell."

Azerial was still hesitant to pursue our relationship.   He was afraid, and I think up until that moment, he never considered the possibility of things evolving the way they did. He, in all of his keen wisdom, had overlooked for so long what my heart, not my mind, had been screaming at him.

"Penelope," he said finally, "what do you think we will

gain from this indiscretion?"

I told him I didn't know, and I kissed him again. This time he turned his head and my lips brushed his cheek. I reached up for him, took his chin in my hand and forced him to look at me.

"I love you," I told him. And at first he was taken aback by my words. He licked his lips and shifted uncomfortably before he admitted his own feelings.

Imagine my happiness, and surprise, when his lips formed the words I'd hoped they would. "I love you, Penelope," he told me. And I knew that he did, could *see* that he did.

I've never felt that way since, not with anyone else. You asked me why I'm so picky, and this is why. When you've had what I had, mortal men are slightly less palatable.

"If two people are in love, should they not express it?" I can't recall his response, or if he even gave one. I asked him another question, this time I held his gaze as I spoke. "Have you ever considered that you're here because of this? Maybe this is where your path led, where *mine* led."

"You talk as though you believe this to be fate. That *we* are fated."

"I believe that we are," I told him firmly, and I pulled back to get a better look at his face. "You said it yourself. You've no idea why you ended up here. *Here* of all places. With me! Perhaps this is why. Me, this love that we both feel for each other. What if this is the way it's supposed to be?"

Despite my plea at his emotions, he hesitated still and found his come back for my speech. "Or what if this is a test of our will. Of our faith," he countered. "What if we make the wrong decision? What happens then?"

"I don't know," I admitted to him freely. I looked into his eyes, *stared* into his eyes more accurately. I was mesmerized by him and the things I was feeling.

I felt my insides turn to Jell-O. I was, quite honestly, melting under a force that was stronger than I would ever be. I couldn't resist the temptation of him. And when I sensed that he was on the verge of succumbing as I was, I pushed my lips to his one more time. Either to seal the deal or end the conversation, the outcome of the kiss depending on his reaction.

His reaction, of course, was what led to your creation. I will say here that I'm going to leave out the more intimate details of what happened that night. I'm sure that you can gather how things transpired as you are sitting here today, living and breathing and thanking us both for your life. Besides that, there are few things that I have left to keep to myself now that I've told you all of this. I would like to keep some of the more beautiful things private, keep them safe and alive in my heart. To continue, however, from that point, it wasn't long before I felt the morning sickness creep in. At first I thought I had gotten sick; there was a flu going around at school and the weather outside was turning sharply cooler. But after two weeks of the same symptoms at the same time of day, I began to realize that something was happening inside my body.

I made up a story about needing a book from the library for a history project, and I took papa's truck to the next town. Instead of visiting the library, I visited the doctor. Before the results of the tests were even confirmed, I knew that my fears were about to be realized. I was pregnant.

When I arrived back home, Azerial was waiting with his arms and his heart, both wide and open to welcome me into the safety only he could provide. As I crumbled into him, I babbled and cried and sobbed for what seemed like hours. "What would do we do?" I moaned, "What will the baby be like?"

Azerial would smooth my hair with his hands, never once showing any fear over the situation we had found ourselves in.   He would assure me that you would be beautiful, and his words comforted me in ways I can't fully describe. "She will be loved and nothing else matters," he would say, and after awhile I believed him.

Still, a problem remained.   How would I tell papa about the child slowly growing inside of me? How would I explain an unexplainable story to a man who was barely coherent?

The weeks passed and as they did my clothes became tighter around my belly, a belly that was protruding more and more each day over the top of my pants.   Papa commented about my weight one night as I cleared away supper from the table.   I cracked and I broke down in tears.   He didn't understand what was wrong with me at first, but somehow through my sobs I choked out my unbelievable story.

Papa sat stone-faced and silent for several minutes until finally he stood and walked to the front door.   I waited in stunned silence for what happened next.   Papa returned a moment later through the same door that had provided him exit.   At first I didn't see *it*, only after he passed me on his way to the stairs did I notice the nose of his rifle sticking out from the top of his jacket.   I grabbed his arm, I pleaded with him to stop, to listen to reason, but he was a man on a mission.

He shoved me aside in his haste to get to the attic, but I stumbled after him, chasing him up the stairs.   I caught him at my bedroom door, his fists pounding hard against the wood, so hard that the whole door frame jumped.   I screamed out to Azerial from behind papa, "Don't open the door! He's got a gun!"

"If you know what's good for you, you'll come out here!" Papa was still pounding, he'd pushed back his coat and the rifle was in plain sight.   I could hardly breath.

I tugged at his arm, I wrestled with his shoulder, but papa stood firm in his anger and ignored my pleas for civility.

Finally, the bedroom door opened inwards to reveal

Azerial's impressive sight.   My heart leapt into my throat and words scurried to my lips, "Azerial, no-"

He held up his hand and stepped confidently from the room.   For the first time, he faced my father.

Papa was shocked at the sight of him.   He stumbled backwards into the wall, thankful I'm sure that it was there to stop his fall.   "What... wh-" Papa couldn't find his words and stuttered out a few more fragments of would-be words before he fell quiet from the disbelief of what he was seeing.

Azerial held up one finger then and it drew papa's gaze as well as my own.   "Put down the gun, Jacob," Azerial said softly.   "You don't want to hurt me."

Papa shook his head and did as he was told, bending at the knees to place the rifle on the floor at his feet.   His mouth was still hanging wide open when he pulled himself upright. Azerial smiled gently and thanked him for coming to his senses.

Papa's knees soon buckled under the weight of Azerial's presence, and he fell to the floor in a prayer like crouch.   He slowly brought his hands together in front of him.   Azerial asked him to rise, and he did so.

"You're an angel." Papa's eyes were tracing the outline of Azerial's wings.   He looked at me, his eyes drifted to my stomach.   "And what of that? You've done this to her?"

Azerial closed his eyes.   "The child will be a great blessing."

Papa's lips moved, but no words came.   He was confused, flustered, and instead of continuing the conversation he turned, walked past me without a word and descended the stairs to the living room.   I looked at your father and he nodded a response to my silent question.

So follow papa I did, and I found him standing over the sink with a bottle of whiskey.   His hands were shaking as he took a swig.   When he removed the bottle from his lips, I took it from his hands and set it aside.   "Papa, I'm sorry.   I can't imagine what you're thinking right now, but I love him, and he loves me and it's going to be ok."

He ignored my words and bypassed me on his way back to the whiskey. He took it up in his hands again, running his fingers over the cool smooth glass. He contemplated a drink and finally took one. He sighed when his lips released the mouth of the bottle and his hand came up to rub his chin. For a long moment he was silent and when he finally spoke, he had already made his decisions.

"You are to drop out of school on Monday morning. I won't have the entire town staring at us."

Despite my protests, papa's mind was made up. He never said another word to me about it.

Without further questioning I did as I was told, knowing that no matter what I said or did, he would stand firm in his decision. So I hid in the attic with your father for another seven months, my contact with papa nearly non-existent. He would grunt out a good-morning, ask if I needed anything from town, but other than that, he was a wall of silence.

When finally the time approached to bring you into the world, Papa set to boarding up the windows. He had trouble with the nails; they would rust and break before he could even get them halfway pounded into the window frames. He cursed and swore, but he didn't give up. Over the course of the following couple of days, he had boarded up every window in the house to shut out the light.

"Never can tell what might happen," he said to me. He feared the birth would be more complicated than most, that perhaps your arrival would be accompanied by something he didn't want anyone to see. A burst of light, a gust of wind, an earthquake that would shake the town's people straight from their beds.

And I was almost as uncertain as he was. My fear grew despite Azerial's attempts to calm me. I was afraid I would die;

I was afraid you would be a monster.   I was afraid that I wouldn't be able to love you and care for you in the manner in which you required.

But no matter how many fears I harbored, I knew there was no escaping that which was already set in motion.

Instead, I braced myself for the pain of labor that was fast approaching.   When the time finally came and my water broke, Papa refused to fetch a doctor as I knew he would.   He couldn't and wouldn't risk the secret getting out.

"We don't need no doctor," he said.   And I nodded my reluctant agreement.   If papa was anything at all, it was stubborn to a fault.   I suppose that's where the two of us inherited it from, isn't it?

Anyway, as I was saying... Azerial, trying to be helpful and make the home delivery as comfortable for me as possible, made a list of supplies for papa to pick up at the store, but papa rebuked your father's attempts at helping the situation.   He boiled a pot of water, gathered a few blankets and left me to fend for myself.

Finally you were ready to make your appearance and papa banished Azerial to the attic.   Papa took up residence in his favorite rocking chair on the other side of the room.   I couldn't see him from my location on the sofa, but I could smell him.   Whiskey and cigarette smoke heavy in the air.

There I was, sprawled out on the couch with a blanket covering my lower half, alone and preparing to face one of the worst pains a woman can imagine.   I puffed and wheezed and panted for hours, gripping the back of the sofa with my hands until my knuckles turned white and my fingers went numb. Several times Azerial tried to come to me, but Papa would quickly jump up from his chair and force him to return to the attic.

Never had I felt anything so intense and never again will I.   I chipped my front tooth that night from gritting them together so hard; soon after, the worst of the labor pains kicked in. I screamed and yelled until my voice left me. The entire time papa sat stationary in the corner ignoring my cries, parting his lips only to imbibe his liquor laced tea.

In the height of the pain, I remember the beads. Next to the couch, the project I had been working on before you arrived. A tray of juniper beads and string, a necklace I had been making for your father.

I knocked the tray over, and I remember them spilling and scattering across the floor. That's where your name came from, not from any place else like you might imagine; you spilled from me like those beads, wildly out of control and unstoppable.

Before I even realized what had happened, you were crying between my thighs. I reached down for you, exhausted and tearful, eager to pull you close to me, to see if you had all of your fingers and all of yours toes.

Papa did me one favor by cutting you loose. Together we examined you, he from a slight distance. Oh Junie, you were perfect! Ten fingers and ten toes, a tiny nose with eyes squinted and hopeful. I cleaned you in the kitchen sink, wrapped you in an old quilt mama had made and took you to the attic. I had never felt so relieved or so happy in all my life.

Azerial had paced ruts in the floor and when I pushed aside the door, he came to us quickly with tears in his eyes.

He said nothing as he took you from me, performing his own inspection of you. You made him nervous with your fragility, but when you wrapped your tiny fingers around his thumb, he was hooked.

"She's perfect." He seemed surprised, but he later called it relief.

But as all of this was taking place, Papa was downstairs quickly gathering our belongings. He already had our suitcases packed and in the back of the pickup truck. He shut off the water, boarded up the empty hen house and only then did he admit to me what he had done.

The state had been on him for a long time to sell the land for inclusion in the Camden Falls State Park. Papa had always resisted, after all, the home had been his parents before it was his, *ours*. There was a history there that he wasn't willing to give up, but that all changed after he learned about you. He sold the land and everything on it several weeks before you were born. We would have left that night if it hadn't been for your father's anguished pleas.

Papa, because of your father's insistence, granted us last requests. He allowed Azerial and I to spend one last night together, with you; he also agreed to take a photo of the three of us, something that Azerial might keep to remember us by.

It was that night when we named you. I suggested Juniper; he thought on it a second and finally agreed. We all fell asleep together that night crammed onto the twin bed in that hot little attic, and the next morning I was woken to the sounds of Papa loading up the truck.

Azerial held you while I packed my things in tears.

"It will be better this way," he said to me. "Better if I'm not around to complicate your life. We both knew that this wouldn't last forever. That someday you would leave and I would go back to Heaven. We've always known this day was inevitable."

I nodded at his words through my tears, avoiding actually facing him. I busied my hands instead with the folding of clothes and the careful packing of pictures; Papa went to town to develop the film, he drove clear to Greenville to find a one hour photo place, and he paid the boy behind the counter an extra $25 to never mention what he saw in the photos.

The kid, in open-mouthed shock, agreed to father's suggestion and bribe. Papa swore until the day he died that he only offered the kid money and kept the threats of physical violence to himself, however I still have my doubts about that. Papa wasn't one to leave anything to chance, and if he felt physical violence would further stress his point, he wouldn't have hesitated.

In the precious few moments that we had left together as a family, we stood in an embrace. Words were exchanged; he told me again that he would be returning to heaven, that time adding that most likely we would never see each other again. I wept without shame into the softness of that cloak, my tears soaking him straight to the bone, until finally I had to kiss him good-bye.

When I pulled back, he turned his attention to you. He placed his thumb at your forehead and brought it slowly down the bridge of your nose. You squirmed and cooed and with one outstretched hand you reached for him, as though you realized what was happening.

He gave himself to you; his finger, his hand and finally he pulled you from me and covered you in his embrace. I held myself at the stomach and lost my eyes to the floor; he kissed you good-bye, whispered something in a language I didn't understand and when he gave you back to me at last, he kissed my cheek.

"I will always love you, Penelope." For years his words woke me from a deep sleep and left me tear-stained in my bed.

I loved him, Junie. And as Papa and I finally pulled away from the farm house, I looked back to the attic window. He was standing at it, one hand across his heart, his head bowed deep to his chest. I watched him until he disappeared in the distance and then I looked at you.

You, the only real evidence of his existence that I would ever have. I held you tight to me, using you to block my tears from Papa.

We lived in Table Rock then, and I attended a local college during the evenings. When Papa finally died, I moved us back to Camden Falls.   The town had grown and housing was going up all along the perimeter of the woods and by the lake.   We lived in a small apartment over the market for a year until a house became available near our old farm house.   I snatched it up immediately and in we moved.

Never once did I enter those woods again.   I would instead stand in the backyard and stare off into the distance, imagining that I could see the house as it was.   Imagining that he was still there, still watching and hoping and- and many, *many* times I thought about sedating my curiosity with a visit.

But something kept me away, Junie.   I don't know what, but something was there between me and the past, something that I couldn't explain and couldn't overcome.

I settled for the longing looks and tried to shake him from my mind.   *You* were my main focus and from that point on, I instilled in you the same fear of those woods that my own parents had put into me.   It was all done to keep you from finding the house, to keep you from finding out exactly what it was we had lost.   I apologize for that now, but I thought that I was protecting you.

I realize in hindsight that I treated you unfairly... but you mustn't hold it against me.   I love you, Juniper.   You are my gift from God and for being blessed with you, I will always give praise.

Chapter Twelve
An Overdue Reunion

Juniper had remained silent throughout the length of her mother's story. At many points she thought of interrupting, but something kept her silent.   Perhaps it was a sense of understanding, or perhaps one of compassion for the struggle that her mother had in telling the story that she'd hidden so close to her heart for nearly sixteen years.

Her mother had dissolved into tears at the conclusion of the story; Juniper wished to console her, but found that her blood had been replaced with slowly-drying concrete. Her feet weighed a thousand pounds each and kept her pinned to the floor and to the chair.

"Thank you," she finally managed to eek out. "Thank you for finally telling me everything I've always wanted to know."

Her mother looked up and blotted her tears absently with the back of her hand. "I'm sincerely sorry, Junie. For keeping all of this from you."

"Oh mama... *I'm* sorry I kept things from *you!*" she exclaimed. "These past few weeks? They've just been hell! Lying to you, keeping you in the dark... I've just been so used to telling you everything that keeping this from you was pure torture."

Their eyes met and held an uneasy silence that Juniper finally broke.

"So I'll ask you again... Is it ok with you? If dad comes to dinner Saturday night?"

"Well I- I can't very well say no, can I?" Penelope's face lost all of its remaining color and she fiddled nervously with her fingers.   "I just don't know what I'll say to him. I never thought, not one time, that our paths would cross again. Sure, I hoped for it, but thought that there was a chance of it actually coming true? Never. *Never!*"

"I'm sure you'll think of something to say, and you've got just about two days to figure it out. I know that isn't much, but it's something, right?" Juniper looked down at her forgotten mug of coffee and frowned at the cold beverage. She pushed it away from her person and crossed her arms on the table in front of her. "Mama? It's time. You know that... It's time to face the past."

Penelope said nothing further on the subject, and a moment later she stood in a daze and stumbled away from the table. She ran into the fridge with her left hip as she moved slowly from the kitchen. The impact did little to snap her out of her fuzzy, trance-like state and she continued her retreat unimpeded.

Juniper remained quiet as she watched her mother climb the stairs. A moment later she heard Penelope's quiet footsteps on the second floor. They traveled away from the top of the staircase towards the back of the house where Penelope's own bedroom was located.

Knowing not what else to do, Juniper followed in the wake of her mother's footsteps until she reached the doorway of Penelope's room. She paused just outside of the room; she was uncertain of what to say, of what to do, and in that moment silence seemed to be her best bet.

Penelope was standing by her bureau with a far off look on her face. Her eyes seemed to be desperately searching the surface of the wood for something and Juniper wondered if her mother even knew what it was she was looking for.

"Mama?" Juniper finally broke her silence and approached Penelope, at first verbally, and with an obvious hesitation. Like a sleepwalker, she turned, blank-eyed and silent. Juniper entered the room fully, but stopped at the end of the dresser. "Mama?" she repeated. "Are you ok?"

Penelope blinked away her stunned stupor and nodded in response to her inquiry. "Yeah… yeah, Junie, I'm fine- I'm just looking for my Bible."

"Your bible, mama?" Juniper furrowed her brow. "Gosh, I don't think I've seen *that* since I was a kid."

Penelope smiled softly. "That's because I've kept it from you… I don't suppose you remember the day I found you reading it in the living room, do you? I'm pretty sure we were still living in the apartment over the market then." She paused and rubbed her temple. A second later she nodded absently at the appearance of the memory she'd been searching for. "Yeah, that's where we were. I remember it now… God, Junie, you were probably only four years old at the time, but there you were. Ignoring Sesame Street, ignoring your toys… You were cross-legged on the living room floor with your head buried inside of that bible. You could barely read a lick, but you seemed to be so enamored by it."

Juniper shook her head slowly from side to side. "I don't remember, mama."

"Of course… you wouldn't… *couldn't.*" She laughed softly at the thought of it. "You'd found it in my room. Back then, one of your absolute *favorite* things to do was to go through my stuff. Heaven only knows why that was, but I'd find you in there all the time, searching, looking… Sometimes you'd go so far as to mark up the walls with my lipstick. Of course I never had the heart to punish you. It was all art to me." She started to sob softly. "I'm sorry, sweetheart. I don't mean to babble on like this. I'm sure it's quite a sight to see."

"It's ok, mama. Really."

"Is it?" She blinked, and in response to her action another wave of tears coursed backwards from her lashes in retreat. "I just feel so silly, Junie."

"You aren't *silly*… I can't even imagine how you-"

Her mother interrupted her as the metaphorical light bulb went off over her head. "The closet!"

She turned abruptly and headed to the other side of the room. Once there, she yanked open the closet door and reached upwards to the top shelf. She emerged a moment later with a cardboard box in her hands. She wiped the dust away carefully from the lid, then carried it to the bed.

"This might sound silly, but this box is the only thing I have left that belonged to my mother... that really *belonged* to her." She paused and ran her hand over the surface of the old, rectangular box. "I remember the hat that originally came in this box. It was the worst color green you could imagine and it had this large black feather coming out of the back." She laughed at the thought of it. "God, Junie, it was an awful hat, but mama...? She pulled it off with such style and grace. Oh, I envied her for that, for that ability she had to turn anything into a thing of beauty. I still do envy her. All of these years later."

"I wish I could have met her," Juniper whispered. "She must have been something else."

Penelope raised her head slowly and revealed a melancholic smile. "You would have loved her! She was a quintessential country mother, right down to the made from scratch pies she allowed to cool on the windowsill." Penelope's fingers found the lid of the box and she removed it slowly. She set it next to her on the surface of the bed and carefully reached inside the cardboard box. "This is your great-grandmother's Bible. It's very old... priceless. Our family history is in here. Among *other* things." She opened the book carefully and leafed through the pages. Finally, the book fell open near the middle and a single white feather appeared between the pages. There it had rested casually for much of Juniper's life.

Penelope removed the feather and held it carefully in her hands. "The reason I took this Bible away from you so quickly that day was because of this."

It was one of Azerial's feathers. Juniper didn't even have to ask.   She'd known immediately what it was from the very first second she'd seen it.

"You came running up to me that day waving this feather at me.   *'Mama, Mama!'*, you were saying. I was used to you bringing me things… bugs, books, drawings you'd made, but when I turned from the sink and wiped my hands on my dress to see what you'd found that time?   Well, I very nearly dropped dead of shock!"

"What did I say?"

"You asked me what kind of bird it was from."   She laughed and held the tip of the feather to her chin. "I told you it was from a magical bird... From the bird that had brought you to me wrapped in a pink blanket."

"And I bought that?"

"You were *four*," she said with a chuckle. She ran her fingers along the edge of the feather and looked up to meet Juniper's eyes. "Why has he returned?" she asked. "Why after all of these years has he come back?"

Juniper gulped back the truth and replaced it with a lie. "I don't know."

Her mother's stare hardened. "Don't you know by now that I can tell when you're fibbing to me, Junie?"

"I know I said I'd tell you everything, it's just that I…" She shook her head and toed the floor absently with her shoe. "I just really think this is something *he* should tell you himself."

"So there *is* a reason for his re-appearance?"   Her mother's brow furrowed in the awkward silence that followed. "Junie? Talk to me here."

Juniper's voice was low when she finally spoke the truth. "He uh- he never actually left, mama."

Penelope's eyes widened; her hand stopped it's twirl of the long, lean feather. "W-what did you just say?" she croaked out. "He didn't-? I don't understand."

Juniper repeated herself, and her words found firmer ground the second time they passed her lips. "He never went back to Heaven, mama. He's been in that old farm house since the day we left him there."

"But that's not... How is that possible?" Her mother closed the Bible but continued to clutch it at her stomach. "He never left? Really?"

"Really, mama."

"I don't know what to think! What to say!" Penelope exclaimed. "Why did he lie to me? Why?"

"So that we wouldn't have to spend our entire lives in hiding," Juniper whispered. "He didn't want that kind of life for us so he did the only thing he could do. He let us go."

Penelope lowered her head and the tears she'd been holding back came quickly to dot the landscape of her cheeks. "I should have known he was still there. The truth is, I've always felt that his presence was near by. I just chalked it up to wishful thinking, to the hope that maybe he was looking over us, like a guardian angel might. But now... hearing these... that for all of these years, he's been right there..." She looked at Juniper with desperate eyes. "Why didn't he leave?"

"Because he can't, mama."

Juniper's mother furrowed her brow and she lowered the bible from her chest. "*Can't?* What do you mean *can't?*"

"There's a lot you don't know, mama." Juniper looked down, then back up almost as quickly. "When I was- when I came into being, something strange *did* happen. The seed that grew inside of you was emulated by another seed, by one that grew rapidly from the ground beneath the house. A giant oak tree now stands in the middle of the living room. It's grown right up through the house, through the second floor and past that to the attic. Azerial suspects that any day now it'll finally break through the roof... and this tree, mama... It's not just *any* tree. It's more or less become his lifeline. It keeps him tethered to the farm house and he can't leave it without dying. He can go no further than the perimeter allows him."

"He's trapped there," Penelope said softly. "My God, Junie... I never knew."

Juniper continued her explanation. "He can go to the river... and he can come as far as the road out front, but further than that, and-" She shook her head slowly. "He explained it to me as though the invisible barrier were a bit like kryptonite to him."

Penelope placed the bible back into the box and pulled the lid back into place to cover it. She placed her hands palm flat on top of it. "We used to look at Superman comics all the time."

"I know," Juniper said with a faint smile. "They were his favorite. Of all the things you read to him, Superman was what he enjoyed the most."

Penelope's smile was weak. "Does he still smell like vanilla?" she asked.

"Yeah, yeah he does."

Penelope closed her eyes and took a deep breath into her lungs. "I loved that scent. Something about it was so soothing. No matter what troubled me, just being near him, near the *smell* of him... it made everything ok again." She paused while her mind formed a second question. "Does he still look the same? As in the photos?"

"Mostly, yeah. His hair is longer, of course. But he really doesn't look much older. Oh, but his hair- it has a touch of grey now." Juniper motioned to her forehead. "It's just at the temples."

"I bet he's still very handsome. Is he? Still handsome, I mean."

"He is," Juniper murmured. "In fact, he's quite beautiful to me. He's everything I imagined an angel *would* be."

Penelope's eyelashes assaulted her cheeks, long and

curled up from her eyes. Her lips still carried her faint smile. "He's going to be disappointed when he sees me. This whole time he's stayed mostly the same, while I've aged and changed and-"

"You're as beautiful as the day he met you." Juniper shuffled her feet and moved slightly closer to the bed. She shrugged when he mother looked up. "At least that's what he said."

"What? How does he know that?"

Juniper forced out a cough to delay her response. "He kinda, sorta, saw you."

"When? Where?" Penelope had drawn her curious eyes from the wall and they were once again focused firmly upon Juniper. They were wide as saucers and matched the O her mouth had fallen into.

"Do you remember the night Mr. Halsey brought me my homework assignment?"

Penelope connected the dots before Juniper had the chance. "*That's* why you wanted to get him out of here so quickly? You didn't want your father to see him here?"

Juniper nodded. "Yeah… I mean of all nights for Mr. Halsey to show up here. It just had to be that one!"

"He really wanted to see me?"

"He did."

"And he wasn't completely repulsed?"

Juniper groaned. "Mama! Come on! You're *beautiful!* He thought you looked amazing."

Penelope lowered her chin to her chest. She didn't address the issue further. Instead, she collected herself; she started by smoothing the wrinkles from the front of her shirt.

"He does regret it, you know. Not being honest with you. He wishes things had been handled differently."

"For what it's worth, so do I," Penelope whispered. "I wish we'd tried harder to stay together. Been more honest with each other about the situation."

Juniper finally took a seat next to her mother on the bed. Their hands met on her mother's knee. "Listen, if you want me to tell him not to come, I'll do that. If it's just too difficult to deal-"

Penelope was quick to shake her head. "No, don't do that." She wiped at her cheeks to clear the salt from her skin. "I'd like to see him again. And if he's willing to see me, willing to be here for *you*, then it would be awfully rude of me to rebuff him, don't you think? Besides, this is *your* birthday... and a very special one, at that."

"Are you sure about this?" Juniper asked. "Because if you aren't, I'm sure he'll understand."

"I'm positive. I'd like for him to come. I want to see him." She nodded vigorously and squeezed her daughter's hand tightly. "I might not be able to change the past, but I can certainly take a go at the future."

The tree grew taller with each passing day. That day, unlike those of the prior week, the branches that hung thick with green leaves had begun to pull themselves up through the attic rafters with their sights set upon the roof.

Juniper noticed it, but Azerial effectively skirted the issue.

When she left her mother that early, rain-soaked morning, she went immediately to the farm house to offer Azerial a hand at getting ready for the upcoming dinner. She couldn't wait to tell him that the bag had been opened and the cat had been freed. Moreover, she couldn't wait to see the look on his face when he learned that the outcome of the truth-sharing had been positive.

When Juniper entered the living room that morning, she

could hear the cracking of the branches. Her eyes were drawn up into the darkness of the attic in search of the offending sound.

"Azerial? Dad?" Juniper peered up into the tree-forged hole curiously and a moment later a voice came down to her from the treetop.

"I'll be down in a minute, sweetheart. I'm just exercising my green thumb."

Juniper said nothing else and took a seat on the small chair by the kitchen window. The sunlight that had momentarily broken through the cloud cover had already begun to smother beneath the promise of another thunderstorm. Accentuating the light's demise, the dust particles that floated past her face lost their sheen and began their dissolve into the backdrop.

A few moments later, with a fantastic swish of his cloak, Azerial appeared at the base of the stairs. He carried with him a smile and an armful of branches.

"The tree has hit a growth spurt," he announced. "I know I can't stop her from doing what she's going to do, but I have to let her know that the rest of my room is completely off limits."

Juniper smiled softly, but didn't meet his eyes. In her lap, she found that her hands had nervously twisted into a fleshy-mound of anxiety. She wasn't sure why it was so, but she felt slightly different in his presence than she had before. Before, that is, her mother's confession had found its way to her mind. She tried her best to shrug away the feelings of awkward discomfort, but found that she had a hard time doing so.

Juniper finally looked up at him and for a brief second she caught a glimpse of the aura that surrounded him, the same aura her mother must have seen that first night in the woods. It was bright and white and refreshing to behold; it pulsed with energy as it swam around his form to cover his bones. As he moved out of the narrow shaft of hazy light, to a less flattening patch of shadow, his glow left him looking normal. He smiled at her curious inspection as he bent to place the branches in a pile on the floor next to him.

He brushed off his hands and ran his palms down the length of his thighs. "I have a lot of nervous energy today. Thought I might as well put it to good use." He fell silent for a long moment as he studied her. Juniper knew that her thoughts were calling out to him loud and clear. She did nothing to stop them. Finally, he confirmed his knowledge of the truth. "You spoke with your mother," he said. "And I take it that it went better than you expected."

"Yeah. It *really* did. I was a bit surprised."

"She still wants me to come," he surmised. He crossed his arms over his chest; he looked more than moderately pleased. "I thought for sure that you'd be bringing me bad news."

"Well, I'll admit, mama was a bit upset. Especially after I told her that you'd never left this place like she'd always thought."

"But she understood." It was a statement, not a question and at the completion of it Azerial extended his arms to Juniper who stepped quickly inside his embrace.

"Are you happy?"

"Happy doesn't begin to describe the way I'm feeling!" Azerial held her tighter. "I'm thrilled, *elated*... not to mention completely and totally unnerved."

Juniper pressed her lips to his cheek. "Then you'll be happy to know that mama is feeling pretty much the same exact way. With an emphasis on the unnerved part."

Azerial chuckled and released her from the hug. He leaned back and tilted his head to inspect her neck. "Well! I see that I haven't lost my touch!"

"You're a miracle worker," she said. "I'm physically

perfect.   Emotionally, however... Let's just say that I'm working on that myself."

"There'll be a time when you don't think of it any more." He whispered his words so softly into her hair that she almost didn't hear him. He kissed her then, softly on her forehead and pulled back to look at her face.

Juniper's forced herself to smile. "I know, you're right and I'm dealing with it... I'm just confused. I don't understand how people can be so cruel."

"You don't understand it because you have no propensity towards it," Azerial said. "Do you know *why* they did it?"

Juniper shook her head, then as an after thought, she nodded. "Sort of, I guess... They a bit scared of me, I think."

"That's part of it." He paused to push her hair back from her face. "Humans are always scared of that which they do not understand. We don't call it ignorance, instead we say that they are simply living in the shadows of the light. There is hope for them yet, some more than others."

"What do you mean?"

He smiled and stroked her hair with the palm of his left hand.   "Believe me when I say that even the most foul of creatures can be rehabilitated."

"Is that what I'm supposed to do? Save them from-from a life of crime or something?"

"I'm afraid I can't answer that," Azerial said.   "Only you can decide who carries within them the light of hope and who does not."

"You *can't* tell me what I should do or *won't?*" Juniper posed the question like one might point the barrel of a gun in the direction of an unknown assailant.

"It's a combination of the two." He dropped his hand to his side and stepped away from Juniper. He turned to the kitchen and his eyes found the window. "I was hoping you might stay for a bit.   That is unless there are other things your mother needs you to do today."

"I'm all yours. What do you need?"

He turned back slightly and gave Juniper a profile view of his impressive form.   "Well, for starters, I could use a little help with a haircut," he said. "I want to look my best for your birthday dinner and I'm afraid that will require a bit of a trim."

"Oh, is that all you need? I'd be happy to do it." Juniper pushed up the sleeves of her shirt.   "I've been giving mama haircuts for years. I'm actually quite good."

Azerial chuckled and didn't seem overly surprised. "She always was thrifty. There were times when I actually saw her wash off paper plates."

Juniper laughed. "That sounds like mama." Juniper straightened her posture and tossed one hand to her hip. "Juniper, there is no sense is paying someone else to do for you what you can very well do for yourself." She dropped the imitation of her mother and giggled. "You know, I was 11 when she taught me how to change a tire. That was the summer *after* she taught me to check and change the oil in the car."

"I knew she'd be a good mother. She's very nurturing." Azerial picked up the scissors from the counter and rubbed the side of the blades against the leg of his pants. "I never once worried about you, or about her ability to do right by you. I knew she'd find a way to raise you right."

"It was hard for her." Juniper pulled the dusty chair from the shadows and pat the seat. "She did the best she could. She gave me everything I ever needed. Of course that didn't leave much for herself. Money *or* time."

"She never married? Never got close?" Azerial took a seat and pulled his pant legs up as he did so. "Never mind, don't answer that. It's none of my business."

Juniper shook her head. "It's ok, you're entitled to ask these things. And to answer your question, no. Never married, never close. In fact, I can almost count on one hand how many times mama has been on a date with a real living, breathing man. Two of those occasions were set-ups." Juniper lowered her mouth to her father's ear. "I went through a matchmaking phase, you see."

A smile tugged at his lips. He pulled a small comb from his pocket and offered it up to Juniper. "She must be lonely."

"She has me." Juniper took the comb and pulled it through Azerial's thick, black, waves. "Until recently, we've always told each other everything."

"You've grown apart because of me?" he asked.

"We've not grown *apart*, per se, we're just taking different paths for a change."

Azerial chuckled. "How did you get to be so wise?"

Juniper placed the scissors at the end of a strand of Azerial's hair. She paused before she closed the blades together. "It's just one of the many benefits of being an outcast. When you spend all of your time alone, you find yourself thinking a lot. About anything, *every*thing." She snipped away another grouping of dead ends and brushed them from his shoulder. "I think genetics might also play a role in the wisdom thing. After all, I come from good stock, as you've pointed out in the past."

"Ah yes, I'm sure that must be it." Azerial laughed and brushed away a hair that had fallen to his cheek. "I must confess that I can't help but feel nervous. About dinner."

"It's understandable, really! Heck, *I'm* nervous and mama is *definitely* nervous. I can't imagine that you wouldn't be a little anxious too." Juniper wiped the scissors on her jeans to clear the accumulated hair from the blades. It fell to join the rest of the fallen strands on the floor around her feet.

"I never thought this would happen. I dreamed about it, of course... but I never actually thought I would be given the chance to speak with her again." He sighed. "I really don't know what I expect to come of this."

"I'll tell you what I told mama when she gave me pretty much the same speech."

"Oh yeah? What might that be?"

Juniper leaned towards his ear. "Don't expect *anything*. Just clear the air and settle the past. What happens from there is anyone's guess."

"That's good advice. But tell me, how does your mother seem?"

Juniper found a tangle in his hair at the back of his neck. She worked it out slowly as she spoke. "At first she was shocked, then sad, then upset... By the time I left her she had moved straight on to panic."

"Panic?"

"Yeah."   She paused long enough to chuckle. "Apparently her wardrobe 'sucks'. Her word, not mine."

Azerial laughed, then winced as the knot Juniper had been working on, caught again amongst the teeth of the comb.

"Sorry," she whispered. She pulled the comb free of his hair and brought her fingers to her mouth to wet them. She smoothed the spit over the comb and then used the remainder to wet his hair around the knot. She returned to her work and her words. "Growing up I always wondered if I looked like my father... like you."

"And am I what you expected?"

"More or less." The comb finally broke through the knot and pulled his hair straight. "I had the idea in my head that you would have an accent."

He chuckled. "I used to have an accent, a bit of a British one. But over the years, it's faded."

"I can still notice it sometimes," Juniper said. "I don't know *why* I thought that, though. I guess it just seemed to fit somehow."

"A child's imagination is a boundless place."

Juniper smiled. "I really wish you'd known me then."

"The feelings are mutual."

"What would it have been like?" she asked. "I mean, if we'd been given the chance to be a real family... What would it have been like?"

"It would have been hard," Azerial said.

"But beautiful." Juniper snipped away more of her father's hair and maneuvered with much difficulty around his oversized wings. "And anything worth doing is hard."

"I believe that things happened the way they had to. I will admit that I get lost in 'what ifs' on occasion myself, but dwelling upon things we cannot change is detrimental to our self."

"I know... and I've accepted all of this, I have. I realize that I'm lucky to have you now. The past doesn't matter any more."

"You're right," Azerial agreed. "The only thing that matters is the here and the now."

Juniper paused. She held the scissors closed several inches above Azerial's head. She reflected on his comment and smiled at the simplicity of it. "It's all we really have, isn't it?"

"Indeed it is."

Juniper kept at her work of trimming her father's hair; Azerial hummed softly and slowly as she pulled each strand through the comb and neatly snipped at the dead ends. The melody that escaped his lips sounded familiar to Juniper, like something she'd heard a million times but couldn't place. She listened intently and cut carefully the ends of his hair until she was satisfied that it was even all around. She moved around in front of him and inspected her work from all angles. She smiled, gave him a thumbs up and brushed off his shoulders with the long sleeve of her shirt.

"All done?" he asked. "How's it look?"

"Not too bad if I do say so." Juniper turned and placed the scissors on the counter at her left. "What was that song?

That you were humming?"

"You recognized it?" Azerial asked.

Juniper nodded. "I can't place it, but I know I've heard it before."

"Well, I must say, I'm surprised you remember." He ran his hands over his face and shook out his shortened hair. "I imagine your mother used to sing it to you when you were a child. You see, the one night that we had together... Well, you were quite fussy. Your little hands were balled up into fists and your face was as red as blood. Your mother couldn't settle you, so I thought I'd give it a go. After bouncing you for a bit to no result, I sang to you instead. In a matter of minutes you were silent. Penelope was amazed, she said I had a gift. I told her that all I had was a *song*."

She smiled. "I wish I could remember that night."

"I wish I had been afforded *more* of them."

Abruptly, Juniper bent at the waist and kissed him on the end of the nose.

A smile materialized at his lips. "What was that for?" he asked.

She shrugged and brushed a stray hair from his forehead. "Just because," she said softly. "Just because I can."

When Juniper finally left him that afternoon, she did so with the promise to be back as soon as she could to continue helping him prepare for the dinner. After she was gone and the house had returned to quiet, Azerial returned to his attic room wrapped up within his own silence to have one more conversation with God.

Chapter Thirteen
A Father's Prayer

In the quiet seclusion of his attic room, Azerial found himself staring at the oak tree. It grew taller every day; some days it grew more than on others. On that day in particular, Azerial measured the growth at just over 3 inches. Three inches in less than two hours.

He surveyed the ceiling above his head. He knew that time was running short and that it would be only a few more days before the mighty tree would break through the ceiling and claim the sunlight in victory. At that point he would be forced to move, either to the room across the hall or downstairs to one of the other dusty, abandoned rooms.

It wasn't something he was pleased about. The attic had been his for years; had been the place where he'd fallen in love with Penelope; had been the place from which he'd waved good-bye as she drove off with Juniper in her arms. The room held for him more memories than he could bear to recall; some fantastic, some awful, but most bittersweet.

He sighed and dropped his eyes from the tree. He swung them around the contents of the room and took an inventory of his life. The few possessions he'd had were mostly gone. They'd either been given to Juniper or were still hidden in places that even he could not recall. For at one point he had been so desperate in his depression that he'd spent several days digging and hiding and burying any and all reminders of Penelope that he could find.

She had left winter clothes in the dresser; he had burnt them for heat. She had left hair in his comb; he had pressed them between the pages of a book and tossed it into the eager flames as well. It wasn't that he had wanted to forget her, but

310

rather the reminders of what he couldn't have became too much to bear.

He regretted it then. Had regretted it immediately afterwards and had wept unashamed until the book had been nothing but ashes and the fire had burned away to nothing but a cherry-red glimmer.

Azerial tossed his regrets aside and crossed the room slowly to his cot. He fell to his knees at its side and at first he knew not what it had been that dropped him so quickly to a kneel. A moment later, he lowered his chin to rest at his chest and he closed his eyes. Like a child taking its awkward first steps, Azerial's fingers found each other and in an odd and almost foreign embrace his hands clasped each other in prayer.

He was silent at first, but soon his thoughts bubbled to the surface and spilled over his lips. "It's been a long time since I've found myself in this pose. For so long I've had nothing to say. For years before *that* I didn't stop talking. I waited and watched and hoped for you to extend your hand to me. I wanted to come home, to be with my brothers and sisters; I wanted you to wash me clean of my sins. But now, now I am here not to beg for your absolution, but rather to tell you that I've found it on my own. The faith I discarded so easily has returned to me in the form of a daughter. She has given me back my ability to understand the greater good. For surely you must have some plan for her, for me, as her father and her teacher. I know that now. I understand. And I must confess to you now, here on my knees in this box-like room, that I regret little, and instead I find I am *thankful* for the opportunity to have lived this life. Thankful for being able to continue doing so. Because after years of waiting, I think you *did* answer me when you brought her back to me, my daughter, my one and only earthly creation. And now... now that I've the chance to see *her* again...? Oh, Penelope, my sweet Penelope..." Her name was the whisper that ended his monologue and opened his eyes.

Azerial looked up at the ceiling. "I *will* make this right; I *will* see to it that Juniper does not stray from her path and I *will* set things to rest with Penelope. On this you have my word, my solemn promise."

"Now, if you might excuse me, I have some things I have to take care of before Saturday night. However, I imagine I'll be talking to you again soon in one way or another."

Azerial, as he pushed himself to his feet and went about his afternoon, had no idea how correct he was in his imagination.

Juniper spent the rest of the afternoon and evening curled up on her bed in the darkness of her room. At first she had fought sleep, but finally she knew that she had no choice but to succumb to its siren song. At dinner time, Penelope finally woke her. She looked like she herself had been asleep until just recently as her hair was disheveled and her eyes wore the distinct red outline of exhaustion.

"Hey… you need to wake up, sleepyhead. You've gotta eat something."

Juniper groaned and rolled onto her other side. "I'm not hungry."

"Yeah, well, I'm not either," Penelope admitted. She sat down on the edge of Juniper's bed and reached out to stroke her hair. "Come on now, we both have to have *some*thing. Anything at all, you name it."

Juniper stirred and she raised her head from the pillow. "Ice cream?"

"If that's what you want." Penelope tapped her gently on the shoulder. "So come on then, get up. We'll go to the store, load up on ice cream and other junk foods and maybe, if you're up for it, we can even rent a movie."

Juniper sat up and stretched free of her sleep cocoon. She wiped the sleep from the corner of her eyes with her fists and then stifled a yawn. "What time is it? I feel like I've been asleep for days."

"It's seven thirty or so. Too early to be late, too late to be early." Penelope stood and looked around Juniper's bedroom with obvious dismay. "Not to nag, but you really should clean this place up. I think I just saw something looking back at me from behind your dresser."

"Oh mama," Juniper groaned. She pushed herself upright in the middle of the bed. She felt slightly dazed, almost as though she was still trapped in the middle of a dream. She pinched herself to clear the remaining cloud of sleep and found herself to already be very much awake.

"I'm just saying that you've really been slacking on your chores lately. I've let it slide because of finals, but I hope this summer you'll take on a little more of that responsibility you promised me."

Juniper had to smile at her mother's request, because despite everything they'd discussed that morning, things seemed to be returning to normal at the Kelly household. In fact, it was the first bit of normalcy Juniper had tasted in quite some time. It felt nice, *comfortable*, and Juniper hoped for more moments just like it.

Down the hall the phone rang and Penelope sighed when the sound hit her ears. "Honestly, that thing hasn't stopped ringing all afternoon! If it's another telemarketer, I'm going to scream so you'd be well advised to cover your ears."

When her mother left the room, Juniper decided to change her wrinkled, too-hot shirt. She shimmied out of the long sleeved t-shirt and tossed it over her shoulder. She scanned the room for a clean replacement and spotted a blue, short sleeve top that was resting on the arm of her desk chair. She took the garment to her nose and sniffed it. When she was satisfied that it was clean, she lifted it over her head and forced her appendages through various the holes.

Once again dressed, Juniper pulled her hair back into a ponytail and rubbed her face. She just couldn't shake her feeling of exhaustion, and before she left the room she cast one longing glance back at her empty bed and the warm blankets that covered it. As tempted as she was to climb back in, she knew that doing so would only tick off her mother and further disrupt their still-fragile relationship.

Penelope, after answering the phone, had wandered downstairs with the cordless held firmly to her head. When Juniper approached from the stairs, Penelope lowered her voice and turned her head. It was obvious that whomever she was talking to and whatever she was saying were not things that she wished Juniper to overhear.

"Well, you'll be happy to know that *that* is *that*," Penelope said as she placed the cordless on the kitchen counter and sighed. "That was your teacher."

"You mean *Nick*?"

Penelope sighed and her eyes rolled back slightly in her head. "He wanted to take us both out tonight for dinner. I told him we couldn't make it."

"You turned down a free dinner?" Juniper reached up to touch her mother's forehead with the back of her hand. "Well, the good news is, you don't *feel* like you have a fever. Should I get out the thermometer just to be certain?"

Penelope swatted her hand away and tried her best not to look annoyed. "Oh now, stop that! You act as though I'm cheap or something."

Juniper put one hand on her hip and shot her mama *the look*. The look that Penelope often threw in her direction when she knew Juniper was trying to feed her an unsavory line.

Penelope relented, but only slightly. "Ok, maybe I am a *little* cheap, but there's nothing wrong with that!"

"So come on, mama.   Spill it already," Juniper said. "You did more than turn down a dinner invite and you know it."

Penelope bit her lip and turned her head to the left so that Juniper could only see her profile. "He's a good man, Juniper, but he's just not the man for me. For *us*."

In her chest, her heart lifted as though suspended by helium balloons. "What are you saying? Are you trying to tell me that you two are-?"

"I'm saying that he and I are over," Penelope confessed.

"Really?"

"Yes, really.   And stop looking so smug! This has nothing to do with your father and *everything* to do with Nick's wardrobe. I mean, my god, Juniper. *Plaid* pants?"

Juniper stifled a laugh. "Yeah, they make me cringe too."

"At first it was part of the charm. You know, I thought he was eccentric, that he marched to the beat of a different drum... but, unfortunately he just has bad taste."

Juniper giggled, no longer able to hold it back. "I'm sorry, mama... I don't-" She laughed harder and bent at the waist to hold back the ache in her muscles. "I don't mean to laugh, but it's funny. Come on, it's *funny*!"

Penelope tried to hide her smile, but she failed miserably, and it spilled across her face quickly and turned into a laugh. "How *do* I get myself into these relationships, Junie?"

"I don't know, but I hope that whatever causes it isn't hereditary."

Penelope picked up a dish rag from the counter and threw it at Juniper's head. She ducked just in time to avoid the rag, still laughing heartily.

Even though she felt sorry for Mr. Halsey, it was nice to know that *some* things didn't change.

Before she even realized that it had arrived, Friday was behind her and she found that she had been deposited onto the doorstep of Saturday evening, her sixteenth birthday. Shortly after the sun had begun its predictable descent into night, Juniper had left her mother in a frenzied panic over the impending evening. Juniper thought that her anxiety was somewhat endearing and as she crossed the gently sloping field towards the woods she wondered how the first awkward moments of her parents reunion would go.

Around her, the air was alive with much of the same electricity she herself felt filled with. It swirled about her, ripe with anticipation, and the humming, buzzing insects of the night added to the mood with their own melodies. All throughout the ever-nearing forest, lightning bugs fluttered amongst the leaves and slowly swarmed the woods and surrounding neighborhood. It looked almost as though they were suspended in air by the sultry, rural, heat that hung tight to the countryside like a wet wool blanket.

Juniper realized then that within her she carried her own fluttering creatures. Butterflies. She found that for the first time since she'd suggested the birthday dinner to Azerial that she was nervous, not so much for herself, but for her mother. All afternoon and evening she had been frantic about her appearance, and had interrupted Juniper's thoughts every couple of minutes to ask her opinion on this dress or that skirt.

It amused Juniper, seeing her mother acting giddy and giggly like a teenager. She realized that under the excitement there was still a lot of residual hurt, but for the night that would be forgotten beneath the hopeful promise of renewed love, or at the least, would result in the burying of the proverbial hatchet they'd both carried strapped to their backs for so long.

Juniper wondered what they would say to each other, in

those first moments, wondered what words they might exchange after a sixteen year absence neither of them had wanted.

Juniper knotted her hands and pulled at her fingers for the remainder of the walk and as the house loomed closer, she found herself anxious for an entirely different reason.

The trees surrounding the house were almost unfamiliar in their shadowy darkness; their bark was no longer welcoming and rich with story, but instead was hard and cold and held back secrets and eyes and hidden thoughts.

She knew she wasn't alone. She knew that she was being watched. But by whom? It wasn't Azerial, that much she knew, and that conclusion left few people to consider. Could it be Ben, Jason or perhaps just a wild animal with an especially penetrating gaze? And then, just maybe, it was something else entirely.

Juniper was suddenly glad that she'd had the forethought to plan for her own safety and protection. With the thought of the near-hanging still heavy upon her mind, she hadn't come unarmed that evening. She had been afraid of just what was happening, and although she had no real intention of using it, she had taken a knife from her mother's room. A hunting knife that had belonged to Juniper's grandfather. It was pressed firmly to her lower leg, shoved down into her sock and shoe to hold it fast to her person. She felt safer for having it there, but worried more that it might be used against her.

She knew nothing of wielding weapons or inflicting harm on other people, but had to hope that if the situation presented itself she would know how to act quickly, justly and without flaw.

There was a light on in the living room as she approached. It was candle light, Juniper assumed and she walked hurriedly up the front steps to the porch. She found herself raising her fist to knock, an action that she knew was unnecessary.

A moment later, the door opened and revealed a rather dapper looking Azerial. Juniper was impressed and visually shocked by his appearance. Her mouth formed an "O" at the sight of him and her hand flew up to cover it. Wide-eyed, she stood there in the doorway, surveying her father, and wondering for a second if it was really him.

The pants Juniper had bought for him at the Good Will store fit nearly perfectly. They were a bit short, but not noticeably so. His feet were in sandals that Juniper had never seen and she wondered about their origin.

"How do I look?" Azerial moved back and welcomed Juniper into the living room. He turned around slowly, arms extended at his sides to provide her a better glimpse at his attire.

Juniper nodded approvingly. He had managed to tailor the shirt she'd brought so that he could wear it in spite of his wings; his tie was hanging perfectly square at his throat and moved up and down with his Adam's apple. He was nervous as evidenced by the gulping and the profuse wetting of his lips.

He wiped the back of his hand across his forehead to clear the rapidly beading sweat, and in the process a strand of his dark black hair escaped its smoothing and fell to tickle his forehead.

With her finger, Juniper moved it back into place and secured it with a dab of spit and a little persistence. "You look great, dad," she said when she was finished, and she stepped back to look him over one more time. *"Really* great."

"I *feel* great, Junie. You'd be amazed what a shave and a new set of clothing can do for a man."

Juniper was still smiling and her eyes were glued to her father's face. "I can't get over how wonderful you look. And not only that, but you seem... *happy*."

He rubbed his hands together and inhaled deeply. "Happy, yes... nervous, *definitely*."

"Don't be nervous! You're with *family.*" Juniper took his hand in hers and held it tightly. "But if it makes you feel any better, I'll tell you that mama has been running around all day like a crazy person."

"What do you mean?" asked Azerial.

Juniper did her best impression of her mother, and placed one hand at her chin and the other over her heart. "Should I wear the black skirt or the blue dress? Is this too revealing? Maybe I should just wear jeans... do I look like I'm trying too hard?"

"She hasn't changed her mind, then?" A glimmer of worry presented itself on Azerial's face and wove itself into his brow.

Juniper dropped her impression, and her hands, to her sides. "Of course she hasn't! She's excited to see you! Oh, and I haven't told you the best news of all." Juniper lowered her voice. "She isn't going to be seeing Mr. Halsey any more. She broke things off with him on Thursday."

Azerial seemed only slightly surprised. "Did she say why?"

Juniper beamed. "Yeah. According to her, he was a horrible dresser."

Azerial had to laugh. "Well, as long as she had a good reason."

Juniper winked at him, then looked back towards the front door. "We should go. We shouldn't put this off any longer."

Azerial hesitated. "You're *positive* that she's looking forward to seeing me again?" Azerial was hopeful, *nervous*, but hopeful.

"She can't wait," Juniper reassured him. "In fact, I don't think I've ever seen her this happy. Or this *nervous.*"

"I can't wait either," Azerial confessed. Juniper noticed him pulling at his fingers and she smiled at the small traits of his that she had inherited.

"Then let's go! You've waited long enough, don't you think?"

Azerial nodded and her words spurred him from his position. "Right, just let me grab my cloak and we'll be off." He turned to the rickety old rocking chair and removed his cloak from the arm. In a few moments, when his wings were fully concealed, Azerial took a deep breath. His eyes were again focused on the front door. "I think I may have forgotten how to walk," he said softly.

"Breathe, *relax*! Just put one foot in front of the other." She extended her hand towards him and as he took it, he squeezed it tightly between his sweating fingers.

"Everything is going to be fine," he whispered. "Everything is going to be *just* fine."

"Who are you trying to convince?" Juniper asked. "Me or yourself?"

With his free hand, he pulled the hood from his shoulders and pulled it up over the back of his head. "Juniper my dear, I'm not sure." He tightened his grip on her fingers and smiled with a glimmer of the confidence Juniper was accustomed to seeing on his face. "Let's give this a shot, shall we?"

Juniper returned his smile with one of her own and the world, momentarily freed of its ominous shadows, lit up before her with hope and promise she'd only previously known in dreams.

Azerial paused in the grass at the bottom of the Kelly's side porch steps. Juniper felt the tug in her arm as he stopped and she looked over her shoulder to question him.

"What's wrong?"

"Nerves," he said simply.

"Dad!" Juniper turned and placed a kiss on the end of his nose. "It's going to be ok. I promise!"

"Would you go in first? Maybe give me a few minutes out here to compose myself?" he asked timidly. "It's not that I'm afraid, it's just-" He looked up at the kitchen window and gulped so deeply that his tie bobbed at his chest. "She's *in* there... and you live here, so I thought if you went in to sort of... I don't know... pave the way?"

"Oh no you don't!" Juniper shook her head and laughed. "The next thing I'd know you'd be high-tailing it back to the woods."

"Do you really think I'd run in fear?" asked Azerial.

Juniper chewed her lip, contemplated his question then nodded her response. "Yes. Maybe."

"I wouldn't. I promise... but you're right about one thing, if you left me out here I would definitely at least *consider* chickening out."

"And that isn't going to happen," Juniper said firmly. She pulled his hand again and finally freed him from his frozen position upon the grass. "Come on. This is what you've been waiting for. This is what you've been *hoping* for since the day mama left."

Without any further words of protest, Azerial followed in Juniper's wake. His sandals clicked on the stairs as he climbed, then stopped as he shuffled to a halt at Juniper back.

"I don't know what I'm doing. Why did I agree to this?"

"Because you love me. Because you still love mama."

He lowered his lips to Juniper's ear and expelled a frantic, raspy whisper. "But I have no idea what I'm going to do! I've absolutely *no* idea what I should say to her, Juniper!"

"How about *hello?* Or maybe, long time no see?" Juniper tossed out her arbitrary suggestions and Azerial took them in. He nodded softly and mulled them over carefully.

"Is that all you've got?"

Juniper chuckled. "I didn't know I was supposed to script this evening. Besides, I thought you had something planned out."

"I do. Well, I *did*," he hissed, "but I currently can't remember what that was. It seems I've lost a rather large part of my mind on the walk from the house to here. I'm lucky I remember my own name."

Juniper stifled a giggle. "Well, I'm sure you'll think of something, and if all else fails, tell her she's beautiful. She'll appreciate that. Most women do."

"Right, beautiful," Azerial muttered. "That *might* work. But you don't think that I'd be... coming on too strongly with that? I don't want her to think that I'm being too forward."

"You two already have a history," Juniper reminded him. "In case you've forgotten, you had a child with her. You can't come on much more strongly than that."

Even in the darkness, Juniper could see his cheeks redden. She tightened her grip on his hand and with her free one she pulled open the screen door and gave the storm door and shove with her foot. Like a photograph, the kitchen developed before them in stunning clarity and color.

Since Juniper's departure, Penelope had hung balloons and streamers throughout the living room and kitchen. She'd obviously taken special time and consideration to make the place look nice and Juniper had to wonder if the extra care Penelope had exercised had been for her or for Azerial.

Penelope herself was no where to be seen as Juniper stepped into the kitchen with Azerial close behind. She instructed him to close the door and he did so with a tremble in his fingers. Juniper gave him a hopeful smile then turned back to the kitchen.

"Hey mama? Where are you? We have company." Juniper bent to take the knife from her sock before her mother entered the room.   She removed it slowly and placed it on the counter, blade towards the wall. Azerial didn't seem to notice the act, a fact that Juniper took great relief in.

Penelope's voice sounded from the upstairs. "Just a minute, sweetheart. I'll be right down! I'm just- I'm having some trouble finding my blue blouse. Have you seen it? I could have sworn I washed it yesterday." Her voice dissipated and Juniper could almost picture her mother standing in front of her closet looking dismayed, a customary hand on her hip.

"No, mama, I haven't seen it," Juniper replied. "Just come down, would you? And wear the green one, it looks better with your hair anyway." She rolled her eyes and looked back at Azerial. "I told you, she's been like this *all* day." Juniper turned back to the hallway and the stairs. "Hurry up, mama! Don't you think you've been waiting long enough for this?"

"I'm coming, I'm coming! Don't rush me! You know how I hate to be rushed." Within seconds, Penelope appeared at the top of the stairs. She'd taken Juniper's suggestion and had decided upon a green, silk blouse, a blouse she'd paired with a modest, yet attractive knee-length, black skirt.

She looked fantastic, more beautiful than Juniper had ever seen her. There was something new about her, something fresh, something that hadn't been exposed to the light in some time. Juniper took it as hope, as excitement and as love that she'd been forced to keep buried for years.

Her shoulder-length blonde hair had been pinned back from her face with two gold barrettes. Juniper recognized them as the barrettes she's given her mother two years prior as a birthday present. As she descended the stairs in her mid-heel, open-toe shoes, Juniper gave her a subtle thumbs up. Penelope smiled beneath her blush at her daughter's approval.

Azerial was silent at Juniper's back throughout the duration of Penelope's descent. He still hadn't removed his hood and hadn't uttered a single word since they'd entered the house.

Juniper glanced back at him and saw that his eyes were downcast. It was almost as though he was saving the first sight of Penelope for when she was right in front of him.

"I'm sorry I wasn't down here when you two got back. I'm afraid it took me a little longer to get ready than I'd expected." She motioned to the kitchen at her left. "I had to decorate and the dog kept attacking the balloons… and the streamers! Have either of you tried to hang streamers without help? It's really a two person job. I just hope everything looks ok. If I would have had more time-"

"Everything looks great, mama," Juniper assured her. "And so do you. I told you green was the right choice."

"Oh, you mean this old thing?" Penelope laughed as her feet finally came to rest on the bottom rung of the staircase. Her hand held the banister with such ferocity that her knuckles had turned white. "The funny thing is, this was my first choice. It took trying on *eleven* other things before I finally came back to it."

"You're *so* neurotic."

"And you aren't? The nut doesn't fall far from the tree, you know." Penelope joked. Her eyes moved from Juniper to Azerial briefly before she pulled them back. "So uh, I hope everyone is hungry, because I think I made enough food to feed the whole town. I just wasn't sure what you guys wanted so I made some of everything."

"I know I'm definitely hungry, although I can't speak for dad," Juniper said. With that, she stepped aside and gave her mother and Azerial a clear and obstacle free path to one another.

Penelope made the first move as she stepped onto the tile kitchen floor. Her heels made a decisive click as they slid into place to support her. At the sound of them, Azerial finally removed his hood, but still he didn't raise his head. Not until he'd removed the cloak entirely and slung it over his arm.

In the bright light of the kitchen Juniper noticed the subtle wrinkles around her father's eyes and mouth. He wore them well, like badges of honor that did little more than make him look distinguished. He was a very handsome man, she realized, and she could see more than a little of herself in his appearance.

With his courage finally gathered, Azerial took several small steps forward. He stopped when only a few inches of air remained between them. His chin was slow to withdraw itself from his chest, but when at last it did, he and Penelope's eyes met after a sixteen year delay.

Penelope was the first to break the trance. "Hello there," she said softly. "It's nice to see you again, Azerial. It's been too long."

Azerial found his own words and reached for her fingers. "First of all, I have to say that you're every bit as beautiful as the day we met, Penelope." Without hesitation he took her hand to his lips for a kiss. He lingered there, her skin pressed to his.

"Oh well, I'm sure that isn't true, but it's still nice of you to say so," she laughed. Her eyes crinkled slightly at the corners as she examined his face, a face she had once known so well. "You look wonderful too, Azerial. Time has been kind."

"Thank you," he whispered. He nodded towards the kitchen and reluctantly released her hand. "And thank you for allowing me into your home."

"Did you really think I wouldn't *jump* at the chance to see you again?" She released a nervous and high-pitched laugh. "I'm glad you could make it. *Really* glad."

Juniper smiled and watched the scene unfold before her in rapt silence. Her eyes couldn't believe what they were seeing; her heart could barely contain its excitement, and it threatened to leap into her throat. Juniper stepped backwards, but didn't take her eyes off of them. There they were, reunited at last under the cool glow of halogen lighting in a place not so far removed from the spot where they'd bid their unwilling farewells. Juniper took a mental picture of the sight in front of her, one she knew she'd carry with her for the rest of her life.

Penelope's lips twisted into a soft, almost awkward smile. "So, uh, could I get you something to drink? Dinner will be a few minutes. I have water, milk, soda, *scotch*."

Azerial clapped his hands together and his cheeks lit like torches around his laughter. "You remembered!"

"Of course I remembered," she said with a wink, "that *was* the first time I got drunk."

Juniper's eyes widened. "Mama!"

"What?" Penelope looked shocked at Juniper's intrusion and then laughed. "I'm against underage drinking for *you*, young lady."

"I see." Juniper crossed her arms over her chest and narrowed her eyes. "So this is one of those do as I say, not as I do kind of things, is it?"

Penelope nodded. "Yes, that's it, exactly!"

Juniper laughed and rolled her eyes. "You're a wonderful role model."

"Hey, you turned out ok, didn't you?" Penelope looked at Azerial and motioned towards Juniper. "What do *you* think of her? She everything you'd imagined?"

He nodded approvingly. "She's fantastic, Penny. You've done a great job, just as I knew you would."

Silence fell between them, but Juniper didn't intercede. The lull in conversation was not one of awkwardness, instead it was one filled with longing looks and unspoken apologies.

Their hands found each others a short time later and they locked fingers somewhat awkwardly. Juniper had never seen her mother smile with such unfettered intensity; she looked young and beautiful, refreshed and at the same time, completely at peace.

"I know that there are a lot of things for us to discuss," Azerial said. "But right now, looking at you, I can't imagine why it was I ever let you leave."

Penelope's eyes widened to make room for a wash of salty tears, tears she struggled to hold back. "We should have come back for you. I should have known you were playing the martyr on our behalf, I just should have *known*."

Their eyes searched each others faces. Azerial stepped closer to Penelope until he was near enough to pull her in for a hug. At first she was taken aback by the emotion, but her shock quickly faded and gave way to a strange sort of comfort and then, reciprocation.

"I've missed you," she whispered into his neck. She placed her lips at the nape and crowned him with a kiss.

"Oh Penelope..." Azerial pulled back and examined her face more closely. He drank in each line and pore in an attempt to memorize her face, to reconcile the two sides of her that he knew; the past and the present.

Juniper cleared her throat and sheepishly, her mother looked over.

"Junie! My goodness, I'm so sorry! This is *your* birthday and here we are, stealing the limelight for ourselves. I just-" She looked at Azerial again and smiled. "I just feel a bit like it's my birthday and I've just received a *fabulous* present."

"There's no reason to apologize, mama. Seeing you two together is the best gift a girl could have," Juniper said softly. "I'll even leave you two alone if you want." She tossed her mother a wink and Penelope's cheeks flushed with color before she shook her head.

"Oh, how! Don't be silly! We have a lot to celebrate here tonight!" She looked at Azerial with a wide smile. "Wouldn't you agree?"

Azerial was grinning like a fool. "I most certainly would!

Tonight has been a long time in the making and as far as I can tell, it's special for more than just a few reasons. That being said, we should get this party started as soon as possible! Now, about that scotch, you mentioned…"

Chapter Fourteen
Burning Up, Burning Down

"I can't believe you're torturing me like this! And on my *birthday* no less!" Juniper exclaimed. "This should be a crime! In some parts of the world I'm sure it *is*."

Penelope opened the second photo album and shoved it across the table towards Azerial. "Oh hush, you! I just thought your father might like to see some pictures of you. You were such a cute kid."

"And what am I now if not *absolutely* adorable?" Juniper asked jokingly.

Penelope reached out for her and pinched her cheek. "You're beautiful, is what you are. A bit annoying from time to time, but beautiful none the less."

Juniper stuck out her tongue.

Azerial pointed to a photo in the red-leather album. "How old were you here?"

Juniper leaned over and smiled at the small Polaroid photo beneath her father's finger. It had been taken several months before her 7th birthday, at a petting zoo in Columbia. In the picture she was petting a rather large, somewhat unhappy looking goat. "I was six, or as I told everyone, six and three quarters. Gosh, I still remember that like it was yesterday! That picture was taken right before that goat decided it was time to use the bathroom."

"Right on my shoe," Penelope added. "Needless to say, that was the last time we went to a petting zoo."

Azerial chuckled and turned the page. "Animals can be quite unpredictable," he commented. "Speaking of animals, where did that dog of yours get off to?"

"Well, if he knows what's good for him he's not in my

room," Penelope said. She lowered her coffee mug back to the table and rolled her eyes. "For some reason he has a fascination with my clothing."

"If you'd learn to pick up your things he wouldn't be able to get to them," Juniper said in a sing-song voice. She leaned over to Azerial and bumped his shoulder with hers. "She's always on *my* case about keeping *my* room clean, but you should see hers! Sometimes I'd swear a tornado swept right through there."

"Hey, I work two jobs and run a household. What's your excuse?"

"I'm sixteen, mama."

"Sounds like a good excuse to me," Azerial chimed in.

Penelope sighed. "If you two are going to team up against me, I'm sunk, aren't I?"

"Quite possibly, yes," Juniper said. She pushed herself away from the table and grabbed her empty coffee mug. "Can I get anyone a refill?"

Azerial shook his head and Penelope consulted the clock.

"Goodness me, look at the time, would you! We've been sitting here for almost an hour looking at photos. I need to stop this and clear the table. It's time for cake and ice cream! No birthday would be complete without it."

"I was wondering if we'd ever get to the cake," Juniper said. She refilled her mug, but left the coffee black. "My sweet tooth is almost as impatient as it is large."

"Then let's get to it! Just allow me a minute to clear off the table and I'll bring in the cake." Penelope glanced at Azerial. "It's chocolate with cream cheese icing, Junie's favorite. I hope it sounds ok to you, too."

"It's been so long since I've had anything sweet that I reckon anything will taste wonderful."

"Good, good!" Penelope stood and began to gather the dinner plates just as Juniper returned to the table.

Azerial quickly offered to help, but Penelope refused his offer flatly and politely.

"You're a guest," she said, and she fluttered her eyelashes at him in a rare flirtatious moment. "What kind of a hostess would I be if I made you do chores?"

Juniper watched her mother with a certain amount of awe as she moved around the table in her work. She'd never seen that side of her mother, and quite suddenly it was easy to imagine her as a carefree teenager, unencumbered by crappy low-paying jobs and mortgages. She surmised that they would have been good friends, even if fate hadn't joined them as a family.

Juniper soon moved her inspection to her father, but he was all but lost to her. His eyes were fixed upon Penelope as she moved quickly from the table to the sink and then to the fridge to store the leftover chicken that Juniper knew she'd be eating until at least the following Monday.

Penelope excused herself when the dishes were soaking in the sink and Juniper took the chance to lean in closer to her father.

"So?" Juniper prompted. "What do you think? How are things going?"

"Well, I'll say one thing. It was certainly nice to have a meal that didn't consist of fish and an assortment of berries." Azerial chuckled and kept his eyes trained closely upon Penelope until she finally buzzed from the room in a bubble of excitement and activity. When she was finally gone, Azerial leaned in closer to Juniper's ear. "Things are going better than I expected," he confessed. "I'm having a wonderful time. It's nice to share this with the two of you."

Juniper smiled and tried to bite the excitement back from her voice with her teeth before it bubbled over the surface of her tongue. "That's good, right?" she asked. "I mean, it's good that you two are getting along and catching up on old times...

on old *emotions*."

"Junie, sweetheart…" Azerial's head swung low to his chest. He kept it lowered for only a second before he pulled it back up and slowly faced her. "I don't want you to get your hopes up here. As much as your mother and I are enjoying this reunion, the problems that befell us sixteen years ago are still present to a certain degree. One meal cannot fix everything."

"I know that, but… is there even a *chance*?" asked Juniper hopefully. She wasn't certain she wanted to hear the answer to her somewhat loaded question and bit her lip to prepare herself for Azerial's response.

"A chance at what? At your mother and I ending up together?" He shook his head softly and his words came cautiously over troubled lips. "I cannot even offer a guess as to where we go from here. To do so would be foolish at this point. Nothing has been discussed, nor decided."

"But you have a good feeling, right?" Juniper's frustration grew up from her feet to her legs. She moved them around restlessly under the table. "*I* have a good feeling. I haven't seen mama this happy since…" Juniper paused to replay the past in her worn-out mind. "Well, since *ever*!"

"I saw her this happy once." Azerial smiled and extended one hand towards Juniper's face. His thumb found the end of her nose and he touched it softly. "When she brought *you* to me for the first time she was this happy."

Juniper felt her cheeks redden slightly beneath her hair. She pushed a few strands away from her eyes and caught her father's gaze. "I know you don't think it can work between you and mama, but-"

"Junie, I told you. There are things that keep us apart that no one can change or control."

"I know, dad. You've said that over and over again… but what *things*?" She licked her lips quickly then rushed on with her speech to avoid her father's conservative rebuttal. "So you're an angel... big deal!"

"It *is* a big deal!" Azerial's voice raised slightly before it plummeted back to a whisper. "Do you think I could live here with the two of you and never be seen? Do you think I could accompany you to school plays? Drive you off to college? Walk you down the aisle at your wedding?"

"Yes!" she exclaimed. "Why not?"

He shook his head and a sigh pressed past his sealed lips. "I wish that I *could* do all of those things for you- *with* you. But Junie, I just *can't*."

"Your coat covers your wings!" she protested, unwilling to allow Azerial to admit defeat, or to make her face it herself.

"Not without looking suspicious." He pressed his eyes firmly against Juniper's. "I love you as much as a father can love a daughter, and I want nothing more than to be there for you *and* your mother, but I'm just not certain that it's possible."

It was Juniper's turn to sigh, a sharp and elongated sigh that pierced her lungs and squeezed her heart like tightly drawn together fingers around a tennis ball.

"I just don't want you getting your hopes up, that's all." Azerial looked over his shoulder to the hall that lead to the living room. "Your mother and I have a lot of talking to do once this celebration is over... and speaking of this celebration." He paused and pushed his fingers to the corners of his daughter's mouth. Carefully, he molded her lips into a smile and then found one of his own. "This is your *birthday* party! Your *16th* birthday party! I'm here, your mother is here... you should be happy for so many reasons, yet here you are, dwelling on the few negative aspects."

"I just can't help it," Juniper said with a sigh. "I mean I am happy..."

Azerial narrowed his eyes as if to stop her from saying what he knew would be lies.

Juniper re-configured her words in the back of her mind.

"I *am* happy. I suppose this situation is a bit like cake. You have one piece, it tastes great and suddenly you're wanting more. A second piece, extra icing, some ice cream on the side. Do you know what I mean?"

"I know what you mean." Azerial kissed her forehead. "Listen, not to change the subject, but there's something I've been meaning to talk with you about for a past few weeks. It's just that we've been through so much that I haven't been able to find the right time to discuss it with you."

"There's no time like the present! What is it?"

"It's about your destiny. About those *tools* I mentioned."

"Oh, right, right, the mysterious *tools*. Are you finally going to tell me what they are?"

"Not they, **it**," Azerial corrected. "Since you're now officially sixteen, you're of age."

"I didn't know there was an age requirement on this."

"There is, sort of. I *could* have given it to you last week or the week before, but sixteen is a special age and I preferred to wait. The number sixteen itself is important in many ways, in many endeavors. It's important in religion, mathematics, astronomy... It also means in a lot of cultures that you've come of age into adulthood."

"Right... but what are you getting at here? The curiosity is killing me."

Azerial sat up straighter and cleared his throat. "When sixteen years have come to pass in the life of a Nephilim child, it becomes time to bestow upon them the gift that will allow them to erase the rift of the Nexxus that accompanied their birth. Their father's halo."

Juniper's eyes widened. "What? Your-? Are you kidding me?"

"I assure you I'm not."

"But if you give me your halo then you'll be without-"

"Yes."

"But how will you stand it? Not being able to heal or read minds? You've had those abilities since the beginning of time!"

"I'm aware of this, but it's what has to be done. It's one of the rules that I was given-"

It was Juniper's turn to interrupt. "Given by whom?"

"By God, of course," Azerial responded. "In the hours after your birth he spoke to me for what would be the last time. He told me the things I must do now that I had fathered a child with a mortal woman."

"So wait a second here... if I take your halo and close this Nexxus, will you be free? Of your tether?"

"I will indeed, for once the Nexxus is sealed I will no longer need to guard it. I'll be free of that duty."

Juniper sat back in her chair and shook her head slowly from side to side. "This is... this is a lot to swallow!" she exclaimed. "I can't believe this. This is... this is-"

"Surreal?" Azerial supplied.

"Yeah, you could say that," she breathed. "I mean, wow. I'll have a halo? I have so many questions!"

"I thought you might, which is why after this dinner is over, I'd hoped we might discuss things in more depth. I'd like to get this halo to you soon so that I can begin teaching you how to properly use it and harness its full potential."

"You want to give it to me *tonight?*" she gasped.

"The sooner you receive it after you've turned sixteen, the better. The longer we wait, the more complications we'll be forced to deal with," he said. He reached out to her and ran his palm down the length of her hair. "It won't hurt, if that's what you're worried about."

"No, no, I'm not worried about that... I guess I'm just a bit overwhelmed."

"That's understandable. If I were in your position I think that I too would be a bit-" Azerial's words were halted as

Penelope breezed back into the room with a handful of candles and a lighter.

"Sorry that took me so long! I could find where I'd put the candles. Lord knows we can't have a birthday cake without candles. How else would Junie get her wish to come true?" Penelope dropped her smile and paused at the head of the table to survey the scene she had interrupted. "My, my! You could cut the tension in this room with a knife. What have I missed?"

"Junie and I were just talking, nothing more." Azerial tossed his arm around Juniper's shoulders and pulled her closer to his chest. Juniper laughed and struggled to free herself so that she might sit upright in the face of her mother's question.

"Is it finally time for cake?" Juniper asked. She expelled her words amidst a choppy sequence of laughter brought about by Azerial's fingers beneath her arm. She shoved him away playfully and extended a long, lean warning finger in his direction. "If you tickle me again, I'll tickle you back."

"I'd leave her alone, if I were you." Penelope took her seat across from Juniper and caught Azerial's gaze. "She's a fierce tickler, this one."

Azerial raised his hands in front of him to admit his surrender. "Then I shall raise my white flag and wave it without shame."

Juniper laughed and turned her attention back to her mother. "So... cake? Soon?"

"In a minute," her mother laughed. "*First*, I think you should open *this*."

Penelope's hands brought forth a small and neatly wrapped box. It was no larger than a jewelry box, and was only slightly more rectangular in shape. Penelope extended the tiny offering to Juniper, who took it carefully into her hands.

"Mama! You didn't have to get me anything! I didn't even tell you what I wanted!"

"It's your 16th birthday, Junie, and not too long from

now you'll be heading off to college... I had to get you *some*thing!" She paused to wave her hand. "Just open it, would you?"

Juniper looked down at the small box and pulled slowly at the red ribbon that held it firmly in its simple beauty. She placed the freed ribbon on the table beneath her hand and ran her fingernail over the end of the wrapping paper until it split at the seam. Juniper pulled the shiny blue paper away from the rectangular object and let it fall to the ground at her feet. She removed the lid a second later and peered curiously inside.

"You got me a... key?" Juniper's face bunched up into a look of absolute confusion. "A *key*?"

Penelope sighed and rolled her eyes. "Well, aren't you even going to ask what it opens?"

Juniper looked up at her mother curiously and a moment later, a notion hit her. "Mama..." Her eyes widened slowly and in doing so pushed her eyebrows up towards her forehead. "Mama! You *didn't*!"

Penelope's tight-lipped secret escaped her in the form of a laugh. "I did! Now go on! Have a look at the driveway already, would you?"

"Mama!" Juniper stood up so quickly that her chair scooted several feet backward across the linoleum floor and nearly toppled over. Azerial caught the back of the wood-slat chair with his right hand and steadied it to the ground.

"It isn't a great car, but I got a good deal." Penelope followed her daughter to the kitchen window and jerked her head towards the driveway. "Happy Birthday, sweetheart. I hope you like it."

Juniper's fingers found the cord of the blinds and tugged. "I can't believe you did this! How on *earth* could you afford to buy me a *car*?"

"Well, it's part of the reason I've been working so much... and you remember Mr. Johnston, right? His doctors told him that he's no longer allowed to drive because of his Parkinson's, *so* he sold the car to me for nearly nothing just to be rid of it." She placed an arm around her daughter's shoulders and kissed her softly on the temple. "It runs great, it has low miles, and *now* you can take that job at the book store this summer. If you still want to, that is."

Juniper felt tears begin to well up in the corners of her eyes. She pushed them away with the side of her hand and threw her arms around Penelope's neck. "Oh, thank you, mama! Thank you!"

"Well?" Penelope pulled away from her daughter's hug and then glanced out the window to the driveway. "What do you think of her?"

Before Juniper could answer, her attention was stolen from the window and was returned to her father. It had been a loud clatter that had sounded first, a clatter followed by a gasp and a decisive thump. Something unseen and unknown had reduced Azerial to a lump of flesh and feathers on the kitchen floor.

"Dad?" Juniper lowered the key to her side and shoved it quickly into the pocket of her jeans. She ran back to the table and hovered over her father's form in a state of shock. "What's wrong? *Dad?* Are you ok? What happened?"

Thick and heavy gasps escaped Azerial's lungs as they tried desperately to procure enough breath to function. He held one hand over his heart while the other was placed palm flat on the floor to steady his rapidly wilting form. "S-Something's wrong, Junie." His chest heaved laboriously around his words before he sputtered out a second series of deep, heavy coughs.

"What?" Juniper fell to her knees at her father's side and reached out to rest her hand on his. "Are you sick? Do you need me to heal you? Just tell me what to do, dad. Just tell me and I'll do it."

Juniper didn't realize that Penelope had joined her vigil

until she spoke. "Azy? What's wrong?" Her words were creased with worry and panic, both emotions that were also etched deeply into her forehead.

Azerial looked up at the sound of her voice. He was pale and gaunt and his eyes bulged from his face like two angry, tightly-bound fists, a reality that gave him the appearance of a choking victim. The hand that he'd previously held over his heart moved upwards to his throat. The action revealed to Juniper a series of quickly-spreading burns that seemed to have originated on the back of his hands. They looked like melting candle wax as they began to move up the lengths of his arms.

Juniper wiped the sweat from his brow with the back of her head, but found that it came too quickly to be stopped. He was burning up with fever. It was almost as though a fire had been set in his chest and was spreading rapidly throughout the rest of his body.   "Oh my- What's happening?" she asked.

"The tree," he whispered, "something is happening to the tree. It's d-dying." His eyes rolled back in his head as the burns pushed up from his chest to his neck and face like angry rivers of boiling water.

"What?" Juniper's arms grabbed for his shirt, but he escaped her fingertips and fell backwards to the floor.

His eyes remained closed and with each tick of the clock his breathing became increasingly more shallow. Penelope raced around the table and came up behind him. Over his pain-wracked body, her eyes met Juniper's.

"Mama! What's wrong with him? What do we do?" Juniper searched her mother's eyes for clues, but came up empty.

Penelope pulled Azerial's head into her lap and her hands brushed the beads of sweat from his forehead. She ignored Juniper's question in favor of her own escaped terror. "Azy?! Azerial, wake up. Come on! Please!"

Juniper felt the panic rise up inside of her. It was hot

and thick and it reached for her teeth like grabbing fingers on an outstretched hand. She raised her palm to cover her mouth, uncertain as to what might come out. When the nausea receded, she spoke through her fingers, her tone frantic. "Dad! Tell me what to do- I don't know what to do!"

Azerial's eyes rolled open and found the ceiling. His lips were so dry that they had practically sealed themselves shut over his teeth. Penelope stroked his forehead with the fingers of her left hand; with her right she fanned him in vain, trying desperately to cool him down. When finally he found a small opening between his over-parched lips he pushed his words free through the crack.

"It's time-" he croaked. "The tree is dying, the Nexxus is opening. You have t-to seal it… **now**." Azerial closed his eyes again, then re-opened them as though a voice inside of his head had prompted him to do so. "Come closer, Junie, please…"

Without hesitation, Juniper did as she was told and leaned closer to her father's fallen frame. She stopped her approach when her face was only a few inches from his.

His eyes were wide, but calm, and somehow he forced a smile. "There isn't much time- I know this isn't how-" He broke off and broke down into a series of heavy-chested coughs. "It was *supposed* to be different, but we can't help that now."

Juniper shook her head as the confusion circled her like long beaked vultures ready to pick at her flesh. "Dad, what are you talking about? I don't understand what-"

He brought his left hand up to find her cheek and Juniper dropped her voice at his touch. He pat it softly, then moved his outstretched finger to her forehead. "It's time, Juniper. You're ready, you can do this. Save the tree if you can, but your main objective- close the portal. It'll be just like when you saved Sam, Junie… Use the energy you've been given." His finger moved slowly down the length of her nose to the tip, where he held it firmly. "Use your *tool*."

A spark erupted from his fingertip and shot straight into Juniper's nose. She gasped at the odd sensation of the liquid light as it rocketed upwards towards the top of her head and quickly dissipated into her mind. Juniper felt it hit her brain and immediately she felt her temperature soar. She wobbled, pulled back slightly and felt for a moment as though she were going to pass out from the fuzzy almost out-of-focus feeling behind her eyes.

"What was that-?" Juniper managed to ask. "I don't-"

"Go," Azerial whispered. "There isn't much time."

"Are you sure I can-?" Juniper began, but Azerial quickly interrupted her doubt.

"I *know* you can." Azerial's peaceful smile faded and his eyelids fell slowly to rest over his eyes. "Hurry... *please*... before the Shadows are freed and all hope is lost."

Penelope whimpered. "Azy?" She looked up at Juniper, her eyes seared with a wildness Juniper had never seen. "He's dying, Junie... He's-" Penelope broke off into sobs, and her hands cupped Azerial's sweat-soaked cheeks. "I don't want you to go, but you have to... I've raised you for this, for this moment, for this *destiny*."

"I'm afraid!" Juniper cried. "I can't-"

Penelope released Azerial's left cheek and raised her hand to meet Juniper's. "Don't be afraid. You have to do this, Junie, or we'll lose him. We can't let that happen... we just got him back!"

Juniper, eyes wide and lips trembling, nodded and extricated herself from the tangle of her parents. As she fought to pull herself to her feet, she slipped and her knee hit the overturned dining chair that Azerial had spilled out of. She cursed under her breath and then quickly regained her footing. "Stay with him, mama. I'll be back as soon as I can."

Penelope nodded and the movement of her chin freed

her tears from their vigil at the corners of her eyes. "Be careful! I don't want to lose both of you."

"Don't worry, mama," said Juniper. "No one is going to lose *any*one. Not tonight."

Juniper pulled open the kitchen door and threw the screen from her path with one swift shove of her outstretched hand. It rattled and banged, and by the time it returned to silent stillness, Juniper was already facing the forest. With her heart beating loudly inside of her head like the over-exaggerated pounding of booming bass, she began her forward movement. At first she didn't see it; it, the giant storm cloud of billowing smoke that seeped through the forest canopy and gathered just above the tree line.

When she finally did see it, she gasped and stopped dead in her tracks. Her mind clogged with fear, a fear that rapidly funneled down to infect every part of her body. For a moment she was immobilized, that is until the memory of Azerial clutching his chest on their kitchen floor rushed back to her; until the look in her mother's eyes haunted her with an indescribable sadness.

He's dying, you idiot, she chastised herself. *Run!*

The wind grabbed her quickly by the hand and pulled her through the night, pulled her across the field of wild flowers and tall unkempt grasses, straight on to the belly of the beast.

Above her the sky revealed her jewels. Jewels that had been set deep in their jet black canopy in a stark contrast to the slowly rising cloud of thick oppressive smoke.

At her legs, the weeds scratched and pulled at her skin as she sliced through them with her long determined strides. She was itchy, hot, and a feeling of dizziness hung tightly around her head much like the noose had previously hung like a second skin at her neck and throat.

Juniper pushed back the panic that welled inside her with the gathering of her fists. Without another moment's hesitation she threw herself into pursuit of the house and ran as though she herself were on fire. She didn't break her stride until she passed the smattering of old oak trees at the forest perimeter. The smoke had begun to stretch out towards her, and it obscured the familiar path she had blazed to the farm house. She knew that the creek lay at her right, and she could almost hear it, *sense* it. A moment later, she found it and she followed the gentle serpentine further into the smoke-choked cluster of trees. She continued, however, at a slower, less confident pace.

The smoke had collected in thick curtains, curtains that parted only slightly in the stale wind to provide her horrifying glimpses of the flames that were quickly engulfing the farm house.

But there was something else, some*one* else, standing in the shadows just ahead of her. The closer she drew, the more movement she saw. There were *two* people and Juniper squinted through the haze to make out who or *what* they were.

As she approached, her legs pumping in time with her arms, the figures heard her. The snap of the twigs and the rustle of leaves beneath her feet had alerted them to her presence, and when she was almost upon them, they parted slightly. Just enough to allow her a path between them.

It was Ben, and at his side stood Jason. They had turned to watch her with wide-eyed amazement as she came at them with an expression on her face that she knew must have looked just short of insane. Her eyes flashed with fury at the sight of them; her hair flowed out behind her, tangled up in the wind, and her chest heaved as though on the verge of collapse. It was all too much, the emotions that coursed through her.

Ben called out to her. "What took you so long?"

She didn't stop to respond to his question at first, instead she passed his stunned-still body without breaking her pace. She called out to him only after she'd passed him by. "You have no idea what you've done! Do you? You *fucking* idiot!"

Her words stirred them both and a moment later she heard the crack of branches rise up behind her as Ben and Jason made chase.

"What do you think you're going to do?" Ben yelled. "It's too late to save your precious house!"

"No!" Juniper screamed. "It's not. It's never-"

Before she could finish her sentence, she felt the solid grip of a hand as its fingers spread out across her upper arm and jerked her from her run into a jog.

She shrugged it off, stumbled, and felt her throat tighten from the increase in smoke. "Stop it!" Juniper bellowed. "Leave me alone!"

A voice rose up behind her. It was Ben's, heavy and pressed through grit teeth. "Juniper! You crazy-" He tackled her and pushed her to the ground. In doing so, his words escaped him and left his thought to hang unfinished.

Juniper screamed as her face hit the cool, hard ground. Dirt and dust jumped up at her mouth and rushed inside to coat her tongue. With her flat on her stomach, Ben scurried up the length of her body until he had managed to straddle her. His hands moved quickly to the back of her head. Once there, he forced her face into the ground with a fair amount of force. A moment later, his hand tangled within her thick locks, he pulled her head free of the dirt.

Juniper winced as he shoved her face a second time into the hard earth with a decisive thump. Her vision blurred from the impact, but didn't leave her fully.

Over the course of the next few hazy seconds, Juniper sensed that something was happening just above her, something she herself couldn't witness. A moment later, however, she found herself free of Ben's sprawled body and she scrambled forward on her knees. She turned as she did so, and found, to her surprise, that Jason had pulled Ben backwards from the spot where they'd been involved in their tussle.

Juniper pulled herself upright just as Ben broke free of Jason's stranglehold. He gasped and stumbled, but regained his footing just after Juniper had regained hers and had broken off into a sprint across the final few feet to the front porch.

The acrid intensity of the fire had grown hotter and more ill-tempered with each frantic footstep that Juniper had placed in front of the other. Her heart popped in her chest like bacon grease, and burned her lungs with an aching sizzle as her chest struggled to inhale, exhale and repeat the process.

Juniper's hand flew up to cover her mouth as a series of coughs sputtered past her lips; her tongue was pressed to the bottom of her mouth, heavy with ash, and in the slowly passing seconds of her panic, she wiped her tongue on the back of her hand and tried to swallow away the burnt-black remains of the leaves she'd ingested.

Her eyes were stinging and she furiously blinked back the water that shimmied to her eyelashes and prepared for its leap; the house was lost to her in the thickness of the smoke. Every tree looked the same, an impressive, shadowy, silhouette smoldering in the scant rays of moonlight that shone as beacons through the chaos.

Behind her, the voices continued.

"Where are you? You fucking bitch!" Ben was lost in the same haze that Juniper found herself squarely in the middle of.

She sucked in a gulp of fresh air and dove into the darkness before her.

Juniper found a moon beam there, and another just beyond it. She pieced them together like a celestial tapestry, and plotted her way through the ethereal mist to the other side where the farm house waited.

A noise caught her attention; the feeling that Juniper had experienced earlier returned - the feeling that she wasn't alone. The shrugging, creaking shake of falling wood, the voices of

Ben and Jason - her concentration was split and frayed like the ends of a cut rope.

In her throat, a cry rose. Frustration and panic took the liberty of assaulting her again, but she withstood their slings and arrows and followed the noises of the crackling flames.

Juniper's sleeve had found her mouth and nose again, and filtered the air she allowed herself. It did little good, but it was better than the alternative which was doing nothing. Finally, her feet smacked into the edge of the porch.

She stumbled over the first step and fell hard to her knees on the rotting wood. She pulled herself up and onward and crawled up the next three stairs until she felt the reassuring flatness of the porch.

The smoke had dissipated slightly; the fire had sprouted up in its place and was working hungrily to devour the contents of the home.

Juniper smelled books burning, heard the pop of a window as the glass shattered under the heat and slithered away broken into the night; the tree stood before her, the base of it surrounded by a solid wall of fire.; dark, heavy, shadows were crawling out from beneath it, their eyes shining red like simmering coals.

She surveyed the situation and searched the growing flames for a path to the stairs. Just as she found it, the voices behind her returned.

Ben appeared in the doorway a second later. His face was smeared with dirt and soot and his eyes were wild, almost as wild as Juniper knew hers must be. She spun to face him and backed slowly away from him with her hands out in front her.

"Please, leave!" she begged him. "You don't know what you've done-"

Ben ran towards her and Juniper turned to make a dash for the stairs. Finally, the steps emerged through the smoke and cleared a path for Juniper's feet. As quickly as the path had opened, it closed again and trapped Ben on the other side. Juniper heard him coughing, but she didn't stop to plead with him further. There wasn't time, and with that thought, her feet led her to the first landing successfully.

"Juniper!" Ben was screaming her name. Over and over he said it, and each time it grew closer.

The air was hot and pregnant with rage, and it billowed out from the doorways at Juniper as she passed them by in her haste. She ignored the anguished cries behind her and tried her best to force them from her mind.

She spun frantically in the middle of the burning hallway. Her heart pounded in her ears with such intensity that she thought her eardrums were going to burst from the intensity.

Ben's feet hit the landing next to her. He had jumped over a small wall of fire, and his arms were outstretched in Juniper's direction. She recoiled, but not quickly enough, and Ben's fingers pulled at the sleeve of her shirt.

Juniper raised her hand to him and narrowed her eyes. A glimmer of darkness snaked across her face and revealed itself to Ben. He gasped at the sight of it, but didn't release his grip on her arm.

Juniper's voice shook as she spoke. "You have to leave, please... Before I do something I'll regret."

Ben threw both of his arms around her waist and pushed her to the ground. She struggled that time by kicking and flailing her arms and legs about wildly in the hope she might push him away.

One of her knees connected with his stomach and he groaned, winced and slightly released his death grip on her torso. Juniper placed her hands on the sides of his face and pushed him away from her person with near superhuman strength. She bit her tongue to hold back the temptation that dwelled there; the temptation to take from him what he was unknowingly taking from Azerial.

His life.

She closed her eyes and sent a silent prayer through the burning rafters to the peaceful heavens above. *Give me the strength... give me the strength to withstand this temptation.*

Juniper rolled Ben over and off of her. They continued their side-by-side scuffle on the landing as the fire raged on around them. Finally, she gathered the whole of her physical energy and directed it to her fists. She punched Ben hard and square on the nose and he rolled onto his back from the impact. His legs found the wall of flames that he'd jumped over at the top of the stairs and a bloodcurdling scream erupted from his lips as he realized that his jeans had caught fire. He sat up, wild-eyed, and tried to pull himself away from the hungry lick of the blaze.

Juniper looked away and tucked her chin into her chest. Ben grabbed for her leg. The determined, angry look in his eyes had been replaced with terror, with panic. He jerked at her again until she felt the flames tickle the hem of her shirt and rise quickly up the front.

With one last burst of energy, Ben jerked her down to the ground so that she was once again on his level. As he did so, Juniper shifted her hips. It was an action that caused her to land on his left shoulder. Ben yelped from the pressure and lost his grip on her clothes. Juniper took that as her chance and scrambled away, breathless, sweating and choking on the absence of oxygen. She rolled onto her left side and tried desperately to get her wits about her. It was only a split second after her tuck and roll when a loud, wooden-sounding, creak erupted over their heads. It sounded like angry thunder, and the clap drew both of their attentions to the ceiling.

Juniper had just enough time to look up; Ben's eyes were also pulled to the noise and its lofty height. From there, everything happened in an instant. The ceiling seemed to pitch, the walls shimmied and the overhead beam that supported the back-half of the upstairs hallway broke free of their combined hold and began its unstoppable fall. Wooden and weighing several hundred pounds, it plummeted quickly and gave Ben little time to react. With his eyes wide and arms thrown up over his face, he moved to the left; the movement, however, wasn't enough to put him out of the path of the falling object. It hit him with a sickening thud and pushed from his lungs a scream that made Juniper's blood run cold.

She covered her ears, but was unable to close her eyes. As much as she wanted to turn from the scene and run on to complete her task, she couldn't move from her spot on the floor. Not until she heard Ben's cries rise up from the flaming wood a second time.

"Juniper! Oh God- please!"

Terrified, Juniper rolled onto her knees and crawled across the wood plank floor to the horrific scene. All she could see from her vantage point was the beam and one of Ben's twisted, presumably broken legs, as it protruded outwards.

"Ben? Can you hear me?" Juniper asked. She reached the beam, reached out to touch it, and was instantly bitten by an angry flame that reared up in defiance of her appearance.

Ben didn't respond to her question, still, Juniper pushed on and wedged her fingers beneath the beam. She huffed, she puffed and with all of the strength she'd been afforded she tried fruitlessly to hoist the wooden beam from atop Ben's broken body.

She knew after the first attempt that it was useless; after the second attempt she knew that trying a third time was an exercise in futility. Still, she tried, and only stopped when she saw the flames leap up the stairs two at a time in pursuit of Ben's fallen body.

Like a well-choreographed ballet, the fire leapt into his hair and onto his clothing and spread out to inspect his skin. Apparently liking what they had found, the ravenous flames proceeded to cover him fully in their embrace. His scream rung out for only a second before he fell away into silence; into a silence from which he'd never arise.

There's nothing I can do for him now, she told herself. *I tried, I did more than most people would have done in my situation. I did my best, but I couldn't save him… and maybe… maybe I was never meant to.*

That sad realization pulled a sob from her chest, but she knew there was no time afforded her to grieve or to bury herself in guilt. So she did what she knew she had to do, and she stood.

At the bottom of the staircase, on the other side of Ben's quickly, burning body, Juniper found Jason. Their eyes met only briefly before she forced herself to turn away from his horror-stricken face.

If he doesn't have the good sense to get out of here, there's nothing I can do for him. I don't have the time to protect him, not now. I have to get to the attic, I have to save dad, she thought, a thought that came quickly from the murky underwater depths of her shell-shocked mind. *The attic… It'll be the only place left where the tree isn't surrounded completely by flames. Hopefully.*

And she ran, ran as quickly as she could down the burning hallway, all else be damned. She paused only long enough to side-step a flame that jumped up at her feet from the floor below in attempt to grab her jeans.

She heard nothing as she made her flight to the small attic room; her heartbeat had replaced everything with its echo, an echo that rattled and shook around Juniper's brain until she felt dizzy and faint.

When finally the attic bedroom door was within her sight, she breathed a sigh of relief from the side of her mouth and then hungrily gulped in the last bit of fresh air she could find amongst the smoldering walls.

With one sleeve over her mouth and nose, the other over the fingers of her left hand, she reached out and quickly twisted the assumably hot door knob.

Her first attempt was unsuccessful, her second however, was not, and when Juniper finally entered the bedroom, she found that she had no time to grab her bearings before the wrath of the flames was unleashed upon her.

The first tackled her by the feet and ignited the hem of her pants; the second took a different approach and instead reached out to play with the thick curls of her raven hair.

Juniper screamed as the fire licked her milky-white flesh and she fell to her knees in the middle of the pulsing inferno. Juniper prayed, unaware of the slowly awakening spark in her chest; a present from her father, on that, her sixteenth birthday.

Suddenly, from somewhere deep within the depths of her soul, the spark coursed from her sternum, upwards towards her head. The heat dissipated around her until the flames that tore at her clothes were cold and unthreatening.

Slowly she stood, surprised by the small amount of difficulty it took to do so. By that point, the room was engulfed in flames. The fire had climbed to lick at the ceiling and the long branch that extended into the room was burning freely like a tightly rolled piece of paper dipped in lighter fluid.

Above her the flames formed a canopy and shot to a point at the peak of the ceiling; her eyes focused on the tree in front of her, her mission at hand.

With palms exposed and offered up for the taking, Juniper walked into the flames and winced only slightly as her body prepared itself for the pain. Instead, she received nothing more than a slight tingling sensation that quickly faded into numbness. The bark of the oak seemed almost to reach out to her in an attempt to pull her close. The moment she touched it, an angry roar rose up from beneath her feet in protest of her actions. The force of it sent her several inches off of the ground and into the air. Another small shock shook the first floor and rumbled into nothing. The Shadows awoke and rose upwards through the second story to the attic, and when they surrounded her, she closed her eyes to avoid the sight of their flaming eyes.

Juniper's fingertips began to tingle as the light crept from her nails and radiated out to eagerly fill the flame engorged corners of the room.

Blinded by awe and drunk on power, Juniper pressed on, and threw herself into the tree with the whole of her body. She clung to its bark and focused her mind to a razor fine point.

Behind her she became aware of a noise. She didn't open her eyes, instead she held fast to the burning tree, her mind concerned with only one thing.

Azerial.

"Juniper!"

It was a voice, and whoever it belonged to was calling her name. Somewhere in the back of her mind, she recognized it.

Strange hands found the back of her shirt, but she resisted the tug in favor of her task.

"What are you doing? We have to get out of here!"

It was Jason, his voice frantic and high-pitched at the back of her head. Juniper lost her concentration and released her grip on the tree. She fell exhausted into Jason's waiting arms and together they toppled to the floor. Juniper landed with her back on Jason's knees, but gathered her wits quickly and twisted around to face him.

"What the hell are you doing in here?" She threw her hands into his chest and pushed him towards the door. "You have to get out of here, Jason! It's not safe!"

"I'm not leaving you here to die!" he bellowed. "I can't watch another person-"

"*I can't leave!*" Juniper yelled, her voice elevated to compete with the loud rumble of the fire. "You don't understand, I don't expect you to… but I can't leave! Not now, not **yet**!"

Jason fought with her and pulled at her shirt until he was

practically dragging her across the room on her back. Juniper, with her arms outstretched towards the tree, struggled like a worm on a hook until she broke free of his weary fingers. She scuttled across the floor, directly into the flames, and again found the tree.

That time, when her fingers hit the bark, she felt a jolt rock her entire body. She heard Jason's voice, heard him scream. Juniper opened her eyes wide to face the wall of fire that had leapt up the trunk of the tree to fill her face with brightness.

She bit her tongue to suppress her own screams, but didn't waver from her task. She pressed onward, and ignored the tickle of the flames as they chewed at her protective bubble seeking entrance. The flames retreated, then advanced, retreated, then advanced. When the struggle finally ended and the flames receded, they did so with quickness and force. The ground seemingly opened up beneath her and parted the rotting dusty boards after it sucked them clean. Suddenly, as if by magic, the unearthly raging beast fell silent into the nothing from which it had come.

Finally, after the smoke had filled her lungs and her peripheral vision had been lost, Juniper collapsed to her back amidst the smoldering wreckage of the farm house.

Beside her laid the silent body of Jason Price.

Juniper, in one last display of courage, rolled on top of him where she placed her hands over his chest. As she began the healing, a surge of pain swept throughout her body; it was the last thing she felt before she collapsed into the ball of light energy that had so quickly covered them both.

Somewhere in the back of Juniper's mind, a voice encouraged her to open her eyes. When she did so, the reality of life came flooding back to her, and filled her nostrils with the smoldering scent of burnt wood and burnt flesh.

Slowly, her surroundings slid into focus; the outline of the flame-ravaged trees, the collapsed and foreboding front porch of the farm house, the moonlight that found her in the dark. Ash fell around her like rain as it plummeted from the tree branches to take its rest at the forest floor.

Juniper realized soon enough that she wasn't alone in her confusion; next to her, Jason sat cross-legged with his head thrown forward into his waiting hands. He was crying, and his chest heaved with guilty, mournful sobs.

"Jason-?" Juniper's voice struggled past her ash-soaked throat and found the thick night air that surrounded them.

The boy froze at the appearance of her words and his cries almost instantly subsided. He pulled his head from his palms and turned to face her. His eyes widened like saucers beneath his brows as he searched her face in obvious disbelief. "You- you're alive!" He seemed surprised, almost shocked, that she hadn't suffered the same fate as Ben.

Juniper sat up slowly and propped herself up on her elbows. "Am I?"

"If *I* am, *you* are," Jason said cautiously. He pushed his soot-covered hands across his face and eyes. "Are you ok?" he asked.

She coughed and expelled thick, black, phlegm from her lungs. She spit it out to the ground and pushed her hands across her mouth. "I-I think I'm ok, yeah. You?"

He nodded numbly, as though still dazed from the events that had transpired. "Yeah, I'm fine. Thanks to you," he whispered.

Juniper rubbed her temples and her foggy headache subsided. "I don't remember what happened-"

"And I'm not *sure* what happened. I- I was trying to get you out of the house, but you didn't want to leave. You-" He shook his head as though confused by the few memories his mind had managed to retain. "I don't know what I saw, Junie. I can't even begin to explain it."

Juniper gulped and glanced back at the house. Her words trickled from her lips like water from a struggling drain. "What happened here tonight... you can't... you can't tell *anyone* what I've done."

"What? Wait a second here! You mean you really- that you really did it?" Jason's eyes were wide again and in the darkness he looked almost haunted. "You put out the fire?"

Juniper wet her lips and nodded weakly. Her head felt like it had been filled with concrete. "You were right about me, ok? I'm *different* than other people."

"You saved my life. Just like that dog... You saved me." His head rolled to his chest and his eyes fell to examine his lap. "After everything I did to you. After everything I *let* Ben do-" He gulped, swallowed and licked his lips as though he couldn't quite figure out what had happened or how to describe it. "I remember passing out, and then the next thing I knew, I was waking up. The fire was g-gone, *completely* gone, and you were collapsed next to me on the floor. You weren't breathing... I thought you were *dead*."

"You carried me out of there?" she asked.

He nodded, but said nothing further on the subject.

Juniper felt for the root of her headache with her fingers and found a thick knot at the back of her skull. She rubbed it to provide relief, but the throb only increased and she dropped her hand to her side. "I don't remember anything after I saw you passed out on the floor. It's all a blur." She looked over her shoulder to the farm house in the hopes that it might reveal to her the pieces of the puzzle her brain had conveniently misplaced.

Thick, black, smoke still billowed out from the attic in the form of angry and determined clouds. Their presence filled the air that hung over them and obscured the tops of the trees, and the sky beyond, from their sight.

The old oak tree Juniper had tried so desperately to save was black and charred. All of the leaves and branches were gone, or almost gone, and they dangled like broken, heavy, appendages over the remainder of the staircase and the back wall of the farm house. The tree was alive, Juniper guessed, but barely.

The rest of the house that had once surrounded it was gone, reduced to nothing more than a collection of broken and blackened boards. The front porch, where Juniper had first realized her gift, had buckled under the weight of the falling walls and was nothing more than a heap of busted boards. All around the charred remnants laid ceiling beams similar to the one that had broken free of the rafters and claimed Ben's life. Between their fall and the crumble of the walls, everything that had remained within the confines of the home had been taken to the dirt and buried beneath the rubble.

Juniper drew in a sharp breath and took her eyes from the scene. She was unable to look upon it any longer, as doing so made her feel a myriad of confusing emotions she wasn't yet ready to face. Ready to escape them, and the scene around her, she stood slowly. She knew her face was pale beneath the smears of ash and soot, as she felt like she was going to pass out at any second. "I have to go," she said quietly. Her voice was tight as it passed over her dry lips. "Are you going to be ok?"

"What?" Jason asked. The shock in his voice evident. "You can't go! Where are you going?"

"I have to go home," she whispered. "I- I have to make sure he's ok."

"Who? What are you *talking* about?" Jason clutched the sides of his head as though something was about to burst free of his skull.

"I'm sorry, but I have to **go**," said Juniper. Her words

were slow like molasses as they poured over her tongue. "I don't have time to explain."

"Wait!" Jason cried out. He jumped to his feet and followed her with surprising agility. "You can't leave me here! The cops are coming! The firemen! Don't you hear the sirens?"

"Yeah, but I *have to go!*" she said again. That time she spoke louder than the first and poured more anger into her voice than she'd intended. When she saw the look of hurt on Jason's face she amended her harshness. "I'm sorry, I am. And thank you," she said, "thank you for carrying me out of there. Thank you for caring enough to do the right thing, even though what you did was pretty stupid."

"Juniper, please, don't-"

She interrupted his pleas with an urgent statement. "I don't expect you to understand this. I just have something else I have to do, something *important*."

Without another word, Juniper scampered across the burnt earth under the approaching wail of distant fire trucks. Her feet skated gracefully over the dirt and soon found themselves on the dew-collecting grass of her backyard in what seemed like only a matter of seconds.

Her head ached and her stomach turned over and then over again in the throws of nausea. She covered her mid-section with one hand in hopes of quelling the pains, but the action did little good and seemed only to increase her trouble. With her chest heavy from smoke inhalation and her body exhausted from the healings she'd so liberally dished out, her breath halted in her throat.

Her feet and legs failed her just as she reached the side porch of her home. Her fingers had but a mere second to brush against the handle of the screen door before she fell away into the darkness of physical and emotional exhaustion.

"Juniper? Sweetheart? It's mama. You have to wake up now."

Juniper felt an odd sensation about her face. It was a gentle sting that pulled her free of the dark water in which she'd been languishing and showed her the comfort of the light.

Her eyes opened slowly to adjust to the brightly lit interior of the room she was in; her mother's face came into focus, tight with concern. Her lips were drawn into a whisper and held tight to her prayers.

"Mama?" Juniper struggled to sit up, but a hand pushed her back to the surface of the bed.

"Shhh, rest, Junie. You've been through a lot tonight," Penelope said. "It's going to take a bit to recover from this one."

"Where am I?" The room around her was white and clean; a sterile-smelling box that beeped, whirred and whistled around her weary mind.

"You're in the hospital." Penelope scooted her chair closer to her daughter's bed side and lowered her voice. "I don't know exactly what happened out there tonight, but there are a *lot* of people who are anxious to speak with you."

Juniper closed her eyes and returned to the darkness. "I can only imagine."

"Are you ok?" Penelope took Juniper's hand in hers and squeezed it gently, almost as though she were afraid to apply too much pressure to her frail daughter's fingers. "It's obvious you worked hard tonight, but are you *ok*?"

"I'm fine... Well, I'll *be* fine. Soon enough." She pushed out a cough. "How's dad? Is he-?" Juniper couldn't bear to say the words out loud. The taste of panic rose up in her throat; it was hot and acidic.

"He's alive. He's in a lot of *pain*, but he's hanging in there. Thanks to you."

"But as long as the tree is alive he'll be fine? Right?"

Penelope bit her lip, and chose her words carefully before speaking. "Juniper, there are some things we need to talk about."

Juniper recognized her mother's tone. It was the one she used when she had bad news; Juniper was no stranger to it.

"Your father..." she said softly. "Well, as I'm sure you know, he did something very noble tonight. Something that I can never thank him enough for."

"You mean giving me his halo?"

She looked at her hands and kept her voice soft. "Yeah, that's what I mean. And I don't know how much you know about him and it, but now that you have that halo... well, quite simply put, everything has changed for you both. Do you understand what I'm saying?"

"Yeah, I think so." Juniper nodded. Her memory had begun to return in waves as her concussion dissipated.

"Then you realize that your father can no longer heal himself? He's told you all of this?"

Again, she nodded. "Yeah, I know how it works." Juniper didn't understand what her mother was getting at. She reached up to touch the side of her face and then examined her hands. She noticed then for the first time that she was practically unscathed from the scorching heat of the flames that had tickled her flesh. She assumed that in healing Jason, some of that energy had also infected *her* flesh.

Penelope glanced at the door of the small white room to make certain it was closed before she continued. "Good. Well, at least you know that much. It might make what else I have to say a little easier for you to understand."

"I just don't understand why he did it. I mean, I *understand*, I just wish that he hadn't done it the way he did. I wasn't ready! He was supposed to have taught me how to use it!" Juniper exclaimed. She found that she was slightly angry at what Azerial had done, and her emotion crept into her words. "He should have kept it for himself and he'd be fine right now, wouldn't he? Oh mama... *why?*"

Penelope finally smiled. "You don't get it, Junie? He did it to save *you*. Don't you see? He gave you his halo so that you would be protected from whatever it was that you might encounter out there tonight. So that you might be able to save the tree and seal the Nexxus. It was your only chance. And his."

Juniper licked her lips. She hadn't realized until that second just how parched she was. "So, I'll just give it back to him," she whispered. "As soon as I get out of this place, I'll just give it back to him for a bit. Just long enough for dad to heal himself, then I'll take it back and he can teach me how to use it. Just like he planned."

Penelope's chin lowered and her head shook gently from side to side. "No, sweetheart. I'm afraid it doesn't work like that. Now that the halo is yours, it's yours."

"I don't understand!" Juniper said with obvious frustration. "He gave it to me, but now I want to give it to *him!*"

"Sweetie, calm down." Penelope stood up and placed both of her hands on her daughter's shoulders. "The halo was his to give and I'm afraid there's nothing that can be done about it now. Once it's passed, it's passed and there's no taking it back."

"Then I'll just heal him myself." Juniper pressed herself back to the paper-thin mattress without further argument. She crossed her arms and Penelope removed her hands from her shoulders.

She turned to the sink and grabbed a small paper cup from the dispenser. She filled it quickly with water and handed it to Juniper.

Juniper drank it thirstily, and asked for more when she

finished the first thimble full of liquid.

Penelope filled Juniper's request, then took her seat. "Juniper, I want you to listen to me, ok? *Closely*. Azerial is an *angel*, sweetheart, and as I'm sure you realize his appearance is deceiving. He's thousands upon thousands of years old! When you think about it, *really* think about it, you'll realize that he's been here longer than any human. He was here before there *was* a here! He was, *is*, an instrument of divine light, an instrument of *God*! That being said, there's one thing your father didn't tell you. I know that he told you that you can't resurrect the dead, but there's one more group of people that you can't heal."

She didn't even have to say it; Juniper already knew what the words would be. However, Penelope said it any way.

"The immortal, Junie. You can't heal the immortal."

"But there has to be a way, there just has to be." Juniper, too tired to cry, fell back to the pillows and closed her eyes. She tried to blink away the constant swarm of thoughts that assaulted the inside of her eyelids with their insistent and presumptuous nagging, but failed miserably.

"I have to warn you, Junie. When you see him... he looks really bad. I need you to be prepared for that."

"I won't lose him, mama. Not *now*, I need him! To teach me!" Juniper's words began to trip over her tongue in an emotional frenzy. "I can't do this alone!"

"Oh sweetheart, I know... believe me, I know." Penelope leaned forward and extended her arms over Juniper's torso like a warm and breathing blanket. "I've been given a second chance here too, Junie. I have as much to lose as you, but you and I both have to start preparing ourselves for the-"

"No! I won't *prepare* myself for losing him, because I *won't* lose him, *we* won't lose him. Because where there's a will, there's a way. This situation is no different, mama. I won't *let* it be."

Penelope pulled away and instead took Juniper's hand

inside of her own. She cupped it gently and her fingers held Juniper's together like a mitten. "I don't think you quite understand the situation we're facing here, baby. Azerial is immortal, you can't heal him and he certainly can't heal himself. Given his current physical state, even the small amount of self-healing left within him isn't enough to pull him back from this trauma... He's progressively weakening and what's going to happen now, is that he's going to continue to get sicker. He'll lose weight, he'll lose his hair, until finally there will be nothing left but bones and wings. No real life, no hope for recovery, just an empty shell of what he was. You must know that I hate to say this, Junie, but if something miraculous doesn't happen to aid him in his recovery, we'll have to-"

Juniper pulled her fingers from her mother's grasp and put her hands over her ears. She squeezed her eyes as tightly shut as she could manage. "No mama, don't say it."

"Juniper, if we have to clip his wings, you have to be able to help me. That's not something I can do alone."

Juniper shook her head and lowered her hands. "I'll never do that to him, mama. Never."

"So you'd rather sit by and watch him wither away to bones than to spare him that indignity?" Penelope's voice rose steadily as her words multiplied. "How *dare* you be so selfish! How can you lie there and tell me that you wouldn't help him? That you wouldn't spare him that sort of a long, lingering demise?" Penelope shook her head and her eyes filled with a tangible sadness. "I am shocked and disappointed, Juniper."

Juniper was taken aback by her mother's anger. She also felt ashamed. She bit her tongue and lowered her head, no longer able to face her mother's eyes. "I'm sorry, mama. I understand what you're saying, I do. But I can't give up on him. I *won't*, and you can't either."

Penelope stood and turned away from her daughter. She was rigid, and stood as tall as she could manage beneath the weight of their steadily worsening situation. "I won't give up, Junie. I've lost your father before and I can't bear to suffer that again. But, sweetheart-"

"You won't have to lose him again. I promise you, mama. Whatever it takes, you'll get your happy ending."

"And what about you?"

Juniper's smile was sadly sweet and held back her tears. "Don't worry about me, mama. I'm a big girl now."

"I've told you before, Junie, and I'll tell you again. So long as there is life in me, I'll worry about you."

Juniper, having found a renewed sense of purpose, threw back her bed sheets and sat up. "I want to see him, mama. Get me out of here."

"Not so fast there, kiddo. Don't you realize what you've done tonight?" Penelope moved closer to the edge of the bed and prevented Juniper from swinging her legs over the edge.

"Of course I do. What of it?"

"There are people waiting outside to speak with you about tonight. Doctors... *Policemen.*"

Juniper's heart skipped a beat then froze solid in her chest. "Am I in trouble?"

"No, but they do have some questions for you," Penelope said. "About the fire, about Ben... about what happened in that farm house and why you were there in the first place."

"Do they know how the fire started?" Juniper asked. She held back her information and waited instead for Penelope to spill the beans on what she knew so far about the investigation.

Penelope shook her head slowly and her blonde hair spilled out from behind her ears. "When the firemen and the cops arrived on the scene, they found Jason. He was sitting there, just crying his eyes out. The poor kid was in absolute shock. As far as I know, they haven't been able to get any sense out of him. *Yet.* That's why they're so anxious to speak with *you."*

"I saved Jason's life, mama."

Penelope nodded. "I assumed as much. And I'm sure that Jason realizes that you had a hand in getting him out of that fire alive. For now, no one else needs to know about that."

Juniper bit her lip. "There's something else, mama. It's about Ben. He uh- he didn't make it out of the fire."

Penelope's brow furrowed. "What?"

Juniper rephrased her words. She knotted her hands together on her stomach and studied them nervously. "He chased me into the house, trying to... to do *what*, I don't know. To stop me from what I had to do, I guess. To kill me, maybe. I really don't know what his motives were. All I *do* know is that a beam fell on him. He was trapped and I- I couldn't save him. I tried, I did, but I just couldn't. And I watched it all, mama... I saw him burning and I heard him screaming and- Jason... he witnessed it all too."

"Oh Junie... I- I don't know what to say." Penelope looked uneasy. She studied the floor, then the steadily beeping monitors that Juniper was attached to via a series of cords and wires. "Just- try not to think about that now, ok?"

Juniper gave her a half-assed nod and the drowsiness kicked up around her like a potent choking dust cloud. She yawned, unable to hold it back. "I'm so tired, mama."

"You've had quite a day, Junie, I'm not surprised." The worry returned to her face and formed ridges at her forehead. "To think, I could have lost you both tonight."

"But you didn't, and you aren't going to, either. I told you that earlier and I'm repeating it now."

Penelope took Juniper's hands in hers and pulled them to her chest. "I'm going to get some coffee, and then I'm going to get the doctor in here to see when I might be able to take you home, ok?"

Juniper nodded. "Ok, just don't be gone long. You

know I'm not a big fan of hospitals."

Penelope kissed Juniper's forehead and smoothed her hair. "I promise, I'll hurry. Just hang in there."

Juniper released her hands, then grabbed for her sleeve as she turned to leave. "Mama, wait!"

Penelope turned back to face her. A new seed of worry had grown quickly in her eyes. "Yes, sweetie?"

"If we do have to... to *clip his wings*... he'll be human, right?" She licked her lips and continued cautiously, almost afraid to say what it was she was thinking. "I can heal humans, mama." Juniper's realization had been slow to come and once it had arrived it hung between herself and Penelope like a rickety rope bridge. They both knew that it could very well prove to be their only exit from the canyon they found themselves in, and it was to it they would cling.

Chapter Fifteen
Halo

When Penelope left the hospital room in search of coffee, Juniper's silence was short lived as a fresh-faced, broad-shouldered police officer skirted into the room a moment later without even extending the courtesy of a knock. He introduced himself and flashed his badge as proof of his clout. Juniper nodded at it and reached back to fluff up her pillow.

"I hope this won't take too long, I'd like to go home soon, sir," she said somewhat sharply.

The officer stood next to the vacant chair, smiled without really smiling and pulled out his notepad. "Miss Kelly, my name is Officer Mark Donovan. I'm from the Anderson County Sheriff's Department. I've just got a few questions for you, miss. I promise this will only take a few minutes. I just need to get your account of the events in question."

His eyes were the brightest color blue Juniper could ever remember having seen and she stared into them as she spoke. "I'll do my best to help you, officer, but you'll have to forgive me. I'm afraid my memory is a bit cloudy at the moment."

He mustered a somewhat sympathetic smile. "I understand, miss. And as I said, I'll keep this as brief as possible." He paused to click his pen and then flipped to a fresh page in his notepad. "First of all, can you tell me how you know Mr. Benjamin Maxwell and Mr. Jason Price?"

"They're classmates of mine," she said simply.

He nodded. "I understand they give you a fair amount of trouble. That maybe what happened tonight was to get back at you for something."

"Well, I- I don't know about that. I mean, *yes*, they pick on me from time to time, but-" Juniper adjusted her position in the bed and moved her hips from side to side before she settled back into the mattress. "It's just stupid high school stuff. Name calling, book checks, you know."

"Nothing more serious than that?" He had narrowed his eyes to further question her claims.

Juniper shrugged. "Boys will be boys, right officer? It's nothing I couldn't handle."

Officer Donovan let the subject drop, despite his wariness in doing so. "The reason I'm stopping by to see you tonight is... Well, Mr. Price has told us a very *interesting* story, Miss Kelly and we wanted to make sure that we got your side of it."

"*Interesting* how?" asked Juniper.

She could see the thoughts behind his eyes as they whirred about quickly in a storm cloud of activity. She crossed the fingers of her right hand under the bed sheets and hoped that Jason had the sense about him *not* to have told the truth. As she waited for whatever vague explanation the officer might offer, her heartbeat increased.

"He uh- he claims that it was Mr. Maxwell's idea to burn down that abandoned farm house. We found the empty gasoline can, and it *has* been identified as belonging to Benjamin's father. However, we aren't quite clear on what role Mr. Price played in the incident."

"Have you found Ben's-" Juniper drew in a shaky breath. "Did you find his body?"

Officer Donovan lowered his notepad to his side and took one long lanky hand to the brim of his hat. He adjusted it slightly, and pushed it back on his head. "At this point, the recovery effort is still underway, Miss Kelly. We really don't-"

"I saw it happen," Juniper whispered. "I couldn't save him... There wasn't time." Juniper felt a sob rise slowly from her chest as Jason popped to mind. "What about Jason? Is he alright? Has he been arrested?"

The officer shook his head. "Mr. Price is still suffering from a fair amount of shock, but other than that he appears to be in good health. I believe his parents just arrived a few minutes ago to take him home. He's quite shaken up by the whole event." The officer finally relaxed and loosened his posture. "As for formal charges, no one has been arrested, not yet. I just- I get the distinct feeling that kid is hiding something. Something he saw. Something that scared him pretty badly."

"What happened to Ben…? He saw it too. It was a beam. It fell from the ceiling and trapped Ben under it. Jason saw it all, just like I did."

Officer Donovan scribbled something down on his notepad before he looked at her again. "Yeah, but-" The officer scratched his forehead and then shook his head from side to side. "I don't know, call it instinct if you like, but I get the distinct feeling that there's something he's not telling us."

Juniper gulped, but said nothing.

Officer Donovan continued. "Like I said, something scared him. Something he can't explain. And I'll tell you something, Miss Kelly, I've lived in Camden Falls my entire life, just like most everyone else. I've heard the stories about those woods, too, you know. That they're haunted and what not… and after tonight? Well, let's just say that I'm a little more apt to believe there might be some truth to those old tales yet."

Juniper laughed, a crooked, jagged, and somewhat guilty laugh. "You're kidding right?"

"What?" Officer Donovan shook himself up into his former position of stiffness. "Well… right, of *course*, I'm kidding… But you have to admit, what happened out there tonight was strange to say the least."

"I'm afraid I don't remember much about tonight," Juniper said quietly.

Officer Donovan toggled his professionalism switch back to the 'on' position. "Do you remember why it was you were out in the forest tonight?"

Juniper gulped and twisted her fingers nervously. "I'd been using the house as a hang out for some time. I wanted to save some things from the fire, that's all."

"So you foolishly ran into a burning house? To save what exactly? A few CDs? Some books?" Officer Donovan raised an eyebrow to illustrate his disbelief in her claims.

"I was stupid, ok? I admit that freely." Juniper crossed her arms over her chest as a shield against the young officer's obviously condescending tone.

"Listen, Miss Kelly..." He took a seat in the chair next to the bed and lowered his voice. "It's just you and me here. So why don't you tell me what *really* happened out there tonight?"

"I've already told you everything that I remember." Juniper looked him straight in the eye to prove her honesty.

The officer didn't drop his gaze as he continued. "Mr. Price tells us that you saved his life. That you administered CPR before collapsing yourself."

Juniper nodded. "That's what I've been told, yes."

"And in turn, he pulled you from the house?" Donovan continued.

"Yes."

"I see..." He nodded and continued, pen poised over paper. "And it was between those two events that the fire mysteriously *vanished?*"

"Yeah, I guess so," Juniper said flatly.

"Do you care to explain that, Miss Kelly?" Officer Donovan asked. "Because it seems to me that's a little bit out of the ordinary, wouldn't you agree? There was no rain, the fire trucks were still minutes away, yet suddenly the flames just went out on their own?"

Juniper was slow to answer, but her heartbeat was quick to jump wildly about in her chest. Officer Donovan waited for her response, and his toe tapped the tile floor impatiently.

They looked at each other; neither spoke.

When finally Juniper broke the silence, she did so by tightening her hands across her chest. "I've said all I care to say for one night. I'm tired and I don't remember anything else. I was *unconscious*, you know. I have a concussion."

Officer Donovan sighed and then slowly closed the cover on his notepad. "I suppose we'll leave it at that and I'll allow you to recover your strength. I'll be in touch soon to finish this, Miss Kelly."

Juniper had no doubt in her mind that he would, and as he turned to leave, she began to wonder exactly how she'd explain herself when the time came. Not only to the police, but to Jason as well.

The doctors vacated Juniper's room scratching their heads, and left her to change out of her ridiculous paper gown and back into her smoke-swollen clothing.

The lump on the back of her head was gone; her lungs showed no signs of smoke damage and the few cuts and scrapes that had marked her cheeks and arms had disappeared without a trace; even her ankles, ankles that had walked across the flaming floor of the attic, were completely devoid of injury. As a fact, the only reminders at all that Juniper had been in a fire were the burnt hems of her jeans and the flame-ripped hole on the right side of her t-shirt.

Having no explanations for her lack of injuries or her miraculous recovery, the doctor had no choice but to sign her release papers and send her on her way.

The hour was late, or early depending on what side of the coin you stood. Three forty-five am and Juniper felt every bit of that, *saw* every bit of that reflected back at her in her mother's equally weary eyes.

The car ride home was silent aside from an occasional yawn and the incessant yammering of the radio DJ. When they finally pulled into the driveway, the tension around them was almost thick enough to be sliced with an oversized pair of scissors, scissors usually reserved for ceremonial situations involving the grand openings of grocery stores and banks.

The headlights of her mother's car fell to rest upon the back bumper of Juniper's all-but-forgotten birthday present. She suddenly felt the small metal key in the pocket of her jeans and noted how insignificant it all seemed to her now.

"Do you want me to go up with you?" Penelope broke the stifling almost choking silence of the car with her simple well-meaning question.

Juniper shook her head and kept her voice low. "I'll go up alone if that's ok with you."

Penelope nodded and then reached across the center console to find Juniper's hand. "I'll be in the kitchen if you need me. I just can't bear to see him again right now. Beside that, I need coffee... And I need a little time to- to I don't know... think? Compose myself?"

Juniper didn't look at her mother, and she offered her no words. Her thoughts had taken flight to other locations and had perched in precarious positions. Somehow through her mental fog, her hand found the door latch and pulled it. Her fingers were numb and in being numb, they matched the rest of her.

It all seemed like a dream to her then. The events of the past several months, the fire, the realization of her self and what she was. It all seemed like a long and peculiar dream and when she looked back on it, it was a bit like a surrealist painting, water colored and misty, and running towards the corners of the page into oblivion.

Juniper drew her breath in close and fast and climbed out of the car. For a moment she stood in the driveway and faced the wind that blew in from the west. It raced down the street and rattled the trees; Juniper shivered, but did not waver. She closed her eyes and drank it into her, its fury and unbridled tenacity; an entity of eternal wanderlust that passed by long enough to whisper a hello and offer an encouraging pat on the back.

The wind was Azerial. The wind was her life. Ticking the seconds, they plagued her then as she knew her time was running low. But there she was, her feet stuck to the concrete as though they had melted there; had melted into the tar and cement and years of trampled-upon, ground-in dirt.

When Juniper was finally ready to face him, after her time of reflection, she noticed that her mother had gone ahead and had already unlocked and opened the side door. In silence, she'd entered and Juniper knew that her mother, much like herself was nervous and unsettled over the possibility of the death that lay ahead of them.

With a heavy, heart-sick sigh, Juniper followed her mother's lead and walked slowly up the driveway towards the house. Once inside, she moved to take off her shoes, but decided instead to leave them on. Her mother said nothing about it and took a seat instead at the kitchen table. She was stone-faced and silent, and obviously lost deep within the maze of her own thoughts.

Juniper didn't bother to ask which room Azerial was in; she already knew, and when she reached the door of her mother's room a short time later, the knob was cold to the touch. Juniper turned it slowly and her heart caught in her chest over the anticipation of what waited just beyond.

The door creaked as she opened it. Juniper placed one hand over her heart and then quickly moved it up to her mouth to quiet any noises that might uncontrollably erupt from her throat.

Azerial's eyes were open when she found him, but he didn't immediately respond to her presence. The floorboards beneath her feet spoke out when she reached the foot of the bed; they did so in the same place where they'd creaked since her mother had originally bought the house.

Juniper winced from the sound and scolded herself silently. *How could you forget that?*

"It's alright, Juniper. I wasn't sleeping." The voice was low and drowsy and rose slowly from the bed sheets.

The room was dark, save for the dulled light of the street lamp that filtered in through the lace curtains. The light fell upon the floor in a familiar-to-Juniper puddle and a nostalgic smile met her lips. As a small child she'd spent many nights in that very spot, curled up under the light and dreaming at her sleeping mother's bedside.

She had thought the light protected her; from harm, from sickness, from evil. Her feet found the light then without being told to do so and she hoped for much of the same protection. As she stood there, Juniper felt much like she had as a child; frightened and helpless. Her heart beat doubled when she realized that she was no longer six, that she couldn't run to her mother and cling to her legs while she waited for her to make everything better. It was up to no one but Juniper to fix what had happened, if a fix was even possible.

Standing there above her ailing father, she suddenly felt the halo he'd given her and she understood all that it meant and stood for. The history, the pride, the ignorance and the bliss... It filled her veins, soaked her muscles and seeped from her pores with a sweet light smell that reminded Juniper of a sun-soaked summer afternoon.

She sat carefully on the edge of the bed and beneath her weight, the box spring squeaked. Azerial didn't look her way and Juniper assumed him too weak for much movement.

His eyes were sunken into his head and were surrounded by charcoal colored circles; chunks of his hair were on the bed sheets and pillow, and even as she looked at him then, she could almost see the deterioration of his muscles.

"You did it," he whispered.

"Yeah, I guess I did."

"I'm proud of you."

Juniper lowered her chin. "Thanks. I wish *I* was proud of me."

"And why aren't you?" he asked. "You saved the tree, you closed the Nexxus, yes?"

"Yes," she replied quietly. She kept her eyes focused upon her knotted, intertwined fingers. "But there's some things you don't know."

He turned his eyes to face her with obvious difficulty. "Such as?"

"The fire... It was arson. Ben started it," she whispered. "He and Jason were in the woods tonight when I went to the farm house... Ben followed me inside... Jason followed *him*..."

"Junie? What's wrong? What happened out there?"

Juniper felt the tears she'd struggled to hold back begin to make their push towards the surface. "Ben... Ben- he- he's dead. He's dead and it's all my fault."

Azerial reached for her and covered her nervous fists with his burned, mottled hand. "How is it your fault?"

"I wasn't fast enough. I wasn't strong enough to lift the beam off of him."

"But you tried? You tried your best to save him?"

Juniper nodded.

"Then I ask you... what more could you have done if you tried your absolute best?"

"I don't know... I... I'm just afraid that I held back because I-"

"Because of all the things he did to you?"

"Yes."

"I don't believe that's true. You're too good to have let him die as revenge for what he did to you," Azerial said quietly.

He squeezed her hand with as much force as he could manage. "And Jason? What of him?"

"He's fine," she said. She finally looked up and met his gaze. "I healed him. I had to or he would have died out there too."

"And now you're worried," he said softly.

"I'm not, not really. I have faith that he'll keep my secret." Her words weren't a complete lie, but rather a slight elongation of the truth.

A glimmer of a smile touched the corners of his mouth. "You're welcome, by the way."

Juniper looked back down to her lap. "Why did you do it?"

"How could I not?" he asked.

Two impossible questions presented themselves to each other from opposite sides of the fence where they proceeded to engage in a staring contest.

"Why can't you take it back? You *have* to take it back," she whispered. "I don't want it. I'm not ready-"

"You're ready," he said softly. As he nodded, more hair tumbled loose from his head and dropped to his pillow. "After tonight you aren't convinced of that?"

"But what did I do? Really? What did I do that was so great?" Juniper protested.

He removed his hand from atop hers long enough to expose his scarred palm. Juniper placed her own palm against it and their fingers laced together. "You put yourself at risk to save my life. And not only did you save me by saving the tree, but you closed the Nexxus on top of that. It might seem to you that you've done little, but I assure you, what you've done is an impressive feat."

"But I could have done *more*! I could have done a better job! I could have been faster! I could have been *stronger*! Maybe I could have saved Ben, too. Isn't that what I was supposed to have done? Shouldn't I have been able to save him so that he'd have had a second chance? To reform, to be- to be a better person?" Juniper rushed on, her words sloppy and eager to spill. "I failed him. I failed him and now I'll have to live with it for the rest of my life... The look on his face, the screams... God, dad! The screams! I'd never heard anything so horrible in my entire life! It was like- it was *hellish*. It was *painful* and *heartbreaking* and I don't think I'll ever forget that sound, not as long as I live."

"Shhh, child. You did all that you could do. You tried, I know that, you know that, and I'm sure that Ben knows that." Azerial's hands warmed beneath hers, but his voice remained weak. "The rest, as they say, was out of your hands. Some things aren't meant to be. Perhaps this is the case with Ben."

To keep her lip from increasing its quiver, she forced out a question that she could already see the answer to just by looking at her father's heaving chest and sweat-soaked brow. "Are you in much pain?"

He tried to laugh, but his injuries trapped the chuckle at his ribcage. "A bit." He coughed and removed one of his hands from Juniper's grasp. He placed it over his heart and tried laboriously to inhale. "The pain... it comes, it goes."

"So is it true?" Juniper asked. "That I can't heal you?"

"Yes, it's true."

"And what happens now?" Her words were weak and approached him slowly; slowly as though he were a sleeping giant and she meant not to disturb his rest.

"We both know there's only one way out of this. Don't we?" asked Azerial.

Juniper took a deep breath and nodded. "Yes, but-" A thought hit her and her eyes widened around the bold idea as it took shape at her tongue. "Wait! Maybe there *is* another way! Couldn't I heal the tree? *Completely* heal it? Since you and it are linked, wouldn't healing it heal you? *Harming* it certainly harmed you, so wouldn't the reverse be true?"

"I'm afraid not," Azerial replied. "The damage has already been done. The tree, much like me, has certain immortal qualities that will prevent such a healing. Forever now, it will bear the markings of the fire."

Juniper's heart sank back into her chest and left her throat empty and dry.

Seeing her disappointment, Azerial squeezed her fingers. "There isn't much time before a decision has to be reached. At the rate I'm deteriorating, it's only a matter of time before it'll be too late. However, I need some time to think, or rather to align myself with my Creator in case I should see Him again soon."

Juniper hesitated before she pulled her hand from his. She wanted nothing more than to savor the feeling of warmth on his skin, but knew that he was tired, frail and couldn't withstand the pressure of her touch. "Is there anything I can do for you? Anything at all?"

Azerial smiled. His voice had grown weaker still. "Pray," he whispered. "At this point, it's all we can do."

"Does that actually work?" Juniper asked.

Azerial's smile widened in response to her query. "Sometimes," he replied, "sometimes."

Juniper passed her mother in the hallway as she made her way to her room for a fresh pair of clothes and a much needed nap. A shower would have to wait, as she knew her bones were too weary to withstand the pressure of the water.

Penelope's expression was somber; in her hand she carried a glass of water. "Is he awake?"

Juniper nodded. "Yeah, he's tired though. And weak. *Very* weak."

"How did he seem to you?"

"As well as could be expected, I guess." Juniper nodded towards the closed bedroom door. "He said he needs some time to be alone. He, uh- he knows what we have to do. He said he had to think, and talk to-" She jerked her eyes upwards, but kept her chin firm. "You know. *Him.*"

Penelope bobbed her head up and down and then pursed her lips into a small tight smile. "I just want to see him one more time tonight, then I promise I'll leave him be for awhile." She quickly changed the subject. "Are you going to bed?"

Juniper nodded again. "I'm going to try and get a little sleep, yeah."

"I hope you succeed. You could certainly use a few hours of shut eye after tonight." Penelope leaned forward and kissed her forehead somewhat awkwardly. "Sleep well, sweetheart."

"Yeah, you sleep well too, mama. You need the rest just as much as I do."

"Sleep?" Penelope asked with a soft laugh. "I don't think I could if I wanted to."

Juniper reached out and took her by the arm. "Promise me you'll try, ok? You're no good to any of us if you're exhausted."

It was her turn to nod. "I will try. For *you.* Goodnight, sweetheart. I love you."

"Night, mama. I love you." Juniper released her, but not until after she gently squeezed her arm and forced a weary smile to her lips.

Once inside of her room, Juniper closed and locked the door. She kicked her shoes off and the left flew under the bed; the right hit the dresser with a thump and stopped silent at the carpet.

Juniper, unaccustomed to praying, took a typical pose and dropped to her knees at the edge of her bed. She clasped her hands together tightly and bowed her head.

At first the words hesitated and all thoughts ceased. She had spent little time in her life speaking to God, and in that moment she felt added pressure to be well versed and eloquent in her pleas.

She cleared her throat and inhaled. Her voice was low when it finally came. "You'll have to forgive me if I do this incorrectly... I was never taught how to pray. Religion has never been something that I took an interest in, probably because I was never exposed to it. That isn't to say that I blame mama for my lack of knowledge, but rather I blame *myself* for not seeking that knowledge out." Juniper hesitated and opened one eye. She cast it to the ceiling, then closed it again quickly. "I'm sorry, I really am... for being so bad at this. I'm just filled with a lot of ... *inner turmoil* right now. About dad, about my life, about *everything*. Being a teenager is hard enough without this. *This*! I mean, it's all quite cruel when you think about it. Putting all of this on me at one time as though I've a spine of steel. Well, I don't, you know. I'm not a superhero, I'm not a hero of any kind. I'm just a girl. I'm sixteen and so far in my life I've had to endure quite a bit of crap. Poverty, ridicule, a near hanging, watching a guy burned alive, finding my father, finding out that father is an *angel* and now... *now* I have to face the very real possibility that I'm going to lose that father, right when I need him the most. And I don't understand it. I don't understand how you can let this happen to him. You, *God*, you're the giver of love, forgiveness and free will, amongst other things of course. As I see it, the only crime my father ever committed was exercising that free will. And what happened once he did? You turned your ear. You ignored him, you **abandoned** him! Don't you see that he needs you right now? He needs you to... to help him! To *save* him!"

"And I know you don't owe me *or* him anything at all, but couldn't you find it within yourself to do *something*? I'm sure my dad was a great angel. He must have been or else you wouldn't be so angry that you'd lost him. If that's true, then I just don't understand how it could be that you'd let this happen to him."

"I sound like I'm blaming you, don't I? Well, maybe I *am* blaming you. Maybe I've *always* blamed you in the back of my mind for me not having a father in the first place. But then I have to ask myself... Have I always known the truth but chosen to deny it? When I found the feather pressed between the pages of mama's bible, did I bury something inside me then that never grew into anything more than a fleeting thought?"

"I know I sound scattered and weak... but I'm tired, that's all. Tired of always running uphill... but if that's what's asked of me? Then I'll answer the call. This day and every day. Because how could I not? How could I let this potential of mine waste away now that I realize how great it truly is?"

"Anyway... I'm not sure what I expect here. An answer would be nice, but I'm not counting on it. I just want you to save him, that's all. Somehow... Just give me a father. Give me a *teacher*! I can't do this without him, you know, and if you take him- if you take him," Juniper sobbed, "I'll be lost. I'll be completely, *totally*, lost... and as I see it, the world needs me to be found. I think we both know that, don't we?"

Juniper dropped her hands to her lap and whispered an Amen. Wearily, she climbed into bed and pulled the blankets up to her chin. She was cold beneath the sheets, but didn't have time to ponder that; her eyelids were heavy and the insistent tug of sleep was upon her.

As soon as her eyelids snapped shut, Juniper was sound asleep and she fell quickly into the deep, dark, rabbit hole of night.

And at first there was nothing more than that, nothing but darkness. Slowly, however, the pitch-black curtains in her mind were split at the middle and pulled back to the sides of the stage.

In front of her, a world opened up. Juniper recognized the scene immediately: it was her house. The angle shifted and moved slowly from the kitchen, up the stairs and towards her bedroom. Juniper found herself following along, as she was unable to steer clear of the vacuum-like pull that grabbed her and dragged her through the dream.

The next thing she knew, she was standing over her own sleeping body and observing her own rhythmic breathing. Upon her brow she could see the beading sweat as she fought needlessly with non-existent sheets; with sheets that had been abandoned and tossed to the floor.

As the sleeping version of herself breathed deeply and exhaled, a small ball of light escaped her lips. It pushed out from her mouth and explored the room in wide, sweeping circles. Juniper watched it with great focus as it bounced from the walls, to the floor, to her desk and finally, to the window. It perched on the sill and sat quietly. It was as though it were waiting for something, and Juniper approached it carefully, slowly, as though it were a timid animal and she was the intimidating predator.

It flinched when she neared it; it pulsed and throbbed and seemed to wink at her suggestively. She placed one hand out to it, and with little hesitation it hopped into her palm.

It was like a sci-fi movie. The light grew in her palm until it covered her entire hand, then her arm, and finally, the whole of her body.

Juniper found herself opening the window, encased in the aura of light. With her knees on the window sill, she leapt outwards from the house and into the night beyond. When she started to plummet, wings expanded outwards from her back and brought her level with the night. The wind found her cheeks and assaulted them; Juniper kept her mouth closed, despite the jaw-dropping awe of the experience at hand. She looked down at her house, at her driveway and life, and suddenly she felt very small.

Her attention was next drawn to a figure. It was a girl. Juniper's eyes followed her as she ran frantic through the field, towards the woods. Her hair was streaming out behind her like so many ribbons. She was barefoot and dressed in a thin white nightgown.

Juniper recognized the girl as herself, and she shadowed her own movements, flying over herself unnoticed.

The other version of herself carried eyes that were wild, wide. She seemed dazed, as if in a trance that she couldn't quite free herself from.

Juniper found herself flying through the trees, past the creek and over the fallen pines. The house was waiting for her there, tall and knowing, untouched by fire.

Juniper watched her other self run to the house, watched the girl fling open the door in a noisy clatter and throw herself to the floor in front of the tree.

The floorboards that she splintered with her hands and tossed aside joined the spider webs and dust balls in the corner.

Her fingers were wild, clawing at the earth until finally Juniper heard it.

Clank.

Her knuckles drummed against the metal surface again and Juniper watched the girl bite down upon her lip and dig further into the earth. She pulled dirt aside in handfuls until finally she jerked the box free from the soil.

Juniper woke up suddenly, and her dream faded quickly around her. It gave way to the familiarity of first-person existence.

Her eyes were alert when first they opened; they found themselves being drawn to her desk.

The metal box.

She remembered she'd placed it under the bed, hidden from sight, and she threw herself to the carpet without hesitation. Her arms flew under the bed into the darkness and fumbled past shoes and dirty clothes until her fingers grazed the cool surface of the box.

She pulled it towards herself, clinging tightly to it as she stood and walked to her desk.

She sat and placed the box in front of her. With shaking hands, she opened it, and pulled out the contents to cover the surface of her desk where she fanned them out for inspection.

A newspaper clipping and the strange unreadable book were the only items that remained. Nothing more, nothing less, and with the exception of the photo her mother had kept in her possession, they were the same items that had always been in the box.

But the dream was persistent and the details chewed at Juniper's curiosity until finally, she opened the small leather bound book.

The first page was blank, the second page was missing and the third was ripped in half. The rest of the pages, however, seemed to be in tact.

Something, was strange about the book she held in her hands. The writing that had once been illegible was then clear as day, bold and black.

It was Azerial's bible and the language was Angelic. With Azerial's halo, Juniper had the proper skills to read it. The right *tool* to interpret the previously puzzling and foreign text.

Hungrily, she began to read.

Chapter Sixteen
Light of Day

After her shower the next morning, Juniper made a feeble attempt at eating breakfast. She quickly realized, however, that her tongue felt metallic and her stomach was incapable of accepting food. After two bites of her scrambled eggs and one of her toast, she placed her plate on the kitchen floor, much to Sam's delight. He gobbled up the rest of the food quickly and carried the bacon triumphantly into the next room where he dropped it on the carpet.

Juniper's mother had finally found sleep; she was curled up on the sofa still fully dressed. Juniper had draped a blanket over her legs, and in her restlessness, her mother had tossed it aside and buried her face in the cushions of the couch.

Azerial was also asleep and had been for some time. Juniper checked in on him every twenty minutes with her lip firmly between her teeth as she did so. She was still mulling over the dream and the decision at hand. She hadn't approached him yet about the situation, and dreaded when he finally did wake for she'd have to ask him for his answer.

Juniper washed her hands in the kitchen sink and dried them on her jeans. She glanced out the window, but overlooked the driveway in favor of an odd, out-of-place bicycle that had been propped up against the garage. A confused look crossed her face briefly, only to be swatted away by a knock on the side door.

Juniper jumped, laughed at her nervousness and walked to the door. When she opened it, her heartbeat increased at the sight of the shaggy haired boy. "Jason, hey there," she said quietly.

"May I come in for a minute?" His face was scratched

up and his hair was singed slightly at the ends from the previous night's fire play.

Juniper looked over her right shoulder towards the living room and then looked back at Jason. "My mama is sleeping, let's step outside."

"Sure." Jason shoved his hands into his pockets and took several large steps backward. He rested his lower back on the railing and kept his head lowered slightly.

Juniper stepped onto the porch and closed the door quietly behind her. "I was wondering when you'd show up."

"I hope I'm not bothering you. I was going to wait and come by later, but, here I am," he said. He removed one hand from his pocket and ran it through his shaggy brown hair. "So am I? Bothering you, I mean."

"No, you aren't, not at all. I was just finishing up breakfast."

He seemed surprised. "You can eat?"

She shook her head. "Well, not really."

"Yeah, same here. Can't eat, can't sleep. In fact, I can't think about anything other than what happened last night."

"I know the feeling," Juniper said.

Finally, he looked up and caught her eye. "I know what I saw. I didn't mention it to the police because…" He shrugged. "Well, because I didn't want them to think I was completely flippin' insane."

"I understand. And thank you, I appreciate it." She extended a smile to which he responded by tearing his gaze away.

"I didn't do it for you," he said abruptly. As if realizing the harshness his words had carried, he recanted. "What I mean is, I didn't do it *just* for you."

Juniper looked down at the porch. She found it difficult to find the right words. "What exactly did you see?" she asked finally. "Do you remember anything?"

He kept his eyes focused on some distant imaginary point. "Ben and I were lighting the furniture on fire in the living room. We'd already spread the gasoline all over the house... Ben made sure to get that old tree nice and soaked. When I asked him why he did it, he just said he got a weird feeling from it. He wanted to make *sure* it burned." Jason paused to wet his lips. His confession had struck him parched. "I told him I didn't want to do it. That he was going too far with the arson bit, but he wouldn't listen, and when he struck the match everything went up in the blink of an eye."

"He wanted to make sure he hadn't left his dad's gas can upstairs, so he ran to check for it. He found it and we rushed outside to watch our handiwork. It wasn't even five minutes after that when you came running up to us, faster than I've ever seen anyone move. I told him to let you go, to leave you alone. I didn't think you'd run into the house, I didn't think... but you *did* and he followed you, and I- I didn't know what to do. It was like a dream, ya know? None of it felt real... and if you want the truth? It still doesn't."

"Anyway... I thought to myself... she's going to die," he continued. "Then I remembered what Brian said that day, the day that we... He said that we'd all die, that none of us would make it out alive. That's when I got scared and turned to leave, but then I heard you screaming. I made it to the stairs just in time to see Ben get hit with that beam, and then the fire was-" He shook his head. "I had to jump over his body to get to you, and I don't know why I did what I did, but I just wanted to save you. I felt like I *had* to... that if I ever did *one* good thing in life, it would be that. It *had* to be that."

Juniper didn't know what to say. She remained silent and instead pulled nervously at her fingers.

"I saw you ahead of me," he whispered. "You were running up the stairs, stumbling through the smoke. I called out to you, but you didn't answer. I don't think you heard me over the roar of the flames. So I just kept following you to the attic and when you opened the door to the bedroom, I stood in the hallway behind you. I saw the flames burn your jeans. Your hair!" He paused again and searched her face with his eager, wide eyes. "But I look at you now, and you're pretty as ever. There's not a mark on you!"

Juniper blushed despite the heaviness of the situation. "I was lucky, I guess."

"That's some kind of luck!" He wagged his finger absently in her direction. "I can't quite figure out what you are, Juniper, but you're definitely *something*."

"A witch?" she asked when she finally allowed herself to meet his eyes.

It was Jason's turn to redden. "I wanted to apologize for that. Ben was- and I was-" He drew his eyes to the horizon, too ashamed to look her in the eye. "Ben was very influential. I went along with a lot of stupid shit just because he told me to."

"We used to be best friends, Jason. And when you, *you* of all people, started treating me the way you did... It hurt. It really hurt." She paused and drew in a breath on which she continued. "But in some strange way, I think I understand."

Jason's brow furrowed with curiosity. "You do?"

She nodded. "Yeah, I do. And for what it's worth, I forgive you, Jason. I just want to move past all of this and try to put it behind me once and for all." She extended her hand for a shake. "No hard feelings, ok?"

Jason shook on it, and the look in his eyes was serious when he approached her face with his. "I am sorry, Junie. You're a better person than me, for forgiving me, I mean. I don't know that I could forgive me... not after all of the things I've done to fuck with you. Certainly not after last night. We all could have died... *you* could have died, and I would be in jail, the shame of my family, of the *town*. I don't even want to think about what would have happened to you. I mean, Jesus, you'd be *dead*. There's no coming back from the dead."

Juniper bit her lip and shuffled her feet nervously across the wood slats of the porch.

Jason continued, "Or so I thought... After you entered that attic room, you went immediately for the tree as I suspected you would. I jumped over the fire in the doorway and called out to you again. But you were already at the oak with your palms pressed against the bark. You cradled that tree and the light- It poured off of you like nothing I'd ever seen. It was so intense that it almost hurt to look at it, but I couldn't look away no matter how hard I tried. It was like being in a trance. And then, before I realized what was happening, I saw the flames shrink into the wood. I *saw* it happen, Junie, and I couldn't explain it then just like I can't explain it now... But that's not the only thing I saw... I also saw the look on your face and the-" He paused and made a circular motion at the top of his head. "-above your head, there was a burning ring of gold. It was almost like you were an angel, like it was a halo or something."

"You must have been seeing-"

"No, Junie. I wasn't *seeing* things. I was seeing *you*, what you *are*." He chuckled and shifted his weight awkwardly. "We were totally wrong about you, weren't we? *Totally* wrong."

Juniper's words were careful. "Can I trust you not to tell this story to anyone else?"

He swallowed heavily, and obviously took her words as admittance to his claim. "So it's true? You're an *angel*?"

Juniper blinked and realized that she hadn't considered her new status. "No, I'm- it's complicated," she said with a laugh. "But, I can *heal* people. You know sick people, animals, plants-"

"The puppy," Jason said softly, as if something in his brain had suddenly clicked on. "You healed him, didn't you?"

Juniper nodded. "Yes, I did."

"And you healed me too," he whispered.

"I think so," she said cautiously. "I remember turning around, after the fire was out, and I saw you lying on your back. You were breathing, but barely. I put my hands on you and tried to heal you, but soon after everything went black. The next thing I knew I was outside... with you."

Jason took her words into himself slowly and then nodded. "I won't tell anyone, you have my word. I mean, God, Junie... you saved my life! After all I did to you, you still- you gave your last bit of energy to *me*. If that isn't enough to buy my silence, so to speak, then what would be? I'm just- I'm glad you're ok. Because, man, when I carried you outside and you weren't breathing...? I thought you were dead, and I just cried like a big dope for what I'd done to you. For every awful, mean, terrible thing I said, or didn't *stop* Ben from saying."

"Jason, I-"

"Let me finish," he said. He held up his hand to halt her words. "Thank you. Thank you for not leaving me for dead. Thank you for what you did."

Juniper caught his eye and they exchanged careful smiles.

Jason quickly changed the subject to avoid a continuance of the awkward moment. "They haven't found Ben's body yet. Everyone is pretty sure that he's dead, but no one wants to say as much. Not yet, anyway. I think they found one of his shoes, but other than that..." A moment of sadness washed over him before he quickly swatted it away. "I'm almost glad that he's gone. I know that sounds awful, but it's true, it really is."

Juniper reached out to him and placed her palm on his cheek. "Don't be sad any more, Jason. Be *free*! Consider this your fresh start and turn over a new leaf."

A brief glimmer of light passed through her and seeped into his skin. When Juniper removed her hand, the bruises and cuts that had covered his face were gone.

"Remember," she said softly, "this is our secret, now and always."

When Jason left, Juniper slipped back inside, careful not to disturb her sleeping mother. Sam had taken up a position next to the door where he was waiting curiously. His eyes were wide and his tail wagged dutifully behind him. He whined as she closed the door and Juniper bent to pet him.

"Hey guy. You stay down here and watch over mama, ok? I'm gonna run upstairs for a bit to check on dad."

Sam stood and trotted off towards the living room with his tail held high. Juniper smiled at his understanding and headed for the stairs. She took the steps two at a time and when she reached the top she detoured from her path and visited her own room instead. She made her way to her cluttered desk where she grabbed Azerial's bible from the spot where she'd previously left it. She brushed a hand over the cover then pressed it tightly to her chest. She continued down the hallway to her mother's bedroom, slow in her steps. She was still nervous about seeing him again, especially with the grace of the sunlight to give her a new view she wasn't sure she was prepared for.

As she approached, she noticed that her mother's bedroom door was slightly parted. With gathered breath, Juniper crept in on quiet feet. She slowed her breathing and held her words behind her teeth as she neared the bed. If Azerial was still asleep, she didn't want to wake him. She assumed he needed his rest, even if the clock was ticking down to zero. To Juniper's surprise and slight dismay, he was awake and was staring blankly ahead at the ceiling.

"You're up. I didn't think you would be." Juniper took her usual seat on the edge of the bed. "Do you need anything? I see that mama brought you water at some point but if you're hungry I could-"

"I'm not hungry, but I appreciate the offer." His reply was even weaker than Juniper had expected.

As she looked at him in the daylight with his condition no longer concealed by shadows, she could assess Azerial's true physical state. A state that was startlingly apparent thanks in no small part to the white bed sheet that clung to his chest and outlined every single rib in the cage.

Azerial blinked his eyes as though pushing away thoughts too heavy to support with his lids. Groggily and with obvious difficulty, he rolled them in her direction. A smile met his lips when he saw her. "You look well rested. What time is it?" His voice was hoarse, almost non-existent.

Juniper leaned in and placed a kiss on his forehead, careful to keep the pressure light. "It's just after ten."

"Where is your mother this morning?" he asked. "Is she home?"

"Of course she's home. She was supposed to have worked this morning, but after last night... well, as you can probably guess she didn't feel much like driving all the way into Greenville to pull down a few hours for crap pay." Juniper scooted closer to his frailty with the bible still unnoticed in her hands. "She's *finally* catching a few minutes of shut eye. Downstairs, on the sofa."

He seemed to take comfort in the knowledge. "Good."

"Yeah, it is good. She needs a little rest." With a touch of hesitation, Juniper placed the bible on Azerial's chest. He looked down at it slowly, but made no immediate comment. "I'm sure you knew I had this, right? I mean, it was in the box and you knew I had that, so I made an assumption."

He smiled as his hand glossed over the worn cover. "You've read it?"

She nodded. "I've started to, now that I *can* read it. But uh, I've just looked over bits and pieces for now. I figure once things calm down around here, *if* they calm down, I'll read it all.

I'm guessing it's just chocked full of interesting stories."

He closed his hands around the book. His tone turned serious. "I knew I could trust you to keep this safe. As I'm sure you realize, this is a very important book."

"Yeah, I kinda got that impression. But what does it all mean? It's a bit confusing to me."

Azerial opened the book to the first in-tact page and traced his fingertips over the page. "Have you read the traditional bible?"

Juniper shook her head. "As embarrassed as I am to admit this in the presence of a real, honest-to-goodness angel... not really, no. I've just never found the time. Well, ok, I guess that's a lie. I should say I never found the want. Does that make me awful?"

Azerial mustered a weak laugh. "It doesn't make you awful, it makes you human. And between you and me? It's a bit hard to grasp at times, especially for children."

"It's nice to get confirmation."

Azerial's smile remained as he continued. "*Your* bible is missing a few key sections, sections that *this* book contains." He paused as a thick cough shook his ribs and prohibited his words. When he continued he looked noticeably weaker. "In between the words of the opening passages of Genesis lies our story, the story of the angels. There are so many words, so many tales, all of them concealed by man in the form of one period at the end of a line of text. That period is *my* history. You see, as an angel, my existence and the existence of the other angels pre-dates the human race. When God announced his plans for the race of mankind, the angels divided themselves in the heavens. Some of them were angry, angry that God would create another race of creatures and bestow upon them the gift of free will; the gift of *choice*. You must understand that choice was something we had no concept of, something we weren't allowed to exercise because until that point, we'd had no awareness of it! Others, me included in that group, realized that God wished not to lessen our importance by the creation of the new race, but instead sought to heighten it." He lowered his voice and cast his eyes to the ceiling. *"This* book is the word of God, *not* the word of men."

"So, it's like an Angel's Handbook?"

Azerial smiled at the simplicity of her explanation. "I suppose that would be a fine way of looking at it, yes." He re-closed the book and smoothed the cover with his palm one more time. "You'll read this book, you'll remember the knowledge it contains and you'll protect it from harm. Will you promise me these things?"

"What, you mean you don't want it? I thought having it might bring you some comfort."

Sadness filled his eyes and he cast them away from her sight. "I'm afraid that I have no reason to keep it. I no longer have a need for it, can no longer read it. The language is as foreign to me now as it was to you the first time you looked through it. But, I am consoled by the fact that I still have my memories. Every word I've committed to memory and I'll never forget what I was... And now, in these last moments-"

"What do you mean? *Last moments?*"

"Junie-"

"No! Don't Junie me. Don't lie there and try to prepare me for the worst case scenario because it isn't going to happen," Juniper said firmly. She reached for Azerial's chin and turned his head back to face her. "Do you hear me? This isn't over! We aren't giving up, not as long as there's still an option we haven't explored."

"I appreciate your optimism," he whispered.

"Yeah, well, I *don't* appreciate your **lack** of it." Juniper lowered her hand from his chin and instead placed her fingers over his; over the hand that still rested on the closed-cover bible. "Are you so sure this is the end? Because we both know there *is* a way. There's no guarantee it'll work and I know that, but that doesn't mean we shouldn't try it! And I know that when we touched on this last night you said you needed time, but I'm afraid if we wait much longer-"

"Shh, child." Azerial placed his other hand on top of hers. "This is something I've given much thought since your last visit. I told you, I needed time to consider-"

It was Juniper's turn to interrupt. "We're running out of *time*, dad!"

He nodded solemnly. "Believe me, of that I am aware."

"Are you? Are you really? I mean, for goodness sake! Look at yourself, dad! You're withering away into nothing right before my eyes!" Juniper exclaimed. She shook her head softly and forced the anger from her voice. "I know how to save your life, dad, and I know that I can do it."

Azerial said nothing for a long moment. Finally, he looked back at her with wide, soulful eyes. "You don't understand, Juniper. I've been what I am for so long that I cannot fathom giving it up. I don't know any other way to exist."

"So what, you'll lie here and melt into the sheets? You'd seriously put mama through the pain of losing you all over again?"

He looked away and his eyes found a crack in the wall. He examined it absently, unable to return his gaze to Juniper's hardened disbelief. "This decision, Juniper... It's not as though I don't want to be with you and your mother, but I do find that I'm anxious and uncertain about living as a mortal. I know and have seen the things they experience. The good, the bad, the worse... and I never wanted to be human, never wanted to feel what it was like to be completely cut off from my divinity. From my *life*."

"But what about *our* life?" Juniper asked. "All of the reasons you cited as to why you and mama couldn't be together?

They'd become null and void! We could be a *family*! *Finally*, after *all* of these years, we could be *together*! I know you have to want that, if only just a little."

"You think I only want it a *little*?" he asked, obviously saddened by her assessment of his character. "You should know by now that I want that more than anything."

"Then why the hesitation?"

Azerial brought his eyes to hers. "If you had to give up the only life you'd ever known to take a chance on something completely foreign, would you do it so easily? Would you put all of your cards on the table and let it ride?"

"After all that I've seen these past few months?" Juniper asked. She nodded quickly. "Yes. Without a doubt I would."

Azerial sighed. "You make it out to be so simple."

"Isn't it?" she countered.

He lowered his head. "I've been an angel for a longer expanse of time than you can even imagine It's what I was created as, what I lived as, and moreover, what I fought and then later fell as. It's who I am! And the decision to give up the last link to what I was- *am*...? It doesn't come as easily as you might think."

"But you can't go on like this... In pain. Lingering on only because of your wings." Juniper sighed and ran her eyes over the length of his sheet-swathed body. "Your condition has been worse every time I've checked on you this morning! And I know you can't see for yourself, so let me run down the list for you. Your hair is falling out in chunks, both of your eyes are black, your skin is pale and hanging off your bones... your stomach quivers from the pain of the burns you've suffered. Your arms, your legs... your..." She began to sob and pushed her hands up to hold her face.

His hand found the top of her head and he smoothed her hair. "Answer me one question. Your mother, she's in favor of this?"

Juniper nodded at his statement. *"Yes."*

"She wants me to stay here? With the both of you?"

Again, she nodded. *"**Yes**."*

Azerial closed his eyes. "You do realize that you might not be able to heal me, yes? That it might be too late for such things?"

"I realize it, and it's not really a risk I want to take, but there isn't another option-"

"Then do it." Azerial's words had crept through his lips and when they'd hit the cool air of the room, they hung suspended between them. "Do it, Junie. Please."

Juniper inhaled slowly and took his words to her brain where she processed them carefully. After they'd been checked and re-checked for errors, she nodded her understanding. "Are you *sure?*"

"I'm sure. Do not ask me again."

Juniper placed a kiss upon his cheek. "Alright, I promise, I won't. Now get some rest, ok? I'll be back shortly. I need to talk to mama and find some- Just uh, rest. We've got a big night ahead of us."

"Are *you* rested?" asked Azerial.

"Yes."

"Have you eaten? Have you recovered *completely* from last night?" He raised an eyebrow to examine her, and when he saw that she was truthful in her claims, he relaxed.

"Yes," she whispered. She understood his concern for her mental and physical state and further calmed his nerves. "I'm totally fine. Never better. Just have a little faith in me, dad. Say that you do. I *really* need to hear it right now."

"Juniper Kelly, I have faith in you."

Juniper squeezed his hand. "I'm going to talk to mama for a bit, but we'll be back for you soon."

He was silent as he slowly moved his right hand over the pages of the bible he could no longer read. "I'll be here." He closed his eyes and Juniper moved slowly to find her feet.

When she reached the doorway of the bedroom, she looked back over her shoulder at her father's gaunt and tired form. Without another word, she found her way to the living room, and to where Penelope would be waiting.

Penelope was awake when Juniper found her. She had finally changed clothing and her hair had been clipped back from her face with several golden barrettes that reflected the light that filtered in through the living room window. On the coffee table in front of her sat an empty crumb-covered plate and a can of soda.

"At least *someone* around here has an appetite," Juniper said as she took a seat on the couch next to her mother.

Sam barked as if to protest her comment and then lowered his head back to the pillow.

"I think he ate more of it than I did." Penelope looked curiously at Juniper, her head tilted slightly to the left. "Is there something you want to say?"

"Do I have that look?" Juniper asked.

Penelope nodded. "You've definitely got the look. So come on, spill it. You've just been to see your father, I take it."

She pulled in a breath and let free a nod. "Yeah. We had a nice long talk."

Penelope sighed and pushed up the sleeves of her blouse as though preparing herself for the news to come. "And? How is he?"

"Not good, but he's agreed to let us clip his wings so that I can try to heal him. He knows that it's the only way and he's willing to do it."

Penelope's eyes widened for a moment, then returned quickly to their normal state. "Is that really what he wants?" she questioned.

"He told me not to ask him again," Juniper said. "This isn't a decision he's come to lightly, you know. It's one he almost didn't come to at all. I uh, I sorta forced his hand."

"He always was a bit wishy-washy," Penelope joked. When her laugh faded she looked at her hands, hands which were folded neatly in her lap. "I can't imagine how hard of a decision this was for him."

"I can't either, mama." Juniper bit her lip, hesitant to continue. "I don't want to rush things, but we really shouldn't wait much longer. The more he lingers on in his current state, the less likely I'll be able to pull him back once his wings are- you know... *gone*."

Penelope's lips pushed forth a glimmer of a brave smile before the whole of her mouth swatted it away with a frown. "What if he resents us for this?"

"It's a chance we have to take if we want to save him from certain death." Juniper paused. Her mind changed subjects and her lips followed suit. "Mama... Do you still love him?"

She looked up then tore her gaze away just as quickly. "Yes. Yes, of course I do."

"All of these years you've loved him?"

"Always, Junie. Every day."

"So let me ask you this... Does the idea of having what you've always wanted frighten you?"

She laughed at the question. "I suppose it does. A little. How about yourself?"

Juniper gulped. "Yeah, it does scare me. A little. And dad? Well, I think it scares him too. So at least we're all in the same shaky boat."

"There's always that."

"He uh- He asked me if you wanted him to stay here, if it was what you *really* wanted. Even though we hadn't discussed it,

I-" She looked down and shook her head slowly from side to side. "I didn't really feel we *had* to discuss it, you know?"

They sat in silence for a long time; neither of them spoke. Juniper finally stood and reached out for her mother's hand in an attempt to shatter the awkward umbrella of silence that had expanded to cover them.

"We have work to do," Juniper said softly. She squeezed her mother's fingers briefly before she released them back to her lap. "If you don't want to be there, I'll understand."

Penelope looked out the window and nodded numbly. "No, I- I want to be there. I *should* be there," she whispered. "I won't leave him again, especially not now when he needs our love and support the most."

Juniper could hardly imagine how her mother was feeling. All of the current heartache that was upon her came after a happy and wholly overdue reunion, a reunion which had been brief at best. It wasn't fair, it wasn't *right*, and Juniper found that anger was starting to grow where only fear and sadness had dwelled.

"Do you think I can do this?" Juniper asked after several uncomfortable seconds had elapsed.

Penelope turned her head, as though slow to wake from a dream she'd been having. "I know you're scared, it's natural to be scared at a time like this! But your father has faith in you or he wouldn't ask this of you. And yes, *I* have faith in you, Junie. I have faith in you and I have faith in God. He'll see us through."

Juniper nodded. "There's just one more problem. I don't really know what to use for this." Juniper didn't know how to continue her sentence without cringing or crying, or *both*. She sucked in a long breath that did little to calm her. "How do I cut off his wings, mama? I don't know what to use or how to even begin with this... I don't- I don't know anything. I'm just a stupid kid!"

"Junie, hey!" Penelope stood and reached for her daughter with both hands.

Juniper took one step forward before she fell into her mother's waiting arms. Her head rested on her shoulder, and Penelope stroked her hair. "We're going to get through this, you hear me? We're going to get through because we're *owed* this, because it would be horribly, *horribly*, cruel to give him back to us, only to take him away again." Penelope pushed her daughter back, but kept a firm grip on her upper arms. She looked her straight in the eye with more seriousness than Juniper could remember ever having seen. "I think there's a pair of branch trimmers on my work bench in the garage. They should be sharp, I've never used them. At least not that I remember."

"Will that work? Are you sure?" Juniper could barely swallow past the thickness of the knot in her throat.

"They should... and we don't really the time for alternatives, do we?"

"No. I don't think we have much time at all-"

"Then hurry. Get the trimmers from the garage. I'm going to speak with your father for a few minutes in private. After all, this could be the l-" Penelope didn't finish her sentence, but rather ended it abruptly and shoved silence into its place. The unspoken words hung between them.

This could be the last time I hear his voice.

Juniper nodded and amazed herself when she found the strength to turn and walk towards the kitchen door. She hadn't thought that her legs were taking any more commands.

Yet somehow she managed to control them and they led her from the house to the driveway and beyond. Once in the garage, Juniper found the branch trimmers in exactly the spot Penelope had promised. They were larger than she remembered them being, or perhaps it was that Juniper felt very small in the grip of what was to come.

The blades glinted against the light as she picked them up; the trimmers were shiny and silver and shook ever so slightly in her nervous hands. Juniper clipped the blades together several times in the air to make sure they weren't rusted, and to determine just how much pressure she'd have to apply to cut through the large, tufted wings on Azerial's back.

She realized suddenly that it would take everything she had, and then some. Physically, it would be exhausting. Emotionally, it would be heartbreaking, gut-wrenching. Juniper wasn't sure which aspect of the upcoming ordeal she dreaded most.

As her final mechanical test, Juniper checked the blade for sharpness by running her finger across their sharpness. It only took a second before a ribbon of red beads appeared across her fingertip in an orderly line. A moment later, the seam vanished in much the same way it had appeared and left no trace that it had ever existed.

Juniper suddenly had a better idea of what exactly her father had, and subsequently, had sacrificed on her behalf. She only hoped that she wouldn't let him down, as she knew she couldn't bear losing him. The only thing worse than that would be seeing the look in her mother's eyes if she wasn't able to save Azerial's life.

It would be heartbreaking; sadness, shock, and disappointment, all mingled into one unbearable pain. Juniper shivered under the fear of having to live with such a look for the rest of her life.

With her hands shaking and her heart racing inside of her chest, she made the long walk to her mother's bedroom where Azerial waited. In her hand, swinging limply at her side, she carried the branch trimmers and their impossible weight.

Chapter Seventeen
The Return

The bedroom door was locked when Juniper twisted the knob and she called out to her parents. Her tongue was hesitant to intrude upon what she was certain was an emotional talk between Azerial and her mother. However, something in her gut told her that their time was shorter than any of them could even realize.

It was her mother who answered her call a moment later. "Just one second, Junie. Your father and I are talking."

Juniper leaned against the wall with the trimmers hot and heavy in her sweat-slicked hands. She, unable to support their weight and herself, rested them against the wall next to her and knotted her hands nervously at her stomach. If she'd actually been able to eat her breakfast that morning, she'd most certainly be on her way to losing it.

Juniper heard their muffled voices and in spite of herself, she listened in. Their words were unrecognizable filtered through the distance and the bedroom door and sounded like nothing more than faint whispers. First her mothers, then Azerial's, then her mothers again. The whispers were followed by a moment of silence that preceded a deep mournful sob. Finally, Juniper's ears perked up at the click of the lock.

Penelope came into the hall with eyes red and a balled up tissue held under her nose. She sniffled and forced out a smile for Juniper's benefit. "He's ready," she whispered. "As ready as he'll ever be."

Juniper picked up the trimmers and held them behind her back. She was careful to shield them from her mother's curiously frightened eyes for as long as possible. "Then let's get this over with so we can get on with our lives. *All* of us."

Penelope shoved the tissue in the front pocket of her jeans and re-opened the bedroom door. Juniper slid past her and walked slowly to the edge of the bed.

Azerial's condition had worsened still. His features looked melted and contorted, as though he were a giant wax figure that had been set too long in the afternoon sun.

Juniper felt her breath catch in her chest as the reality of what she was about to do hit her squarely in the ribcage like a bag of rusty hammers swung at her from a high cross beam.

Azerial eyed the trimmers. "You know-" He struggled to speak. "You know what to do?"

Juniper nodded and behind her she heard her mother sniffle, then sob. "I think so, yes."

"Penny... Come to me, please." Azerial reached out for her and she obliged him. She rounded the bed to the far side and took his hand. She closed her eyes and Azerial did the same.

A moment later, he broke the silence and found his weak words. "Juniper, grab my left shoulder. Penny, you get the right. Sit me up slowly. My pain is quite intense."

Juniper and Penelope exchanged a nervous glance, but did as they were told. Juniper put the trimmers on the floor next to the bed and took Azerial's left shoulder in her hands.

"One... two... *three...*" Penelope counted. When she reached three she nodded at Juniper and together they hoisted Azerial to a sitting position.

He cried out, groaned and then fell into a loop of deep choking breaths. He hunched forward and his head fell forward to hang close to his outstretched, blanket-covered legs.

"Take the trimmers," he whispered. "Near the base- where the wings meet my back, you'll want to place the blade there."

Penelope held him while Juniper picked up the trimmers and raised them to the spot Azerial had indicated. Juniper felt the sweat erupt at her brow as she positioned the blades as close to her father's back as she could manage.

The long, white, feathers that comprised his wings seemed to realize what was about to happen, and they rustled slightly as if to protest. Juniper closed her eyes.

I can do this, she thought. *I have to do this, it's the only way.*

Azerial took one last deep breath before Juniper made the cut and a word struggled to the light. "Now."

Despite his earlier request, Juniper gave him the question one last time. "Are you sure this is what you want?"

"Be quick with it," he said, ignoring her question effectively. "As soon as- as the first wing is clipped, move on to the second. When the second is freed, release me to the sheets. You'll have only a matter of moments to begin healing me before my heart stops and I-"

Penelope interrupted with a sob. "Oh God, Azy. I can't stand this. I can't stand it!" She said nothing more, instead she bit her lip and turned her head towards the floor in an attempt to hide her falling tears.

"Hurry now, Junie, before it's too late," Azerial commanded. "Remember, I love you both. Please, don't forget that. Know that I've *always* loved you and I always will."

From behind her hair, Penelope whispered a reply. "I love you, Azy. I will until the day I die."

Juniper could hear him smile, but from her position at his back, she could only see the bald patches on his head where the hair had fallen free. "Are you ready, dad?" As much as she didn't want to interrupt their moment, she knew that the longer she waited, the more impossible it all became.

"Yes," Azerial whispered. "Please continue."

"I love you, dad. It's going to be ok, I promise."

Azerial said nothing more and Penelope's sobs kicked back up briefly before she squelched them with an iron clad clenching of her lips.

Juniper licked her own lips and brought the blades of the trimmers closer together at the base of her father's left wing. One feather fell free as the sharp blade grazed it, and Azerial allowed a sob to escape his lips.

Juniper wanted to close her eyes for the snip, but couldn't bear to look away. She bit her tongue between her teeth and with all of her strength she quickly closed the blades onto each other.

Azerial went limp as the first wing left his back with a wet crunch and fell nearly silently to the bed. Penelope's right hand caught his chest; her left was still pressed firmly at his back. Her tears were flowing freely over her cheeks in salt-laden streams, all of the shame having left her.

Juniper quickly worked to move the blades to the second wing. The trimmers caught on the bone at first, but with a slight repositioning of the blade, quickly snapped through it.

When the second wing was finally severed from its base, it fell awkwardly to the bed sheets and laid to rest next to the first. The blood that poured from Azerial's back was so red that it was nearly purple. It flowed quickly and without pause down his back to the sheets where the threads soaked it in quickly and spread it about evenly.

"Lay him back, mama." Juniper dropped the blood-covered trimmers to the floor and they clattered against the wood.

Juniper looked at Azerial's silent face. He was pale and cold. His lips were parted slightly and his eyes were open and fixed, staring blankly upwards at the stucco swirl ceiling.

Juniper placed her hands over his chest and brought her knees and legs up to rest on the mattress next to him.

She began her work and moved her fingers quickly towards his heart. She pulled up and aside his blood stained shirt and repositioned her hands against his bare flesh. Penelope stood by the bed in silence, tears frozen in her eyes and waiting for the thaw of spring to permit them their leave.

The light came slowly from her fingertips and moved over his chest. The pure white intensity of the energy was strong and thorough at first, but then, as suddenly as it had appeared, the light waned before it slowly turned blue. Azerial made no movement and his chest lay silent and heavy. His eyes remained empty and fixed upon the ceiling.

"What's wrong?" Penelope asked. "Why isn't it working?"

Juniper felt the panic rise up within her and it ceased her actions. Her hands lay limp on his chest. "I don't know... I don't understand-" She pressed her palms over his heart again, but the light remained blue and weak. "It's not working. Mama, it's not-"

"Oh my God, Junie. No... **no**!" Penelope dissolved into tears. "This isn't happening. Junie...?"

"Mama, I'm trying!" Juniper's voice broke loose of words and turned instead to desperate whines and frustrated sighs.

Her hands found Azerial's quickly fleeting warmth and tapped into it. "Come on dad! Don't do this, don't you die on me!" She pressed herself into his flesh and waited for the healing to begin.

But nothing happened.

Nervous and confused, Juniper's eyes cast themselves towards her mother's. They met in an uneasy silence over his quiet body.

The fear rose up to her throat and Juniper could taste its bittersweet notes heavy at her tongue. "Mama..."

Her simple word was ushered quietly into the room, as though it were made of glass and wished not to drop itself onto the stone cold atmosphere surrounding them.

The alarm was rising in her like water over the banks of a swollen, storm-soaked creek until the tears fell from her eyes and assaulted Azerial's lifeless face and chest.

Her tears hit his flesh and sizzled. Tiny puffs of smoke rose up from his skin to mark the spots where they had struck him.

"Papa, please, please don't die!" She pressed her hands to him and sobbed and she threw herself across his chest like a second skin. "God, oh God, *please*! Do something! Help me! It can't end like this- it can't!"

The air in the room seized up with a hot, heavy sensation. Penelope felt it first as it grazed the top of her head; Juniper felt it next as it touched the back of her neck like a reassuring hand before it quickly faded to nothing.

Penelope pushed her daughter aside and lowered her own hands to rest on Azerial's cheeks. She slapped him softly several times, all the while spewing her own desperate plea under her breath. "Don't leave me again, don't you *dare* leave me again! You told me it would be alright! You promised me we'd finally have it all! After all these years!"

Juniper found the scene unbearable to watch. She sobbed softly behind her curtain of hair with her hands folded in her lap like the useless objects they were.

"No, Azy, please! You can't be dead. This isn't happening…" Penelope's words fractured at the edge of her sharp tongue and her angry disbelief turned quickly to despair. Her hands clung tightly to his, hands that Penelope brought slowly up to her own chest. She sobbed with such intensity that Juniper feared she'd flood the state.

"Mama… He's gone, mama. He's gone. There's nothing more we can do." Juniper could scarcely say the words without her voice cracking and receding like the defeated tides of morning.

"No, Junie! He can't be. He can't leave us again. He *promised-*" Penelope shook her head and hiccupped. "Why can't you heal him? I don't understand… he's mortal now… he's

mortal!"

"I don't know why, mama. I don't-"

"Try again," Penelope interrupted.

"Mama."

"Junie... *please*!"

Juniper sighed, nodded once and moved back to her former position at her dead father's side. She raised her hands over him. She pressed her tongue awkwardly against the back of her teeth in an attempt to prevent its escape from her mouth, and escape that would flood her mother with protests.

That time, when her hands touched his chest, there was a spark. Not a white spark, nor a blue one, but instead the color was reddish purple, nearly the same color as the blood that was still leaving Azerial's body. It burned like an electrical shock and Juniper recoiled. She attempted to shake the sting from her fingers, but the numbness didn't dissipate.

"What happened?" Penelope asked. Her eyes had witnessed the same spark and held the same glint of curiosity.

Juniper shook her head. "I don't know, I-"

Her words were halted by the shattering of the light bulb in the lamp next to the bed. The thin pieces of frosted glass rained down to the table top and floor like delicate shrapnel.

It was only a second later that the blinds on the windows snapped shut, closed tightly by the presence of unseen hands. The curtains fell into place over them and enveloped the room in unnatural darkness.

"Junie? What's going on? Are you doing this?"

"No mama. It's not me"

An eerie silence and the smell of death hung low over the room, but both sensations were soon replaced by a steady, low-pitched hum that not only seemed to grow in volume, but in *color*.

Juniper turned to the doorway behind her, where her eyes focused themselves to fine points. "Mama...? Something weird is about to happen and I have no idea what it's gonna be." Juniper felt the truth in her statement as it raced through her bones to her teeth where it caused her gums to quiver.

Her hands found her sides and she moved from Azerial's body, then from the bed entirely as though in a daze. She turned her full attention to the doorway and to the intruding, unknown presence.

When the light parted, Juniper fell to her knees at the bedside through no choice of her own. Her hands came quickly together and found solace in their union at her chest. To her right, Penelope had also been reduced from her former position to take up residence in a new one.

Unconsciousness. Head against the wall, arms and legs spread out across the cool surface of the hardwood floor, she was silent and spent.

From out of the light, the stranger stepped. He was wearing a dark blue robe with gold piping. At his back, he carried a familiar sight. Wings. The only difference in them was that his wings were larger than Azerial's had been, and were as clean and white as the light from which he had appeared. His lips were curved slightly upward into a soft smile and his eyes were already cast towards Azerial's silent face.

"You may stand, Juniper." The angel's voice was deep and heavy, but comforting in its authority. "Tell me, what of this?" The angel motioned towards the bed with one perfect finger. More importantly, he motioned to the clipped wings that lay crooked and tattered on the mattress; to the trimmers that lay forgotten on the floor.

"I tried to save him, but I couldn't. He was already too far gone-" Juniper choked on her words and lowered her eyes to the floor. "He's dead..."

"That I can see." The angel stepped closer and removed his hood. The face that was revealed looked as though it had been finely sculpted from clay; smoothed and fired to a golden bronze color. He extended his hand to Juniper, and she took it carefully and without fear.

"W- What is your name?" she asked gently.

The angel smiled, and the smell she had grown to associate with Azerial reached out to calm her. She felt her pupils dilate under the soft vanilla scent as her brain released a series of chemicals that relaxed the muscles of her face and upper body. Juniper found it hard to keep her grasp on the angel's hand, harder still to keep her eyelids open. Sensing her relaxed state, he squeezed her fingers more tightly between his own.

"I am Gabriel," he said softly. "I've come with word from God."

Juniper swallowed, and in doing so, her fear tumbled back to the empty pit of her stomach where it proceeded to flop around madly like a fish left on dry land. *Gabriel?*

"The one and only." His features softened beneath his crown of honey golden hair and a question followed. "Do you know why I'm here?"

"For Azerial," Juniper whispered. "You're here to take him home."

He nodded once. "Your father was a great angel. A great *man*."

Juniper glanced to her right to gauge her mother's reaction to Gabriel. Only then did she notice her mother's body slumped between the wall and the bed. Juniper made an attempt to pull away from Gabriel's grip, but he didn't release her.

"Mama?" Juniper's eyes, widened with shock, shot back to Gabriel. "What's wrong with her? Is she ok?"

"She's sleeping, Juniper. Do not worry. She will wake when she is ready."

"Sleeping?" Juniper felt her brow furrow. "Sleeping? I-"

"Some things it is best she does not see," Gabriel

explained. He squeezed her fingers gently and his smile warmed.

"Oh, I- I see." Juniper lowered her eyes. "But she'll be fine?"

Gabriel laughed softly. It sounded melodious. "Yes. She'll be fine, just fine. You've my word."

Juniper relaxed briefly only to tense immediately back up into a tight ball as her eyes roamed her father's cold, slowly stiffening form. "And what about dad?"

"Ah yes. Azerial." Gabriel finally released her hand and he stepped past her towards the bed. "Do not worry, child. Everything is under control."

"Are you here to save him?" Juniper asked.

His words came evenly. "I am here to give him a *choice*."

Gabriel bent slightly at the waist and lowered his lips so that they were just above Azerial's left ear. He whispered something that Juniper couldn't hear, a series of words spoken in a tongue she recognized vaguely as Angelic. Then with the slight waving motion of one hand passed in front of Azerial's face, Gabriel restored to him what Juniper herself had not been able to. Life. Blinking, twitching, wonderful life. In addition to that, all of the distortion and burns that had scarred him disappeared as though they'd been nothing more than a bad dream. In an instant, Azerial was as he'd been before the fire. Unblemished and reformed.

Azerial's frozen wide eyes snapped shut when Gabriel lowered his hand. His chest shook and rumbled like a water-flooded engine fighting for gasoline as breath coursed over his lips and raced to fill his deflated lungs.

Juniper fell again to her knees as her shell-shocked bones turned to quivering gelatin.

Gabriel smiled at his old friend and extended his hand to find council with Azerial's. Azerial was in shock; his mouth moved but no words came, and instead he expelled only a series of soft grunts between coughs.

"Easy, old friend. Easy there!" Gabriel's hand pushed itself into Azerial's sternum. "Rest now. You've been through quite an ordeal."

Finally, Azerial found his tongue. "Gabriel? I-" Tears raced to fill his eyes. "You've come for me."

"Of course I came! Did you think we would let you end this way? After all that you've done?"

Azerial, too ashamed to reply, lowered his chin to his chest.

"Azerial..." Gabriel stroked his cheek lovingly with the back of his hand. "Why have you doubted us? Why have you doubted *Him*? After all of these millennia, you chose now to lose your faith? When perhaps you needed it the most?"

"I'm sorry, so sorry." Azerial finally looked over and found Juniper kneeling at his bedside. Too shocked to smile, she only cried.

Gabriel took a seat at his side and drew Azerial's hand into his palm. He placed his other hand on top of it. "Did you think we would allow you to die this way?"

"I've not been sure of your plans for me for some time now," he admitted. "The silence has been deafening."

Gabriel's serious look softened. "You have suffered so because of these burdens. But I am here to tell you that we have seen and have understood your struggles."

Azerial began to cry again, that time more loudly. "I'm sorry."

"Shhh, my brother, all has been forgiven." Gabriel removed his hand and buried it in the folds of his robe. "You gave your everything to your daughter so that she might live to fulfill her destiny. You were selfless in that action, and that selfless action of yours begot another, and another... We are proud of you, Azerial, so proud that we have come to offer you a choice."

Azerial stopped his sob and looked up. "What?"

Juniper felt her heart tighten in her chest as though it were being held in a vice grip.

Gabriel continued. "If you choose to return with me to Heaven, you will be fully reinstated to your former position. If, however, you choose to become mortal and stay with your family, then you will be given your health and all attributes that accompany humanity."

Azerial's words were raspy from the emotion is his heaving chest. "I have been forgiven? After all of this time?" His voice was barely classifiable as a whisper.

Gabriel nodded and his smile widened. "You have done well, Azerial. God rewards the faithful, you know that."

Juniper finally found the courage to speak. "If he decides to return to heaven, we'll never see him again, will we?"

Gabriel looked at her and shook his head slowly. "I'm afraid not, child."

Azerial's gaze met with Juniper's. He held it only briefly before he dropped it and looked away. Azerial instead raised his eyes to meet Gabriel's once more.

"There was a time when I would have given anything to be welcomed back; to have been forgiven of the sins I'd committed? It was something I wanted so for such a long time. But now? Now that I learn my slate has been wiped clean... Well, I take little hesitation in making my choice."

Gabriel paused to read Azerial's unspoken thoughts and when he'd gleaned his answer, he nodded. "Your answer is final?"

Azerial closed his eyes. "Yes."

"Then I will give you one last chance to say your farewells before I make it so. If you would like, that is."

Juniper felt her heart sink quickly to the soles of her feet. It was followed closely by her hopes and her dreams. It took all of her might to roll her eyes up to meet Azerial's face.

However, when she did so, she found there a smile so contagious that it leapt quickly to her own lips.

"Tell your mother I'll be back soon," he said softly. "I just have some loose ends to tie up."

Her eyes widened in disbelief as her father's decision sunk into her frazzled mind. "You'll be b-back? You really mean it?"

"Of course I'll be back!" he said; it was a sentiment that was followed closely by a series of soft chuckles. "You didn't think I'd leave *now*, did you?"

Juniper blushed, almost ashamed to admit that had been exactly what she'd thought. She finally mustered a nod.

"Oh, Juniper…" Azerial sighed softly, as though saddened by her lack of faith in him. "After all we've been through and talked about? We need each other! *All* of us! That is of course, if you two will have me."

Juniper's held breath escaped her teeth and she threw herself to her feet. Her arms went quickly to wrap around Azerial's neck. "Are you kidding me? Of course we'll have you!" She pulled back and examined his face again. She was looking for further confirmation of his decision. "You're *really* staying? *Really?*"

"Indeed I am! There's no other place in all of existence I'd rather be than right *here*." He kissed Juniper on the end of the nose.

"Azerial, we have to go now." Gabriel tapped his wrist where his watch would have been, had he been wearing one.

Azerial nodded at his old friend. "I'll be back soon, Junie. Tell Penny not to worry *any* more." He squeezed his daughter tight and whispered into her hair. "Everything is going to be just fine from here on out."

A moment later, hand in hand, Azerial and Gabriel left under the blinding cover of light. It had been the same intense light that had carried Gabriel into the room. With them gone,

Juniper looked at the bed sheets. She was only moderately surprised when she found that they had been bleached white and smoothed flat. They were, quite possibly, cleaner than the day they'd been bought.

She smiled at the sight and shook her head in amazement. She next went to her mother's side and lowered herself to her knees.

Penelope's eyes opened slowly when she sensed Juniper's presence at her front. "What happened?" she asked. She yawned as she did so and pressed her hand to cover her lips. "Was I asleep? How did I fall as-?" It was then that her eyes found the pristine and empty bed. "Where is he? Where-?"

"Shhh... It's ok, mama." Juniper pulled her shaking mother into a hug and gathered her explanations on her lips. "The most wonderful thing has happened, mama. As it turns out, we finally got our miracle."

Epilogue
A New Life

In the days following the fire, the town of Camden Falls buzzed with gossip.

Most of the stories centered around Ben's disappearance and assumed death, and although none of his remains had ever been found in the charred wreckage of the farm house embers, a funeral was held to mourn his passing two weeks to the day after the fire.   Juniper had decided not to attend, Jason had stopped by to see her after the service. He informed her that his father was sending him to military school and they exchanged an awkward good-bye hug in her driveway. She watched him pedal away on his bike, and found that she was almost sad to see him go.

Aside from the stories of Ben's demise, a handful of other tales hit closer to the truth of what had happened that night under the unspeaking canopy of the forest trees.

Juniper ignored the stares and questions of the town's people, questions that picked at her clothes and poked at her flesh, and she chose instead to live the life she had always wanted.

Azerial was quick to adjust to his new-found mortality. He learned to cook, he watched TV, he helped with dishes in the evenings. Juniper even spent her Sunday's teaching him how to drive in the abandoned-for-summer parking lot behind the high school.

One afternoon, several months after Ben's funeral, Azerial and Juniper found themselves walking through the forest hand in hand. Azerial's feet stopped at the sight of the fire-ravaged remains of the farm house that for so long had been his home.

"When I first saw this house, I had never seen a place so foreign." His words found their footing slowly. "Heaven isn't anything at all like you would imagine. It's nothing like the stories."

"What *is* it like?" asked Juniper. "You've never really talked about it much."

Azerial smiled faintly. His eyes were still fixed upon the burnt black, branchless oak at the center of the rubble. "Do you know how it feels to wade into the water until your feet lose the bottom?"

Juniper nodded.

"It's kind of like that," he whispered, then he tossed a casual smile to his lips.

Juniper responded in kind. "I hope I see it someday."

Azerial squeezed her hand. "You will, but not for a very long time. You have a lot of work ahead of you, young lady."

"Do you think I can do it?" Juniper asked cautiously. "You know, whatever *it* turns out to be?"

He nodded firmly and without pause. "I *know* you can do it. You've proven nothing to me if you've not proven that."

Together they stood there, hand in hand, with the wreckage of the past tossed haphazardly around their feet. Several long moments passed before Azerial sighed and they continued their walk towards the serpentine creek.

Had they instead ventured closer to the house, they would have seen it.

It. One single, white, feather that stuck out of the rubble as a sort of flag of surrender. A flag that was left to point towards the heavens as a solitary reminder of the places they had been and the places they were certain to go.

The End

Coming in Late Spring 2007...

THIRTY-SIX STEPS
Mark of Darkness

Nearly five years after the tragic fire in her hometown of Camden Falls, Juniper Kelly wakes to find that destiny has found her.

A healing, a crowd of curious onlookers and a handsome stranger intersect on the campus of her university, and suddenly, the normal life she'd been trying to live vanishes. In its place she finds a dangerous new reality that will threaten to destroy everything she's ever known, including herself.

In the company of a handsome British stranger, Juniper embarks on a cross-country road trip to find a way to overcome the dark forces that pursue her. What she finds along the way will forever change her world.

www.ingramcontent.com/pod-product-compliance
Lightning Source LLC
Chambersburg PA
CBHW020505020726
47493CB00001B/194